Hunter's Soul

Stacey Oakley

HUNTER'S SOUL by Stacey Oakley

Copyright © 2017 Stacey Oakley

ISBN 978-1-7750407-0-5

Background image on cover taken by Darlene Oakley

Cover design by Stacey Oakley

Written in Canada by Stacey Oakley

Printed by IngramSpark

Visit writershaunt.wordpress.com

Part 1
Home

Rain sat at the table eating her supper while her parents and Uncle Damien were talking about something that sounded serious, but she didn't really understand why.

"The Fiends have been drawing closer for a while," her mother said. Her voice sounded like it did whenever Rain was caught doing something that wasn't safe. "We need to kill them before…" she glanced at Rain and her sister, "before anything happens."

"We'll go out tomorrow and see how bad it is," their father told her, tapping his fork against his plate. "Then we can take it to the Council and get a team together for an eradication mission."

"They don't like Fiends too close to the villages, so it won't take much," Uncle Damien added. "Hell, maybe we'll take a group of students out with us, let them get some experience."

"But won't the Guardians keep them away?" Storm wanted to know. Their dad was a Guardian, mostly. Sometimes he was a Hunter, like their mom or Uncle Damien. They went out to fight the monsters while the Guardians protected villages, towns, and cities. It didn't matter if those places belonged to humans either. They were still protected, even though humans didn't like her people.

"They'll do their best," their mother said, "and us Hunters will do what we can to make sure they don't have to work *too* hard," she added with a wink as she looked at her husband. More than anything Rain wanted to be a Hunter, even if there were some times when Hunters were sad when they came back home, or when they were scared even if there were no Fiends around. She wasn't allowed to try to scare Hunters or sneak up on them because of it. Everyone knew that.

"How much longer until I can go to the Academy?" She asked. When she was fourteen she could start at the Guardian Academy where Keepers, Guardians, and Hunters trained for four years. At the end, she would be able to fight the Fiends, just like her parents and her uncle. She could fight the monsters and go on adventures with her friends, just like they did.

"Nine years, sweetheart," her father told her. Rain pouted, it seemed like she would be waiting forever.

"I only have to wait seven years," Storm said, earning a glare from her younger sister.

"But you hate fighting!" Rain protested. "It's not fair!" Storm didn't want to be a Hunter, not really, not like Rain did. Storm didn't even like to fight when they were playing pretend.

"You can always be a Keeper," their mother suggested.

"Wouldn't that be boring?" Storm asked, frowning. Keepers studied spells and history.

"It's still important. Without them we wouldn't get very far," their father explained. "They also find new ways to help us fight and stay safe." Rain considered that for a moment while the adults went back to their conversation, talking about things like strategy and tactics. She tried to pay attention but too much didn't make sense to her. Not yet, anyway.

"So, what are you two little monsters going to get up to today?" Uncle Damien asked the sisters, breaking off from the conversation with their parents.

"I'm gonna fight monsters!" Rain exclaimed, thrusting her fork like a sword. "Me 'n Kestrel are gonna save the village!" Kestrel was her best friend. They were going to go to the Academy together and save everyone when they grew up.

"Oh really?" He said, eyebrows raised, humour in his mercury coloured eyes.

Rain nodded. "Yeah!"

"Okay kiddo," he said with a chuckle, "I believe you." He turned to Storm, "what about you? Are you going to fight monsters too?" She just shrugged.

"You can save the village with me 'n Kestrel!" Rain offered. Sometimes Storm would play with them, sometimes not.

"Fine, but I'm not going to be a damsel in distress this time!" She insisted with a glare.

"Okay," the younger girl acquiesced. "But I can't promise you won't get eaten."

The glare deepened. "You better not!"

"Girls," their mother warned, and they quieted. "Maybe later we can practice some real Fiend fighting moves, that way no one will have to get eaten." The girls cheered. Rain hoped they wouldn't get called out to work at all, because then she might be able to talk her mother and uncle into sparring after. It was so cool to watch, their weapons moving almost too fast for her to follow. She wanted to be able to do that someday; to be brave and strong like they were. Then the monsters would be the ones running scared.

"Will you practice with us?" Storm asked their father and uncle. The two men exchanged a look, shrugged, and nodded.

"Are you gonna stay here a while?" Rain asked Damien. He usually travelled with her mother, but he went out on his own a lot too, or with her father when he decided to go hunting.

"Dunno," he replied, taking a long drink from the silver and leather flask he always carried. She knew it was liquor –something only adults were allowed to drink- but whenever she asked he would give her a different answer. "Maybe a few days," he said, exchanging looks with her parents. She guessed that it had something to do with the Fiends they had been talking about. She wished she'd been able to understand more of that conversation. "Maybe a little longer; there might be some work around here for me to do." She clapped her hands together and he smiled slightly.

"Can I go with you?" Rain asked. She'd always wanted to go on a hunt, but no one ever let her, always telling her that they would when she was older, when she was a Hunter, never mind that that was forever away.

"Not yet, kiddo. Maybe in a few more years," he said, laughing as he reached over to ruffle her dark blue hair. "What about you, Storm?"

She frowned. "I can wait." She'd probably read instead. Storm loved to read. Rain did too, but she wanted to fight Fiends a little bit more.

"Well, neither of you will grow much if you don't finish your dinners," their father said gently. Rain quickly resumed eating, and Storm did as well, though much more elegantly, for all she was only two years older.

Then the screams started.

Both girls jumped as a vicious roar tore through the air, making Rain scream in fear. The adults looked at one another before jumping to their feet, hastily pulling on armour and activating the protection spells they always wore. Rain broke free of the terror that was keeping her frozen to the spot and ran for her mother, who'd just finished strapping her sword on and was already heading for the door, Uncle Damien a step behind.

"Mommy, stay!" Rain pleaded, afraid as she clung to her mother's leg. Her mother picked her up and kissed her cheek, wiping away her tears. Her leather gloves where soft against Rain's skin.

"I can't sweetie, I have to save the village with Uncle Damien," she said with a smile. "But don't worry, we'll be back before you know it and Daddy will be here and keep you and Storm out of trouble."

"Promise?"

Her mother nodded. "I promise."

She looked to her uncle. "Promise?" She wanted to make sure that he came back safe too. She knew that sometimes Hunters left and never came back.

"I promise," he vowed, ruffling her hair again. Rain allowed herself to be handed over to her father as Storm hugged her mother and uncle as they ran outside. Rain could hear their battle cries not long after, rising with the voices of a hundred other Hunters and Guardians who lived in the village.

"Everything will be okay," her father said, grinning. "We've just got to remind the Fiends why they don't want to be around our village." They nodded. The sounds of fighting grew louder, and Rain couldn't help it, she started crying again. Her father picked her up and held her close while she clung to him, weeping into his armour, ignoring the bumpiness of the chainmail against her face

Then the door came crashing in. Rain found herself on the ground beside her sister in an instant as their father rushed at the monster that broke in. It was bigger than he was, with rough green skin and horns that stuck out from everywhere. Both girls shrieked as it roared and lunged at them. But their father was faster. It had barely taken two steps when its head came crashing down onto the floor, blue blood spraying over the room and their father. The body started to shrivel up, like everything inside was being sucked out, and he kicked it back outside, his sword held at the ready. He turned back to them, and went pale. Rain felt sharp claws dig into her side and twisted to see that a Fiend had come in through the kitchen door and grabbed both her and Storm, who was screaming and kicking to try to get away. Their father lunged and managed to cut off the arm holding Rain, but the Fiend ran with Storm still in its grasp.

Her father took one look at the door, then back at her. He grabbed her and took her into her parents' room and pushed her into the closet where their weapons were kept. "Don't come out, don't make a sound until one of us comes for you," he ordered tightly, gripping her shoulders for a moment. She nodded and he closed the door. She felt a ripple as the spells on the closet activated and listened as his footsteps faded away. She curled up in a corner as far away from the doors as she could get, hands over her mouth to keep herself from screaming and sobbing as the sounds of battle raged around her, though she couldn't stop herself from crying. *Please come back Daddy*, she begged silently. *Mommy, Daddy, Storm, Uncle Damien, don't leave me alone, come back!* She wanted to leave, to run and find one of them. But Daddy had told her to stay, so she stayed, hoping the monsters didn't come in and find her, trusting that her father had put her somewhere the monsters couldn't reach her.

She stayed even when the sounds of the fighting and the screaming faded and there was only silence.

Rain had no idea how long she'd been in the closet. She was cold, tired, hungry, and her side hurt where the monster had grabbed her. And she could smell smoke. At least she didn't have to go to the bathroom yet. It had been a while since she'd been able to see light though the crack between the doors. No one had come near her hiding place, and although she'd heard footsteps in the house they had left quickly, barely getting farther than the living room. She didn't like this, not at all. When she became a Hunter she was never hiding again, and she wouldn't let any Fiends come close to her village. She would kill them all, and keep killing them until they all ran away, so far away they couldn't ever come back. She wouldn't be scared of them, they would be scared of her!

She waved her hand through the air, making a thin rope of water appear. At least she wouldn't go thirsty. Most of her people had some kind of magic; hers had to do with water, like her mother's and her sister's magics. Her father's magic had to do with plants, while her Uncle Damien's magic was in metals. She curled up tighter, wishing someone would come for her. The closet wasn't very big and most of it was taken up by weapon racks and hooks, and it felt like it was getting smaller and smaller with every passing moment, the darkness a heavy weight on her small body.

She jumped when she heard noises outside, but it was just rain falling, her namesake. Normally that would have made her feel better, but not today. Today it was a reminder that she was alone. She wrapped her arms around herself, tears falling again. Where was everyone? Where was her sister so they could go out and play in the rain, jumping through puddles and trying to spray each other using their magics. She could imagine it now: Storm and Daddy would come back in and get her, and then she and her sister would run outside. Then Daddy would follow them after he put his armour and big sword away. While they were looking for the biggest puddle to jump in Uncle Damien would sneak up behind them and jump in another, splashing them both while their mother shook her head, laughing and then drenching him with her own magic while the girls laughed and he pretended to fall down dead in defeat. Later, when they were all soaking wet Daddy would make a fire in the fireplace and they would sit by it, warm, dry, safe and together while her parents told funny stories about when they were younger, and ordering Uncle Damien to shut up a lot when he started to tell a story that Rain and Storm weren't supposed to hear until they were older. They would let her and Storm stay up past their bedtime, and then Mommy and Daddy would tuck them into their beds and there wouldn't be any nightmares.

That's what would happen. That's what had to happen, she decided as she wiped away her tears. Any moment now, Storm and Daddy would come through those doors. She just had to wait, just had to be quiet and be patient. Any moment now…

"Rain!" She bolted upright at the rough shout, but it wasn't her father. Uneven footsteps staggered across the wooden floors. "Rain! Fuck!" Something crashed into the wall. She covered her mouth with her hands to keep from making any kind of sound. "Fuck… Rain!" Her parents wouldn't swear like that, though her uncle would. But shouldn't he have been helping her father look for Storm if they weren't back yet? Her mother should have been the one to get her while they searched, or her father, since her mother was more powerful. The footsteps drew closer, into her parents' room. She whimpered. The closet doors were wrenched open and she screamed as torchlight showed a tall figure covered in torn cloth, metal, leather, and blood. She lunged to her feet and tried to run, but she only made it a few steps before she was caught. "Hey, kiddo, it's me, I've got you," Uncle Damien's voice was a rough rumble as he held her tightly, careful to hold his torch away from her with an arm that shook. She stopped fighting and clung to him instead. "That's right, I've got you." He stepped away from the closet, but swayed and fell against the wall with a gasp, swearing again. He paused for a moment before righting himself, though he still leaned against the wall, taking deep breaths.

"I want Daddy!" She cried, shaking. It was still dark, she could still smell smoke, and the front door was still broken apart, rain falling into the living room, and Daddy and Storm still weren't back. Everything was wrong. Damien froze, then slowly sank down the wall to the floor, his head dropping until his forehead was on her shoulder and he started shaking. That wasn't right. Something was wrong, this wasn't how Uncle Damien acted ever. "Where's Daddy and Storm?" She asked. They should have come right back. "Where's Mommy?" If Uncle Damien was there, then her mother should have been back as well. Whenever they left on a hunt together they always returned together.

He flinched and held her tighter, lifting his head to cover his face with one blood-splattered hand. "Uncle Damien, where are they?" He just kept shaking. "Uncle Damien!" She tugged his hand away and froze. Her uncle, her strong, dangerous, fearless, laughing uncle was crying. "Uncle Damien!" That scared her more than the monsters ever could.

"I'm sorry," he said, his voice cracking. "I'm sorry." She shoved at his shoulder and froze when he gasped in pain. The torchlight showed her hands were covered in red. She started shaking and sobbing again, afraid. This was all wrong. This wasn't what was supposed to happen. She should have been playing in the rain with Storm. Damien gently shifted her so her head was on his other shoulder.

"I want Mommy!" She said again. She didn't understand why he was apologising. "I want Daddy and I want Storm!" She wanted her family back together, all of them. Right now. "Where are they?"

Mercury eyes met sapphire, tears falling freely as he took a ragged breath. "Your mother is dead."

"But Mommy promised she would come back..." Dead people didn't come back, she knew that, like her grandparents, and Uncle Damien's parents, and Raven. "She promised!"

"I know she did, she wanted to, I swear she wanted to, but Rain, sometimes no matter how much someone wants to keep their promise... they can't."

"She promised!" Rain insisted again. Mommy always kept her promises. Always. "She promised me she would come back!"

Damien closed his eyes for a moment and seemed to come to a decision when he opened them again, holding her gaze with his as he spoke in a low, serious tone she'd never heard him use before. "The Fiends killed your mother. She wanted to come back to you, she fought so damn hard, but there were too many of them." She stared at him for a few moments.

"You couldn't save her?" She knew he had in the past, just like Mommy had saved him. He flinched like she'd hit him.

"I couldn't," he said, looking away. "I couldn't do anything." She didn't like this. He wasn't talking to her like he normally did. He was talking to her like he would talk to Mommy or Daddy or another grown up now.

"But you're the best!" She'd heard so many times that her uncle and her mother where the best Hunters in the village and among the best Hunters alive. Elite was what everyone called it. They were elite Hunters

"Yeah, Rain, but sometimes that's just not enough." She put her head back against his shoulder, exhausted and confused. There was too much she didn't understand, and too much that she did. She wanted to ask if she could go home, where it was safe. But she was home, and it wasn't safe. Not anymore.

After a while Uncle Damien stood, keeping her in his strong arms, though he staggered.

"Where are we going?" She asked, no longer crying. She was tired, her head ached and her eyes burned. She didn't really know what was going on. Nothing made sense anymore.

"We're going to find your dad and Storm," he replied, stumbling and almost falling again, only catching himself by grabbing onto the wall. "Godsdamnit!"

"I can walk," she said, and he put her down, though she kept a tight grip on his hand. The leather of the fingerless gloves he wore were soft and his rings digging into her hand, but she didn't care about that. She couldn't help but stare at the red puddle in the kitchen where Storm had been taken but her uncle gently pulled her away, leading her out of the house and past more blood. Outside it was dark and raining, and there were people all around, carrying others, holding them up, or shouting names while they ran around. Most of the wooden houses had broken pieces, a lot of them doors or windows. One or two were on fire, but mostly the fire came from where the bodies of the Fiends were being burned or from the torches people carried.

"This way," Uncle Damien said, gently directing her to where a group of people were gathering. She could tell that many were Hunters from the way they dressed, while others wore the uniform of the Guardians who served the Academy. Sometimes her father wore that uniform, but mostly he stayed in their village, especially if her mother and uncle were gone. Damien caught the attention of one of the Guardians and soon his wounds were being bandaged. Rain looked down at her clothes and saw a lot of red marks on them. "Don't worry," he said before she could start to panic. She knew she didn't have any cuts where the Fiend had grabbed her, only bruises.

"Can you ride?" The Guardian asked, tying a final bandage around his leg.

"Yeah," he replied, though he was almost grey under his light gold skin. "I'll take the kid with me." The Guardian didn't protest, just found a horse and helped them both on, getting Rain settled in front of her uncle and finding a waterproof cloak to wrap around both of them. When she was older and learned how to use her magic she would be able to make the rain move where she wanted it, just like her mother could.

"When are we going to see Daddy and Storm?" Rain wondered when he didn't move, for all he looked as impatient as she felt.

"We have to wait for a few other people and we're all going to go together."

"But I want to go now," she protested.

"I know, so do I, but we need to wait." His voice was calm but she could tell there was something more, something he was hiding from her. "Why don't you close your eyes for a little while and try to get some sleep?" She nodded reluctantly and closed her eyes.

Next thing Rain knew, she was waking up and they were moving. The sky was just starting to grow lighter and the rain had stopped. Uncle Damien still held her, his eyes red like hers were whenever she'd been crying.

"Hey kiddo," he said softly when he saw that she was awake, his voice hoarse. She looked around. There were other people on horseback too, and more being pulled in wagons. Most were battered and bandaged, some were crying or moaning. She shifted so she could hide against her uncle. He wrapped the edges of the cloak around her so she wouldn't have to see.

"Where are we going?" She asked, disoriented. For a moment she was going to ask if they were going to see her mother, but then she remembered that her mother was dead. She wiped at her eyes as tears started falling again. Damien shifted so he could hold the reins in one hand and hold her with the other.

"We're going to the hospital," he reminded her. "We're going to see Storm and your dad."

"Are they okay?" She needed to know, had to know they wouldn't die. He hesitated a moment too long and she started to panic.

"Woah, kiddo, Rain," he said, gently rubbing her back. "Your dad'll be fine, he's a tough old bastard," Damien pointedly ignored the disapproving looks from other adults, "it'll take a little while, but he'll be fine. Your sister... she was hurt pretty bad. It's going to take a long time before she gets better, and she won't be the same as before."

"I don't get it." She felt tired still and all dried out like she didn't have room inside to feel anything more.

He took a breath. "The Fiend messed her up pretty bad. She lost a leg, and even when she's better she's not going to be able to move around like she used to."

"Can she still be a Hunter?" Damien shook his head. "She never really wanted to fight monsters," Rain told him. "I guess now she won't have to."

"Don't worry kiddo, there's plenty of stuff your sister is good at. She'll figure things out. It'll take a long time, but she'll make it work." Not 'it'll be all better'. She knew enough to know that there was a difference.

"What about Mommy? What'll happen to Mommy?"

"Once your sister wakes up we'll have her funeral," Damien said, swallowing hard.

"The Fiends didn't eat her?" That's what happened in a lot of the stories she'd heard. Not from her parents, but others, other kids who had Hunters in their lives.

He closed his eyes for a long moment again. "No, they didn't. I couldn't save her, but I wouldn't let them eat her."

"Thank you," she said, then curled up against him and closed her eyes once more.

Damien woke her up when they got to the hospital. Their village only had a few healers because it was small and close to the city. The hospital was part of the Guardian Academy, the large stone building beside a big castle with many towers. She'd been there a few times, but never inside the castle, no matter how much she'd begged. She looked up at the imposing building where Hunters were trained, where she'd always wanted to go. Normally she would have been excited, but now she just felt sad. The group they were with stopped and Damien dismounted without his usual grace, wincing as his feet hit the flagstones, then held an arm up for her.

"Here, let me help," a young man wearing a healer's robes said, reaching for Rain. She moved away, trying to get to Damien. "Come now, I won't hurt you."

"No!" She protested loudly, kicking at him. "No!"

"The poor child's been traumatised, Roderick," all three turned to see the healer from Rain's village approach. He looked tired as well, his tunic and pants stained with blood. "You can't expect her to react well to an unfamiliar face."

The younger man hesitated. "Ah, yes." He turned to Rain as the other healer left to attend to someone else. "I'm sorry my dear. Your..." He looked from her to Damien, taking in the lack of family resemblance.

"Uncle," Damien supplied.

"Yes, your uncle is hurt and it would hurt him more if he lifted you off the horse. Will you let me help you down so he doesn't get hurt more?" Rain looked from him to Uncle Damien. Her uncle was standing weird, his hand pressed against the thick bandages at his side and she could see that some of his other bandages had started to turn pink. Plus, he hadn't been able to carry her earlier, either. She nodded reluctantly and let the healer lift her down, though she immediately reached over and clung to Damien's good leg the second her feet were on the ground, watching the healer, who held up his hands in a gesture of surrender. Damien ruffled her hair, making a noise that was something between a laugh and a sigh.

"Didn't your parents teach you manners?" He asked her.

"Thank you," she said quickly.

"Now, we're here to find two people, Storm Undine and Ash Glade," he said. "Do you know where they are?"

Roderick frowned. "Perhaps you should look to your own wounds first?"

"I'll be fine, we just need to see them first," Damien said shortly, glancing down at Rain. Roderick gave in with a sigh and turned towards the hospital. The moment his back was turned Damien took a long drink from his flask, grimaced, then took Rain's hand and they followed the healer.

Inside the hospital was very clean, the air scented with blood and medicinal herbs, with healers in white and grey robes moving quickly from person to person and room to room. Even the hallways were crowded with people who were hurt. Roderick stopped to ask for directions and then took them to one of the upper floors. He knocked on one of the doors and another healer came out, red on his robes. Rain edged closer to Damien, who gently squeezed her hand. Questions were asked and answered, and then they were allowed in. Her father stood and staggered over, falling to his knees as Rain ran to his arms, sobbing again.

"I'm sorry I left you there for so long," he said. Rain didn't care about that. She just cared about the familiar scent of evergreen trees and her father's embrace.

"Daddy!" She cried. "Daddy, Mommy is dead. The Fiends killed her." He looked up at Damien for a moment then back to her.

"I know sweetie," he said quietly and she was alarmed to see tears in his bright green eyes. "I know."

"Why didn't you and Storm come back?" She asked, trying to see her sister over her father's broad shoulders but even kneeling he was too tall.

He swallowed hard. "Honey, Storm was hurt, and so was I. The healers wouldn't let me leave."

"Oh."

"That's why you were stuck with me. Your dad wanted to make sure someone you knew would find you. Besides, we all know I'm your favorite uncle," he added, winking as he moved to sit in one of the chairs with a grimace. "I wasn't hurt too badly, so I could sneak away from the healers."

"But Mommy always said to listen to the healers," Rain said.

"Yeah, but sometimes even the healers can be wrong." He didn't look at the healers who were still in the room as he spoke.

Just then the door opened and a man in an Academy guard uniform came in. "You!" He shouted when he saw Damien. Rain noticed that his face was badly bruised. "Why haven't you been arrested?"

"Maybe I didn't 'sneak' away, per se," Damien amended.

The older healer in the room spoke up. "Shut up or get out." The guard turned to glare at him but the healer didn't back down. "I don't care, I really don't. There's a badly injured girl who doesn't need your shouting, plus two injured warriors and a girl who's been through more than enough today."

"You'd better listen to the healer," Damien said with a smirk. The guard turned an odd shade of red, but stomped out all the same.

"Are you in trouble?" She whispered when the door closed.

"Nah," he said. "Still, I should get it straightened out. Why don't you stay here for a bit? I'm sure your sister would like it if you did."

"After you get it straightened out are you coming straight back?" Her father asked, and there was something in his tone she didn't understand.

"You don't have to worry about me tonight, Ash," Damien said. "I'm going to the morgue to get things sorted out for Tempest, then I'm coming right back." He rose with a grunt and limped towards the door, still holding his side.

"Don't go!" Rain protested. If he went, there was a chance he might not come back, just like her mother wasn't coming back. She wanted everyone to stay together. If they were together, they were safe.

He stopped and looked back. "There aren't any Fiends here, Rain. I'll be back before you know it. I promise."

"But you said sometimes promises can't be kept," she reminded him.

"Yeah, I did say that." He sighed, rubbing a hand over his face.

"Rain, Damien has to go just for a moment," her father said. "He's not leaving the hospital." She looked at Damien, who nodded. She held his gaze for a long moment before she nodded. When he left she pushed past her father to get to her sister. Storm was asleep in a large bed, and she was almost covered in bandages. Rain frowned. Something didn't look right.

"Where's her other leg?" She asked, looking at the flat space that shouldn't have been just below Storm's knee.

Her father sighed and managed to get back into the chair, his face twisted with pain. "She lost it," he told her.

"Shouldn't we go look for it?" Rain asked, confused.

He shook his head. "No, sweetie, it doesn't work like that. She'll get a new leg."

"Uncle Damien said that she'd still have trouble moving for a long time."

He nodded. "Yes, she will, even after she gets the leg."

"I'll help her," Rain decided.

"I'm sure she'll appreciate that."

Rain looked back at her sister. "When will she wake up?"

"I don't know." She looked up at her father, who looked at the healers.

"Tomorrow we'll wake her up," he said. "For now she needs to rest so we can get to work on mending the worst of the damage." He looked like there was something more he wanted to say, but when he looked at Rain he stopped himself.

As promised, Damien came back a while later. He was wearing different clothes and wasn't covered in blood any more. Roderick trailed behind him, Rain hadn't noticed him leaving. "Hey kiddo," he said when she ran to him before returning to her father, climbing into his lap and curling up again, careful of the bandages. Damien's eyes were red again, and she noticed his shirtsleeve was a bit damp. He went back to leaning against the wall by the door.

"When's the funeral going to be?" Her father asked, voice cracking.

"Sunset." Damien looked at the healer. "Can you wake Storm up then? It's her mother's funeral."

The older healer paused for a moment, looking at Storm. "For a short time might be fine, but I need to clear it with the Head Healer," he said, walking out.

"He's stressed," the younger healer said. "We don't normally see Fiends attacking our villages like this, not so close to the city, anyway. We just got word that two others were hit as well, so we're going to be seeing even more patients flooding in before dawn." He looked at the Hunter and the Guardian. "Will they come after the Academy, the city?" Rain could tell he was scared.

Damien sighed. "No, they won't. They're not exactly mindless beasts, they seem to be able to learn, since they only rarely attack villages in the territories where you have tons of people able to fight them. Besides, the human territories are far more populated and easier targets."

"Something like this happens every twenty years or so," her father added.

"I heard about the last one," Roderick said, nodding. "It happened just before I was born."

"My wife…" her father's voice cracked and he clenched his hands into fists. "She lost her parents in that one, and that time they actually did attack the outskirts of the city."

Rain took all of this in from the safety of her father's arms. She wasn't going to let anything like this happen again. She would become a strong, powerful Hunter. The adults kept talking for a while, until the older healer came back. "She should be stable enough, but the important thing is that she stays calm, and both of you will need healers to accompany you." He gave Damien a considering look. "You should stay here for a few days as well, but I'm afraid the hospital is no place for a child who does not require our care. We can find somewhere for her to stay during your convalescence."

"No!" Her father wrapped his arms tighter around Rain. "You can't take her and I won't let you hand her over to strangers!" Rain had another uncle, but she'd only met him once. He lived in the city but never visited and she didn't think anyone liked him very much.

"There's no other choice. You need to rest, the wounded girl needs quiet. Besides, we're getting at least two more waves of patients, and the other villages didn't have the same population of Hunters that yours did."

"I don't want to go away," Rain protested, panicking again, clutching at her father.

"I'll take her," Damien said at last.

"You need to stay here," the healer protested. "In case you didn't notice you're still bleeding and you have broken and bruised bones among your other wounds."

"You want to take a traumatised child away from her family? Weren't you watching what happened when I was about to leave for a few minutes?" Damien snarled, stepping forward and nearly falling, but he didn't back down. "Either she stays or I go." His hand was on his sword hilt. Rain shivered and couldn't hold back a whimper of fear. Damien glanced over at her and took a deep breath, removing his hand from his sword. "You can't keep me here. I'll get a room at an inn or something for tonight." His voice was far calmer, though the threat still wasn't entirely gone.

"There's no need," Roderick spoke up and everyone looked at him. "I live in the staff apartments at the Academy. You can stay there for the time being, since I doubt I'll be home, and you'll be close by." He looked at the older healer. "I trust that'll be suitable? If he has any complications from his injuries we'll close by and I can check on them."

The older healer sighed and ran a hand through his thinning grey hair. "I can't naysay any of that, but Ash can't leave for a few days yet, and Storm could be here for a month or more." He looked at Rain's father. "What we're doing tonight is basically putting a very temporary plug in a leak. She won't be able to move much."

Her father nodded, then turned to Damien. "Are you sure?" He asked, and again, there was something behind the question that wasn't voiced out loud. "Are you sure you can handle this?"

"Yeah," Damien said roughly. "I will."

"I'll show you to the apartment, you can get something to eat and rest for a few hours before the funeral," Roderick offered.

Damien nodded and looked at Rain. "Want to come along, kiddo?"

She hesitated. She didn't want to leave her father and Storm again.

"Go on," her father encouraged her. "We're not going anywhere."

"But I am."

"I'll protect you," Damien said, holding out a hand. "Between Roderick and me, nothin' bad'll happen." She wanted to point out that something bad had happened, her mother had died, but something told her that wouldn't be a good thing to say, and she didn't want to hurt her uncle's feelings. He was already sad.

"There's a market near my apartment," Roderick said quickly. "Why don't you see if there's something your sister would like? It might help her feel a little happier."

"You did want to help her," her father reminded her.

"Okay," she said reluctantly, hopping down and taking Uncle Damien's hand as they left.

That night she went to a funeral.

It was different from the other funerals she'd attended. When her grandparents had died there had been a group of people, and when Raven had died it was just Uncle Damien, her parents, Storm, and her, and some people had come by later. She didn't remember it that well anymore. Uncle Damien had left for a long time after that, though Storm said it was only six months. She'd been confused at the time, why none of the people who'd stopped by had gone to the funeral, but her mother had said she would explain later, when Rain was older. She'd guessed it had something to do with Uncle Damien, who'd acted really weird but really sad the whole time. Then he'd disappeared and six months later her mother had gone away for a week and came back with him and he'd stayed with them, never moving back to the flat he'd lived in with Raven.

This time things were different. There were lots of funerals happening all at once, lots of pyres burning along The Cliff, smoke hiding the stars. Even though there were a lot of fires, it was still cold because of the brisk wind, but she stood next to Damien, almost hidden in his cloak. Beside them her father and Storm sat in chairs with wheels. Storm looked strange, like she wasn't really awake, and she was strapped to a lot of things to keep her still while Roderick stood by her side. Rain still wasn't sure how she felt about him, though he'd helped her pick out a bracelet for Storm, which her sister now wore. She kept her eyes on the burning wood that held her mother, wrapped in a cloth.

"Does it hurt?" She asked Uncle Damien as the edge of the cloth caught fire, holding his hand tighter. She didn't want Mommy to burn, because then she would never see her again. Her ashes would be scattered over the cliffs behind the Academy, her sword stuck into the ground as a marker, like all the other Hunters who'd died.

"No," he said quietly, slowly kneeling down beside her. "It doesn't hurt." She glanced up to see that he was crying again. They all were, even Daddy, even Storm.

"I-I don't want M-Mommy to b-be g-gone," she cried. Damien pulled her into a tight hug.

"Neither do I."

"Uncle Damien, you're one of the best Hunters, right?" She asked, pulling back so she could look him in the eye.

"Yeah." He didn't sound happy about it.

"I want to be the best Hunter *ever*."

"Why?" He asked after a pause, the firelight reflecting in his mercury eyes.

"Because I don't want Fiends to take anyone away ever again. Not from me or from anyone else." She'd seen all the people who'd been hurt, bandages where arms and legs were supposed to be, everyone covered in blood, crying. Everyone was crying now too. She could hear the people at the other pyres.

"You can't save everyone," he said gently. It was a lesson she'd learned already, watching him try to save Raven, and it was reinforced now as she watched the pyre burn, the cloth steadily turning black as it was eaten up by the hungry flames.

"I don't care. I'll save as many as I can!" She said fiercely, more determined now than ever.

"It's going to take a lot of work."

"I know. Will you help me?"

"I promise," he said. "I promise I'll help you." She threw her arms around his neck and sobbed as the flames rose high into the night.

Part 2
Hunter

1

Beginning

Rain shoved a lock of midnight blue hair out of her face, ignoring the pain in her wounded arm as she watched the Fiend she'd just beheaded, her sword at the ready. She didn't relax until it started to shrivel up until it was little more than a fragile leather sack of bones. Then she let out the breath she'd been holding and let her sword arm fall, though she didn't drop her weapon. She glanced at her wounded arm, wincing at the sight. Her protection spell had kept her arm from being clawed off, but that was about it. She sighed; it served her right for not renewing the spell when she should have. She was also pretty sure that at least one of her ribs was broken, if not more.

"Not bad, kiddo," a voice behind her said. Rain spun around, sword rising again, and regretted it when her head kept spinning. She hadn't quite realised how much blood she'd lost. She staggered, and a moment later a hand caught her uninjured arm, steadying her.

"Uncle Damien!" She reached up to throw her arms around his neck like she always did, only to be stopped by a wave of pain. She swayed and Damien took more of her weight, helping her to the ground as he looked at her blood-covered arm. "How long were you watching?" She asked, looking up at him. His messy black hair was longer than normal, and he had a short beard instead of his usual shadow. Her uncle fell somewhere in between hating facial hair and generally not giving a damn about his appearance. There were fine lines at the corners of his mouth and eyes, there was a little silver mixed in with his black hair, though that had always been there. His mercury eyes were sharp and defiant though now she could still see a glimmer of pride.

"Long enough, though I almost stepped in when the bastard got your arm, but you handled it well." High praise from the Hunter who'd started her training while she was still a grief-stricken child to help her combat the monsters in her nightmares. He pulled a battered old flask from his pack along with a roll of bandages. He opened the flask and poured the dark amber liquid over the deep cuts that covered most of her upper arm from shoulder to elbow.

"Fucking hell!" Rain gasped as her vision went fuzzy. "A little warning would be nice next time!" She had to look away when she could see white bone in the wound. She was a Hunter in training and tough as nails like the best of them, but there were still some things she just didn't need to see, like her own bones. If it had belonged to someone else it would have been fine.

"Next time remember to renew your protection spells," he said, taping his ear, which was pierced a number of times, like her own were. Hunters and students both kept spells in jewelry for later or prolonged use, and Rain was no different. The jewelry allowed them to use spells that their own innate powers wouldn't normally allow them to cast. They ranged from single use to being able to last for a period of time. Some Hunters also got their spells as tattoos, which tended to be far more powerful and lasted a lot longer, but were also a lot more expensive. Since most students and even early Hunters were still growing into their powers only Hunters who were three years past graduation could start getting them. Rain knew her uncle had his armour spell as a tattoo on his back and a few others, mostly on his arms or torso. She tended to get her spells in earrings or beads she could put on small hoop earrings since she found other kinds of jewelry more irritating when fighting and dreamed of the day when she was allowed to get tattoo spells. Her uncle wore rings, but he was also a metal mage. When the spells were used up the beads would turn a burnt black, which was what her uncle had noticed.

"Yeah," she said, looking away, embarrassed.

"It happens to everyone, just make sure it doesn't happen twice," was all he said as he turned to look at the Fiend. "You got a fang?"

She shook her head, so he finished tying the bandage and went over to the corpse to snap one off. It was as long as her thumb. "I wonder how much I'll get for it." She knew that the people who dealt with Hunter's kills could find out what kind of Fiend it was from a fang and figure out how much to pay them, but she didn't know how. That wasn't really explained it in class except that magic was involved.

Damien looked down at the body for a moment. "A few silver pieces, I'd say." He tapped a red gem than hung from one of his own earring, and fire appeared in his hand. He threw it at the Fiend, which burst into flames for a few seconds before turning into ashes. It would have gone away to dust after a few weeks, but the corpses tended to attract more Fiends. "First we get you to a healer." He reached down and helped her to her feet, sliding an arm around her shoulders to help steady her when she stumbled, the blood loss starting to take effect. Breathing didn't feel so fun either. He handed her a flask, and it was the one of the stuff he'd poured over her wounds. "Take a drink, it'll help with the pain until we get there." She did, tipping her head back like she'd seen him do, only to cough and sputter as the liquid made her throat burn like the body they'd left behind.

"What the fuck is that?" She gasped. "You drink that stuff?" She was almost certain she could use it to clean rust off a blade.

"Nope, that stuff is strictly medicinal. I'm a functioning drunk, not a suicidal one," he reminded her. "I get that shit made special, it'll kill any infections and clear your head, as long as you don't drink too much."

"Right," she said as they began walking towards the village. The liquor did help dull the pain a bit, though she knew she'd be paying for it later. Damien Lance might be one of the best Hunters around, but he was also one of the most infamous for drinking and being a walking tragedy. She couldn't say they were wrong about the first, though she felt that much of it was exaggerated. He didn't get truly drunk often, and never when he'd had to take care of her and her sister. As for the latter, well, few Hunters had many happy stories to tell once they left the Academy, one of the reasons why many of them were drunks or had other issues. Her uncle had seen and been through more than most of them as an elite Hunter. It was kind of a miracle he was as sane and functional as he was from what she knew, and that was only a fraction of what he'd been through, bits and pieces picked up as she grew older and more able to understand how fucked up the world was. Some of it she would likely never know: things too awful to be repeated except in whispers and rumours she sometimes heard.

"So, have you figured out who you're going to ask to mentor you?" All Hunter students spent their last year in the field with an experienced Hunter. The Guardians did a mix of field and class work, and as far as she knew the Keeper students did mostly classwork. Passing meant surviving the year and proving to her mentor that she could survive, kill Fiends quickly and efficiently, and had the mental strength to withstand everything else. It was to the advantage of both the student and the mentor that they paired with someone they could get along with, and the school finalised the decisions. Mostly they got it right.

"Hey, you could have changed your mind," he said when Rain just gave him a look.

"As if," she replied. "Anyone else ask you about being a mentor?"

"A few; the Academy asked me to be a mentor and I finally said yes, but surprisingly there haven't been as many long, awkward letters to reply to than usual." He sighed dramatically. "Alas, I made a promise once, and I'll be damned if I break it." A promise made to a young child in front of her mother's funeral pyre.

"They know you're my uncle," she reminded him. "Most of my friends knew you were going to be my mentor before we even started at the Academy." Most of them also forgot that she and Damien weren't related by blood; he'd met her mother when they joined the Academy as orphans and had quickly become the only family the other had ever known. Then when she had died he'd practically been a second parent to them, especially when they were younger and needed someone home with them, though he'd still been away often once her father and Storm recovered from their wounds. He was a Hunter, it was his job and his duty to hunt and kill Fiends wherever they were, and for the most part the territories were safe, so he had to go farther.

She smiled as they walked through the village gates. Twelve years ago it hadn't been fortified; those walls of wood reinforced with magic had been added too late, a reaction to a tragedy rather than a move to prevent it. Rain stumbled as a particularly nasty wave of pain came from her side. Damien adjusted his hold and sighed. "First thing tomorrow morning you're going to see the mages about that protection spell." Rain nodded silently. That sounded like a very good plan.

They were lucky, there was no one else looking to see a healer when they arrived. There were two healers in their village, and both worked out of their shared home. "What have you done to yourself now?" Jaques sighed when he saw her. Most of the exasperation in his face and voice was fake. Most of it. Of the rest, maybe half was deserved.

"You should see the other guy," Rain said as they followed the older man into one of the rooms. Damien helped Rain onto the table before leaning against a wall.

"I'm sure," he said, cutting away the bandage on her arm. His bushy grey eyebrows went up. "You're lucky you didn't lose the arm," he said as he ran light fingers over the deep cuts and Rain bit the inside of her cheek to keep from crying out. "Where were you?"

"Just outside the walls." She'd been on her way home from the Academy. She could have stayed in the dorms, she supposed, but she'd opted instead to take the hour-long walk instead. He shook his head and did a quick but thorough examination of the rest of her body.

"You have one broken rib, and another two are bruised. I'll fix the break and I can stop the bleeding in your arm, but you're going to have to take it easy for a week, especially the next two or three days," he said at last, stroking his beard.

"Will I have scars?"

"Yes," he answered, "and before you ask, yes, they will look cool." He looked at Damien and rolled his eyes. "You Hunters and your scars…"

"Hey, we're supposed to be awesome, roguish warriors, we'd better look the part," he said, taking a drink from a more familiar worn and battered flask that would contain regular –albeit still strong- liquor instead of the rust remover he'd had out previously.

Jaques just sighed and moved so that one hand hovered over the wounds on her arm and the other over her broken rib. "Try to relax," he instructed. Rain gritted her teeth and tried to do just that as his magic rippled over and through her, and she felt muscle and bone move and knit back together under her skin. It didn't hurt, the magic dulled the pain to almost nothing, but it was highly unpleasant nonetheless. A few minutes later he took his hands away. "How's that?" Rain sat up slowly and looked down at her arm. The wounds were still angry and raw, but mostly closed and not bleeding anymore. She was just happy not to have to look at her own bones again. She carefully raised her arm and tried to move it around. It hurt like hell, but the skin didn't tear and it didn't make her want to pass out.

"A lot better, thanks," she said. He picked up a small pot of a bitter smelling salve and rubbed some over the wounds before bandaging her arm again. She could feel the power in the concoction seep into her flesh.

"Put on a thin coat of this twice a day for the next week," he said, closing the pot and handing it to her. "That'll set you to rights. It'll work for any kind of wound, so make sure you keep it with you when you're in the field." He gave her a dry smile. "I'm sure you and your uncle will make excellent use of it."

"Thanks," she said again and hopped down, only to clutch the table as vertigo hit.

"Take it easy," he repeated sternly. "I'll send a message to your instructors." She nodded and walked out slowly, Damien a step behind her.

"So, mages in the morning," she said as he closed the door behind them.

"Yep, now let's get you home."

Her father and sister were both home when they arrived. Her father looked as he always had, though like Damien there were some fine lines around his mouth and bottle green eyes, eyes that went straight to the bandage around her arm as she sat down at the kitchen table.

"What happened?" He asked, looking from her to Damien.

"A Fiend attacked me and I won," she replied, keeping it simple and leaving out the part where her spell had failed because she forgot to get it redone. She'd taken the bead off her earring before they'd arrived and stuck it in a pocket. Damien hadn't said anything, just shook his head.

"She did well," Damien added, hugging Storm when she jumped up. Her sister still bore signs of the attack that had shattered their childhood, and not just in the metal leg she wore. A line of scar tissue went from below her eye to the base of her neck, the only visible scar over her clothing, but Rain knew that her arms and back were covered with spider webs of scarring, almost as bad as their father and uncle for all she'd been in one fight and they'd been in thousands. Her leg was a mix of magic and metal, allowing her to walk easily and with only a slight limp, though she couldn't run because of damage done to her back and the upper part of her missing leg.

"We weren't expecting you for another week!" Storm said, sitting back down. They hadn't seen him in a little over four months. There had been many letters exchanged, but it just wasn't the same.

"Why does everyone expect me to arrive at the last minute?" He wondered, running a hand over his short beard.

"Because normally you do arrive at the last minute," Rain's father pointed out, putting a large arm around Damien's shoulders for a moment as he walked past. He still limped slightly from injuries sustained in the same fight that had almost killed Storm, though as far as Rain could tell the damage didn't impede his fighting. "Unless there's an open bar," he added with a grin.

Damien glared at the other man, opened his mouth to protest, then closed it and sat down with a shrug. "I got nothing," he told the girls, who shook their heads, laughing, as he took a drink from his flask.

"So, are you ready to be run ragged for the next year?" Rain's father wondered as he checked on dinner.

"I've been preparing for this for years," Uncle Damien answered heavily, leaning back in his chair. "I think I might make it. Maybe..." He winked at Rain when she glared at him. "Anyways, I have a job lined up for us, so we'll be leaving a few days after the ceremony at the Academy."

"Really?" Rain asked, forgetting she was annoyed. Hunters could sometimes get hired out for odd jobs, usually when people wanted serious protection while traveling without dealing with dangers of hiring mercenaries and with something better than Rangers.

"Yeah, we're escorting one of the princes of Glask to the capital of Landaia. He's acting as an ambassador of some kind, and his royal parents are worried enough about political enemies and Fiends that they'd look to hiring a couple of demons instead of using their own guards." Humans called her kind demons, and had for centuries, no matter what the legends said about how her people had come to be, that they were humans who'd given up their souls for the power to fight the Fiends that were threatening to destroy everything. As it was, they didn't call themselves demons, at least those who grew up in the territories never did. No one had ever asked what they would have liked to call themselves, and as far as Rain knew none of her own people had tried to put a name on what they were.

"I think I heard that bandit activity is also on the rise in that region," Storm said, frowning. "Phantom mentioned it yesterday when he was dropping off some books." She'd graduated from the Academy as a Keeper a year before and as she had difficulty traveling they let her do a lot of her work from home.

"Did he also bring the flowers on the windowsill?" Rain wondered, raising a brow. Storm's glare was enough of an answer for her.

"He's nice," she said defensively.

"I think he's cool –for a Guardian," Rain said with a shrug. "He's also totally into you."

"How would you know that?"

"He was asking about you a few days ago." The Guardian had graduated the same year as her sister and worked in the city and the Academy, though the latter was where he was most often found, and Rain was certain it wasn't a coincidence. "It was totally obvious and Kestrel will back me up on it."

"I've met him a few times, he's a good kid," their father remarked. He didn't interfere in his daughter's love lives, not like some parents she knew. He trusted them to make decisions for themselves, though he still liked to be kept in the loop of who they were going out with.

"Anyway," Storm said, bringing the conversation back to the more important topic, "the important thing is that the bandits are actually dangerous, as in targeting our kind. He said that the Council was considering warning Hunters to be careful." Rain sat up a little. That was news. Bandits were a normal part of life for anyone outside of a major city, and all Hunters ran into them at some point, but they were never desperate or stupid enough to try to target someone with magic who made a career of killing monsters that sent humans running. Her people were faster, stronger, and had more acute senses than humans, among other things. Even aside from that, their magic was stronger and less limited than that of human mages. Yet more reasons humans feared and shunned her kind.

"They can try to target us," Damien said with a derisive snort. "But I can tell you now that if they don't up their game then we won't have to worry about them for long."

"How many did you kill?" Rain wondered, catching on to what he wasn't saying.

He grinned slightly. "Ten. They knew I was a Hunter, but that didn't seem to stop them. Hopefully now they've realised that the phrase 'it takes a monster to fight a monster' has some merit."

"Did they know who you were?" Ash wondered.

"Dunno, they didn't do a lot of talking, especially once they were dead, and two just up and ran after the first few fell. Didn't seem worth the effort to chase them." He shrugged. "They'll think twice about pulling that shit again, especially if they find out who I am." It wouldn't be a hard thing to do either, even most humans knew who the elite Hunters were.

"That's going to come back to bite you," Rain's father predicted, his tone grim. Damien shrugged carelessly. "Dinner's ready," he said a moment later, still shaking his head at his friend.

A week later Rain stood among her classmates on one side of the auditorium's stage while their mentors stood on the other. The contrast between the two groups was startling: the students looking like children next to the scarred, tattooed, pierced, and battle-hardened warriors. All of the Hunters on the stage had at least ten years of experience.

The Headmistress of the Academy stood front and centre, reading out her usual speech. Their audience was made up of family, visiting Hunters, some off-duty Guardians, Keepers, and younger students. Rain couldn't focus on the words, she was too excited. This was the last step, just this last year and she would be a full Hunter at last. She surreptitiously looked around, noting that she wasn't the only one who was a bit antsy. She spotted her father and Storm out in the audience, but not her father's older brother Vine, though that was hardly a surprise. He was a businessman of sorts who stayed in the city and didn't talk much to his younger brother, let alone his nieces. The few times Rain had met him she'd thought he was mean, cruel even. She glanced over at the Hunters, and Uncle Damien caught her look and winked. He'd gotten rid of the beard and once more sported his usual stubble, and he'd cut his hair as well.

It seemed like forever before the pairs started getting called up. Of course, it went in order of the student's last name, so as Rain Undine she'd be near the end, one of the downsides to having her mother's last name. Both Hunter and student walked to the front where the Headmistress and a few of their instructors stood. The student was presented to the community as a candidate, and the Hunter was announced as their mentor. Then they were both given medallions. The pendants had the Academy insignia and both of their names on one side, and on the other was a strange mirror-like black gem. The pendants acted as a kind of licence before they got their Hunter medallion, and they were spelled so that mentor and apprentice would be able to find one another at all times. There were other rumours about the pendants as well, but their instructors hadn't set any of them to rest, except that there was no magic known that could cause the pendants to falter or fall off. In a year's time she would get a new medallion, one all her own, with her own crest to tell the wold who she was.

"Rain Undine," the Headmistress, a retired Hunter, called at last. Rain walked forward to the spot where students had been instructed to stand. "Her mentor: Hunter Damien Lance." Uncle Damien ambled forward, and Rain could almost hear the sighs of her classmates and held back a shudder. She'd had to listen to them all week going on and on about him. It was nauseating. He stood beside her as the crowd applauded, her father and sister loudest of all. She'd be lying if she didn't wish that her mother had been there to see this. Her uncle would still be her mentor though, since parents were not permitted to be mentors for their children, not with the fatality rates. Still, they were lower than they would be after graduation. She tried to keep her expression schooled and serious like she'd been instructed to as the Headmistress slipped the medallions over their heads and Rain felt a slight buzz of energy as the magic settled over her. The next time she stood on this stage she'd be receiving her own medallion. She and Damien clasped hands, raising their arms high. The wounds on her arm had completely healed, with only faint, jagged scars across her upper arm to mark the damage and earn the jealousy of her classmates.

"Your mom would be so proud right now," Damien murmured just before they went back to their seats, quietly enough that only she could hear. Rain had to try to hold back tears as the last few pairs were called before they all went to the celebration in the Academy's great hall. Later the students and their mentors would go to the city and there would be a less formal, more drunken celebration. She tried not to think too hard about the fact that this would be the last time she would see some of her classmates, her friends. There were always a few deaths during the training year, and then a handful more over the next two years. By their tenth year as full Hunters, only about half of them would still be active. The others would be dead, burnt out, quit to raise families of their own or to try to retain what remained of their sanity. Those who remained had a good chance of living long lives as Hunters, like her uncle, as they'd proven they could handle themselves and the hardships that came with the job.

"So, any idea of what you're going to do now?" Kestrel asked, sidling up to her.

Rain nodded. "Already got a job lined up, actually. You?"

The taller girl shrugged. "Amber said that she's looking at a few leads, but none of them look promising, so it's likely we'll go on a hunting trip." She grinned. "We'll get to save the world, just like we always wanted to."

Rain grinned and waved to Kestrel's parents as her friend went over to them. She found her father, Storm, and Uncle Damien quickly as well.

"I'm so proud of you!" Storm said, wrapping her sister in a tight embrace. Her sister had inherited more of their father's height than Rain had, so her eyes were level with Storm's chin. "Let's see the medallion," she ordered. Rain held it up, a round gold pendant the size of a copper piece that hung from a long silver chain. A full Hunter's medallion was silver, a metal that was more valuable magically than gold. She could have done a handstand with the thing around her neck and it wouldn't fall off, part of the spells that kept it with her. The stylised crossed sword and bow that were the Academy insignia fit between Damien's name and her own. She turned it to the other side where the glossy stone was attached. Two dots, one silver and one blue, were next to one another in the center.

"They used our blood to finish the spell, so you're the blue and I'm the silver," Damien said. Rain nodded. Keepers had gathered blood from students and mentors once their partnerships were finalised. "Now there's no way for me to get away from you." He sighed miserably.

"You're the worst." Rain informed him with a glare.

"And you can't get away from me either!" He replied cheerfully, ruffling her hair. As with calling her 'kiddo' he was the only person in the world who could get away with it.

"Just remember that you picked the diabolical one," her father muttered, exchanging a grin with Storm.

Damien froze, an expression of horror on his face. "Shit, I take it back!" He pretended to try to pry the medallion off his neck.

"The *worst*," Rain repeated.

"It's too late," Storm said cheerfully. "I'll write a nice eulogy for you though."

"Thanks, I'm sure my ghostly self will appreciate it," he said dryly. "I'm writing both of you out of my will."

"I thought you already did," Rain said.

"Six or seven times now," Storm added.

"Save me," Uncle Damien begged their father.

Rain's father looked from his daughters to his friend, and quickly turned his attention to the stained glass windows. "What pretty glass," he said.

"*You're* the worst," the other man accused.

"What? It's not like I can win if I pick a side."

"Just think of how much you could lose if you don't," the Hunter threatened. "Remember, I know *everything*."

"Girls, leave your uncle alone," he said. The sisters sighed. "For now." They both grinned as Damien scowled. Other Hunters who knew the two men came around and talked to them, and Storm followed Rain when she went to join a group of her friends. They all knew and liked Rain's older sister, especially considering how she'd helped a number of them with their schoolwork. Not that those grades mattered this year.

"So, everyone ready for tonight?" Tristan asked the group when there was a lull in the conversation. "I mean, we've only been hearing about what it will be like forever."

"I don't know," Kestrel said, nervously playing with her medallion. "I mean, what if we make fools of ourselves in front of our mentors?" Not everyone got to have their uncle as their mentor, and some barely knew the Hunters they were paired with. Those who didn't have someone to ask approached a Hunter suggested by Hawk, who was in charge of the mentorships. He'd been doing the job since her uncle had finished at the Academy and the number of bad matches had gone down drastically.

Rain spoke up. "I'm pretty sure that's the point of tonight, to break the ice, isn't it? We're not going to learn or fight at our best if we're always worried about appearances, not to mention that they'll be relying on us to some extent since we'll be with them in dangerous situations."

"That is true," Adrian said, considering her point while the others nodded. None of them wanted to think about the other reason, that for some it would be a final farewell.

"So, where are you heading to?" Kestrel asked him

"Out around Kelaroon, they seem to be having a problem with Fiends in the area," Adrian said. "You?"

"Not sure if it's going to be hunting Fiends or a job," she replied.

"Well, whatever it may be, let's party hard tonight and not worry about tomorrow," he advised. "Looks like our mentors are gathering." The others in the group looked over and saw that it was true, so they went and joined the group. Rain hugged her sister before she left. Her father waved as she fell in step with Damien, Kestrel, and her mentor Amber, the medallion shifting against her skin with each step, bringing her closer to her dreams. She didn't want to think about how many of them were being brought closer to their deaths.

2
Life Lessons

Two days later Rain was double-checking her horse before they left to escort the prince. She'd made it through the celebrations two nights before relatively unscathed, unlike many of her classmates and a number of Hunters after the night of drunken revelry. Even Uncle Damien had been a little worse for wear. She couldn't wait to go. Sure they'd done some hunting exercises at the Academy, but it was different, safer. Now it would just be her and Damien out in the world. This trip alone would be the longest she'd ever been away from home, since she normally went back and forth to the Academy and the city, with occasional trips to the Hunter's memorial site, and even that was in the Academy's shadow. It would also mark the first time she left the territories, the lands her people had claimed for their own thousands of years ago, lands free from human rule and prejudice.

"All ready?" Storm asked, coming outside.

"Yup, I double checked everything, and I'm just waiting for Uncle Damien. He said he had to pick something up," she replied, fighting to sit still.

"I can't believe my baby sister going off as a Hunter." Her older sister sighed. "I can remember the day you were born like it was yesterday."

"You can't."

"Actually I can. It was a traumatic event for me," she said with a grin. "Come inside, Dad's got something for you."

"Bitch," Rain said without heat, following her sister inside. She caught her reflection in a window and couldn't hold back a grin. She looked like a Hunter now. Instead of wearing the Academy uniform or practice gear she wore black leather pants and a black shirt under a dark blue and black corset. She had two leather belts that hung crooked on her waist for her pouches and weapons, along with knee-high black boots, plus black vambraces and fingerless gloves. Her corset was reinforced with chain mail, and her boots had steel plates over her shins and steel over her toes. Her new armour spell would protect her, but a little backup never hurt. A neat row of silver hoops lined both ears, ready for spell beads if she didn't already have one in. She'd also gotten a special nose ring enchanted so that it would keep her from inhaling smoke. Around her neck she had her Academy medallion, which fell between her breasts so only the chain was visible unless she pulled it out of her shirt. She'd left her dark blue cloak with her horse. Few Hunters wore bright colours, let alone bright cloaks. Dirt and blood showed too easily and someone who hunted monsters didn't want to make themselves an easy target.

For weapons she had a sword, a few daggers, and a bow. Students were allowed to choose what weapons to specialise in, though they were trained to be at least competent with most others, most of them choosing some type of sword in the end. It was customary for students to receive the weapons they would be relying on in the field in their third year, so they could master them before going into the field. Like Uncle Damien she fought with a longsword and he'd taught her to use daggers even though she didn't have the metal magic that he did to make them useful against Fiends. Her sword was the most impressive of her weapons; the steel had an odd blue hue to it and there was a rippling pattern that reminded her of waves and she hardly felt worthy of it. She knew that both her uncle and her father had had a hand in its design, both wanting to do anything they could to keep her safe.

"You look like a Hunter ready to go to battle," her father said, hugging her tightly. She returned the embrace fiercely before letting go. He handed her a jeweler's box. "It belonged to your mother," he said, voice thick with emotion, "it was passed down in her family and was one of the few things she managed to hold on to." Rain opened the box and found a silver ring heavily inscribed with runes she didn't know, though she knew the ring well. Tears pricked her eyes as she remembered playing with it on her mother's fingers, and her mother showing her what it did. She reverently picked it up and slipped it on, feeling the powerful magic seep into her skin. She twisted it, and the charms around the house glowed with power. She would be able to see any magic around her. She twisted it back and the glow faded.

"Wow," was all she could say for a moment, and then she turned to Storm. "Are you okay with this?"

Her sister nodded. "Something like that is made to protect the wearer. I want you to stay safe.". Rain hugged her sister tightly and her father again.

"Hey, what'd I miss?" Damien asked, walking in. He was also dressed for the road, with black leather pants, a black shirt, a black leather vest that Rain knew was armoured, heavy black boots with steel over the toes, and a long black leather coat. He also had a wide belt and forearm guards that had thick steel plates inside that he could manipulate and shape with his magic.

"I got Mom's ring," she said, holding her hand up to show him.

The corner of his mouth kicked up, though his eyes were sad. "Oh I remember that one," he said. "I used to threaten to steal it from her in the night." He shook his head, laughing softly. "We should get going, I want to make Fiorn by nightfall." Rain nodded.

There had been so many times in the past where she'd said goodbye to her uncle, her father, and her mother; standing at the door watching them until they were out of sight. Now she was the one leaving. She'd said her goodbyes, and now she twisted in her saddle to wave to her father and Storm until she couldn't see them anymore.

They rode in silence until they were well past the village gates. Rain had looked back before the forest swallowed them, unsure of when she would see them again. It could be weeks, or months. She didn't want to think about the other option; the one where she would never see them again. Damien was the one who finally broke the silence, "we can relax for a little while," he said. "But once we're past Fiorn things get far more interesting." Fiorn was the last village of their kind heading westward, the last place with a high concentration of Hunters and Guardians. "You'll really start putting your skills to the test then." He grinned. "This is the first trip I've had in a long time where I can take it easy." When he saw her scowl he shrugged, his grin growing wider.

"Well, at least now I know why you started training me so early," she said dryly. The fighting lessons had begun once Damien's wounds had healed, three months after her mother's death. Her sister hadn't even been out of the hospital.

"It's best to think ahead with these things," he said. Rain knew the truth though, so there was no heat to her glare.

"What was your field year like?" Unlike her father, her uncle had never talked much about his training year, but he'd also been away far more often, once for nearly a year when she'd been eleven. He'd written letters frequently though, if only to let Rain and Storm know that he wasn't dead. She also didn't know much about her mother's field year either. Her father had never answered when she or Storm would ask, changing the subject on them. Eventually they'd stopped asking. But now Rain figured she just might be able to get an answer. She knew that they'd shared a mentor who Damien still kept in contact with and Rain herself had met a time or two, but that was it. It was a very unusual circumstance, so she knew that there had to be something to it.

Damien sighed. "I thought you'd let that go."

"It's a reasonable question to ask, considering I'm in my field year," she said. "I've heard stories from a lot of other Hunters, but nothing about you and Mom, not from anyone." While the Hunters were spread out across the globe, news still made its way around, and most Hunters could be counted upon to tell stories of their victories and follies, especially when they'd been in training for the benefit of students or if a Hunter who'd made a foolish mistake was in earshot.

"Yeah, I guess so," he acknowledged, reaching back to pull his flask out of his saddlebag. He opened it and took a drink.

"What, is it bad?" She asked, frowning.

"Your mom and I approached a pair of hunters we knew worked together a lot, so we wouldn't have to spend the year on opposite sides of the planet." Hunters were encouraged to work in pairs or groups to increase their chances of living to an old age, like Damien and Rain's mother had before her death, or her father when he'd worked as a Hunter before Storm was born. "They accepted us, of course. We were the top students in our class. Your mother's mentor was Eida Flood, while I apprenticed under Gold Tailor." Rain froze, accidently stopping her horse as well. Damien turned to look at her. "Yeah, those two."

"But I heard that they…" She trailed off, unable to believe it. Not her mother and her uncle.

"Heard that they sold their apprentices to a Thief King to pay off their debts?" Damien finished for her. "Yeah, that happened." Eida Flood and Gold Tailor were among the few Hunters in history to be formally stripped of their medallions and cast out by their people. Damien sighed again when she didn't say anything. "It wasn't as bad as it could have been," he continued. "The thieves were harder on me than your mother; she was just a guard. One of them recognised me from before I went to the Academy." She knew her uncle had lived on the streets in a human city until he travelled to the territories and enrolled in the Academy at fourteen. "So they figured I could be dragged back into a life of crime. I didn't want to." His tone made it clear that his rebellion hadn't gone over well. He took a long drink from his flask. "Anyway, it was four months. Then word started to get out about how the Thief King of Dagani had a pair of apprentice Hunters in his hands, and eventually Eida and Gold confessed and other Hunters came and got us out of there." She knew that Eida had committed suicide and Gold had never been heard from again.

"Was that when you got assigned to Ember?" Rain asked. She didn't really know what to say.

Damien nodded. "Ember Free took us both. We were only three months away from graduation at that point, so the Academy allowed it." Rain had met Ember a few times, when she'd been a guest lecturer at the Academy. She lived farther south in the territories, nearer to the desert, which made sense seeing as she was a fire mage. Her uncle forced a laugh. "It's not a taboo subject, but not one anyone wants to talk about. I mean, we're supposed to be above that shit." He glanced at his flask and smirked. "But nope, we're just as flawed as everyone else. Eida and Gold were just better at hiding their gambling problem until it was way too late." He looked at her. "I'm sorry if it's not the story you wanted, but it's the one that's true."

Rain shook her head. "I'm just sorry that Storm and I kept bothering you about it for years."

He shrugged. "It was a lifetime ago, and like I said, not as bad as it could have been. We were two kids who'd actually lived on the streets, so we knew how to survive it." When Rain didn't say anything he continued. "I will admit that having contacts among the thieves can be useful, though. Sometimes you'll find that as a Hunter you need spells or things that aren't really legally available among humans and occasionally among our people too. I'll introduce you to a few who are worth knowing." Rain nodded. She'd known that a lot of Hunters dealt with human criminals, it was a reminder of how humans regarded their kind that those were the humans they got along best with. She also figured he was thinking more of the thieves he'd known growing up rather than those who'd held him captive.

"Is the Thief King one of your contacts?"

"Not really, he died about a decade back, some kind of sickness, or poison. It's hard to tell the difference with humans. I do know his successor though, and he's not so bad, though the Thief King in the city where I grew up is better."

"You and Mom didn't have it easy, did you?" She asked, nudging her horse forward again.

He shook his head with a dark laugh. "No. It was better when we met, because everything is easier to bear when you have someone else with you, but it's just a fact that life isn't easy. You already know that part."

Rain nodded. "Yeah." They rode in silence for a while, though it wasn't uncomfortable. Rain was about to ask something else when one of her earrings started to grow warm, the one with a warning spell. She looked at her uncle, who gave her a wolfish smile.

"Time to earn your keep," he said as Rain dismounted and drew her sword, watching her surroundings carefully. Fiends were fast, so she wouldn't have much of a…

The Fiend leaped out of the trees on her left. She shifted back so that its claws went past her, and brought her sword down hard on its neck. The creature twisted as if fell in two pieces, knocking her over. She scrambled to her feet and watched as it began to wither before plucking a fang from its mouth and putting it in one of the pouches hung on her belt. She moved back to her horse to collect her flint and steel.

"Wait," Damien said, tossing something to her. Rain caught it and smiled when she saw what it was: a spell bead with a tiny rune for fire. She looked up at him. "Ember makes 'em for friends. You have ten seconds to throw the fire before it starts to burn you." Rain nodded, and felt for the power in the bead, drawing it out with her own magic. It fought for a moment because her magic was in water, but it answered to her in the end, letting her pull a stream of fire out like Damien had in the clearing a week before. She didn't hesitate, throwing the flame at the corpse and watching as it caught and burnt until nothing more than a pile of fine grey ashes remained.

"Was that acceptable?" The Fiend had been a little shorter than her, but far broader.

"I'll keep you around a while longer," he said after a few moments, "though I think I could get a good price from pirates."

"Have I mentioned that you're the worst?" Rain wondered, remounting her horse. Trust her uncle to make a joke out of a situation like that. Her instructors often said that dark humour was a coping mechanism that was basically part of the job. They'd all had fairly dark senses of humour as well.

"Hey, it's in the job description. I read it in the fine print before agreeing to become an uncle the first time, let alone the second."

She shook her head and kicked her horse forward. He was right, though, he'd chosen to be an uncle to her and Storm, and kept choosing to fill the role. He had no blood ties to them, could have walked away -especially after her mother's death- becoming a distant memory of her mother's cool friend. Instead he'd brought Rain home while her father and Storm were in the hospital, despite his own wounds and grief, and took care of her.

It hadn't been easy either, for weeks she'd woken up screaming from nightmares, panicking at the slightest noise. The first few nights he'd come running into her room, sword in hand even as blood seeped through the bandages around his wounds. She could still remember it clearly, Uncle Damien looking around with lethal intent, only to find that the monsters were in her mind. His sword arm had dropped, the point gouging the wood floor while she lay curled up in her blankets and ran a hand through his hair, roughly pushing it back from his face as he sighed.

"Nightmare?" He'd asked. She'd nodded.

"They took Mommy and Storm and Daddy and you and they were going to take me," she'd cried as she trembled.

Damien had sat down on the edge of her bed with a groan. "Well, I'm still here, and Storm and your dad are in the hospital, and no Fiend will get into the Academy," he reminded her.

"But they did take Mommy," she'd said. He'd covered his eyes with his free hand for a moment.

"Yeah, yeah they did," he'd said roughly. "But they won't be back."

"How do you know?" She'd asked. His hand had dropped into his lap, and she'd never forgotten his expression then. She hadn't known the word for it at the time, but now she did: despair. Absolute and utter despair.

"I don't," he'd said. "I don't know." His voice had cracked. "But they won't get you, don't worry."

"Why?"

"Because I'm here. I'll protect you."

And he had, sitting by her door, sword in hand until she went to sleep. When she'd awoken the next morning, he was still there, and for the next few nights he would return and stay when she woke screaming and crying. On the fifth night he'd simply hauled a chair up to her room and slept there for the next several weeks, though it couldn't have been comfortable or painless. Still, she couldn't remember one instance where she'd woken from a nightmare alone, or that he hadn't responded to her cries. Eventually it had gotten easier, and she'd let him go back to sleeping in his own room, once her father started returning home from the hospital. Damien had started teaching her to fight to help her deal with the nightmares, to give her some sense of confidence and safety. He'd brought her to visit her sister every day, and stayed sometimes so Rain could spend time with her father and so he could try to cheer Storm up a little as she slowly recovered. As far as both she and Storm were concerned Damien was more their uncle than their father's older brother had ever been.

"Are you sure?" She asked now, pulling herself back to the present, a midnight blue brow creeping up. "I'll have to get a copy of it."

"A Fiend ate the last one, sorry." The words spoken with an unrepentant grin.

"I'm sure. So, what do we know about this prince?" She turned her mind to their job. They had a few days before they made it to Ankira, the capital of Glask, but she still wanted to know all she could about what they had to do.

"Not a whole lot, I don't pay too much attention to rulers and human politics," Damien said. "I do know he's some kind of up-and-coming ambassador. I think he's the same age as Storm." He shrugged. "I know he's been around Hunters a bit, they seem to think well of him and that was when he was a few years younger." It was generally in a governments' best interest to stay on the good side of the Hunters and Guardians they relied on to protect their borders from Fiends, whatever their personal sentiments about 'demons' might be. Still, Hunters, Guardians, and Keepers did their best to keep the peace as well, for the most part. It was a fragile situation at best, and if it turned sour no one would win.

They made Fiorn just as the sun was starting to set behind the mountains and Rain had taken down two more Fiends, both small. Damien took her to the town hall, where she over handed the fangs she'd collected and received a small purse of coins in return.

"There you go, the makings of your very own riches," her uncle said as they walked to the inn, leading their horses. "Except for the fact that you have to pay for food, lodgings, weapons, weapon repairs, spells, armour, clothing, medical help, healing balms and salves, horses, and everything else Then if you decide to settle down at some point you'll need a house, with furniture, all the attendant spells that make life so comfortable, and all that."

"Or I can live with my best friend's family for fourteen years," Rain mused.

"That is also an excellent option," he agreed with a grin. "Realistically it was much longer than that because once your parents had the house I spent far more time there than the flat I was renting in the city. Until I moved in with Raven, anyway. Of course, I doubt your sister would throw you out."

"No, she wouldn't," Rain agreed. Despite their differences they were and always had been close.

When they made inside the tavern she wasn't surprised to see a few of her classmates. It was a popular inn with Hunters both leaving and returning to the demon territories as the humans called her people's lands. They just called them the territories and stuck with that. Maybe there was a hint of defiance there, resisting the human need to label absolutely everything. She and Damien got rooms and stored their things before joining the group.

"Who's that behind the bar?" Damien asked as they sat down at a table across from Kestrel and Amber, eyeing a pretty woman who looked to be in her early thirties.

"Anita, the innkeeper's younger sister," Amber answered.

"You know, I think I ought to go introduce myself. I'll get the next round," he said as he got up. Amber rolled her eyes at him and he just grinned.

Rain wrinkled her nose. She knew her uncle had lovers, but that wasn't something she wanted to know a lot about. Anything, really.

"You know, I always thought it was a damn shame he never got to have the life he wanted with Raven," Amber said, watching him for a moment before turning her attention to the two apprentices.

"You knew her?" Rain asked. "I don't really remember her." She'd only been three when Raven had died.

The Hunter nodded. "She was close to my older sister –they both worked in the apothecary- so I knew her better than most. She was pretty quiet about where she came from, but I do know that Damien located her family not long after she died."

She knew he'd vanished for a few months after the funeral. "I don't think he or Dad moved on from their loves dying, not really."

Amber nodded again. "Relationships are hard for Hunters; the longer you're in this the more shit you see and the darker and more cynical you get. Besides, just think of how hard it would be to always be leaving them behind for days or weeks at a time and they have to wonder when and if we're going to come back." She looked guilty as she said it and Rain wondered if she was thinking about her own partner, a healer in the hospital. Rain was fairly certain that Amber and Willow had been together before she was born.

"Yeah, I know what that's like," Rain agreed, thinking of her parents and her uncle

"And honestly, there comes a point when you just don't want to see one more person you love die." She leaned back in her chair. "I'm not saying it's not worth it to try to make things work, it is, and having someone who understands you makes what we deal with a lot easier, but that someone is hard to find and harder to lose." She looked at both young women. "I know they don't sugar coat things at the Academy, but there's still a lot you need to learn if you want to survive physically and mentally in this line of work."

"What are we talking about?" Uncle Damien asked, returning to put their drinks down in front of them.

"How doomed relationships are in our line of work," Kestrel replied.

"You just have to find what works for you and make sure you don't make any promises you can't keep," Damien said. "And never expect a happy ending."

Early the next morning Damien was knocking on her door, telling her to get up and get ready to go. Rain moved quickly, packing her things and going down the stairs. Not many were awake yet, including her friends, though considering how much some of the Hunters had had to drink she wasn't surprised. She sat down across from her uncle, who'd actually paced himself well.

"I was asking around last night and it sounds like if we go south west to Cannor and then north to Ankira we can go around the bandit's territory. It'll add two days of travel, but right now it's the better decision." He said as Anita put food in front of them.

"I thought the bandits didn't scare you."

"They don't, but I'd rather your first experience with bandits not be with those who probably want to use my skull as a wine cup." He took a drink from his flask. "As a rule bandits are tricky to deal with, more so than thieves."

"Okay," she said, putting her fork down for a moment. "When do we leave?"

"As soon as we're done." Rain started to eat faster.

"Happy hunting!" Anita said as they left, giving Damien a very flirty grin.

"Always," he said with a wave as they left. Rain just rolled her eyes.

3

A King

They made it to Cannor with few incidents. As expected there had been more Fiends as they got farther from Fiorn and outside the territories. Rain had never been so far away from home before, and didn't quite know how she felt about it. She'd known this was coming, had looked forward to it, but it was still different from anything she'd expected. No matter how often her instructors had warned them not to, she'd always dreamed of the action-packed adventures she heard about it stories or from Hunters, who obviously left out the parts where they spent hours looking at a dirt road and trees, though close to Cannor they left the forest for hours of looking at rolling hills. Still, she knew better than to complain too loudly, because the boredom allowed them to make it to the village, though they arrived well after sunset. Things had gotten tense after dark. Though their kind could see far better in the dark than a human could, many Fiends had perfect night vision, or something akin to it, some sense that made the night their domain. She'd stayed close to her uncle, bow in hand as she'd watched the sun set over the trees. Hunters and anyone with any kind of sense avoided camping as much as possible, because even with the spells Hunters used there wasn't a lot of warning before an attack. Luckily the Guardian at the gate had recognised Damien and let them in right away, directing them to the only inn. It was a little smaller and a lot quieter than Fiorn, hardly anyone in the tavern.

"Food, bed, up at dawn," Uncle Damien said to her after handing over the money. Rain nodded tiredly; it had been a surprisingly long day. They ate in silence then went to their rooms. Rain let herself fall onto the hard bed, hoping she would adjust quickly to constant traveling that was somehow more exhausting than fighting, or it could have been that the traveling had been broken up with periods of quick, intense fighting in which Damien had let her do all of the work and then that was followed by hours of tense watchfulness, waiting for the next period of fighting. She forced herself to rise and make sure everything was ready to go in the morning, and then fell asleep as soon as she lay back down.

As promised, Damien pounded on her door at dawn. She rose, readied quickly and went downstairs to meet him. He was already drinking, a glass of some dark liquid in front of him. Part of it might have been tea, but not a large part, judging by the colour.

"Rough night?" She asked as she sat down across from him.

"Happens to the best of us," he said, downing the liquor in one swallow and gesturing to the innkeeper, who quickly brought over another. "We'll stop in Beyrron tonight. We could make Hask if we pushed it, but even with the extra day we added by coming this way we're still ahead of schedule. We should make it to the city walls of Ankira the day after that."

"I dunno about that, a weather mage said it was supposed to rain today," the innkeeper said, putting a plate of food in front of Rain.

"How long can you keep the rain off us?" Damien asked her with a sigh.

She shrugged. "I've done the better part of a day before, but I have trouble holding it and fighting at the same time." Their professors had made sure that they had trained in every kind of weather and knew how to use their magics.

"That's fine," he said. "You'll get it in time." Rain was exceptionally powerful, as was her sister. They'd inherited that strength from both of their parents, though they had their mother's type of magic. Their father might not have been as good a fighter nor as powerful, but he knew how to use his magic well enough to take out stronger opponents.

"Want to talk about it?" She offered tentatively when he downed the second drink as quickly as the first.

He shook his head. "Things just tend to build up over the years. That's all."

They got back on the road quickly. Rain raised her arms and made a parting motion, so the rain fell on either side of them. Redirection like that took little power compared to actively manipulating water or changing it to ice or steam. It helped that they were on a well-traveled road, so she didn't have to deal with. She knew that in these areas there was also a risk of flooding, especially farther south.

"Shouldn't we have a map?" She asked a while later when all the trees had looked the same for the last hour. The forests got thicker outside the territories where the trees weren't so battered by the ocean winds of the coast. It was also warmer here than her homeland, for all they hadn't covered a huge distance. It was strange though, being so far from the sea.

"I'm from Ankira, remember? I don't go back when I can avoid it, but I do know the way." She remembered that he hadn't been raised among their kind, he'd grown up around humans, but she'd forgotten the city. Most in that situation tended to avoid the places they'd come from since few had good memories of those times, especially orphans. Her warning spell heated up just as a small Fiend scurried in front of their horses. Damien flicked a dagger at it, pinning the squirrel-sized monster to the dirt. It started withering right away. He flicked his wrist and the dagger returned. Rain could just make out the thin silver wire that ran from the hilt of the dagger to one of the rings he wore on every finger. He didn't collect a fang, but that wasn't surprising. A lot of the smaller Fiends were lethally venomous, just because things weren't hard enough already.

"So you do work after all!"

"Sometimes," he drawled. "It'd look bad if I made you do everything, after all, I am supposed to be teaching you."

"Nice to know you take your job seriously."

"Of course I do! I need to be able to get a good price from the pirates, remember?"

She had to ask. "Why pirates?"

"You have water magic, makes more sense than land-locked thieves. I thought it would be obvious." She let the rain pour on him for a second. "That was just mean."

"I'm supposed to be a bit of a nuisance, it's in the job description for being a niece."

"I'd like to see that."

"Sorry, a Fiend ate it," she said, throwing his words back at him. Another small Fiend scurried across their path, and this time she took action, forming a sharpened piece of ice in the air and using her power to launch it at the creature. She got it.

"Not bad." Damien gave her a considering look. "Tell you what, whoever can get the most of these fuckers by the time we get to Beyrron wins. Loser pays at the inn."

"You're on, old man!" She agreed.

"Not old," he protested, just as she knew he would. For someone who was so confident and self-assured he had a weird thing about his age.

"Have you looked in a mirror?" She wondered, raising a brow.

"I'm a *metal* mage, it's only natural that there's going to be silver in my hair," he said defensively. "Come on *kiddo,* let's see what you've got."

In the end Damien won, so Rain forked over the money to the innkeeper in the busy town of Beyrron. It was bigger than Cannor but not fortified, and there wasn't as much traffic from Hunters. She did spot Guardians on their way into town, as well as human warriors and even a few Rangers, the human attempt at a Hunter equivalent. Still, the humans in the inn's tavern starred at them like they'd never seen their kind before. Rain moved closer to her uncle, who either didn't notice or didn't care, the latter being far more likely. She'd been around humans before, but had never so many of them at once with so few of her own kind to balance the numbers. They all had softer features and rounded ears, their hair shades of brown, blond, black, red, and grey, and their eye colour was dull, faded compared to her kind. They didn't have fangs or claws, and there was just something so fragile about them, though she knew they had the potential to be even more monstrous than the Fiends. She'd expected that, what she hadn't expected was that they would be so damn *loud.* She knew that their hearing wasn't nearly as good as hers, but still, this was excessive.

"You'd think they've never seen a Hunter before," Rain said quietly as they found an open table and sat down. Her uncle would be able to hear her, but none of the humans. He also saw through her meager attempt at bravado.

"Or they remember me from the last time I was here," Damien said, frowning. "remind me to ask your father when we get home. He was with me and far more sober." He watched her shift uncomfortably under the weight of the human gazes. Her midnight blue hair really stood out here, unlike Uncle Damien's greying black. She tried to surreptitiously pull her hair to cover her face from their gazes. "Sit up straight and don't let them see they're getting to you," he advised her quietly, leaning forward so she was the only one who could hear him. "You're going to be a Hunter, one of the best, and you'll be smiling as you face down monsters that would have those bastards pissing their pants."

Oddly enough, that did help. She sat up and squared her shoulders, pushing her hair back behind her pointed ears. "How's that?"

"There's my niece," he said, grinning slightly. "This isn't a hot spot for Hunters so they wouldn't have seen many of us." Guardians tended to wear heavier armour and looked more like knights, while Hunters probably looked closer to the kind of people from whom they would need a knight's protection. One of the servers came by and took their order, his disapproval clear and directed at Uncle Damien. "So it is mostly me that's the problem," he noted as the young man walked away. "I will definitely have to ask your father about that." He didn't seemed bothered by it, just curious. It made her wonder just how often this kind of thing happened to him.

"How long ago was it?" Rain wondered, mentally sorting through all of the Drunk Uncle Damien stories she'd heard over the years.

"Ah, let's see… two years, two and a half?"

"I think you got rather drunk and started a brawl because some guy looked 'so punchable' and essentially caused half the tavern to be destroyed. Dad wouldn't tell me what he said though." There were a few stories about her uncle that went like that, but fewer than his reputation would lead people to believe.

"That does sound like me," he agreed, leaning back and looking around. The humans wouldn't meet his quicksilver gaze. "Did your father tell you what he was doing at the time? Normally he stops me before things get that bad."

"He agreed with you."

"Then I have no regrets."

"You beat the shit out of the last innkeeper and he sold the place to the new owners," the server said from beside them, having returned while they were talking. "Worked out for almost everyone, though please don't do it again."

"So why the sour looks?"

"Because I had clean up the mess," he replied, putting a glass of water in front of the Hunter with a saccharine smile.

"That's fair," Damien said, pulling out his flask and taking a drink. The server left with a sigh. "Well that explains that. Don't worry, I won't pull any stunts this year –probably. When you're older all bets are off."

"Good to know. So, what do we for the rest of the day?" She wondered as the servant brought their food and they began eating.

"Rest, resupply, make sure everything is in good order. I know we've only been away for three days, but you'd be surprised at how quickly and how horribly things can go wrong on the road." She nodded, having heard horror stories. "I'm going to the marketplace for a bit, since they obviously want to keep me dry here. Do what you want, just be back around sundown, we're up at sunrise again. Trust me, when we're on the road for three weeks straight you'll be longing for some time away from me." He grinned. "Hell, even your mother and I needed some time apart once in a while."

They finished and he left while she went up to her room to double check her gear, then headed to the marketplace herself. The village might not be a hotspot for Hunters, but that didn't mean merchants didn't go through it. Most merchant caravans avoided the territories, for all it was probably one of the safest places in the world to travel. She did her best to keep her head high amidst the stares and the noise, pretending she didn't hear the comments about her clothing, her looks, the number of piercings she had. They could talk all they wanted, but when push came to shove Rain knew that they would come screaming to her for help when the Fiends came.

They pushed hard the next day and made it to Ankira shortly before sunset. The city was both larger and busier than Lysee, with people all over the place, different languages and scents filling the air and most of the buildings were quite tall and lavish, especially near the gates. If she'd found the tavern the night before alarming, the city was overwhelming. "Stick close," Uncle Damien said. "This city is a maze." She had no problem listening. Ankira was a capital city and a major stop along trade routes, and that was all she knew about the city itself. She knew a little more about its criminal underworld from the few times she and Storm had managed to get their uncle to talk about his childhood. She knew he was the child of a Hunter and a human. There were no half-bloods, children from those pairings were always demons. In the territories it might raise a few brows, just because they all knew how the humans felt about them, but it didn't last more than a moment. A child of such a pair born into one of the human cities, though, tended to go through absolute hell. A lot of parents eventually moved their families to the territories to get away from persecution. Those who slipped through the cracks often became criminals and bandits or journeyed to the territories and the Academy as soon as they were old enough.

"Where are we going to go?" She wondered as she looked around.

"Well, I told you I would introduce you to some of my contacts," he said, leading her off the main road. They ventured further away from the chaos and Rain relaxed. The buildings became shabbier, clothing became patched and worn, and people watched them more closely as they passed by, but she could breathe again.

"Why if it isn't Lance, you old bastard!" An older man called, jogging over to meet them. "What are you doing back here?"

"Tam, it's been a while," her uncle said, gripping the man's forearm before indicating Rain. "This is my niece and apprentice, Rain Undine."

He looked at her with sharp brown eyes. "By Gods, for a minute I thought I was looking at your mother. I was sorry to hear about her death." Rain didn't know what to say, so she just nodded.

"How's the Thief King?" Damien asked. Rain knew it wasn't the same Thief King that his mentor had sold him to; most major cities had their own court of thieves.

"He's getting on in years, but still strong," Tam replied. "You want to present the kid?"

"I'm a Hunter, not a kid." Rain objected before she could stop herself.

"My apologies," Tam said, bowing deeply, then turned back to Damien. "You want to present the Hunter to his majesty?"

"I suppose so, I am supposed to be helping her network," Damien said and the human snorted. "Hey, you can't tell me that the underworld isn't the best place for information."

"So long as you can hold your own," Tam said absently, giving Rain a once over. "I told you that years ago."

"She'll do fine," Damien said, nudging his horse forward. Tam walked beside them to a large stone building that had once been beautiful, but was now cracked and covered in soot, the windows either yellowed with age or boarded up. "You'll watch our horses?" He asked Tam, who nodded. Rain dismounted when her uncle did and silently followed him inside, passing beggars and children running amok. He led her through an old and sagging archway to what might have once been a grand hall. Music played under shouts and raucous laughter and cheers erupted from one corner while another held a small group that seemed to be holding some kind of vigil. "If you ever run into trouble in the city, come here first," her uncle said as they made their way to the platform at the front of the room, where an older man sat on a heavy wooden chair that looked like a throne. She guessed him to be somewhere in his fifties though she wasn't the best when it came to human aging, but still strong and carried a presence of authority. A slender young woman a few years younger than Rain stood beside him and caught sight of Damien. She bent to whisper in the Thief King's ear and he looked at them, then stood, laughing loud enough to gain everyone's attention. Or perhaps it was because he was the ruler here.

"Damien, it's been too long!" He said, stepping down. The humans around him scattered. Rain couldn't help but wonder how much of that was respect and how much was fear.

"Dagger," her uncle greeted him, clasping forearms before the human pulled him into a bear hug, "and I have with me my niece and apprentice, Rain Undine." Dagger turned to her, his blue eyes crafty.

"Are you anything like your mother?" He asked her.

"I hope so," she said with more confidence than she felt.

"We're fucked!" Someone nearby remarked to more laughter.

Dagger laughed. "Tempest set me on my ear a time or twice. Before I had my crown, though it wouldn't have made any difference to her what was on my head. She was a special woman, your mother."

"Yeah, she was," Rain said. Damien and Dagger took her around the room then, introducing her to people and mentioning the ways in which they could be useful, like Werick the smuggler, or Yasia the Finder who could find anyone anywhere in the world through forbidden magic. The thieves were clearly uncertain about her, but respected her uncle and their king enough that they seemed willing to give her a chance. They stayed for a long time as people came up to talk to Damien, though a few cast him looks of fear and gave him a wide berth. His amusement at their actions only made them move faster.

"So, you're escorting the princeling to Landai?" Dagger asked as they ate. The food was surprisingly good, though Damien had warned her not to look too closely or question what was in it.

"Yeah," he answered. "What's the climate like? Anything I would need to care about?" He wasn't talking about the weather.

The thief shrugged. "It's pretty neutral right now, there's some tension, but it hasn't reached a breaking point yet. The real problem isn't Glask or Landaia, it's Phasoia." Ankira was the capital of Glask, and Landai was the capital of Landaia. Rain knew that Phasoia shared the northern border of both countries, a wide, thin band of a country. "They've been making some moves and threats that might not just be sword rattling."

"I was hoping to go north," Damien said, scowling at the map that someone had put on the table. "Are the bandits still taking up the borders of Glask and Landai?"

"They are, and they're becoming a real pain in the ass, even to us." Dagger sighed. "They've become a wee bit full of themselves and soon I'm going to have to send some of the boys out to teach them respect." He turned to Rain. "Even though they live in the wilds they still rely on my court for a few important things." In that moment she realised that no matter how genial he was, this wasn't someone to be crossed without dire consequences.

"Okay," she said as she looked at the map, then turned to her uncle. "Couldn't we still go north and skirt the mountains instead of taking the pass?" She lightly traced the path with a claw. "It wouldn't add on a whole lot of time."

"It'd be an extra night in the woods," Damien pointed out, his eyes following the path.

"It looks like there's a village that's been crossed out here," she said, pointing to the spot.

"Yeah, they got hit hard by Fiends about five years ago," Dagger said. "Some of the buildings are still standing, but the only living souls that go there are those wandering through. I know Werick has stayed there in the last year." He gestured at the smuggler, who hurried over and confirmed what Dagger had told them.

"Any supplies left are long gone," Werick said, stroking his short beard, "but there's still a few sturdy buildings, even after the floods last summer."

"Are you sure the King and Queen would let you take their precious child that way?" Dagger asked with a cynical grin.

Damien snorted. "I told them that if they wanted to question what I decided they could choose someone else to escort the prince." He looked at Rain, "I wouldn't normally advise talking to royalty that way, though. They can be a bit tetchy sometimes when you won't let them do as they will."

"Not that it's ever stopped you," Dagger said dryly.

"Well, they requested me specifically, so I don't know what else they were expecting."

"A loyal citizen?" Both men laughed. As a general rule, most kingdoms didn't recognise demons as citizens, and Glask was no exception. However, even though he didn't exactly keep his heritage a secret, Rain doubted the monarchs knew that her uncle was from Ankira.

"Well, they're paying well, so I don't really care," he said. "Is *The Bloody Goose* still standing?"

"And still the finest inn in the city," Dagger said with pride. "I'll send someone over to let them know to expect you and your apprentice." A few words to the slender youth who'd been at his back initially and the girl ran off. "My granddaughter," he told them as they watched her run. "She's learning the ropes." Rain wasn't sure what to say, she knew that for the most part rulership of the underworld wasn't dynastic; thrones were won in blood spilled, not in bloodlines. That Dagger had held his throne for so long was impressive in itself. "She's a little like you, I guess," he said to Rain. "Hopefully her chances at life will be just as good."

"I don't know if you've heard, but Hunters don't have the best life expectancy."

He shook his head. "You've got Damien for a mentor and you are your parents' daughter. You'll live a long life. I'm an old crook, we can tell these things." He winked.

"What's the age difference between you and Uncle Damien?" She asked brightly.

"Let's go, *kiddo*," Damien said, standing quickly while Dagger laughed.

"She'll do fine," the Thief King of Ankira decided, echoing her uncle's words.

"I like him," Rain said as they walked out. Tam handed over the reins to their horses and Damien slipped him a few coins.

"Yeah, he's pretty good, as far as thieves go," Damien agreed. "Just never forget what he is and how he got there and stayed there."

"I won't," she promised. "So, what is *The Bloody Goose*?"

"The hidden gem of Ankira; it's an inn and tavern in an out of the way corner of the city that no decent human would ever visit. They have the most comfortable beds though, if you're on good terms with the owner, or with Dagger. We'll rest up and tomorrow at noon we need to present ourselves to the royal court." He didn't sound too thrilled about that.

"How bad is it going to be?" She wanted to be prepared.

"Depends. I haven't actually had anything to do with the royal family, we communicated by messenger or one of their servants. I know that there's going to be some sort of farewell party for the prince, and our presence has been requested." He sounded even less thrilled. Rain wondered just how the invitation was phrased, since Damien was normally all for any occasion where the liquor would pour on someone else's coin. "It'll be a formal event, apparently." That explained it.

"Oh fun." Rain wasn't overly fond of crowds or formal events herself. A night on the town with friends was one thing, but faking polite small talk with total strangers was a special kind of hell. Moreover, these strangers would be human and many would hate or fear her for existing.

"Yeah, hopefully they'll keep the wine pouring." Damien sighed. "With any luck the nobles will ignore us and just judge us from a distance to cover their fears."

"So we're not going to try to blend in," she guessed.

"Why would we?" He asked, frowning at her.

Rain considered it for a long moment "Can't think of a reason," she said at last. She didn't want to hide what she was, and the monarchs knew what they were dragging into the party. If not, it was their own damn fault.

He grinned. "Good."

As promised, the rooms at *The Bloody Goose* were very good, even if the strange goose that wandered through the halls was prone to attacking guests. That night she quickly checked everything and pulled out a length of cloth. It was plain black and could be tied at the hip, creating a slit skirt that went to her ankles. It was what most female Hunters wore when they needed to dress up, or just felt like wearing a skirt but still needed to be able to fight. She laid it over a chair along with softer, though still fitted, black cotton pants to wear underneath. In the morning she would ask Damien about weapons, because she knew from her lessons and stories that most human monarchs frowned at outsiders or even their own subjects being armed in their presence. She just had to make it through the next day and after that was when the real fun would begin.

The next morning she woke before Damien arrived to rouse her at dawn again, telling her to meet him downstairs. She quickly dressed and headed downstairs to where he was flirting with a maid, though he stopped when she approached, rolling her eyes.

"I thought we didn't have anything to do until the afternoon," she said as they found a table.

"We don't, but you still need to train," he reminded her.

"Doesn't fighting on the road count for something?" She wondered, drinking the juice the maid handed her. She watched as Damien emptied his flask into his mug. It wasn't that she minded the practice, but it seemed redundant to do anything more than her regular warm up routine.

"Maybe if we met anything that put up a real fight," he said as he took a drink from his flask. "Besides, it'll keep you from worrying about your first public function as a Hunter."

"The King of Thieves didn't count?"

"Dagger is an old friend, so that doesn't really count, though you did well. This time we both have to behave, though we won't be pandering to the humans. We don't want to give them a reason to decide that the world doesn't need two more Hunters, because us escaping from their prisons would create a lot of paperwork for the Council and generally make life harder for the rest of our people."

"Who did it before?" That tone could only be brought on by experience.

"Jerek." He named Aiden's mentor . "It was about a decade ago and we still have to be careful about the Republic of Kechna. However if you do have to get thrown in jail somewhere, breaking out is pretty easy."

"No way," she said. She couldn't see the ever-proper Jerek fucking up that badly. Her uncle having to break out of prison and succeeding wasn't quite as difficult.

"Yup, and I also like getting paid, so we're going to behave."

"Good point," she acquiesced. "What would you rather deal with, bandits or nobles?"

"Bandits," he replied without hesitation. "They're at least honest and will openly try to kill you. Most nobles aren't that courteous, and no matter how good the monarchs are, every court is a nest of vipers cloaked in silk." He paused when the food came to their table.

"Will we spend the night here or in the palace?"

He chuckled darkly. "They're not going to let wolves in among the sheep at night."

"You just said they were vipers."

"They're venomous sheep," he decided. "Cute until they decide to bite." At her look he laughed. "You know what, I like it, and I'm sure your dad'll get a kick out of it too. Thanks kiddo." Rain resisted the urge to bang her head against the table. She knew better, she really did. Storm would be ashamed of her when she heard of this, and she would hear of this, because Uncle Damien wasn't going to forget it. Sometimes it was awe-inspiring to be around by an elite Hunter who walked the fine line between sanity and darkness, a real and terrifying badass. Then there were other times where she wanted to push her uncle into a lake.

4

The Prince

"You cheated," Uncle Damien accused as he stood, both fighters bent and breathless in the open space behind the inn. Rain had finally beaten him in a sparring match.

"Have you met my teacher?" She asked with a wide grin, catching her breath.

"He's a rotten old bastard to teach you to fight like that." He straightened and looked up at the sky. "Okay, that's enough for today; we should get ready to go." Rain nodded and headed inside. She washed quickly and put on the outfit she'd set aside. She also pulled the top part of her hair back using a pin that Storm had given her a few years ago, letting a few locks hang to frame her face, it was a pretty thing, with tiny blue crystals that dangled from silver chains, like raindrops.

Damien was downstairs and had like her had eschewed leather pants for cotton. He also wore fitted black tunic and he'd kept his vambraces. Of course, both of them were armed. If nobles were venomous sheep –damn her uncle- then Hunters in court finery were wolves in sheep's clothing and neither she nor Uncle Damien felt a need for such subterfuge.

"Don't we look nice," she said as they went to get the horses.

"We still have to do justice to the title." Rain followed suit when he mounted his horse and stuck close as he led the way through the city. The bite of fall was in the air today, and she could almost smell snow. It was luck that the cold didn't bother her, a benefit of water magic.

With Damien's knowledge of the streets it didn't take long for them to reach the palace. Rain wasn't sure what to think; it was certainly grand, but she didn't think it was as grand as the Academy even though it was prettier. She said as much, but Damien just shrugged and kept going. The guards on the gate were all human, and they eyed the Hunters with open suspicion but let them pass without issue. A servant in gold and orange livery was waiting for them in the courtyard.

"Hunter Damien Lance, their most royal majesties bid me to welcome you and your apprentice to Ankira," he said with a small bow. Damien dismounted, and Rain followed. The servant's eyes went to her and her attire.

"Rooms have been made ready should you wish to… prepare before seeing their majesties." She resisted the urge to punch him in the face. Barely.

"We're fine," Damien said with a smile only a fool would describe as friendly. "We can meet the King and Queen at once." The servant paled slightly as he nodded and gestured. Somehow a young man and woman appeared.

"These two will take your horses." He looked at their swords and the knives they wore openly. "Your weapons can be left with the master-at-arms. Their majesties will permit no weaponry in their presence."

"Yet they will permit us to take their son across dangerous terrain?" Damien asked, canting his head slightly.

"Let them come in," a well-dressed man said, riding into the courtyard. "Hunters are not going to harm anyone here."

"Yes, your highness," the servant said as he bowed, though he clearly still disapproved of the Hunters. Rain turned to look at their unexpected supporter. Damien had said that the prince traveling with them was around Storm's age, and this prince looked older, early thirties. She could have been wrong though, humans aged faster than her people did, and she hadn't spent enough time around them to really figure it out. "Crown Prince Axiel, may I present Hunter Damien Lance and his apprentice…"

"Rain Undine," Damien supplied.

"Rain Undine," the servant repeated.

"If you like I can bring you to my parents," he offered as he dismounted. He didn't wait for them to bow, and Rain guessed it was because he knew they wouldn't. Smart human.

"That would be welcome," Damien replied, the formal words sounding strange.

The prince turned to the servant. "Go and announce our guests to Mother and Father." The servant nodded and scurried off. Axiel moved as if to offer an arm to Rain but stopped short, turning the movement into an awkward gesture for them to follow. Rain met her uncle's eyes and both looked away quickly to avoid laughing. Apparently the prince only knew how to handle Hunters in theory. "Have you been to the city before?" He asked, making a quick recovery to once more become the charming man who'd met them at the door.

"I haven't," Rain replied.

"I've been around here a few times," her uncle answered blandly. Rain wasn't surprised by the lie. The prince kept up a stream of small talk as he led them through the labyrinth of hallways that made up the palace. Servants and courtiers stared as they walked by, bowing to the prince, but Rain remembered to keep her head held high, a slight, confident smile quirking the corners of her lips.

Prince Axiel brought them to a throne room that apparently was an informal reception hall, though Rain found it was still too fancy to be called informal. The King and Queen were seated on ornate wooden thrones and a young man stood between them. The monarchs rose as the Hunters approached and Axiel bowed to his parents. Rain watched more closely this time. It was a human custom, one rejected by her people when they'd claimed their own lands and independence. Her people bowed to no one, especially those who had grown up in the territories as she had. It was a sign of submission and her ancestors had sworn never to submit again. They would protect the humans as they were living beings and no one deserved to be destroyed by Fiends. In the Academy they were taught to stand their ground, even the Guardians. The humans weren't going to treat them as equals, so why play their games?

"May I present to you Hunter Damien Lance and Apprentice Rain Undine." Axiel gestured to each of them in turn. There was an awkward moment as the royals clearly expected them to bow.

"We are very grateful that you have accepted to escort our son," the King said at last, letting it go without comment. "This is Prince Schuyler, he will be our ambassador to Landai." The young man stepped forward. He was tall, almost as tall as Damien, and slender, with short brown hair and green eyes. She could tell from the way he moved that he was no warrior.

"Thank you for agreeing to be my escort," the prince said with surprising sincerity, his voice warm and deep. More formalities were exchanged, and while Damien did the talking Rain paid close attention. They had two weeks to get the prince to the palace in Landai and they weren't expected to escort him back to Ankira, since he would be staying there for a few months and it was insane to expect Hunters to stay in one place for that long unless there was an issue with Fiends or it was their home. They reiterated concerns about the monsters and bandits, which Damien calmly and firmly put to rest. This was what she wanted to be when she was older, she reminded herself. She wanted to be one of the elite Hunters, the ones who could fight anything and commanded the respect of even the humans who believed themselves above everyone else. She was certain that had it been someone younger or weaker the monarchs wouldn't have acted the way they had with her uncle. That kind of status and skill didn't come without a heavy price, but she was willing to pay it and willing to carry the burdens.

After more formalities Prince Schuyler escorted them to a study where they could talk in private before the party, since there wouldn't be another chance before they left at dawn the next morning. He didn't say much as they walked through the halls, though Rain wasn't sure if that was because he knew that anyone within earshot would be trying to listen or if he was just quiet. Another young man joined them as Schuyler opened the door, shorter and much broader in build than the prince.

"This is Warren, my servant and body guard," the prince introduced the other human. "He will be traveling with us."

"So, how much have you traveled before?" Damien asked as Schuyler closed the door behind them.

"Some," the prince answered. "But never with so small a group."

"Any encounters with Fiends?"

"A few, but we had Rangers and guards who managed to take care of them." Damien snorted derisively. Rangers were essentially humans who aspired to become Hunters. They never lasted long. "What?"

"How many of the bait died in the attempt?" Her uncle wondered dryly.

The prince frowned. "Those men and women are very highly trained. None of them died."

Her uncle wasn't impressed. "Then it couldn't have been a very big or powerful Fiend."

Rain tried to be more tactful since they would be stuck traveling with the humans for a while. "They don't have the advantages that we do, physically or magically. We were meant to do this, you humans just, well, aren't." Humans couldn't use their kind of magic; at best it wouldn't work, at worst the human would die horribly, possibly taking the lives of those around them as well.

"Perhaps," Schuyler allowed, considering her words. "So, how long have you been doing this?" The question was directed at both of them.

"I've been a full Hunter for twenty-four years," Damien answered, "and while Rain may be a year short of being a full Hunter, she can be expected to act as one." Rain felt her chest swell with pride. Not that her uncle had been stingy with praise when it was merited, but still, it was one thing to be complimented on a fight and quite another for him to vouch for her to a client as a true Hunter and not just an apprentice.

"Very well," the prince said, nodding. "How long do you actually expect the journey to take? I know we have two weeks, but I just want to know what we're realistically looking at."

"If we meet no trouble at all it would take us six days," Damien replied after a moment of consideration. "I'd put it at ten if we're being realistic, maybe a full two weeks if the weather turns bad, and there's a good chance of it this time of year." Water mages could have some influence over the weather, but it was discouraged since it was also dangerous and could have unpredictable effects on top of being difficult.

Warren spoke up at last, his voice not quite as deep as she would have expected. "How many Fiends do you expect to face?"

"There's no real way to predict it." Rain spoke up before her uncle could. "There just isn't. We have warning spells and we pay attention to talk when we travel, but that's about all we can do." The creatures just seemed to show up out of nowhere most of the time.

"And against humans? The royal family is not without enemies, and Phasoia would definitely benefit if the negotiations weren't able to take place." Maybe she should have just let her uncle answer. So far she wasn't overly fond of Warren.

Damien looked skyward for a moment before answering. "We said we'll make certain that you reach Landai alive."

"And what if an agent from Phasoia offered you money to kill the prince?"

"You seem to be under some false impressions here," her uncle said, and his tone gave her shivers for all she wasn't on the receiving end. Warren looked like he wanted to run. "We are Hunters, not mercenaries, not assassins. We have agreed to guide you across borderlands that are known to be dangerous because there are monsters that would love to rip you to pieces and eat you. This is not outside of our realm of regular duties. Your monarchs could have also hired out a Guardian to do the same." Hunters led more nomadic lives, so humans considered them to be more expendable than Guardians. Damien didn't say it, but she was sure he was thinking it.

"You can't pretend that there aren't some of your kind who don't fill those roles." It seemed like some strange pride or false bravado kept Warren talking.

"I never said that," Damien reminded him. "But those people are not Hunters, they have no medallions, they are mercenaries and assassins." Sometimes a Hunter went bad, like Damien's mentor and her mother's; it didn't happen often, but it wasn't unheard of. Hunters took it very personally when it did happen, and those individuals didn't tend to live very long. "Do you have any other questions?" His voice hadn't changed from that cold, polite tone.

"I do," Schuyler answered, giving his servant a look that had him moving back and standing straight once more. "How long have the two of you worked together?"

Damien's tone warmed considerably, though it still had a cold edge. "Officially? A week." Unofficially it was more like her whole life.

"Well, I have no objections with the route you've chosen. Will you be staying here tonight?"

Damien shook his head. "We're staying in the city. We'll be here for you at dawn." The prince nodded and talk turned to last minute questions about supplies and funds. Warren stayed silent, though Rain could tell he was listening just as intently as she was. She wasn't certain how she felt about him, but the prince seemed decent enough. Clearly not a fighter, but very intelligent; he reminded her a little of her sister.

Finally it seemed that they had everything settled. Schuyler sighed. "I suppose there's no more avoiding it, it's time to prepare for the party tonight."

"Not a party animal?" Rain asked, quirking a brow.

Warren snorted and the prince glared at his servant. "No. I'd rather be reading. Yet I will be seeing you later." He opened the door and summoned another servant who escorted Rain and her uncle to a sitting room where they could stay until the party started. It also held a powder room and a bathroom, should they need to 'freshen themselves up'.

"More like, 'let's keep the Hunters locked safely away'," Damien said with a smirk as he drank from his flask. Rain sank into an overstuffed and overly ornate chair. It wasn't comfortable and made her feel trapped.

"How is that thing always with you? It's like, no matter where we are or what's going on, you manage to keep it with you." Whether she could see it or not, and there had been times where she could have sworn it wasn't on his belt only for it to be in his hand moments later.

"Magic," he answered, wiggling the fingers of his free hand. She glared at him. "No, really, I've put a lot of work into it over the years." He handed her the flask so she could see the runes carefully etched into the metal and stamped into the leather.

"Are you really that worried someone will poison you?" She recognised a lot of the runes and combinations, including a few meant to misdirect the gaze of someone looking at it and others to negate poisons and drugs if the bearer drank the contents.

"Unfortunately the Fiends aren't our only enemies," Damien said darkly as he sat in one of the chairs, making a face as he sank into the cushion.

Rain nodded. She knew that, but it was something she would have to remember. "How long do we have to stay at this thing?"

"Long enough for the courtiers to gawk at us and for the brave to ask stupid questions; then we can go back to the inn. Or to the Thief King's court. That could actually be a fun evening."

"Will we actually end up back at the inn if we do that?"

"We will," he waved away her concerns.

Luckily it wasn't long before someone came to get them and brought them to a ballroom, though again, it was an informal ballroom. Rain didn't understand the difference, and when she asked Uncle Damien he was just as clueless. When they entered the ornate room they were announced to the crowd. The humans were dressed like characters out of the fairy tales Rain had read when she was younger, in colourful and overly elaborate gowns and suits that definitely hadn't been made with any practicality or possibility of facing danger in mind. There were long tables full of elaborate dishes, far more food than anyone in the room could possibly eat. Everything was so… lavishly decorated. It was frivolous, especially when she'd seen how many people in the rest of the city were in or near poverty.

"Are all courts like this?" She asked, keeping her voice low and trying to keep a neutral expression. But then, it wasn't just the courts, she'd seen it in the human towns among the regular folk as well, though not as bad as this. Then again, that could have been the human hierarchy at play.

Damien looked around without trying to hide a slight grimace at the excess. "To some extent. A lot of nobles and merchants are just as bad. Granted, I haven't been to many courts. Luckily they try to avoid having people like us around." The most formal events she'd attended back home had nothing on this. Everything looked so overdone, so fake. Every look, every gesture seemed calculated and practiced. She could see it in many of their eyes, the schemes, the plots, the lust for power and money. It made her feel a little sick. Everyone was watching for someone to misstep and say the wrong thing to the wrong person so they could jump in and gain something.

She turned her attention away from that and focused instead on the music. There was a band playing, and though the music was very different from back home it wasn't unpleasant. She watched the dancers, carefully mapping out the steps in her mind as she tried to figure it out.

"Want to join them?" Damien asked, finishing off another glass of wine. "I find dancing usually makes human parties less painful."

"I don't know the steps," she replied. She was almost certain she had most of it figured out from watching. Dancing was a little like fighting, really, just with more rules and less blood. Usually, anyway.

Damien placed the empty glass on a table and grabbed her hand to pull her onto the floor. "Just follow me, and let's show these courtiers a thing or two." She nodded and concentrated on the music, letting it flow through her like water as she moved, following her uncle's cues and within a few turns she had it down. "That's it, now turn." She did, aware of the eyes on her. Compared to the Hunters, the humans looked clumsy and slow. When the song changed they were both approached by other partners. Rain found herself facing Schuyler while some noble lady twirled away with her uncle.

"You dance very well," the prince said as they moved into the opening steps. It was similar to the last one, enough that she managed not to stumble while scrambling to figure out the steps.

"Thanks," she said. "You're not half bad yourself."

He grinned. "I think you're the first person to tell me that. Most tell me I'm amazing."

"Is that because you're a prince?" Perhaps not the best thing to say, but she was curious.

"I'd like to think some of it is honest," he said. "After all, I'm neither the heir nor the spare, so I'll never have the throne. People tend to kiss up to me less than my brothers and sister."

"Does that bother you?" She wondered. In some of the stories she'd read, one of the younger siblings ended up overthrowing the heir.

He shrugged. "I wasn't brought up to expect it. I was given the choice of becoming a knight and commander, a scholar, or a diplomat. I chose the latter two. What about demons? I don't know much about your rulers."

"We don't really have any," she said. He looked surprised. "We have the Council, but they mostly just make sure that the things that need to be done get done by the right people, they don't necessarily have much power outside of emergencies. They earn their place, too." She said before realising that maybe that wasn't the best thing to say to a prince either. However, he looked intrigued rather than offended. "In the villages and smaller towns we just work together. There is a mayor in Lysee, which is the only city in the territories, but that's because it's quite large."

"What's it like living there? I've heard that there aren't many humans."

She shook her head. "There aren't. For the most part your kind don't like mine too much. As for what it's like… we do things differently, and it's not so loud or… well, we don't have events like this." Her people admired beauty and beautiful things as much as humans, but this was just too much. Gaudy was the right word, though she kept that to herself.

"Have you spent much time among humans?"

She shook her head. "No, at least not humans who weren't always around my people."

"How do you find it so far?"

Ah, hell, how to answer without possibly making the trip extremely awkward? "Different," she said slowly.

He snorted and called her on it. "A diplomat's answer."

"We're going to be stuck together for two weeks, I'd rather not make it painful," she informed him. "How about I go with 'undecided'?" But she could definitely see why Hunters preferred the company of those who lived on the wrong side of society.

"Why become a Hunter?" She could tell that that was what he'd really wanted to ask her. "I've always wondered, especially since they don't seem to have very long careers for the most part."

"To protect the people I care about and to hopefully keep others from losing loved ones as well," she answered honestly.

"Not for the glory or the riches?" He asked with a small smile.

She laughed. "No, actually in my village there are a lot of Hunters, so growing up I knew exactly how little glory there was to be had in it." Not to mention how much pain there was. "The money is pretty good, but between protective charms and weapons it can get pricey."

"I would also like to apologize for Warren's behaviour earlier, he gets a little overzealous and protective sometimes, especially when he's nervous."

"We're used to it." The song changed and they followed the new beat. "So, what do you study as a scholar?"

"History, other cultures, languages, different laws and customs; I want to see the world and maybe help everyone get long a little better, be they human or demon."

"Admirable," she remarked, though she wasn't certain it was possible.

"I hope so, I don't have much else going for me. Does it ever make you nervous? The fighting?"

She shook her head. "They beat that out of us pretty quickly at the Academy." She was half-joking. Nervousness caused people to make foolish mistakes or hesitate when it could get them killed.

"I guess they would have to. I find them terrifying, but I'm also abysmal with a sword," he admitted sheepishly.

"Don't worry, I'll keep the nasty monsters away," she teased. It wasn't that she had no fear of them, because she did, ever since she'd watched her sister dragged through their kitchen door, watched her father chop off the arm that clung to her own body. But there was a difference between letting that fear paralyse her and using it to fuel her need to destroy them.

When that song finished they were separated by different partners. A few dances later her uncle appeared before her again. "Is that lipstick on your neck?" She asked as the other pairs bowed to one another. He pulled out a handkerchief and rubbed at the spot she pointed to. "It's gone."

"Thanks. That explains the last five minutes," he muttered, irritated. Rain decided not to ask. Apparently her uncle drew the line at noblewomen. "How's your evening going? You and the prince seem to be getting along well."

"He's curious about us. He kind of reminds me of Storm."

"Okay." He looked like he wanted to say something else, but decided against it. When she asked he just shook his head. "It's getting late," he said instead of answering. Rain glanced out the large windows that lined one wall. The sun was starting to descend towards the mountains, setting the sky on fire. "I think we've been here an acceptable length of time. Let's go have some real fun."

"Sounds good to me."

That was how she found herself learning how to pick locks an hour later while her uncle played cards with some rather unsavoury looking humans who may or may not have been either mercenaries, bandits, or assassins.

"What the fuck? Are you psychic?" A heavily scarred woman demanded, slapping her cards on the table and glaring at Rain's uncle.

"I swear, my magic is in metal, not minds," Damien said, waving his hand and getting the coins to slide themselves across the table to his pile. He glanced over at Rain and frowned.

"Where did you get that?" He asked as he looked at the lock she'd just opened.

"From me," Tam told him with a mischievous grin

"No, you're not," Damien protested with a look of horror. "Not again!"

"What?" Rain asked, looking between the two men.

"I taught your mother how to pick locks," Tam said with a grin.

Damien glared at him. "And I believe we have had words about how much trouble that caused me over the years."

"Sometimes you need a little trouble in life, keeps it from being boring," the thief said with a wink to Rain.

"Just what do you think being a hunter involves?" He demanded, exasperated.

Tam's grin widened. "Well, it's too late now. She's as much a natural as her mum was." Rain grinned at her uncle's dismay.

"Damn water types, always getting into everything," he complained with a melodramatic sigh. "I don't know why I put up with it for so long."

"You kept coming home," Rain pointed out. "You have only yourself to blame."

"Well, someone had to make sure you only fell into the right amount of trouble, kiddo," he said, reaching over to ruffle her hair, laughing when she glared at him. "Ash is an excellent father, but every kid needs a crazy uncle."

"I know about a hundred different places to hide a body in this city," the scarred woman offered to Rain.

"No, I need him to get my medallion," Rain replied. "I'll get back to you in a year." The thieves laughed.

"I helped raise you and your sister, I trained you, and this is the thanks I get?" He asked, shaking his head. "Anyways, we need to get going, we do have to meet the prince at dawn." He said, looking out a window as he swept his rather large pile of coins into a small leather bag.

"Taking the bookworm to Landai should be an easy job," Tam said as he leaned back in his chair and drank from a mug of ale.

The scarred woman frowned. "I don't know, the stories going around haven't been that good."

"Be on your guard," she warned both of them. "I don't want that one to die before I win my money back," she added with a glare at Damien.

"I wouldn't dream of dying without seeing you again, Calai," he said gallantly. She shooed him away so he and Rain could make their way back to the inn.

"I wonder what it says about humans that their thieves are more honest than their nobles?" She asked as they walked down the dark streets. She knew there was no one in earshot. "Well, I mean, you know, they're not as..."

"Not as much like venomous sheep?" Damien supplied with a crooked grin.

She rolled her eyes. "Not that again."

"Don't think about it too hard," he advised as they entered the inn. "Just be glad that we're dealing with a human who seems like a decent sort." She nodded and went to her room. That night she dreamed of dancing with a green-eyed prince.

5

The Road to Landai

Damien woke before dawn, the sun's light just barely beginning to hide the stars. Everything was quiet as he sat up and reached for his flask, taking a deep drink, feeling the familiar burn of liquor as it slid down his throat. He set it aside and readied for the day and their journey with well-practiced efficiency. He took another drink and sat down on the bed, rubbing a hand over the stubble on his jaw. Just enough to take off the edge, to hold off the darkness that threatened to swallow him whole again. Just that much and no more, that was what she had told him so long ago.

He double checked all of his weapons and made sure that his charms and amulets were working order before grabbing his bags and leaving the room. He knocked on Rain's door and his niece emerged ready to travel and fight. She looked so much like her mother, but he knew she wasn't Tempest. Tempest was gone forever. Still, she would have been so proud to see what her daughters were becoming, how strong they were. Storm was already gaining attention as a scholar and Rain was going to be an amazing Hunter, one of the elite.

He'd lost count of the number of times people had asked him if it was out of some sense of debt or duty to Tempest that he did so much for the girls. Many seemed to think that with her dying breath she'd made him swear to take care of her girls. That wasn't true. His best friend, the first family he'd known, had already died by the time he'd fallen to his knees at her side that night. Maybe at first he'd cared about the girls because they were hers and Ash's, but long before she'd died they'd wormed their way into his heart, creating spaces of their own. So while he'd never wanted to be a mentor, taking Rain on as an apprentice was no burden, and hell, he'd have been hurt if she'd asked anyone else if he was being honest. He also did his best to help Storm, testing out her spells and helping her find obscure books or writings, something his rather unsavory contacts came in handy for. They were the closest he'd ever come to having kids of his own, and the closest he would ever be, so Damien would do his damnedest to make sure they both survived and got to have the lives they wanted, that they had some chance of being happy. No matter how he knew that the two didn't always overlap, especially for Hunters. Elite Hunters faced even worse odds on that score. Then again, considering that they dealt with the most powerful Fiends it was no wonder most of them weren't exactly sane.

They ate a quick breakfast as they rode to the palace where a sleepy prince and his irritating servant met them at the front gate. With a quick greeting exchanged Damien led them northward out of the city. The prince and his servant followed, with Rain at the back. Fortunately the scholar had some sense, wearing sturdy clothes that would offer some protection on the road. Travelers who insisted on wearing fine clothing on the road were the reason why he normally avoided escort jobs and stuck to just hunting. The latter was also far more satisfying because he could stab Fiends all he wanted. The servant, however, was wearing the kind of amour favoured by Rangers, an attempt to make heavy plate metal as light and flexible as chainmail that was only moderately successful and inhibited speed. The best defense against Fiends was an armour spell, but so far no human mage had managed to get one to work against more than a single blow and humans couldn't use demon magic; at best the spells wouldn't work, at worst the human foolish enough to try it died horribly. They just couldn't physically handle the amount of power, one thing that helped fuel the legends that his kind gave their souls for the power and magic to battle the Fiends. Damien's armour spell was the most powerful that had been created, made into a tattoo placed where his neck and shoulders met and spreading across his upper back. It drew on his own power to fuel it, which meant that the spell couldn't burn out like Rain's spell beads, but it also meant that he had to be more careful about conserving his strength in a fight. Still, it was worth it.

"So, how long until we start seeing Fiends?" Warren wondered as they reached the edge of the city. The guards at the gate bowed to the prince while the Guardians waved to the Hunters.

"Any minute now," Damien said, glancing back at the human. "I hope that gaudy armour isn't giving you any ideas on what you can do." He ignored Rain's frown.

The young man gave him the human equivalent of a fierce glare. It wasn't very effective. "This is what Rangers wear against Fiends."

He snorted. "It's going to get you killed; steel won't help when your foe can rip through it with claws the length of your forearm."

"And your spells will?" Damien could see he was starting to waver despite his words.

"Yes, actually," he replied. "Hell, the minute the Fiends realise there are gaps in your armour you're going to be ripped to shreds."

"I thought they were mindless beasts."

"Some of them, sure, but others? You'd swear they were as smart as we are. Luckily there aren't normally too many of them around." That was when things got very interesting in very bad ways.

"Uncle Damien?" He turned to look at Rain and nodded. His warning spell had been triggered too. The Fiend came at them from behind, but his apprentice was fast; before the Fiend cleared the trees one of her arrows was ripping through its neck, the barbed tips designed to shred as much flesh as possible. She tore out half its throat and kicked her horse back as it kept moving forward, jumping as the horse reared and bringing her sword down on what remained of the Fiend's neck. A moment later she had a fang in hand and the monster was on fire. She looked up to see both humans staring at her, open-mouthed, and gave them an actor's dramatic bow before mounting her horse once more.

"You should have been able to do that with just the arrow," he remarked. The less effort it took to kill a foe the better. She needed to improve more than she needed her ego stroked, especially if she wanted to be an elite Hunter someday.

"Yeah, the angle was off a little, but I didn't realise that until it was too late," she admitted, lips thinning as she considered her mistake.

"We'll practice shooting later." She could use her magic to create deadly attacks over a distance, ice blades as sharp as razors shredding her enemies, but that didn't mean she could set aside her weapons. Magic wasn't infallible.

"Are you kidding? That was amazing," Schuyler protested, shaking slightly.

"Not against a Fiend," Rain replied with a sigh. "Any of my other instructors would have said the same." She sounded annoyed with herself, always a good sign in a beginning Hunter, a sign she knew that she still had a long way to go.

"You'll get it, you just have to work a little," he told his niece, getting the group moving again.

The further away they got from the city and the more densely populated areas, the worse things would get, so it was better to make up time before they lost it. They only stopped briefly to rest the horses, taking advantage of the rolling hills to watch for Fiends, though they soon found themselves once again in a thick forest. Warren seemed to have put his pride away and he and Rain debated bow styles while though the prince didn't say anything he paid close attention to the conversation. Maybe he ought to give the kid a chance, Damien decided as he listened. He was clever, if a little misguided, and seemed willing enough to learn after a few stumbles. He couldn't say the same about many humans.

Every time he left Ankira he wondered why he ever returned to it. When he'd left the first time he'd been so sure that he wouldn't, that he would never go back to the streets where his blood had been spilled, where he'd nearly died of hunger on more than one occasion. It wasn't easy for a demon in a human city, especially when born with one human parent.

He supposed his parents had loved him, the memories he still had of his mother certainly supported that fact, despite her deep depression. His father had died before he was born, and his mother had died when he was still young, killed by thieves one dark night, though she had given up on life long before then, likely when his father had died. If it weren't for the fact that when he was a child he could be mistaken for human at first glance there was no way he could have survived, not in Ankira and not even among the thieves. When he was fourteen he managed to muster up the courage to go to the city gates and ask a Guardian about becoming a Hunter. He'd seen them in the Thief King's court when he'd snuck in with Dagger and listened to their stories about fighting Fiends, their comrades, and their families back home. He learned about a whole country of people like him, where he wouldn't be hated because of what he was. The Guardian had sent him to the demonic territories with a comrade who was returning home for a visit. Damien had been dropped off at the Academy gates and for the first time since his mother's death he'd been welcomed somewhere. He'd been given a room in the Academy dormitories, the first home he'd had in eight years.

Then a day later someone moved into the room next to him: a girl with sapphire blue hair and pale blue eyes. Their bond hadn't been an instant thing, though there had been an undeniable connection as they had more in common with one another than the other students, including their mutual tendency towards misanthropy. Those things had made them uneasy allies at first in the days they struggled to adjust to an entirely new way of living and for him a new culture as well, both of them learning how to read and write while keeping up with everyone else and just trying to make a new identity. That alliance had held and turned into something far more lasting, each becoming what the other needed so desperately: a family. Before they graduated many had forgotten that he and Tempest weren't related by blood. If only she could have lived, how far they could have gone... How far she could have gone, her spirit far less fragile than his own.

His warning spell went off an instant before a particularly large Fiend came charging down the road, oversized fangs jutting out of its ragged mouth. Damien leaped off his horse while drawing his sword and rushed the monster, jumping over the jagged claws that came at him and using the Fiend's arm to propel himself past its neck, severing the head. He landed neatly behind it and collected a fang as a second Fiend burst through the treeline, though Rain's arrow took its head off before it could get near Damien. He took out a third that came behind it, throwing a dagger on a slim silver thread. He could put power into metals so that they could do far more damage than they ought to, and he did so now, killing it instantly. The Fiend fell on top of the other. He collected the fangs and quickly set them on fire, tossing Rain the fang of the one she had taken down.

"Better," he told her as he mounted his horse once more, and she smiled slightly, both of them trying not to look at the slack-jawed humans.

"Now I get where you're coming from," Warren admitted as they rode away. "It would have taken several Rangers to kill those things, and not all of them would have lived." Damien smiled grimly and drank from his flask.

"How much longer before we get where we're going?" Schuyler asked.

"A few hours yet," he replied. He heard the prince's tired sigh. "We can't stop now and we can't push the horses any faster." It was the closest he would come to an apology. The scholar was doing his best to keep up with the rest of them, but just didn't have the same endurance as Warren did, let alone anything close to Rain or Damien.

"I know," the prince said wryly. "I'm sure I'll get used to this by the journey's end."

"It's probably a better idea to adjust closer to the start or else you're going to have a bad time of it, especially when the weather turns," Rain advised with a sympathetic look.

Damien turned to look at his niece. Those with water magic could sometimes detect shifts in the weather that allowed them to accurately predict what it was going to be. "Will it turn?" He couldn't keep the plaintive note out of his voice. He was a true Hunter. He could last through all but the most extreme weather, but that didn't mean he enjoyed it. Especially wet weather.

"Maybe," she answered after a moment. "It feels like there might be a storm forming." In an area like this it could be difficult to tell. It was worse on the coast or in a rain forest.

"Excellent," he muttered, taking a drink from his flask. "Well, let's just hope it doesn't come upon us when we're camping in two nights." Mud was annoying, even if Rain could keep them from getting soaked.

"Do you always drink?" The prince asked, watching him.

"No, I need to breathe sometimes," he quipped. The prince proved his future diplomatic potential by saying no more on the subject. Conversation fell away as they went on, a natural effect of travel. A few smaller Fiends attacked, but between Damien and Rain they did fine, though one managed to knock Rain off her horse. "You okay, kiddo?" He asked as she took a few seconds to stand and dust herself off and breathe again. It had looked like a nasty spill.

"Winded me, that's all," she replied, taking a few deep breaths as she set the thing on fire before mounting again. "It was heavier than it looked. A lot heavier. I'm going to have bruises."

The prince was staggering when they finally made it to the village inn after the Hunters traded the fangs for coin. They'd agreed that he wouldn't use his titles on the road, even if it would have gotten them preferential treatment because it would have also gotten them far too much attention. Rain laughed at his expression when a maid brought them food, a thick stew.

"What is this?" He asked, poking around the trencher with his spoon.

"Don't think too hard about it," she advised with a grin, obviously delighting in his discomfort.

"Actually, at a place like this you're probably safe," Damien said. "Though when winter comes don't look at the meat too closely." The prince took a moment to clue in, then looked horrified. Warren was faster, and Rain just grimaced slightly. "Hey, it's winter, you're starving, what are you going to do? Properly spiced you won't even notice that you're eating rat." Gods knew he'd eaten worse as a child.

"I suppose," the prince agreed reluctantly. The food was actually rather good here. "Will we be leaving at dawn again?"

Damien nodded, taking a deep drink of ale. "Unless I tell you otherwise, just assume that you're rising with the sun. You travel with Hunters, you keep our hours."

"Aren't demons in your line of work also notorious for partying and drinking?" Of course Warren would ask that.

"We've worked damn hard to earn that reputation," he agreed, raising his glass. It was one of the few ways they stayed sane. Nothing like drunken revelry to help one forget about all the shit in the world for a few hours.

"What's it like at the Academy, anyway?" Schuyler asked. Damien let Rain answer that one. She was good, only giving them information that would have been easy enough to find out anywhere. Their people weren't exactly secretive, but why tell everything to those who could potentially become enemies? Their relationship with humans was always on the edge of a knife, much like he was. He finished the mug of ale and signaled for another. It was weaker than he would have normally liked, but considering that it was a human establishment it would suffice. The humans went to bed quickly after finishing. Warren may have been trained as a fighter, but his place at his master's side meant that he hadn't done much traveling either.

"What do you think of them?" He asked Rain as she swirled water around a glass, giving it the tiniest nudge with her magic to create a miniature whirlpool. She and Schuyler had been getting along particularly well. A little too well, actually.

"They're okay," she said as she toyed with it, changing the speed and direction at random. "I think once Warren's been around us for a few days he'll settle down. The prince is nice though."

"Nice," Damien repeated, raising an eyebrow.

"Fuck off," she told him, blushing.

He held up his hands, "hey, your words," he said, then sighed. It was better to have this conversation sooner rather than later. "Rain, just remember that they're our clients."

Her lips thinned. "I know."

"They're also human and the prince is a godsdamned nobleman, neither of which mix well with our people, let alone a Hunter." No matter how mature they acted, he could tell they were full of the fairy story idealism that came with a sheltered upbringing. No matter how poisonous the courts were, the world was far more dangerous and far less forgiving than they knew, especially growing up in Glask.

She frowned, getting defensive as she caught on to his point. "I noticed. Look, I'm not going to fall in love with him or anything."

"Okay," he said, holding his hands up in surrender. She understood, he didn't need to push it.

"I'm going to bed," she decided, leaving him alone. He shook his head as she made her way to the staircase and leaned back with a sigh. There was no question that she wasn't a child anymore, but she still had a ways to go yet.

"Hey, looks like you're all alone now," the maid said, coming back around.

"Yeah, I guess I am," he agreed, looking up at her. He could see the interest in her eyes.

"You're a Hunter, aren't you?" She asked, gathering the dishes.

"That I am, and I've got the scars to prove it."

She grinned, undressing him with her eyes. "Oh really?"

"Yeah," he said with an easy grin. "Some of the stories are pretty impressive too."

"Well, I'm off in an hour if you plan on sticking around I'd love to hear them." She walked back towards the kitchen, a flirty sway to her walk. Damien watched her go. Tempest would have rolled her eyes at him if she could see him now. Raven... well Raven would have been disappointed in him. He'd never tried to find someone he could make a life with, who he could be happy with. The truth was that he couldn't take it. He always seemed to be the one left behind in the end, the one left to live with the pain and grief. His heart wouldn't survive the loss of anyone else he cared about. He didn't know whether to call it good luck or bad that he was the consummate survivor. Moreover, he just didn't think he had it in him to care about another like that, not anymore. Even Raven had been a rare miracle. A one of a kind miracle. He was okay with that. Or at least he'd learned to live with it.

Rain gasped as she woke up, pulling the knife out from under her pillow. A deep breath later and she put it away. It had just been a nightmare. Luckily she didn't have them often. She rose and stretched before going to look out the window to see that it wasn't quite dawn yet. She knew it wasn't worth trying to fall asleep again so she grabbed her sword and went down to the fenced yard behind the inn and practiced drills, concentrating on the movements, starting slow and then speeding up until her blade was a silver blur. She didn't often dream of the night her mother died, when she'd learned that the heroes didn't always live and that monsters would rip apart a child as easily as an adult, but when she did... After she finished with the sword she started on her daggers. She imagined herself to be water, graceful, flowing, fast. Then she started using magic as she moved, heating the blades using the moisture in the air, lengthening the blades with icicles. She was careful not to overdo it though, she would need her strength. Rain could feel eyes on her, but didn't look up until she was done. Schuyler stood in the doorway, watching her.

"Couldn't sleep?" He wondered, walking over to her.

She shrugged. "You?"

He shook his head. "I'm not used to it being so quiet. Even at night there's always something happening in the castle, servants and guards going about their duties. I'll also admit that I'm a bit nervous the farther away we get from home. With everything going on with Landaia and Phasoia I'm half-expecting something to happen." She could see that was only part of it, and guessed that he missed his family as well. She certainly missed hers.

"You mean aside from getting attacked by monsters that want to rip us apart and possibly eat us?" Rain wondered, raising a brow.

"You have a point," he allowed, "but I also have to worry about people using me against my family for political gain. The ransom for a third prince may not be all that high, but I've worked to make myself an asset to my family and to my brother."

"It's strange, your kind choose to attack each other and waste resources on fighting each other when there are far more important problems to deal with. I don't get it."

"I'd like to defend my species, but you're not wrong," he admitted wryly.

"There are legends say that we're the same species."

"Legends say a lot of things, who knows if they're true?" He shrugged. "It's certainly possible, but I honestly have no idea if it is or not. What do you think of it?"

"You'll have to do better than that if you want to succeed as an ambassador," she said with a slight grin. "I don't know either, I might care more if I thought knowing would make a difference, but…" she shrugged.

"Oh don't worry, I can lie with the best of them, but part of my job is knowing how to get people to like me." She let her expression speak for her. "Well, it's true, and I am quite certain that you would like me for being who I am."

"Which is?"

"Oddly enough a somewhat awkward bookworm." She snorted. "Am I wrong?"

"No, you're not wrong," she admitted, looking up at the sky as she sheathed her weapons. "We ought to get ready to go."

"Do you think you could teach me how to do any of that?" He asked as they turned to go back.

"Do what?"

"Fighting with knives."

"I thought you princes were more about swords." Knives were usually a thief's weapon of choice.

"Well, yes, normally, but I am terrible with a sword and it's generally frowned upon for a diplomat to walk around openly carrying a sword, whereas no one would say anything about a belt knife," he explained.

"There's not a whole lot I can show you in less than two weeks," Rain cautioned. "Wouldn't it be a better idea to ask Warren how to fight?"

"Maybe, but then I wouldn't have a really good excuse to spend time with you," he told her. That brought her up short.

"I don't think this is a good idea," she said carefully, remembering what her uncle had said the night before. He was a human prince, she was a Hunter. Maybe they could be friends, but never more. "Now let's go, we have a long road ahead of us yet." She waved him inside ahead of her and looked up. The storm she'd started to feel the day before was still brewing, and something told her it wouldn't be pretty when it unleashed itself. That made her happy, though no one else would feel the same.

"Wait." She paused. "I'm sorry, you're right," he admitted. "But this doesn't have to be the end of everything."

"No, but it does draw a line." He nodded in agreement and they went inside.

She knocked on her uncle's door. "Uncle Damien? We're getting ready to go." It was yet a little before dawn, but she figured that he would rather get as far as they could before the storm hit. She was good with her magic and could have a limited influence over weather, but it was difficult to control. Add a storm into the mix and it got even harder. He opened the door, half-asleep and only wearing pants. Scars marked his arms and torso, crossing over or under tattoos. Her father had scars, so had her mother and other Hunters. Soon she would probably look the same. The marks on her arm were certainly a start in that direction.

"Give me twenty minutes and I'll meet you downstairs," he said blearily and shut the door again.

They made good headway for several hours with no sign of Fiends. When they stopped for a rest by a creek Rain started training the prince, much to the amusement of her uncle and Warren, and herself for that matter. While the prince was a fair dancer he was an utterly graceless fighter.

"You know, you could always use that as a diversion tactic. Your opponent will become so confused that you can just run away," Damien suggested as Rain tried to get Schuyler to punch in a straight line. The prince glared at the Hunter and tried again, forcing Rain to duck as his strike veered far to the left. Had their audience not been seated they would have fallen over from laughing.

"Wait, that wouldn't have hurt you, would it?" Schuyler asked, horrified.

"My armour spell would do far more damage to you than that hit would do to me." He gave it a few more valiant attempts and sat down on the grass with a sigh.

"I'm going to guess that if I can't manage this I won't be able to fight with a knife, am I?"

"No." The Hunters and his bodyguard spoke in unison, eliciting a glare from the prince.

"Just leave the fighting to me, your Highness," Warren advised, patting his friend on the shoulder. "It's for the best."

Rain looked up as her warning spell went off. A large Fiend came crashing out of the treeline and she pulled water from the creek, directing it like a wave as she froze the edge into a razor-sharp blade. The Fiend's head rolled neatly to her feet and she took a fang before setting it on fire as she sent the water back into the creek.

"Let's go," Damien said, standing with a sigh as the humans stared at Rain. "I want to get to Kadinor as soon as possible. As of tomorrow things are going to get tough." When they left Kadinor it would be two days before they reached another occupied village, and even then, they would have to push to avoid having to camp in the open again. They rose and got back on the road. "Anything more on the storm that's brewing?" He asked a few minutes later, but Rain just shook her head. It was an imprecise skill at best, and reliant on her interpretation of a number of factors and even with practice there was a limit to how accurate she could get. The closer they got to the mountains the more the forest would start thinning out as well, offering less cover from the rain.

Despite concerns they made it in good time, arriving well before sunset. Kadinor was a thriving small town, and there were a few shops near the inn where they could purchase supplies. Rain recognised one of the Guardians as a water mage she'd met at the Academy and asked him about the weather. While he had a decade more experience he was almost as uncertain as she was, though he did know that the storm would be headed northward.

"That's just fucking great," Damien sighed when they were at the inn. It was a little larger than the last one, and busier.

"Should we stay here and wait it out?" Schuyler asked, stirring a cup of tea.

"No, because even though I can say it's going to be going northward, that's pretty vague, so it could still bypass us altogether. We might not even see a cloud," Rain replied, playing with her medallion. "I'm sorry, I can't do any better than that."

"You're doing pretty well," her uncle assured her as he drank. "Weather's a tricky thing. Even if the storm catches us, there are enough buildings are still standing that we'll be able to find a decent shelter."

"How do you know that?" Warren wanted to know, arching a brow.

"A smuggler told me in the Thief King's court," Damien replied bluntly.

"You trust a smuggler?" Schuyler demanded, looking scandalised. It was hard for Rain not to laugh. Warren's expression was almost funnier. They were sheltered humans, no matter how educated or sensible they might seem.

"More than I trust any of your father's men," he said. "You forget, we're *demons*. We tend to get along better with those in the underworld for a reason." The prince and his servant both looked uncertain.

"How do we know we can trust you if you're with the likes of them?" Warren demanded.

"Warren, if they housed any ill-will towards us they could have done away with us at any point after we left the city and blamed it on Fiends,"

Schuyler pointed out as he thought things over. "We may not like it, but we have to accept that this is the way the world works."

"I always heard you were smart," Damien said as he took a drink.

6

Storm

The dawn came cold and grey. Damien gave an inward as his apprentice and clients gathered at the inn's stable. They all looked so young, not one of them over twenty. It made him feel old, so very old for all he was only forty-two. Though for a Hunter one year could feel like a hundred, making him ancient. Rain still couldn't quite figure out what was going on with the brewing storm, so they had to push forward. He could tell that the last few days were wearing on the three, even Rain, though as expected she showed it the least. So far she was meeting his expectations and he was lying if he didn't admit they were higher than what most other apprentices had to measure up to, but he also believed they were fair, since she had always said she wanted to be the best.

"Let's go," he said. One benefit of experience was that he wasn't feeling the strain of travel, which made him feel a little less old. They rode as they had since they left Ankira, with him in the front and Rain guarding their backs, though today he also took out any Fiends they came across, fighting with brutal efficiency, as he chose to prioritise speed just in case the storm did come upon them before they reached the abandoned village and set up some kind of defense against Fiends and weather as they slept.

"The storm is heading in the same direction we are," Rain spoke up after a few hours. "At this rate we'll probably cross paths with it late this evening, though that could change." She sounded certain now.

Damien nodded. "We need to get to the ruins ahead of it." He pushed them even harder. They barely stopped mid-morning to give the horses a rest. "Rain," he said around noon.

"What?"

"No, rain," he held out a hand to collect water droplets, grinning. Her glare would have sent Fiends running for safety. She raised a hand and parted the rain over her and the humans as the rain started pouring. He raised a brow and she waited a few seconds before extending her magic over him. He pushed his damp hair out of his eyes. "That wasn't nice," he said.

"Neither are you."

"Oh come now, you've known that for seventeen years, dearest niece," he reminded her as he looked down the road. "Do you know if there's anything ahead of us?" Tempest could sometimes use water like a bat used sound to orient itself, getting an idea of what was around them, though usually nothing more than a general shape and size. Still, it had saved them more than once and he knew that Rain had been training herself to be able to do the same with the help of her sister, who'd mastered the skill early on.

She closed her eyes for a moment, focusing. He tapped a stud earring high in his ear and blinked as his vision changed, trying to ignore the fact that the rain had started falling on them once more. It wasn't as good as the ring Rain had, and it would give him a headache if he left it active too long, but it worked well enough. His niece was enveloped with a deep blue glow, one that was echoed in the heart of every raindrop he could see. He'd have to get her to use her ring when Storm was doing this sometime soon, he decided, tapping the stud again to deactivate the spell, since there was no sense in wearing it out.

"There's riders," she said at last, opening her eyes. "They're coming up behind us." He hadn't expected to meet anyone on this road; it only led to the abandoned village and to some of the more remote passes through the mountains. It was also too late in the year for smugglers to be operating in this part of the country as the weather could make travel difficult and soon impossible once the snow started coming in. Soon he could hear the horses, running on the muddy road. The only reason anyone would risk a horse's legs in mud was because they were escaping something or they were after something, and his warning spell hadn't gone off. He twisted so he could watch them come around the bend in the road they had just crossed. The riders had drawn weapons and were headed straight for them. He was about to shout at the humans and his apprentice to run when Rain wheeled her horse around and held both hands in front of her, slowly moving them upward. A thick wall of ice rose between them and the riders. He could hear their shouts and curses, calls to find a way around and get the prince.

"Go!" He shouted, wheeling his horse around. Schuyler and Warren didn't hesitate, spurring their horses into a gallop. Rain drew up beside Damien as he let the humans get ahead. Rain hadn't sensed anyone coming at them from the front. They hadn't gotten far before he heard and explosion and cheers. He reached over and grabbed her reins. "Run," he hissed. "There's too many of them and they know what they're at." He'd gotten a glimpse of their gear, and it had been a far higher quality than he would have expected of normal bandits or even a typical mercenary. It was also clear that their target was the prince. "They're going to capture us. You need to run."

"Uncle Damien..." He could see how scared she was, but this was the only plan he was willing to consider.

"Someone needs to be the hero," he reminded her. "Now go!" She nodded reluctantly and rose until she was crouching on the saddle before leaping into the trees. It wasn't entirely a lie, someone would probably need to rescue them and he was certain she would be up to the task, but this would also ensure that she, at least, would make it out of this unscathed. He had no idea how these people would treat a Hunter hired to protect their target, and he wasn't about to let Rain be the one to find out.

Rain hoisted herself up into a tree and jumped to the next and the one after before dropping to the ground and running until she couldn't hear the sounds of the riders or her uncle's shouting, heading towards the river. She stopped when she reached its edge, wrapping her arms around herself as she pushed aside the panic that wanted to swallow her, focusing on her training. She was a Hunter. She had people relying on her. She had to think and act quickly but carefully to make sure they all came out of this alive and as unharmed as possible. She pulled up her medallion and watched the gemstone in the back. Her uncle's silver dot moved away quickly for a while longer before stopping. Her heart rose to her throat when it started moving again, at a much slower pace. She swallowed hard. They'd been taken. Uncle Damien had known this would happen, would have been coming up with a plan before he told her to run. He was good, one of the best, and she'd grown up hearing stories of all the trouble he'd managed to get out of, so this would be no different, right? She took a deep breath and started running to catch up. She settled into pace she could hold for a long time and suspected that the riders were headed to the abandoned village they'd been trying to reach. The rain started to fall harder, and suddenly she was very, very glad for the weather. The storm was almost upon them.

Damien turned his head to spit blood after the riders dumped him on the ground far more roughly than the prince or Warren, trying to figure out what was hurt and how. Though to be fair, he had killed seven of them before they'd managed to cover his mouth and nose with a cloth doused in some kind of drug that had knocked him out, repeating the process three or four times until they got here. He felt weak, his brain full of clouds, and his hands were bound behind his back, with rope, not chain, and all of his knives and armour had been removed, including his vambraces and boots. So whoever these people were, they'd done their work on figuring out who would be with the prince. The sky was darker than before, though that could have just as easily been because of the rising storm as the passage of time. Looking around, he suspected it was a mix of both, because they were in an abandoned building. He didn't see Rain either, but that didn't necessarily mean that she got away. Granted, even if she hadn't these fuckers would soon learn that it was a lethal mistake to try to hold a water mage during a storm. He couldn't find it in himself to feel sorry for them, with the internal bleeding he was sure he had there just wasn't any room left for sympathy.

"Where's the girl?" Damien demanded, rising unsteadily to his feet despite the fact that it hurt like hell. Their guard jumped back, drawing his sword.

"Fuck, help!" He yelled, pointing the blade at Damien. He gave the man a look that Ash had once termed his 'executioner stare' and slowly walked forward, making the sword bend in on itself. The drugs made using his magic difficult but he pushed through it as the guard let go of the sword to cower against the wall. Damien kept it hovering and straightened the blade, positioning it to slit the human's throat. He wished for the mercury he kept in his saddlebag in a jar. He could wield quicksilver like Rain used water. Neither silver nor gold were very good for weapons, though silver was the best metal to hold magic.

"Where is she?" He asked slowly as the guard's comrades rushed in. One lunged at him and he kicked the man's sword away and quickly moved into another kick at his head, sending him flying to the floor unconscious and bleeding heavily as Damien staggered to keep his balance, using his magic to finish off the cowering guard and stepping out of the way of the arterial spray. Three of the riders grabbed him and dragged him back forcefully. He snarled, barring his fangs. They paled but didn't relent; one punched him where his ribs were broken and it was a struggle to stay conscious, let alone breathe. Naturally the drugs also impaired the armour spell that relied on his own magic as a power source.

"Your apprentice?" A woman asked drawing close. Apparently they had done their research. He snapped his teeth at her and she stepped back, but quickly covered her fear with a smug arrogance. "Don't worry; we're looking for her, though I doubt you'll like what we do when we find her."

He relaxed. "Oh, okay." He leaned forward slightly, as if to tell her a secret. "Just between you and me though, you're all fucked." He felt something stab into his neck and a burning agony flood his veins. "Fuck!" He gasped, falling unconscious.

Rain stopped briefly to re-braid her hair as the wind pulled strands free, blowing the curls into her face. She'd managed to catch up easily, because the three captured men were apparently not the best prisoners. She'd wanted to leap out and kill them when they'd started beating her uncle after he was drugged into unconsciousness, which also kept his armour spell from working. Had he been merely asleep or knocked unconscious he would have been fine, but she suspected that the drugs they used were laced with Fiend venom to keep them in his system longer. But she'd waited, knowing they would have just caught her as well. She'd needed to come up with a plan, and now she had one.

She crept through the ruins, drawing the water in the air around her and filling it with her power, manipulating it until she created a mirage around herself. It was something she'd worked on for years, playing hide and seek with her uncle and father until it was almost impossible for them to find her. Of course, it worked better in some environments than other. She made no noise as she examined the situation. She found her uncle and the humans in one of the larger buildings. Schuyler and Warren were sitting against the wall, watching her uncle who was slumped over on the floor, their pale faces tight with worry. There were two guards at the door and one more inside. She hid as all three were replaced, complaining about the weather and wondering how long they would have to wait for something, though they didn't really elaborate enough for her to figure out what it was except that this was politically motivated. Lightning struck nearby, and she felt a sizzle go through her. Humans drew magic from within themselves, one of the reasons why it was so much weaker than that of her kind. Rain drew her magic from her environment and channeled it through herself. As someone with water magic, this often included weather and not just lakes, rivers, ponds, or even a puddle if she got desperate, and each kind of source had a different feel to it. So for her, a storm like this made her feel like goddess, the wild energy filling her to the brim, waiting to be let out. She focused on that rather than the fact that a number of the buildings were full of people who would gladly harm or kill her. She moved to a hidden space behind a crumbling wall and began her work. Visibility was already poor for most beings, but now she used her magic to manipulate the moisture in the air into a thick fog, sending it creeping through the whole village. She heard cursing, and that made her smile, especially once the more superstitious among them got going. Thunderstorms weren't supposed to include fog. She kept it up until the whole village was blanketed in a thick white shroud. She kept a small thread of her power in it, just enough that she could see through it and keep it contained to the village, otherwise she would have been as blind as anyone else and it would have kept moving and thinning out.

She went to their horses first, swiftly killing the humans who stood guard, any sounds they made muffled by the fog when she slit their throats, trying not to think about how she was killing the beings she was supposed to be protecting. Quickly checking that everything was in their packs, she released the horses and led them to the edge of the village, tying them to a post just beyond the fog. Then she went back and freed the horses the riders had been using, leading them out of the village before making them flee, the fog muffling the sound of their hooves. Most would probably become food for Fiends, but she couldn't afford to be followed when they escaped, no matter how much she regretted having to do this. She went back to the building that held the captives and killed the guards outside before they realised she was there, and made short work of the third guard inside since the fog filled any space it could get at.

"Warren, Schuyler," she whispered just loudly enough that they'd be able to hear. "It's Rain." Both humans had bruises, and Warren's nose was bleeding, but otherwise they appeared fine.

"Rain, they did something to your uncle, he's not doing so well," Warren said, trying to find her in the fog. She cleared the room with a hard gesture and went to her uncle. He was pale and gasping for breath, she could see the veins in his neck, his pulse rapid and shallow. When she gently shook him, he moaned and shifted away from her touch. Rain cut the ropes binding him and sat back on her heels.

"Whatever they used to drug him is laced with Fiend venom, it's the only way to make the effects last longer than a few minutes on our kind," she said quietly, trying to stay cool and clinical. "If he's not dead by now then he'll be fine, he'll just be in one hell of a mood when he wakes up." She moved over to the humans and freed them as well. All Academy students were poisoned with

Fiend venom in their third year so they could recognise the symptoms and treat it effectively, when they could, anyway. Often there wasn't enough time.

"Do you need help with Damien?" Warren asked. "He's solid muscle, he'll be heavy." Rain managed to get him over her shoulders while he was still talking.

"Not human," she reminded him. Her uncle was more awkward to carry than heavy, because he was almost a foot taller than she was. "Schuyler, grab my belt, Warren, hold his hand." The prince was a liability in a fight, so it was more important that Warren be able to use a weapon. Rain would use her magic to fight if it came down to it while still carrying her uncle.

"What about the rest of these bastards? Are we just going to let them go?" Warren asked.

"How many are there?"

He thought for a moment. "There were about twenty five when they came at us, this village was empty when we got here. Damien killed seven, I got three others in the initial fight, then he got two more on the way here, so that's almost half."

"I killed five, so there's eight or so left," she figured. "Were any of them wounded but not killed in the fight?"

"Four or five, including one that your uncle knocked out when we got here," Schuyler added. "At least one of them might have died since, her wounds looked really bad." He was pale and shaking with fear, but still clearly determined to help. Warren was better off, but then he was also trained to respond in this kind of situation as Schuyler's bodyguard. Humans what he'd been trained to face, and they were far easier to kill than Fiends. Almost too easy.

"That's half down again. Would they leave their wounded to follow us?"

Schuyler shook his head. "Not all of them, anyway, one or two at most. There did seem to be some kind of bond there more than just being paid to work together. They didn't really tell us all that much, though they did know a lot about us."

"Then they won't dare come after us with only one or two people. Not two humans against a pissed off Hunter, and if they've truly done their work then they ought to know that when Uncle Damien wakes up there'll be hell to pay if he sees them again."

"You don't look pissed off," Warren remarked as they started to leave. He'd found his weapons in the corner of the room. Rain turned at looked at him. Her words may have been calm because they needed to be, but she knew her rage showed in her eyes. "Lead on, I'll be shutting up."

She led them out of the fog to where she'd left the horses. "Hang on; I need to deal with the poison they gave him first." It might not be enough to kill her uncle, but the sooner she acted the less damage he would have to recover from. The humans waited while she quickly found her vial of antivenin and a syringe, injecting the dark green liquid into Damien's arm as soon as she had it prepared. He jerked once and was still again. Most Hunters carried a dose of antivenin with them. It was difficult to make and expensive as all hell, but worth the money considering that time was of the essence. Warren helped her tie Damien to his horse. She wanted them to be gone before anyone could think of checking on the guards, so she just slung him facedown over the saddle with a silent apology as they secured him and mounted their own horses, securing Damien's mount to her own by a lead line. She cut her power from the fog and set the group galloping down the road as it started to spread past the edges of the village like it naturally would, driven by the wild winds. "We're not stopping until we get to Gyroi," she told them. It was the nearest village, a day's journey away.

"What about Fiends?" Warren asked.

"Hunter," she reminded him shortly as lightning flashed through the sky. She focused her powers, drawing the moisture out of the ground so the horses wouldn't slip, allowing them to go faster as se shielded them from the rain. She relied on the storm's energy to fuel her magic, even though she knew she would face consequences later, but that didn't matter. Just because she could draw power from around her didn't mean she was without limits. Still, all that mattered was making it to Gyroi and getting to a safe place, from both the people who wanted to capture them and from the Fiends. She was sure that Damien wasn't going to die, but there was still that little bit of fear that lurked in the back of her mind. A Fiend came charging down the road towards them and she pulled up the water she'd collected from the earth, forming it into a spear and throwing it, forcing it to explode when it was lodged in the Fiend's throat. She ignored the splatters of blood and flesh that mixed with the rain water soaking into her skin and didn't slow down. She was ruthless, relying more heavily on her magic then she ever had, fighting Fiends and keeping the elements from slowing them down. Thunder roared, scaring the horses, but she spurred her mount ahead as lightning flashed above. If she had to, she could use it and direct it since water was a conduit, but it would hurt her badly and likely kill her without the right protective spells, which she didn't have time to cast and couldn't be put into a piece of jewelry.

Another Fiend, the largest she'd ever faced came upon them, its eyes glowing. Rain leaped into the air, forming ice beneath her feet to push off of until she could get to its head. It struck, but she grabbed its arm, digging in with her claws as she turned the raindrops into darts of ice that became imbedded in its skull as she pushed off, propelling herself past its neck and slicing through it as she went. She hit the ground rolling and got back on her horse as it ran by. She twisted and threw fire the moment her seat was sure, burning the body.

Warren drew up beside her. "How long can you keep this up?" He looked amazed, and she was fairly certain that Schuyler was also slack-jawed again. But this was what she'd trained for, the kind of excitement she'd wanted when she was in the Academy. Granted, not quite under these circumstances.

"Until the storm stops or we get to town. Watch our backs." He fell back without a word. She couldn't think right now, she just had to act and make sure they all made it to safety.

She had no idea what time of day it was when they reached the gates of Gyroi, the storm still turning the sky a murky black. There were no Guardians at the gate, but the soldiers there let them in without protest and even escorted them to the inn, disconcerted as they were by the fact that no rain fell on them.

"How many?" The innkeeper asked, brows raised as he took in the state of Rain and Schuyler.

"Do you have a room with four beds?" She asked. She had no idea what the kidnappers had planned, so she wasn't letting Warren or Schuyler out of her sight until her uncle was well and they could leave this town.

"No, two is the most I've got, sorry."

"I'll get two bedrolls," Schuyler said before she could say anything. Warren had stayed outside with her uncle, who was still unconscious. Rain nodded and took the key the innkeeper handed her.

"If anyone is looking for us, we aren't here," she said with a smile that showed her fangs. He nodded, a little afraid of her. Smart human.

She hurried back outside and got Damien while Warren and the soldier who'd escorted them dealt with their horses and Schuyler took the bags inside. She got him on one of the beds and realised that there was blood on her clothes that hadn't been there before. She cut his shirt off, and saw more bruises and cuts from where the bastards had beaten the crap out of him. She hadn't noticed before because the rain had washed the blood away. She forced herself to take a deep breath and do an examination like she'd been taught. Hunters weren't healers, weren't doctors, but they were often the first to find the wounded, so they were taught something akin to the skills a field medic would have. Luckily she found no signs of internal bleeding. If there were no Guardians then sure as hell there were no healers either.

"What do you need?" Warren asked.

"The medical supplies in my bag, and I need you to get a vial of dark green liquid and a needle out of Damien's pack," she said, though she didn't think she'd need it. She quickly treated his wounds with bandages or salves and laid a cold cloth on his burning forehead, then pulled the chair in the corner next to his bed. The fever was caused by both the venom and the antivenin she'd given him.

"You two get some sleep," she ordered. Both young men were swaying and pale with exhaustion.

"And you plan on staying up all night?" Schuyler asked. "After everything you did today? Don't give me that scary look, it won't work." Rain hadn't realised she was doing it.

"Do either of you know how to treat Fiend venom?" They paused too long. "Look, go to sleep, I can hold out a while longer yet." Then she would crash and crash hard, but by then things would be okay. They must have seen her resolve in her expression, because there were no further arguments. "You'll be okay," she whispered to her uncle when the other two had all but passed out. He'd been wounded before, worse than this. Hell, the day her mother had died he'd been in far worse shape. In a few hours his body would burn through the drugs, the antivenin would deal with the poison, and he'd wake up with a hangover from hell. She kept glancing toward the door, waiting for some disturbance or sign of trouble. The other reason she'd insisted she was the one to stay up was in case they were attacked. She was getting close to her limit, but she could still draw power from the storm. She heard a moan and her head whipped around as Damien moved slightly, shaking. She covered him with a blanket and cooled the cloth on his forehead with a touch. She supposed she should have thought of this before, that there might come a time when she would have to be the one in charge, the apprentice taking care of an injured mentor. All her life he'd always taken care of her, keeping the monsters away when she was a child, teaching her to fight, staying with her and her sister during the times her father went hunting. She'd known he was only mortal, had seen evidence of that, but still, he'd always been a giant, infallible figure in her mind who couldn't be brought down by anything. She looked out the window, watching as the storm transitioned back into heavy rainfall.

Damien moaned and shifted, his eyes opening an hour later. He tried to sit up, only to fall back down. "I'm going to be sick," he said, turning on his side and Rain got him a bucket just in time, but he just dry heaved for a while. "Fucking hell."

"Welcome back," she said, handing him a glass of water.

"How long was I out?" He asked, drinking it in one gulp.

"All night... I think it's close to sunrise?" She hadn't yet managed to figure out what time it was.

"Have you slept?" He asked, sitting up slowly and examining his wounds. She shook her head. "Worried about them coming back?"

"A little. There's not many left, so I didn't think they'd consider it worth the risk. Besides, they'd have to find their horses first and who knows where they wound up?"

"Good one," he said with a slight grin, shifting so he could lean against the wall and remain sitting upright. He looked exhausted, dark circles standing out against his still-pale skin.

"How do you feel?"

"Like I got trampled," he replied with a huff of laughter followed by a grimace. "Don't tell me you were worried about me?" She couldn't meet his gaze and shrugged, unsure why tears suddenly threatened to fall. "Aw, kiddo, it's okay," he reached out and tugged her hand until she sat beside him. "You ought to know it would take more than that to kill a mean old bastard like your uncle," he said, wrapping an arm around her shoulders and pulling her close. Rain choked back her tears. He was okay, they were all okay, there was nothing to worry about. "You've never had to deal with anything like this before," he reminded her. "It's okay to react like this."

Damien felt like shit. His stomach was doing gymnastics and he was certain that someone was trying to hammer a large spike through his brain, not to mention the pain from his wounds. It was like every hangover he'd ever had or avoided was coming back to haunt him. He really wanted to find the genius who figured out diluted Fiend venom would make drugs effective on their kind and eviscerate them slowly with a very dull and rusty blade. As for the bastards who'd given him the drugs... they would die slowly. Rain was shaking slightly beside him and he gently squeezed her shoulder. She looked exhausted, physically and emotionally. She just huddled against him like she used to when she was younger and he would read stories to her and her sister. It seemed like ages ago at that moment, though it had only been a few years, five or six at most. He kissed the top of her head. "It's going to be okay. You're going to experience far worse things in life. Soon this will look like nothing."

She frowned. "Is it weird that that's actually reassuring?"

"Welcome to life as a Hunter," he replied as the humans stirred and woke up.

Warren's eyebrows went up when he saw the Hunter. "You were almost dead a few hours ago."

"What do you think I am? Human?" He growled as he moved to stand and regretted it. Rain helped him find his balance, and he was forced to lean heavily on her.

"I see what you meant," the human said to Rain in a dry tone. Damien glanced at her but she just shrugged, looking far too innocent.

"Is it really a good idea to go downstairs?" The prince asked as he changed behind the privacy screen in the corner. "What if the group that targeted us are there? I mean, I know they shouldn't be, but still..."

"That would actually make my fucking day," Damien replied grimly, sliding a pair of knives into his boots with Rain's help. He could still use enough magic to kill someone. They made it down to the tavern as the last drunken patron was stumbling out. So it was a little before dawn then.

"Feeling better?" The innkeeper asked cautiously, looking them over. He seemed like he couldn't decide whether to be more afraid of Damien or Rain. Damien decided that he'd have to ask what she'd done later since most humans wrote her off as a threat because of her age.

"Ask me later," Damien replied. There wasn't much left since the cook had gone home, but between the innkeeper and his wife they managed to procure a respectable meal for the group.

"How long do you want to stay here?" Rain wanted to know, clearly fading fast. He'd managed to get the story of what had happened out of the three young adults, so he knew that Rain had used a fairly substantial amount of magic on top of being awake for over twenty-four hours. She probably had an hour or two before she crashed hard.

"We'll leave tomorrow morning," he decided, shoving his hair back. "I need to rest and recover, and you need to sleep," he looked at Rain.

"Are you sure? You could barely make it down here," Warren asked. Actually he could barely sit upright on his own yet, but the humans didn't need to know that.

"Yes." He said it in a tone that brokered no argument. It wasn't necessary to mention that he would be stiff and sore until probably the morning after they reached Landaia and his broken ribs would take longer to heal, he'd still be able to fight before then. He glanced at Rain, who nodded silently, accepting that she would be doing most of the fighting. It would be good practice for her. He took a drink from his flask, the one with the strong stuff, not his normal flask. He coughed as it went down, but it would help set him to rights. "So, Schuyler is going to stay here with us, and Warren will go get supplies from town," he decided, looking between the two humans. There was a slim chance that some of the bastards would have the courage and stupidity to make it into town and he wasn't going to risk the prince in the open. Besides, Warren was a warrior of some talent, as he'd seen when the young man had jumped into the fight. The prince had been useless at that point, though he had managed to distract them enough that the drugs had worn off three times before they got to the ruins and someone had gotten hold of that fucking syringe. Besides, at the end of the day Warren was expendable to the humans. Their job was to get the prince safely to the capital of Landaia, and that's what they would get paid for. Warren nodded in agreement, and the prince merely looked resigned, both deeply aware of that fact.

$$7$$

Landai

Rain woke sometime after noon, stiff and aching all over. Schuyler and Warren were playing a card game in the corner of the room and her uncle was asleep in the other bed.

"How do you feel, great Water Witch of the East?" Schuyler asked, looking over when she sat up with a groan.

"Like someone dropped a castle on me," she replied, pushing back the tangled mess of midnight blue hair. That was going to be hell to set right again. She combed through it with her fingers as best she could and tied it back before forcing herself to rise and move to the middle of the room so she could do a stretching routine she'd learned at the Academy to help with stiff muscles. "What did I miss?" She asked when she was done, all but collapsing back onto the bed.

"Not much," the prince said quietly. "Damien woke up for about an hour this morning and was rather..."

"Ornery as hell?" Warren suggested. "I got everything we needed, and there was no sign of the group that took us," he added, putting down a card that made Schuyler scowl. "It's been quiet."

"I think your issue of controlling what comes out of your mouth might have contributed to that," Schuyler remarked, drawing a card and slapping it down with a satisfied smile as Warren scowled.

She rose again and changed behind the screen, thinking that later she ought to get a bath. That would definitely help with the soreness and remaining fatigue. "I don't know about you guys, but I'm starving," she said when she stepped back out. Her clothing had at least been cleaned, which was a welcome surprise. She didn't bother with her armour yet. "Want to join me?" She looked over at her uncle. His colour was a lot better than it had been before, as was his breathing. He looked like he was sleeping soundly, so she left him as he was and the humans followed her downstairs.

While the weather had improved, the tavern downstairs wasn't busy. A few patrons sat around the heavy wooden tables, most of them soldiers and guards who'd apparently come off duty. She now remembered Uncle Damien mentioning the day before that there were no Guardians in this town, not since the Landaian military had established a base nearby a few years before. Still, the soldiers didn't seemed perturbed by the sight of a Hunter in their midst. At least, she was pretty sure that being a Hunter wasn't why they kept glancing at her, since they didn't seem threatened by her. Her blue hair seemed to be the thing most humans couldn't get over. Still, at least it wasn't as light as Storm's hair.

The soldier who'd been their guide to the inn walked over to the table they'd chosen, which was as far away from the other patrons as they could get. "Everything turn out okay?" He asked, his concern sincere.

Rain nodded. "All good."

"It's strange; we don't normally get too many kidnappings around here, especially not in the last seven years since the base was finished."

She shrugged, keeping her expression pleasant and hoped that the humans at the table would keep their mouths shut. "I dunno, most people aren't stupid enough to target Hunters, though I have heard that bandits have been a problem lately around the border."

"That's farther south," the soldier said. "They wouldn't come this close to an army base."

She shrugged again and they chatted for a few moments before he walked away. "Shouldn't we tell him the truth?" Schuyler whispered, watching the soldier sit down with his comrades.

Rain looked at him, raising a brow. "How would that help us? What would the military do if they knew a prince was in town? You would be at the centre of attention and if any of them are against a deal with Glask it would be the perfect opportunity for an 'accident' to occur."

"She has a point," Warren admitted, backing her as a maid came over to their table. They ordered food and drink. "So, spend the rest of the day relaxing here then?"

"When my uncle wakes up I'm kicking all of you out of the room so I can have a bath," she said. Normally she would just create a concentrated shower of hot water, but a bath sounded more and more like heaven. They looked at her for a moment.

"Is it a water magic thing?"

"Yup." Mostly, anyway. Enough that she wasn't lying.

"Fair enough," the prince surrendered without argument. They chatted until the food arrived, then an argument broke out over the best plants to use in healing balms, something that Schuyler actually knew a fair bit about. "If I'm terrible at fighting people I might as well be good at saving them," he said when she mentioned it.

There was a crash and a scream from upstairs. Rain and Warren had their blades drawn before the soldiers had gotten over their surprise. Warren moved by the prince and she bolted up the stairs to find the door to their room open. She skidded to a stop in the doorway and dropped the point of her blade with a quiet sigh. A maid had gone in, and Uncle Damien now had her pushed against the wall, a blade to her throat.

"Uncle Damien," she called out gently, stepping into the room and sheathing her sword. His head snapped towards her, mercury eyes wild. "Uncle Damien, that's just the maid," she said, taking a slow step forward. He was shaking.

"I just came in t' change the sheets! I thought you were all out!" Fear had the maid babbling.

"Quiet," Rain cautioned when she saw her uncle tense up. The maid fell silent. She walked over with slow and deliberate steps. "Let her go," she said. "She's no danger to us." He stepped back abruptly, covering his face with his hand, and Rain had to grab the maid to keep her from falling over as she scrambled away, letting go once the poor woman had her feet under her. "I'm sorry, I thought you'd be asleep until we came back up," she said, feeling guilty. He shook his head as he picked up his flask and Rain was certain he drained half of it. This happened to a lot of Hunters and Guardians; they had problems being startled or waking up from nightmares, past traumas coming back to haunt them. Her uncle wasn't as bad as some, but he'd had episodes like this before. Most of their kind who grew up around any Hunter or Guardian learned what to do at a young age, even if they didn't understand what was happening until they were much older. Her uncle didn't say anything, just looked anywhere but at her. "Do you want something to eat?" She asked. "I can have something sent up or you can come down with the rest of us."

He finally looked at her. "Sorry," he sorry, taking another drink. "I'll be down in a few minutes." She nodded and took the hint, leaving him alone and pretending she didn't hear a blade being lodged into a wooden plank at a high velocity. The soldiers were a few meters away in the hall, weapons drawn.

"Nothing to worry about," she said cheerfully.

"Maybe we should check in… will this kind of thing happen again?" One of them asked, a general she thought by the stripes on his uniform, but she wasn't entirely certain. She'd never paid much attention to hierarchies.

"Nope. Now, I'm sure you'd rather get to your meals before they cool." She stood casually in the middle of the hallway, a 'don't fuck with me' smile firmly in place and her hand resting very casually on her sword hilt.

"Rain, its fine," Damien came to stand beside her, wrapping an arm around her shoulders and pushing his hair back off his forehead with a clumsy motion. He still wasn't wearing a shirt, and dark bruises bloomed under his scars. He was slurring his words, but she could tell it was deliberate, just like how much he leaned on her. "They're just doin' their job, kiddo. Don' worry 'bout me though, I'm jus' an old Hunter." He said the latter part to the soldiers, giving them a drunken wave.

The general sighed and signaled for his men to go back downstairs. "Keep an eye on him," he ordered Rain, who nodded and gave him a saccharine smile as he left.

"How often have you pulled that one?" She asked quietly as he straightened with a wince.

"As many times as I've had to," he answered. "Having a reputation as a drunk helps." They listened as the soldiers left the tavern. "Let's go, I'm starving."

"Do you want a shirt?" She asked.

He glanced down at his torso. "Probably a good idea," he agreed, "though I know plenty of ladies love the wounded warrior look." Rain just rolled her eyes as he went back into the room.

She got the bath she wanted after lunch. Damien had decided that he needed to exercise, and the best way to do that was sparring with Warren, which really meant beating poor bastard into the ground ten or fifteen times despite his injuries. Schuyler had decided to accompany them to make sure that her uncle didn't break his bodyguard too badly. She sighed and leaned back in the tub, impressed with how large it was. A small touch of magic kept the water steaming hot, heavenly for her muscles. She rinsed her hair and let the midnight blue locks float around her. She wondered if that would be her someday, so used to being on guard that she could never relax, that she could never really leave the fight behind her when she was in a safe place while the ghosts of her past haunted her, making her panic over something as simple as the sound of a door closing.

But maybe that was the problem: by that point Hunters learned that there were no truly safe places on this planet from the Fiends. Hadn't she learned that already, when two had broken into her home that day? She ducked under the water, letting it envelope her as she slowly breathed out. Some Hunters dealt with it better than others. Her father was one of them, Amber was another, they managed to do their job, deal with the consequences, and found a way to stay above the darkness that threatened to swallow all Hunters. Others, like her uncle, skated by on the edge of a knife, struggling to stay afloat. Some fell into it and became almost mindless killing machines, utterly ruthless, efficient, and grim warriors incapable of real emotion. Those empty-eyed men and women had always scared her a little, living only for the hunt, for the next kill until the day something killed them. She didn't want to be like that. She knew she wasn't going to get a happy story-book ending, but she didn't want to fall into the darkness or spend every day on the edge fighting for her sanity either. She resurfaced and lingered for a few more minutes before getting out and dressing, feeling not only clean but a hell of a lot better than she had that morning.

After she braided her wet hair she headed downstairs to find that Uncle Damien was now playing poker with a group of soldiers and taking them for all they had. She sighed and went to join them. After all, who knew what they were going to do after they got to Landai? They needed all the money they could get, and she doubted the soldiers would stop and think that just maybe her uncle had taught her to play cards.

At dawn they set out again. After the night before Rain was surprised the soldiers let them through without issue and only a few glares, considering how much money she and Damien had won off them. Her uncle was a lot better, though they did have to stop more often than before. Luckily they only faced two Fiends by the time they made it to their final stop before Landai. She was almost sad it was coming to an end.

"Today was shockingly easy," Warren said when they were sat down at the inn, eating. "In comparison to the last few days that was a fucking cakewalk."

"Sometimes you do get that lucky," Damien replied. "I've even had days where I didn't see a single Fiend on the road, and I wasn't even in the territories." He grinned. "Of course, when you're on the fourth day with nothing happening and you're staring at trees or hills you almost wish something would attack you to end your boredom."

"What will you do after we get to Landai?" The prince asked, sipping his tea.

He shrugged. "We'll figure it out tomorrow, when nothing else can go wrong with this adventure."

"It seems like a rather abrupt end to our journey," Schuyler said with a sigh.

"Of course, not all journeys involve being kidnapped, drugged, and beaten," Damien added.

"Not all of them? You mean this has happened to you before?" The prince demanded, wide-eyed. Rain wondered if her uncle was thinking about the time he'd been sold to a Thief King, but she also knew that her uncle and her parents had kept a lot of their darker adventures from her and Storm.

He shrugged again. "What can I say? Hunters live exciting lives."

They were early to bed again that night, rising at dawn to finish the trip. Landai was a little smaller than Ankira, limited both by the ancient wall built around the city to keep Fiends and invading armies out as well as the mountains that flanked it on three sides. No one was willing to build outside of those natural barriers, so the buildings tended to be taller and set closer together, especially in the poorer parts of the city. The palace was a sight, with its towers and windows of stained glass.

"It's pretty impressive, though the government building in the capital of the Republic of Takalam is even more amazing," Uncle Damien said when she mentioned it. They brought Warren and Schuyler into the palace, with the requisite stares from nobles, servants, and guards who apparently hadn't spent much time around Hunters. Landai wasn't the most welcoming place to her kind, but it also wasn't the worst.

"So, looks like this is it," Schuyler said, rubbing the back of his neck as they stood in the hallway outside of the throne room.

"Yeah," Rain said. "I would say it's been fun and we should do it again soon, but I don't want to have to rescue you again."

He chuckled. "That's fair. Are you going to be sticking around the city for a while?"

She and Damien had discussed it while the humans had been racing across an open field a few hours earlier. The land around Landai was an abrupt shift to rolling grassy hills from dense forest. "We're going to stay here for a day or two and then decide," she said. "So far the choice is between going back home for a while or just roam in a general westward direction for a month or two before making our way back home." She would have to remember to write home about their decision while they were somewhere that kept messenger falcons, along with her letters to her friends. She hadn't received any so far, but they weren't even a month in so it was hardly a surprise. Besides, sometimes no news was good news.

"You'll still keep in touch though?"

"I'll try," she told him. She hugged him and Warren before the four of them were presented before the King and Queen of Landaia. To her relief Damien even managed to get out of having to attend another court function. Once that was dealt with they left the humans and headed back into the city.

"Let's go exploring then, shall we? I haven't been here in about ten years." She nodded and followed her uncle through the streets. They got rooms at an inn off the main thoroughfare where the innkeeper didn't think twice about the fact that they weren't human and left their horses in the stables before they went exploring. It was just as loud and chaotic as Ankira had been, though this time Rain had been braced for it.

One thing that Landai was famous for –as demonstrated by the palace windows- was stained glass, and glassware in general, with an entire street dedicated to workshops where people could go in and watch wares being made. Rain had seen a glassblower once in a workshop in Lysee, but this was different, because very little magic was used by the human craftspeople and everything had to be done by hand, making the skills of the masters all the more impressive. Some craftsmen and women even made a show out of it, trying to attract more customers. She could have stayed there for hours, watching them work. Her uncle appeared interested as well, though she knew he would have preferred to watch metalsmiths. There was just something about the way they worked the molten glass that reminded her of moving water, and then to retain its shape afterward it had to be cooled.

But what the beauty of the crafts couldn't do was hide the tension that gripped the city. While Ankira had been relaxed, the people here were starting to worry. Rain wondered if something had happened while they were on the road.

"Don't worry about it," Damien said when she asked him about it as they bought food from a street vendor. "It has nothing to do with us."

She sighed. "I know." Human politics were of no concern to Hunters.

"Hunters have enough to worry about just dealing with Fiends and the occasional fool," he reminded her. "If we worried about the politics of countries who would never give a damn about us we would truly go insane. Humans have to figure out things for themselves, just like we did. We can't tell them how to live any more than they can tell us and if they want to go off and kill each other, well, that's not up to us to stop it."

Her instructors at the Academy had said as much. "Have you ever been near a war?" She knew better than to ask if he'd been in one, because that would never happen. Any Hunter or Guardian who wanted to get involved in human conflict had to surrender their medallions and were never allowed to take up either position again. There might be one or two every few decades who did it, but it was a lot to give up, and word tended to spread quickly, with most of their kind disapproving. Whoever took sides in a human conflict could expect to be ostracised on some level. It might not be fair, but they'd sacrificed much for their independence, for the ability to be free of senseless wars.

"Twice," he said. "Once before your parents met, so it was just your mom and me, and the second time was after, and we were all traveling together. It was... horrible. There were bodies just lying everywhere being picked apart by animals. Some of them weren't even fully dead yet." He took a drink from his flask. "We could hear fighting going on just over the top of the hill and turned around. That's when it was just me and your mother. The other time your parents and I wound up in the middle of a civil war in Yakan," he glanced at her.

"That's to the southwest, isn't it?" Rain asked, trying to picture maps she'd seen.

He nodded. "It is. We were there just before everything started and it was hell trying to get out, because suddenly all these other armies were coming to support one side or the other and it was just a mess. Sometimes we ended up having to fight our way out of a town, so we actually took the risk and camped whenever we could."

"Didn't that happen just before Mom and Dad got married?" She'd heard it mentioned before.

"It was just before they were engaged... maybe a year before?" He pushed his hair back. "Just... it's not worth it. I don't care what anyone says, I don't see how that many bodies and destroyed cities can mean a victory for anyone." They walked in silence for a while as she thought over what he'd said.

She stopped when Damien did, her uncle starring at a man writing something across the street for a moment before dragging her over to him. "Forger, you old bastard! Where've you been?" He asked when the other man looked up. He was one of them, his ears pointed, eyes the same odd silver as a mirror, and looked to be about Damien's age.

"What the hell are you doing here?" Forger asked, grinning as the two men embraced.

"Just finished a job," Damien replied. "We were actually in Ankira a week ago and I was wondering why I didn't see you in Dagger's court."

The other man grinned, showing his fangs. "Got meself into a bit of trouble two months ago, so Dagger sent me here until things cool down some."

He turned his gaze to Rain. "Who's this young thing that looks so much like Tempest? It can't be Rain, because that would make me old."

"This is my niece and apprentice, Rain Undine," Damien introduced her. "Rain, this is Forger. If you ever need any kind of paperwork made up he's the guy to go to." She shook the other man's hand. He was only a little taller than she was and rail thin, but strong.

"Ah," he said. "I hope you're giving this old bastard hell."

"I'm going to sell her to pirates," Damien remarked when she grinned.

Rain gave him a look. "After I saved your life?"

"I'll let you pick the ship," he offered generously.

"You are the worst."

"I do my best," he said before turning back to his laughing friend. "And of course, her older sister is just as bad. I'm surprised I've stayed sane after all these years."

"I hate to tell you this old friend, but you lost your mind when you decided to become a Hunter," Forger said, laughing again.

"You might not be wrong," Damien allowed. It wasn't the first time she'd heard that opinion and likely wouldn't be the last. Even Guardians thought Hunters were a little crazy, and to be fair most of them were.

"Are you from Ankira as well?" She asked Forger.

"Born and bred," he replied. "Never felt the need to go to the territories though, I like a life of crime just fine." He winked while her uncle just shook his head. "How long will you two be in town?"

"Two days at most," Damien replied. "So, what's there to do in this city nowadays?"

It turned out that in the two months he'd been in Landai, Forger had actually found quite a bit to see and showed Rain and her uncle around, taking them to some neat shops, including a mage who made charms for the city Guardians, though Rain couldn't understand how the other woman stood being among the humans. The more she learned and experienced the less she wanted to be around most of them. Both Rain and Damien bought warming charms as winter would soon be upon them and Hunters couldn't wear heavy clothing without sacrificing speed and mobility and there wasn't a decent tattoo that worked with the spell. Then they went to see the metalsmiths at work. That's where her uncle was in his element, literally.

"You do realise we'll be here until dark now," she said to Forger. The other man grinned.

"Why do you think I left this street for last? It hasn't been *that* long since I last saw your uncle. How's your Da, by the way?"

"Good," she replied. "He was just finishing a rotation as an Academy Guardian when we left, so he'll probably be out hunting soon, though he won't go far during the winter." Most Hunters stayed closer to civilisation if not home during winter, venturing out for most of spring, summer, and fall. Winters in the territories weren't as bad as those in Phasoia, being on the coast helped a little except when it came to ice and somehow they were colder than either Glask or Landaia during the rest of the year.

"I dare say not," he said. They made small talk for a while as Damien watched the smiths work and talked with them, or in some cases argued.

"I'm going back to watch the glassblowers," she decided eventually. "I'll meet you at the inn." She loved weaponry, but she had her limits. Damien nodded and she left, picking her way through the streets. Luckily she had a good sense of direction. Kestrel and Nathan even better, and they made sure that Adrian always had a map with their route very clearly marked along with sketches of landmarks and a compass. When they became full Hunters she'd make sure to take them here. It was one upside of spending a year apart, they all got to find places to show one another later. She and Kestrel were going to be hunting partners, and Aiden was one of those people who could get along with anyone and had made himself a part of her group of friends as well. Nathan was another she would enjoy having on a team, though he lived in a different town and had always planned on returning to the far north. Still, if the chance ever came up to hunt with him she wouldn't turn it down, though his rivalry with Kestrel for being the top archer was the stuff of legend at the Academy and comedic fodder for their friends, especially since the pair got along well as long as there were no bows or targets involved.

She was halfway there when she realised she was being followed. She'd taken the shortcut they'd used earlier, so there was no one on the street that she could see. She paused as if to look in a baker's window, actually looking at the reflection in the glass. There. She could see two people in an alley, watching her. She turned to see them scurry deeper between buildings and decided to ignore them and just head to a busier street.

"Hey pretty girl," someone behind her called. She ignored it and turned down an alley that would lead onto one of the main streets. "Hey, don't be like that." Two people walked towards her, humans wearing cloaks. She moved aside to pass them, but they spread apart, parting their cloaks to show mismatched armour and battered swords. Bandits. No thief would target a Hunter.

"Going somewhere?" One asked. Rain put her hand on her own sword hilt.

"Do you really want to take on a Hunter?" She asked, barring her fangs.

"Yes, but not you. You're just bait." She started to turn, cursing that she'd let one of them get behind her, but a damp cloth covered her mouth and nose before she could do anything, the fumes clouding her mind. Last thing she knew, one of them caught her as she fell.

Damien and Forger laughed as they made it back to the inn well after dark. He didn't see Rain in the dining area, which he would have expected.

"Something wrong?" The other man asked, then caught on. "The girl probably just went up to her room," he suggested, glancing around.

"Maybe," Damien allowed, but that wasn't like Rain. "I'll see if she wants to come join us. If you don't mind?" He glanced at his old friend.

"No, not at all. The kid's almost as good company as you are," he replied. "She's going to make one hell of a Hunter."

"She's not a kid," Damien said absently as he started up the stairs.

Then something happened that made him freeze, panic gripping his heart in an iron fist.

His medallion had grown hot.

It was true that they kept a lot of secrets about the medallions that bound mentor to apprentice. He hadn't even learned them until the Academy approved him to be Rain's mentor. When a student was hurt, badly hurt, the mentor's medallion would heat up. He yanked it out from under his shirt, looking at the blue dot. Rain was nowhere near where she should have been, not even within the city.

"Damien?" Forger asked, slowly walking up towards him.

"Someone's taken Rain," he snarled.

"Get your weapons, I'll get information," the man hissed, running back down. Damien rushed to the room and readied in seconds, and luckily Forger was already there.

"Bandits," he said quickly. "They took her and snuck out of the city. What do you need?"

"Get a healer, I'll bring her back here," the Hunter said quickly. Ash had been right: letting those fuckers live had come back to bite him.

He wouldn't make that mistake again.

8

Taken

At least her blood was warm as it slid over her skin. For a few moments, anyway. She shivered and tried not to cry out in pain as the small movements caused the knife in her side to shift, cutting deeper, its magic burning like a brand. Rain was curled up against a tree, watching the bandits laugh around their campfire as they discussed all the things they were going to do to the 'metal bastard' when he showed up, and all the things they were going to do to *her* while they made him watch.

She was terrified. They'd taken her weapons and her armour before the drugs wore off, binding her wrists and ankles with a heavy rope before stabbing her with a blade made to destroy spells and bind magic, even the magics of her kind. She would never forget the pain, like a thousand jagged shards of glass being shoved into her body at once. She'd never been so helpless, not even when she was five years old, hidden in the weapons cupboard, waiting for someone to come back and get her. At least then she'd known the monsters couldn't get her and she'd been able to use her magic. She'd tried to escape, she really had, but they caught her again, and that was when they'd stabbed her instead of using more drugs. She shivered again, tears running down her cold face.

"Go check on the soulless demon bitch," she heard one of the bandits say, laughing. "We don't want her to die too soon." Raucous laughter. One of them came lumbering over.

"So," he said, kneeling in front of her. "You're still alive." Rain lifted her head and spat in his face. He gripped the hilt of the knife and twisted, making her scream. She felt a sudden, sharp stab and it became hard to breath. "Oops," he drawled, running his hand down her body as she coughed, tasting blood. "Hope your mentor hurries." He rose and went back, laughing. Rain glared at his back as she gasped for breath. She had to get rid of the knife. If she got that out, she would have a chance of getting away. She twisted her head to look around, trying to ignore the dizziness that washed over her. She'd lost a lot of blood already and the drugs and other wounds weren't helping at all. She spotted a knot in the evergreen behind her, one that looked about right. Slowly and carefully shifting back and up, she moved so that the hilt of the blade rested on the wood, almost passing out from the pain. She had to do it fast, and she couldn't scream. If she screamed they would notice and it would all be for nothing, they would just stab her again, likely somewhere worse. Her body gave a particularly violent shudder and she felt the knife's edge scrape against her ribs. She gritted her teeth and dropped, twisting as she did. The knife cut through skin and muscle like paper, but she was free, the knife falling behind her and slicing a shallow cut on her arm. She lay, silently sobbing from the pain as she tried to gasp for breath, her vision blurring and her head spinning. Trying to focus, she used her own blood to make a blade that cut the ropes binding her wrists and feet and struggled to stand, leaning heavily on the tree. The bandits hadn't noticed anything; they were more focused on sick fantasies of rape and torture while watching for her uncle. She managed to get her feet underneath her and staggered away from the camp, wishing for a storm, or even rainfall. But luck wasn't with her and the night was cloudless. She pulled her medallion out from under her shirt; it had somehow escaped the bandits' attention. The silver dot was rapidly drawing closer to where she was. Rain stumbled further into the woods. She just needed to hide from the bandits until he got there.

Uncle Damien would find her after the monsters were dead, just like last time.

Damien could see the flickering light of a fire through the trees. He jumped, pulling himself onto the branches of an evergreen and checked his medallion. The little blue dot was almost in reach. He was certain it had moved slightly, but that didn't matter. All that mattered now was that he destroyed the threat to his family and his kind. His initial panic had subsided into a rage that burned with cold malice. He went through the trees until he was right above the bandits.

Then he dropped, drawing his sword as his feet hit the ground, daggers attached to wires shooting out in all directions like vicious silver birds.

It was chaos. Bloody, bloody chaos. He cut two down quickly, their blood a warm arc in the cool night air as he relieved their heads from their shoulders, others impaling themselves on his daggers as they tried to get to him. He turned and directed the blades to spread apart, shredding the fuckers before they realised what was going to happen to them. Blood sizzled as it landed in the fire and he jumped over the flames, landing on another man, bones cracking under his boots as he cut off the hands of a swordswoman before slitting her throat. He punched down at the man beneath his feet, the iron in his vambraces slicing out to form a blade that went through his skull. Damien turned, slashing through someone's chest before stabbing another through the heart. The bandits cursed and shouted as they scrambled, unprepared for a massacre. He wondered what they'd expected as he directed two daggers through a pair of eyes before recalling them and pinning another bandit to a tree. That he would come before them begging for them to return his niece? That he would surrender? He almost smiled at the thought as he brought his hilt down on a bandit's temple before ramming the point through the neck of another. An arrow came at him from beyond the treeline, but the fools used steel for their arrowheads. Then again, they were probably stolen. He directed it around himself and back into the trees. The archer dropped fast to avoid it and received one of Damien's daggers through his eye as a prize. At last there was only one left, desperately trying to pull out the blades that pinned his shoulders to a tree, but he wasn't strong enough.

"Please-" he started, but Damien took his head off in a clean slash. He spotted Rain's armour and weapons and took one of the bandit's bags to store it in, then pulled out his medallion once more so he could follow that little blue dot. He stopped when he came to a tree that had a long silver dagger at the base. He knelt, wiping the blood off the runes etched into it, and felt his fury redouble as he recognised them. He had to find his niece, fast, especially if all the blood at the base of the tree was hers.

"Rain!" He called, walking towards the blue dot. He was within a few meters of her. "Rain!" He searched the shadows. As long as the medallion didn't become cold he had time. "Fucking hell, *Rain!*" Was she conscious? He looked back at the stone, then remembered who he was dealing with. He reached up and tapped the charm that would make magic visible. His heart almost stopped.

Rain lay on the ground, a mirage around her bound to the rune she'd drawn on her hand in her own blood. He staggered over and gently wiped it away, ending the spell. He turned off his charm so he could see clearly again and swore. She was barely breathing, her heartbeat fast and erratic, her skin like ice and deathly pale. He pulled aside the torn part of her shirt and saw the huge, deep cut that still oozed blood. He had to act fast or the blood loss would kill her before he could get her to help. His kind could survive a lot but they were still only mortal in the end. Very carefully he lifted her into his arms, trying not to let her moan break him. He'd failed. He'd failed her.

"Hey kiddo," he murmured, "it's me, I've got you." She shifted, her eyes opening slightly. "That's right, I've got you." Her head fell against his shoulder after a moment and she relaxed a little. He set her down against one of the felled trees around the fire, trying to pick the least bloody spot. Then he took out a dagger and held it in the flames. His magic enabled him to handle molten metals, so a campfire was nothing. He waited until the blade was a bright red. "Rain?" He said, shaking her shoulder gently with one hand as he held blade in the fire with the other, hating himself for what he was about to do. "Rain."

"I'm here," she managed to say, eyes opening though he could tell she was barely holding on. He wished there was another choice, but...

"Rain, I have to stop the bleeding."

"What?"

He took a deep breath. "You're going to bleed out. I have to stop it." He saw her eyes follow his arm to the blade and her eyes went wide as her breathing sped up even more. "There's no other way. Do you trust me?" He asked, meeting her sapphire eyes. She nodded without hesitation. "Don't fight passing out." He pulled one of her leather vambraces out of the bag. "Bite down," he said, putting it against her mouth. She did, squeezing her eyes shut, tears falling. He took a deep breath. He didn't see any other option, since a bandage would only soak up the blood, and she'd already lost so much. "I'm sorry," he said, taking the knife out of the fire. Before he could hesitate he pressed the heated blade against the wound. Rain bit down hard on the leather, screaming for a moment before falling back, unconscious. Damien was having some trouble breathing himself as he pulled the knife away, pressing it into the ground to cool it faster. "I'm sorry," he said again, voice cracking as he pushed his hair back. He quickly scavenged medical supplies and bandaged the wound as best he could, quickly checking her for other injuries. There were bruises, small cuts, including one along the right side of her face and her lip was split, but nothing else that required immediate attention. Very carefully he lifted his niece into his arms and went to the bandits' horses. It took some effort, but he managed to get her settled securely in front of him before he spurred the horse forward, going as quickly through the forest as he dared before getting onto the main road and setting the horse into a flat-out gallop. Rain was so still in front of him, the only sign of life her ragged breathing. He was sure one of her lungs had been damaged, but the bleeding had taken priority, since it would kill her faster. He prayed to whoever was listening to save her, to keep her alive long enough to get help. Was this how Ash had felt when he'd saved Storm when the Fiends had taken her? If it hadn't been for that fucking knife he wouldn't have been worried, but it had been spelled so that the longer it was in contact with someone the longer it would take for the effects to wear off, which included impeding her natural healing ability. It had been a few hours at least, but as long as he acted fast she would live. He couldn't afford to listen to the doubts the shadows in his mind whispered to him. Not now.

It felt like an eternity before he made it before the city walls. The Guardian who'd let him through before was waiting outside. Everything was a blur after that, returning to the inn where Forger waited with a healer, sitting outside the room door while said healer went to work without the 'terrifying and surly Hunter' around. To his surprise Schuyler and Warren showed up shortly before dawn.

"We heard what happened. How is she?" The prince asked, looking from Damien to the door.

"I don't know," Damien said shortly. He supposed it shouldn't have been a surprise that word of an apprentice badly injured by bandits would travel fast. "I don't fucking know." His hands clenched into fists, claws digging into his gloves.

"If she's anything like her parents she'll be fine," Forger said from where he leaned against the wall, keeping his voice calm and light as he watched Damien.

"You didn't see how much blood there was," Damien said. "There was so much..." He covered his face with his hands. "I fucking *burned her* to make it stop." His friend decided to shut up after that, realising that nothing he said would help. Rain his apprentice, he was responsible for her, he was supposed to keep her safe. He'd failed as a mentor and as an uncle.

"Is there anything we can do?" Schuyler asked. "I mean it, anything at all."

"Actually there is," Damien said, pushing a hand through his hair as he tried to regain his composure around the humans. "I need to get a few messages out, fast."

"I can use the royal messenger falcons," he replied quickly.

Damien nodded. "Then I need three pieces of paper, a pen, and sealing wax." Whatever the healer managed to do now, he knew that they would have to go back to the territories as soon as she was stable enough to travel. He also had to let Ash know what had happened. His stomach clenched into knots at the thought. Warren left and returned with what he'd asked for. He wrote three letters, one to Ash, one to Roderick that they would need him as soon as they arrived at the hospital, preferably as soon as they arrived in Lysee, and one more.

"The Guardian Shipmasters at Port Lacoren?" Schuyler asked when Damien told him who the messages were for. "But won't that take over a week, even going with the current?"

Damien shook his head. "Two days, including the time it takes to get to Port Lacoren."

"We couldn't have taken that to get here in the first place?" Warren asked dryly. "That would have avoided a lot of trouble."

He shook his head. "Use is severely restricted. The ships are meant to get Guardians where they're needed fast in case of an emergency." While they had a better life expectancy than Hunters, Guardians still faced significant dangers. "They will also take severely wounded Guardians or Hunters back to Lysee or the Academy. Anything else and you have to go by road." The ships were powered by water and air mages, which was how they could go so fast, regardless of the current.

"Oh."

"Yeah." He finished writing the letters to the shipmasters and Roderick quickly. But the letter to Ash... how the hell did he explain this? What the fuck was he supposed to say? He settled on something fast, that Rain was hurt and they were returning, that he would explain when they got there. It was almost as bad as when he'd had to tell Ash that Tempest was dead. He pressed his Hunter medallion into the sealing wax, his insignia two daggers crossed over a sword. He handed them over to Schuyler, and the prince and his body guard hurried to send them. The falcons would be able to cover the distance in a day, the one to the port ought to return in a matter of hours. He hoped the Shipmasters would grant his request because he had no idea how he would make the journey with just the two of them, and he had no illusions that Rain would be in a shape to ride, let alone fight Fiends for some time. At least with the ships, the Guardians would obliterate any Fiends that came near.

"Want me to see how things are going?" Forger asked. The man had all but dragged him out of the room and forced him to sit in the hall once the iron candle holders started shuddering on the walls and the healer ordered him out of the room. Damien nodded tightly. It felt like he'd been sitting out there for hours. Forger reached for the door as it opened and the healer's assistant, a young woman, all but lunged out.

"We need you, now," she said. Damien was on his feet and in the room before she could move. The healer, a stern-looking older woman, was frowning as her hands hovered over the wound in Rain's side. He felt sick just looking at it, knowing that part of it was his fault.

"What's wrong?" He demanded, his voice ragged.

"She's fighting me," the healer snapped, worried rather than angry at anyone. Damien went over and knelt by Rain's side, holding her hand. It was like ice and she was barely breathing.

"Can you wake her up? She was stabbed with a blade meant to bock her magic." If she was conscious enough to know something was happening to her she likely didn't know it was a healer trying to help her.

"I need her still so she doesn't make her wounds worse," the healer warned him. "Panic also doesn't help."

"I'll keep her calm." She nodded and waved her hand over Rain's face. His niece woke wild-eyed and gasping for breath. He gently turned her face to look at him. "I'm here, kiddo," he told her. "It's okay, I'm here, and I'm not going to move." She locked her eyes on his and gripped his hand tight. "You have to stop fighting the healer, remember?" She closed her eyes for a moment and struggled to take a deep breath, relaxing slightly.

"Much better," the healer said. "I know this isn't fun." She turned to Damien. "There's not much I can do aside from sealing the wounds. Unless you get her to the hospital in the territories there will be serious and lasting damage, especially to her lung. She's not healing like she should be." She pursed her lips. "I don't know what that blade was spelled with, but it did a number on her."

He nodded grimly. Healers were a precious resource and were guarded fiercely. They weren't forced to stay in the territories, but few ventured out. Add the fact that they were unable to help humans and most couldn't take being in a place where they could do so little despite their instincts to help the wounded or sick. Those who did go out went to help Guardians and passing Hunters, either dealing with minor issues or getting them in a stable enough condition that they could return to the territories. "Guess what?" He said to Rain, who's eyes had locked onto his once more. "We're going home." A tear tracked down her cheek.

"She can't talk while I'm working," the healer remarked. "Now, this part is not going to be fun. I patched the holes, but I have to release the air trapped in her chest."

"What the hell have you been doing this whole time?" He snapped before he could stop himself, then forced himself to rein in his temper. He had to stay calm for Rain.

"There were more pressing concerns," the healer snapped. She pulled a scalpel out of her kit. "Now, I have to make a small cut, okay Rain? It'll make it a lot easier for you to breath." Rain nodded and squeezed Damien's hand like she had when Ash had to pull a giant splinter out of her foot years ago.

"We'll go back to the Academy and see Roderick," he told her quietly. "He'll set you to rights in no time, and then we can go back to hunting Fiends, and you'll have a cool scar to show off." The healer made the incision as he spoke and blood bubbled out of the cut as Rain gasped in a breath. Almost immediately her breathing was a lot better. The healer quickly bandaged the wounds.

"That's all I can do, I hope you understand," she said, putting Rain into a deep sleep once more. He nodded. There were at least fifty Guardians in the city, all under her care, and she wasn't strong as it was. "Let her rest and she'll wake up naturally later today."

"How soon can we travel?"

"As soon as you can," she said. "Be careful with her. It won't take much to reopen those wounds and I don't know how quickly the residual magic will leave her system and she'll start healing like she should."

He pushed his hair back. "I've already sent a message to the Shipmasters."

"Good, and good luck," she told him, leaving after a quick glance at Rain. Her apprentice followed close behind.

"Well?" Forger asked, sticking his head in the room.

"I need a drink," Damien said, resting his forehead on their joined hands. "Once she's okay I'm going to need a drink." A strong one.

When Rain woke up she wasn't alone. She could see her uncle out of the corner of her eye, asleep in a chair. She took a careful breath. It hurt like hell, but it was possible. She felt weak and everything still hurt, but she wasn't dead which she supposed was the important thing. She turned to look out the window and saw that the sun was setting once more. The last thing she remembered was the healer putting her into a deep sleep the second time, when her uncle had been by her side. She recalled waking up in a panic but it was blurry. Before that… She remembered the magic knife, getting it out, hiding, hearing screams and fighting, being found, fire… it was all a bit of a jumbled mess after that.

"Hey kiddo, how're you feeling?" She glanced over and saw that her uncle was awake, stretching from where he sat.

"I've been better," she said, her voice hoarse.

"I'm sorry." She could remember him saying it more than once. "That should never have happened."

"What now?" She knew he'd said they were going home the night before, but couldn't remember the specifics.

"We're going home," he said. "The healer here did what she could, but you know how it is in human cities, and you're not healing as well as you should. We do get to take a Guardian Ship, though."

"Cool." She'd seen them coming into the harbour in Lysee and had toured one with her class, but that was about it. "Did you tell Dad?"

He pushed his hair back and ran a hand over his stubble. "I told him you were hurt. Some things are better explained in person." He sighed, shoving a hand through his hair. "We'll leave in the morning, Port Lacoren is about a four hour ride from here and the ship is going to wait for us."

"What did Dad say?"

"He'll be at the harbour, waiting for us."

"What's wrong?" She asked, seeing something in his expression.

"Nothing," he said, but as fuzzy as her mind was she could tell it was a lie.

"Uncle Damien…" she started, but he held up a hand to stop her.

"Don't worry kiddo, just rest. Everything will be okay. Do you want to try eating something?" She considered it and nodded. "I'll be right back." He left her alone. She struggled to get upright, but any movement sent waves of pain stabbing through her side so she gave up. He returned a few minutes later, a tray in hand.

"Okay, now for the hard part," he said, setting it on a small table. Slowly and with her uncle's help she managed to get upright enough to eat, propped up against several pillows.

"What about my weapons and armour?" She asked, refusing to remember how they'd gone missing, "and the ring." It seemed trivial to worry about those things since she'd nearly died, but they meant something to her.

"Don't worry, I have everything," he said, setting up a small table that went over her legs and putting the tray on that. There was a bowl of some kind of broth that smelled good and a glass of water. She managed to eat some of it. Damien had also brought up food for himself.

"Are the bandits all dead?" She recalled seeing blood and a severed hand, but she'd been too focused on other things to pay much attention.

"I made certain of it."

"And the knife?" She didn't want to see it ever again, but she also didn't want it to end up in the wrong hands. Just thinking of it made her feel those jagged shards of glass ripping through her skin as her magic failed her.

"I have it. I'm going to find out who made it and bring it before the Council. They ought to know that weapons that can be used specifically against us are being manufactured." His voice held a dark threat. "The drugs are one thing, but this…" Rain had the feeling that whoever made the knife was going to very deeply regret their actions very shortly. "I'll probably destroy it after we get to the bottom of it all." They finished eating in silence and Damien helped her lie back down.

"Will you stay?" She asked as he moved to bring the tray back downstairs. "Just until I fall asleep." That chair didn't look overly comfortable. It was stupid, but she needed someone there. She couldn't remember the last time she'd been so afraid, and as long as her uncle was there, she knew that nothing else would get her, just like when she was five.

He nodded slowly. "I'll be back in a minute." When he came back, he was holding his sword. He set it carefully against the table and settled down in the chair. "Just like old times, eh?" He asked with a crooked grin, drinking from his flask, which had been on the table as well.

"Yeah," she agreed, letting herself relax a little. If the sword was there it meant he would be staying all night, a guardian at her side who could scare away the monsters, both the real ones those in her mind. "Thanks."

The grin widened. "It's part of the job description," he said, settling in. "So, do you still want to be a Hunter?"

"You're not getting rid of me that easily," she informed him.

"Good." He wasn't quite able to hide his relief. "Now, get some sleep. Traveling tomorrow is going to be a nightmare." She knew he wasn't joking either. The steady agony punctuated by sharp stabbing pains in her side told her as much. She tried to get as comfortable as possible and let her mind drift until sleep took her, thinking of home.

9

Safe

Damien was in hell. His hand shook slightly as he drained his flask and looked out the window. The sky was just beginning to lighten, the sun drawing close to the mountaintops. Rain slept on, her breathing laboured and face pained even in sleep. He had no doubt that when she woke she would feel worse than she had the night before; she might not be on the verge of death anymore, but she was still in serious condition. Forger was in the next room, having volunteered to accompany him as far as Port Lacoren. His old friend was just getting what sleep he could before their escorts arrived. Damien would sleep when they were home and Rain had been seen by the hospital's healers. He'd received replies to all of his letters. The shipwrights had readily agreed and sent two Guardians to escort them and ensure their safe arrival, while Roderick had decided to meet them at the harbour. Ash was understandably distressed over the news and would also meet them there. Warren and Schuyler had also had the foresight to locate a stretcher and a wagon to transport Rain. Damien could have carried her, but there was a risk of reopening her wounds. As it was, he'd requested a potion that would keep Rain unconscious until they made it to the port, where she would be able to draw power from the river to help her heal, keep the pain down, and get back to normal faster.

A soft knock on the door had him on his feet in an instant, and he opened it to find two Guardians with the Port Lacoren insignia on their cloaks led by the innkeeper. He nodded to the man, who turned and left. The Guardians were an interesting pair, one with the look of an experienced and hardened warrior, the other young and earnest, no more than two or three years out of the Academy. "I am Geneva Hawk," the elder of the pair introduced herself. She was around his age, maybe a few years younger. "This is Silver Tailor," she indicated her younger companion. "We're here to escort you and your apprentice to Port Lacoren. We are ready whenever you wish to depart."

He ushered them into the room and quickly pounded on the door to the room Forger was using. "Thanks for coming," he told the two Guardians sincerely when he returned. "We have a wagon to transport Rain." Forger stumbled in, pulling on a heavy leather jacket. "This is Forger, he'll be driving the wagon but will not be accompanying us to Lysee." He would be returning to

Landai on his own after they arrived and the Guardians would most likely remain in Port Lacoren. Damien would be in the wagon with Rain to monitor her, and he would also help in dealing with threats, if only because it would help him deal with his nerves.

Geneva nodded. "When do you want to leave?"

"As soon as possible."

"We're ready now."

"Then now it shall be." He looked at Forger, who nodded that he was also ready. The Guardians helped get Rain onto the stretcher, handling his apprentice with a care that won his respect. Geneva used her air magic to lift the stretcher and direct it down the stairs and to the wagon, a far smoother ride than any of them could have managed while carrying it. Rain stayed asleep through the whole process.

"What about your horses?" The younger Guardian asked.

"They belong to the Academy," Damien said. The Academy kept horses ready for Hunters to use. Most of them didn't own their own mounts, they traveled on foot more often than by horse and were away too often to be able to take care of one.

"We'll ensure that they're returned," she promised as they went slowly and carefully down the stairs.

"Thanks," he said again. They had no trouble getting Rain into the wagon and Forger quickly hooked up one of the horses while the other was put on a lead line. Damien hopped in the back and put his unsheathed sword beside him, ready if anything happened.

"Ready?" Geneva asked as Forger got into the front of the wagon. They all nodded and started forward. They had no trouble at the city gates, the Guardians on duty waiting to ensure they got through quickly, and they sped up once they were on the road, going as fast as Geneva was willing to allow. Damien didn't protest; she knew the roads and she knew about traveling with the wounded, so he forced himself to trust her judgement.

They were left in peace for almost an hour when a Fiend came charging down the road at them. Damien leaped from the wagon, sword in hand, and ran to meet it. He sliced off the Fiend's bulbous head in a vicious attack before taking a fang and setting the quickly withering corpse on fire. He ran to catch up with the group and leaped back into the wagon without rocking it. Forger huffed a quiet laugh while Silver looked at him with awe. When he caught Geneva's gaze the Guardian just gave him a nod, expecting such action from a Hunter of his experience.

"Can't sit still for a minute, can you?" Forger asked.

"Nope," he replied as he checked on Rain for the hundredth time.

"I thought the point of traveling with an escort was that you let us do the work," Silver remarked.

Damien just shrugged, leaning against the wall of the wagon. "Call it restlessness."

"You'll find that all Hunters have that problem," Geneva said dryly. Damien toasted her with his flask; he'd had it refilled before they left the inn. "They make terrible patients and are even worse when it's the person with them who's injured." Forger and Silver both looked at Damien.

"She's not wrong." He, Tempest, and Ash had certainly proven it often enough. "But we do have way more fun," he added with a wink.

The younger Guardian looked amused. "I'm happy as a Guardian. I value my sanity."

"Sanity is overrated," he argued. He'd always thought the Guardians were the insane ones, always waiting for the monsters to attack. Even Ash, the most level-headed and patient person he knew, found it hard on the nerves. But then, Ash had always been a Hunter first.

"How can you know that if you were never sane to begin with?" Forger wanted to know.

"Like you're one to talk," he replied, raising a brow at the career criminal.

"Hey, being a crook is a far safer occupation," he argued. "I get in trouble, I just have to face human police. You get in trouble, you get killed by a monster."

"But I'll just die while you have to be on the run for several months waiting for people to forget that they've seen your face on a wanted poster," he pointed out.

Forger shrugged. "Fair enough."

Rain stirred and woke, grimacing in pain. Damien pulled out the potion he'd gotten from the healer. "Drink this," he said before she could say anything. "Don't worry, we're on our way home." She nodded and let him tip the contents into her mouth. A few seconds later she was out cold once again.

"Did you know her before you took her on as an apprentice?" Silver asked.

"She's my niece," he replied. In many ways he'd helped raise them.

His warning charm went off a few more times, but they didn't face any other Fiends. The most likely reason was that the monsters were attracted to something more interesting than their small group, which was cause for concern but at the moment he couldn't complain. They reached Port Lacoren in good time and made it through the town in even better time; the people here knew to get out of the way when someone had a Guardian escort. It was funny, he'd never been to Port Lacoren before, though he'd traveled through Landaia frequently enough. While he had been injured badly enough to require a ship back to Lysee on more than one occasion, he'd been elsewhere on the continent or overseas. Their escorts took them to the port healers to clear Rain for travel and soon he was waving farewell to Forger while Geneva was floating the stretcher carrying Rain onto the small ship that would take them to Lysee.

"I hate it when it's the kids," he heard one of the ship's mage mutter as she looked down at Rain. He tried to resist the wave of guilt and went to let the captain know they were ready.

"Have you been on one of our ships before, Hunter?" The captain asked. He was older than Damien, probably in his seventies, but there was still a gleam of wild youth in his pale grey eyes.

Damien nodded. "Granted, there are some trips I don't remember too well."

"Well, we should be at the Lysee harbour in a day and a half, provided the weather doesn't offer us any surprises."

"Sounds good to me." The captain nodded and began calling out orders to the crew, who moved with an efficiency of a team that had been together for a long time.

Moments later they were on their way, the world turning into a blur round him. He watched for a moment before heading below deck to check on Rain. They would be home soon, and she would be safe.

For a little while, anyway.

"Hunter, we've arrived." Damien looked up from the book he was reading and nodded at the water mage. He'd felt the boat come to a surprisingly gentle stop a few moments before. Rain looked a little better for having been on the water, but not much. He'd woken her up for a little while, but she was still in intense pain. A few seconds later Roderick came onto the ship. The lanky healer hadn't changed much over the years. Somehow he'd become something of a family friend and Damien knew he was closest to Storm out of all of them.

"She was taken by bandits and stabbed with a knife spelled to block magic. It punctured her lung," Damien recounted quickly and without preamble. "I had to cauterise it to stop the bleeding. The healer in Landai did what she could, but Rain's body wasn't healing like it should have been."

Roderick nodded and quickly checked under the bandages. "Impressive," he remarked. "It looks like the knife was twisted around."

"She somehow got it out herself," he said. There were wounds around her wrists where they'd been tied, so he knew it had to have been excruciating and difficult.

He frowned. "That doesn't explain the twisting." Suddenly Damien wanted to go back and kill the bandits all over again. Slowly. "Let's get her to the hospital. There aren't too many patients right now so we should be able to speed things along quite nicely."

"Is Ash out there?" Damien asked after the healer called for assistance.

Roderick nodded. "He's worried, but he knows she was in good hands. Storm is already at the hospital." Well if that wasn't a knife to the heart... "What?"

Damien raked his hands through his hair and waited until the mages that came down had grabbed The Hunters' bags and left. "The bandits got her because they wanted to harm me," he admitted. "If I hadn't let some of them get away…" he couldn't finish. Roderick gripped his shoulder.

"No one can know the future," he said. "Stop beating yourself up over it, it's not going to help Rain, it's not going to help you, now let's go." He stopped when a mage came back to help get Rain above deck. Damien took the other side and the healer followed.

Ash ran towards them the moment they stepped off the ship. He looked pale as he looked down at his youngest daughter. "What happened? Will she be okay?"

"She'll make a full recovery," Roderick said calmly. "She'll have some scars, but it'll be surface damage only, and as long as they 'look cool' she'll be happy." He gave them a wry grin, shaking his head as they loaded the stretcher onto a carriage. Ash's relief was palpable as he relaxed. "I can give you a better timeline when we get to the hospital." Both Hunters nodded and climbed into the carriage behind Roderick. Ash sat by Rain's side, holding her hand.

"I gave her a potion so she would sleep while we were traveling," Damien told them, handing the bottle over to Roderick. The healer examined the remains of the contents.

"Probably for the best," he said. Damien knew Ash was waiting for an answer as to how this had happened. He also knew it was probably best to wait until they were somewhere with more space.

"You know, she actually rescued me and the humans," Damien said. "A few days ago from some group that wanted the prince." He glanced at Ash. "You'd have been proud." Ash nodded and brushed back a lock of Rain's hair.

"She's her mother's daughter," he said.

"And yours." Damien thought about how she'd dealt with his little episode at the inn afterward.

They pulled into the Academy courtyard, where a group of healers took Rain, leaving Ash and Damien. He knew they would have to wait until the healers did their work see her again. "It's my fault," he said once the healers were gone. "The bandits that attacked me? They targeted Rain and took her to try to get revenge on me. When we were in Landai they overpowered her and stabbed her with a knife meant to block her magic and disable any protective spells. Somehow she managed to get the knife out and hide before I found her."

Ash stared at him for a moment. "I fucking told you! I told you that would come back to get you and you were so fucking careless about it!" He threw a punch, and Damien stood still, letting it catch his jaw and was thrown back several meters. He rose slowly and faced his friend once more, ignoring the pain radiating through the left side of his face. All other activity in the courtyard had stopped, and he saw Storm running out to them. Very few people had ever seen Ash angry.

"I'm sorry," he said, though he knew that nothing he could say would make any difference right then. Ash stepped closer to him, a tower of muscle and rage. There wasn't much difference between them in height, but Ash was much broader than Damien's lean build.

"Dad!" Storm stepped between them, hands out. "Look, what's done is done and I'm pretty sure that nothing you can say is worse than anything Uncle Damien's already thought of himself." Actually, that wasn't true, and Ash and Damien both knew it, but Damien also knew that Ash would never cross that line, no matter how furious he was.

Ash walked around Storm and Damien to go into the hospital without saying anything else. Anyone even remotely in his path found somewhere else to be very quickly. Damien stopped Storm when she moved to go after him. He knew what Ash was like, and right now the other man needed space.

"He's right to be pissed," Damien told her, rubbing his jaw. "Once he knows for sure she'll be okay he'll calm down."

"Will she be okay?" Storm wanted to know.

"Don't worry, she'll be hunting again soon enough." Storm nodded, relaxing slightly.

"We should go in, I want to see her." To make sure that she really was okay, but Storm didn't need to say that. The scars she'd gotten on the day of her mother's death hadn't only been physical, and were just as permanent and damaging. She was absolutely terrified of Fiends, and of losing anyone she cared about. If he or Ash ever returned injured it took a long time to assure her that they would be fine. If Rain was hurt over the course of her training and Storm happened to be the one to get the message she was a wreck until she saw her sister safe and whole again. They'd been lucky so far. He wasn't sure he wanted to see what would happen the day someone wasn't going to be okay, wasn't going to make a full recovery.

"I'll stay here. Your father will do better if I'm not around for a while."

"Where will you go?"

"I need to see a mage about a knife," he said, holding up the blade. He'd cleaned it carefully on the ship, removing any trace of blood that could cover the etched runes. Storm held out her hands for it. "Be extremely careful," he warned, "this'll destroy any spells you're using and block you from using your own magic." Storm's leg was powered by spells. He quickly pulled a spare pare of leather gloves from his bag and handed them to her.

"Thanks," she said, pulling them on before she took the knife. Immediately her brows went up. "This is a nasty piece of work," she said, turning it over and looking at it carefully. "I only recognise about half the runes and combinations." She handed it back along with the gloves. "Who the hell would make something like that?"

"That's what I want to find out," he replied, yawning and wincing when his bruising jaw protested the movement. "Go on, see your sister. I'll be along later and I'll tell you what I find out." He was fairly certain he'd end up staying at the Academy for the night, just to give Ash space. He was also fairly certain he hadn't slept more than twenty minutes in the last three days. He would have preferred to go home but he'd settle for anywhere with a bed. Or just a flat surface. Hell, any surface would do.

When Rain woke up she felt better, the stabbing agony only a dull throbbing ache, and breathing was far easier and less painful. She opened her eyes and found herself in the hospital, her father and Storm speaking in whispers, quiet enough that she couldn't make out what they were saying. It was funny, she'd almost grown used to being able to pick up everything humans said, whether they wanted her to hear it or not.

"Hi," she said, her voice a croak. They both looked up and hurried over. "Where's Uncle Damien?" She was surprised he wasn't there as well.

"He had to find out more about the dagger," her father told her. She could tell he was angry with his old friend. "How do you feel?"

"A bit better," she replied. "Are you mad at him?"

Her dad paused for a moment, sighing before answering her. "I am. You were almost killed because of his mistake." He sighed again, rubbing a hand over his face. "I'll forgive him… eventually. If I ever thought he would be deliberately reckless I never would have let him near you girls, and neither would your mother." Both sisters nodded.

Roderick came in then with a cheerful wave. "Good to see you've finally decided to wake up," he said. "So, the bad news is that you're going to be stuck at home for about a month, but the good news is that once you've healed you can go on merrily slaying Fiends to your heart's content once more." When she opened her mouth to speak he added: "Yes, the scars will look cool." Rain grinned. "You bloody Hunters and your scars…" He shook his head. "Actually, Guardians are just as bad, and even the Keepers who happen to end up wounded are starting to catch on to the trend!"

"But can you really blame them?" Storm asked, standing to strike a pose. "I mean, look at what they see every day. How could they resist?" The healer gave a helpless sighed as Rain laughed, then coughed and moaned at the pain. He looked to her father for help for a moment before he remembered there was no point.

"I'm a Hunter and a Guardian," he reminded the healer.

"Anyway," Roderick drawled, pulling them back to the matter at hand. "I want you to stay here tonight, but in the morning you can go back home, just return twice a week so I can monitor how things are going and I'll see if I can't speed things up a little."

"Sounds good," Rain said and he left.

"I'm on night shift, so I'll be around," her father said. "I got the hospital post for tonight, so I can come up and check on you." He turned to her sister. "Storm, you can get Damien to bring you home when you're ready." Both sisters nodded. They talked for a while longer after that, wanting to hear about what Rain had done during her first time in the field.

"How have things been here?" She asked when there was a lull in the conversation.

"Not much has happened around here," her father said with a shrug. "Some students lured a moose into the courtyard, but that was about it."

"A moose?" Rain repeated. He just shrugged, clearly as confused as she was.

"I'm starting a new project," Storm said, catching both of their attention. "I don't know if it'll go anywhere, but I'm going to see if I can put together a spell that can trace the origins of magic. I started looking into it a few weeks ago, but I think I'm going to take it on."

"Is it because I got stabbed by a magic knife?" Rain wondered, raising a brow.

"That did turn it from a 'maybe' project to a 'for sure' project," Storm admitted, "but right now there's not much we can get from stuff like that unless there's some kind of signature mark that can be recognised, and there often isn't."

Rain frowned. "But they've tried doing stuff like that before and it's never worked."

"I know, but I think there might be a way," she said. "You know I've been doing a lot with ancient runes the last year and a half, right?" Rain nodded. "Well, even though the runes we use now are based off ancient designs, the ancient designs often had subtly different meanings, but different enough to make a difference in the spell, like different dialects of a language. A number of them are old enough to have a kind of power of their own, which is why humans prefer using them for spell work over more modern runes, even though they are harder to work with. Well, one of the reasons anyway." Storm could have gone on all day if they let her, and Rain was more than happy to. After all, Storm had taught her more about using her magic than the Academy instructors had, especially in the last few years as she finished her Keeper training. Rain's sister may not have been one to fight on a battlefield, but she was definitely a force to be reckoned with.

Somehow Rain managed to stay conscious during the ride home the next day, though it had hurt like hell. Uncle Damien had appeared before they left, acting as an escort along with her father, the bruise on his jaw looking worse than it had the night before when he'd stopped by to see how she was doing before he took Storm home. He and her father didn't talk much, but the tension wasn't as bad as what Storm had described the night before after their father had left to take his post.

"Are you going to go hunting now?" She asked her father when they were back home and she could breathe through the pain again.

"In a few days," he said. "You just got back, after all. Unless you don't want to see your dear ol' Dad?" He gave her a look of mock-hurt.

"Of course I do." Enough had happened in the last two weeks that she didn't even roll her eyes when she said it.

"Also, I saw Kestrel last night when she and Amber came in, she said she'd be by to see you in a day or two," her father added.

"Is she okay?"

"Fine, they were just picking up some supplies." Rain relaxed a little.

Being injured among Hunters didn't mean getting to slack off, even if she was still technically in training, especially since her magic had returned to normal. By the end of the day they had her up and moving, not enough to cause damage, but doing as much as she could. There would likely come a time when she was in bad shape and totally alone, with no one to rely on but herself until she could make it to safety, which could be a few hours or days away. So she had to learn to work through pain and around injuries. She also got to watch the budding romance between her sister and Phantom. The Guardian was around often, and the two were clearly interested in one another. Rain liked him well enough, and enjoyed Storm's blush when she pointed it out with all the tact of a younger sister. Her father went out hunting and her uncle stayed home while she recovered, working on her fighting and how to get out of traps, enlisting other Hunters around the village and Academy. If she could get away from them, humans would never be able to capture her again, and she would stand a better chance against Fiends as well. She worked hard, impatient to get back in the field.

10
Sorrows

"I'm cleared to hunt!" Rain announced as she burst through the door. Almost a month had passed since she'd been rushed home. She pulled up short when she saw her father leaning against the wall, an envelope in his hand and a grim expression on his face. "What's wrong?" She asked, the words feeling like they were being pulled from her. He held it up so she could see the wax seal that closed the envelope. She felt her heart drop a little as she reflexively stepped back. Black wax meant that someone was dead. Black was only used for the letters that notified friends and family that a Hunter or Guardian they knew had died. The letters were made up by the Academy but sent out by the next of kin, generally someone close enough to the person to know who would need to be notified. She'd seen many of them growing up, sent to her parents or her uncle because that was the world they lived in. Friends and family members went out and never returned, or went to guard their post and never left it again.

"It's for you," he said grimly, holding it out.

Her heart plummeted and she started to tremble. She'd known this day would come, when one of her classmates would be killed. She'd known it, but that didn't make it any easier. She swallowed hard as she stared at the envelope that turned blurry from the tears that threatened to fall already. She didn't want to take it, didn't want to read it. She made herself walk across the room and take hold of the heavy parchment, dread a weight on her heart. Rain broke the seal and pulled out the letter. It was formal, a template where the name of the dead could be inserted. "No…" she groaned as she read it, falling back against the wall. Not Adrian. She hadn't seen him since the party after they'd been paired with their mentors. He'd been killed in combat. She slid to the floor, dropping the letter as she started crying. She heard her father sigh before he sat down beside her and put an arm around her shoulders, hugging her tight. Adrian had always been a cheerful joker, even when they were almost falling over from a brutal practice, grinning as everyone threatened to throw him off the cliffs for being so damn happy when they were barely able to walk.

Now they would throw him off a cliff, only he would be a pile of ash they were setting free.

"The memorial is tonight," her father said, having picked up the letter and looking it over. "He'll be given the rights of a full Hunter." They acted like Hunters in their field year, so they were sent off from this life as Hunters. It was the least that could be done.

The door opened, but Rain didn't look up. "So, I guess you heard too," Uncle Damien said. "I just saw Jerek at the Academy. Apparently they underestimated the Fiends in Kelaroon." He paused a moment. "I know you two were friends, Rain." She nodded. "Tonight we'll go to the memorial service, then we'll go to the pub, have a drink in his memory and give his soul a proper send off. Tomorrow we'll do the only thing we can: keep hunting, keep killing as many Fiends as we can." It really was the only thing they could do.

"I knew this was going to happen," she managed to say. Just not... just not Adrian and not so soon."

"I know," her father said. "But it's always going to be someone's friend who dies. I'd like to say it gets easier, but it doesn't."

"It can, actually." They both looked up at Damien. "And if it does it means that you're in trouble." He didn't back down from her father's quelling look. "To be able to mourn isn't a bad thing; it means that we're more than the monsters we kill. You just can't let it overwhelm you. It's a fine balance, especially if you want to be an elite Hunter, kiddo. You'll be getting a lot more of those letters."

"I understand," she murmured. Harsh words, but true.

"Does she really need to hear this now?" Her father hissed.

"Better to be forewarned," Damien replied in a dark tone. "I'm supposed to be teaching her how to be one of us, and that includes dealing with the deaths of our own. Maybe she'll be lucky and her friends will live, or maybe her class will end up like Amber's did." Her father sighed but didn't disagree.

At sunset Rain stood with her friends on The Cliff overlooking the ocean near the Academy, the spot where the ashes of Hunters, Guardians, and Keepers had been scattered for thousands of years. Their mentors and other full Hunters stood nearby with Jerek, Adrian's mentor. He was heavily bandaged, his expression stricken as he leaned on his friends. Adrian's family was there as well, his parents clinging to each other as they cried and the Keeper of the Dead spoke. He spoke of Adrian's training, his cheer, his determination, his endless loyalty to his friends. Rain and Kestrel gripped each other's hands tightly through the whole thing, Nathan standing on Kestrel's other side. The cold wind that was always present pulled at their hair and clothing, but they didn't move.

Then it was time, and Adrian's parents stepped to the edge of The Cliff and released his ashes to the winds and waters. It was done. He was well and truly gone, the first victim of the endless battle they fought. Rain's classmates looked around at one another through tear-filled eyes, wondering who would be next, and who would ultimately be the last to survive. Rain didn't know what to be more afraid of, that it wouldn't be her or that it would be.

True to his word, Uncle Damien had her back on the road the next morning. All her spells and charms had been redone days before. "Where are we going?" She asked, trying to focus on the present rather than the friend she'd put to rest the night before. Her mild hangover helped, muddling her mind.

"Anywhere," he said. "We have no mission and the Council hasn't said they wanted us anywhere, so it doesn't really matter." He pulled a dagger out of his boot. "Everyone has their own way of deciding in these cases; often your mom and I would throw darts or icicles at a map if we couldn't agree on where we wanted to go. Of course, she would always want to go straight into any storm, or rain, or snow, or sleet, or any kind of weather that could make things difficult." He paused and looked at her with an expression of horror. "You're going to be the same way, aren't you?

"Water mage," Rain said with a shrug.

"I can't even say that I wish you were born with your father's magic because I've had to retrieve things from very tall trees on too many occasions." He sighed. "I'm doomed. Anyway, sometimes I'll just see where a dagger falls and head that way. Your mom would do the same with iccicles." He carefully balanced it on its point and let go. It fell with the hilt pointing north-west.

"What if the dart lands in the ocean?" Rain asked, bringing the conversation back around. Crossing wasn't usually too bad, the Fiends that lurked in the depths didn't rise too often.

"Then we'd be getting a ship," he replied. "There's some pretty neat islands, and things are really different on the Estavian continent." She couldn't tell if it was a good or bad kind of different. Storm and her father had already left for the Academy that morning, so it was just her and her uncle home. "We'll go for two weeks and come back. It's getting too close to winter to risk going too far, especially northward, unless you want to end up stuck in a tiny village for several months." She nodded. "I know you're still mourning Adrian," he added gently, "but trust me, this is the best way to do it; keep fighting, keep moving forward. He might be the first, but he sure as hell won't be the last." She nodded again and they started walking.

They'd been on the road for a few hours before they encountered a Fiend. It was about a foot taller than Damien, with rough orange hide, five glowing eyes, and too many teeth in its wide mouth.

"This one is mine," she hissed, drawing her sword. The monsters had taken one of her friends. It was time to get back to her own mission: to kill as many as she could, until they learned to fear her shadow and ran for the most remote places on the earth.

"Don't let your emotions cloud your mind. Feed off them, but don't let them take over," her uncle warned, moving away to give her space. Rain lunged at the Fiend, turning the ground beneath her feet to ice so she could duck and skate under its strike. As she went past the arm, she twisted, slicing off the limb with a smooth slash and continued the attack downward to hack at its knee. While her blade didn't go all the way through, she did do substantial damage, and the Fiend swayed, off balance long enough for her to cut its head off, ducking the arc of blood. The head hit the ground and she plucked a fang before setting it on fire.

"Well?" She looked to her uncle.

"Nice move with the ice," he said, nodding in approval.

That night they wound up camping, taking turns guarding while the other slept. This was more like what Rain had imagined things would be like as the days passed, though she had to admit that escorting the humans had been good experience -kidnapping and horrible enchanted knives aside. They stopped in villages to exchange fangs for money, gather supplies, or stay the night. Her uncle introduced her to people he knew, valuable assets to add to her network should she need anything, especially among humans. Shockingly, the trip passed without any major incident, and she returned home with a nice sum of money and a number of kills to her name. She was almost a quarter of the way through her final year.

A kind of routine developed over the next six months; Rain and her uncle would venture out hunting, occasionally taking missions for the council, though they didn't act as escorts again. As an elite Hunter the former was something Damien did frequently, though where he had Rain around now he had to be more careful. No amount of raw talent could make up for the knowledge and skill that came with experience. Sometimes they would be with other Hunters, sometimes on their own. She would write letters home to her family and friends, making plans with the latter group about hunting trips when they graduated, and she kept in touch with Schuyler and Warren. The prince had made quite an impression on the Landaian court and was quickly gaining influence as a diplomat. Rain honed her skills, determined to become a force to be reckoned with. She loved what she did, for the most part, but there was pain and sorrow as well. Three more of her classmates died, and she was only able to attend one of the memorial services. The others she had to mourn alone. They weren't the only Hunters who died in those months. She'd seen other Hunters die, or helped send their ashes back home more than once.

It was the villages that were the worst, those that were attacked by the Fiends. Not every village was like hers, brimming with mages if not actual fighters. Sometimes they arrived in time to help, other times they arrived in time to help clean up the damage. It never got easier, trying not to step on bloody corpses or tripping over limbs far from where they should be. She knew her uncle would tell her not to dwell on it, to just keep moving forward, pushing through the darkness that surrounded their work. It was the only way for a Hunter to survive.

"She seemed… different," Rain said shortly after they parted ways with another Hunter. It had been an odd encounter. Normally when they met a Hunter on the road they would travel together for a time, swapping stories and tips, either for a few hours or days. Uncle Damien knew a lot of the Hunters they encountered –even if they didn't get along all that well-, and Rain recognised almost as many, having seen them around the Academy or Lysee. But this time… there had been something off, something that made Uncle Damien keep things short and drag her in the opposite direction once the other Hunter left, the flat, empty look in her eyes creeping Rain out.

"You mean suicidal," Damien corrected her, taking a drink from his flask, his expression grim, though he hadn't been very cheerful all day. "There's no point in sugar-coating it. She's just fighting to die. If you ever meet Siobhan, she's the same way." Siobhan was another of the elite Hunters, though Rain knew she and Damien had avoided one another for years.

Rain was quiet for a long moment as they walked. "Do any of them come back from it?"

He shook his head, his expression grim. "They don't want to. Something gets broken in them that can't be fixed."

"How close did you get to that point?" As soon as she opened her mouth she realised it might not be a question he wanted to answer. "Sorry, you don't have to answer."

He gave a rueful grin that didn't reach his eyes. "I figured one of you would ask that sooner or later." He sighed. "All Hunters flirt with darkness, some do better than others, like your father. Others are like me, and manage to get by for the most part. Some… some just get swallowed whole. I've been pretty damn close, more than once." He looked over at her. "So if you want to be like any of us, be like your father."

"What about Mom?"

He thought about it for a moment. "I'd say Tempest was somewhere in between me and Ash. She had her moments where she got pretty close, but she always managed to hold the darkness at bay in the end." Rain could vaguely remember her mom coming back sometimes and she would be depressed for a few days, but it had never lasted long. As for her uncle, well, that had never been a secret, even when the adults had tried to hide it.

They walked on in silence for a while longer, in part because the hill they were trying to hike was both steep and rather treacherous, the snow a light coating over loose rocks that could easily send them sliding down, and in part because she felt like she'd pushed her uncle enough for now. She loved the winter, loved the fall, and even the spring, just any season with some kind of precipitation or weather that wasn't hot. Of course, this led to repeated threats to drag her through a desert whenever she got too enthusiastic about what most would call 'awful weather'.

"When will we get to Avern?" She asked when they reached the top of the hill.

"Few more hours," he said, taking another drink. Rain frowned. She could tell that something had been weighing on him for the last few days, getting steadily worse, but she couldn't figure out what it was, and she wary of asking, especially after just having a conversation about suicidal Hunters and that had likely not been the best choice either. "We'll go West from there, I heard some rumours about problems with Fiends near Cadma, then we can probably go back home for a break. We should have time for a few more good hunts before you graduate." She had a little more than three months left. Time seemed to just fly by.

"Will we just pass through or are we stopping there for the night?"

He shook his head. "We'll be there for two nights." She could see Avern from the top of the hill, a small but quickly growing town by what they'd heard from others who'd travelled through it. "They have a decent inn that won't frown on a couple of Hunters." It had been surprising how many places did have the gall to turn them away. The first few times it had hurt, but Rain couldn't say that she hadn't been warned. She'd stopped letting it get to her after that, accepting that whatever problem humans had with her kind wasn't going to vanish. So she kept her expectations low and rolled her eyes when they muttered insults.

"Okay…" Rain didn't argue, and after three weeks straight on the road, it would be a welcome reprieve, though given Uncle Damien's deteriorating mood, she was certain that a break wasn't why they were staying more than one night. She still felt like she ought to know what was wrong, it was just on the edge of her mind, a memory she couldn't retrieve, no matter how she tried as they entered the town. It was busy this early in the afternoon and she made sure to stay close as her uncle led the way to the inn, which had been named *The Drunken Ranger*. "I thought we had cornered the market for notorious drunks," she remarked as they both stopped and looked at the sign, canting her head slightly.

"So did I," her uncle agreed, frowning. "Last time I was here this was called *the Soldier's Sweetheart*. That was what, eight years ago? Maybe seven?" He pushed his hair back, trying to remember for a moment before giving up. "Fuck it. As long as their liquor hasn't changed I'll forgive the name." He led the way inside where they found a welcome surprise in the form of Schuyler and Warren.

"I thought you'd have gone back to first rate inns, your Highness," Rain said as she snuck up behind Schuyler and Warren while Uncle Damien dealt with getting rooms. The prince and his bodyguard jumped.

The prince gave her a wry grin as she laughed. "I'm to stay with my escorts, and apparently my escorts had too much fun in this town in the past and this is the only place that will take them in," he told her, looking over at a small group of men and women who grinned unrepentantly before turning back to a card game. Some were soldiers and others looked like they were trying really hard to imitate Hunters but not quite managing it.

"Your uncle was right about the Rangers," Warren muttered when he saw where she was looking.

"Maybe that explains the name change here?" Uncle Damien suggested as he joined them. He smiled slightly, but it failed once more to reach his eyes.

"Wouldn't surprise me at all, but the Warlord of Kelaroon insisted on sending a squad to escort us who had experience with Fiends." Warren sighed. "She reached out for assistance because they've been having a horrible year and there's a pretty bad famine. The prince is to conduct a survey and decide what kind of assistance Glask can provide."

"I can't say I'm surprised, they've been having a bad time with Fiends," Rain said. It was where Adrian had been killed, and he wasn't the only Hunter to fall in that valley over the last year, and a number of Guardians had fallen as well. There was talk that the Council was going to form what would amount to an army of Hunters and send them to deal with the issue. It had been done a few times in the past, but the cost was always high, both in terms of their people and the humans who fell because there were regions left unprotected.

Schuyler nodded. "That's what they're blaming for the problems. How long are the two of you staying in town?"

"This night and the next," she replied. "You?"

"Same. We need to get our supply wagon repaired. The joys of traveling with a large group." He sighed. "Have you been out to see the markets?"

"Looking for an excuse to leave your escorts behind?" She asked, arching an eyebrow.

"I'd be safe with Hunters," he said innocently.

"Fine," she said, grinning, and looked at her uncle.

"You go on," he said, waving her off. "Have fun, cause havoc, don't get kidnapped, and don't get arrested."

"I can manage three of those for sure."

"I'm not going to ask which ones," Damien decided with a slight twitch of the lips that may have been a weak attempt at a smile. The humans rose and she left with them, glancing back to see her uncle let out a deep breath and lean back against his chair. Schuyler's escorts gave Rain a considering look, but made no move to stop them.

"I half-expected a fight to break out considering the way Damien goes on about Rangers," Warren remarked once they were outside.

Rain shrugged. "It's early yet. There seem to be three kinds of Rangers: the ones who think they can do better than us because they're human, the ones who have a creepy obsession with us and want to be us, and those ones who are just humans who desperately want to do something, anything, to help win the fight."

Schuyler considered that for a moment. "I'd say most of the Rangers in that group are the third type, though some might be the second type. Warlord Ladinia doesn't tolerate any kind of discrimination among her people. Not to say that it's perfect or anything, but it is better than a lot of places."

Rain nodded. "I've heard that." Kestrel had just returned home from Kellaroon. "Still, there's no place like home."

"True," both humans agreed.

Sometime later she found herself looking at silk paintings in a shop. Schuyler had wanted to see if there was anything his younger sister would enjoy. She kept checking her medallion, worried about her uncle. He was staying in the area around the inn, but that didn't mean much, not when there were a number of bars around. She tried to remember when she'd last seen him in this kind of mood because she had and there had been a reason for it.

"Something wrong?" Warren asked, leaning against a heavy stand. He spoke so only she could hear him. They both watched as Schuyler brought the painting he'd chosen to the shopkeeper.

"I don't know," she replied, playing with her medallion. She used to have a habit of playing with the hoops in her ears, but once she started using spell beads she'd had to give it up fast. It had been the laces of her vambraces net but as soon as she had the medallion she switched to that. "Maybe we should head back to the inn for a bit."

He frowned. "You're not worried about your uncle, are you?"

"And if I am?"

"Did something happen?"

She shrugged. They might be friends, but she'd only known them for a few months and they were human besides. "Nothing unusual." He was trying – and failing- to hide it from her in a parental kind of way, like he or her parents would try to hide when something bad had happened on a hunting trip. Except that made no sense now, she was grown up; she could handle things like that. Hell, she'd seen things like that.

"Well, he doesn't seem like the most open kind of guy anyway," the human remarked. "But that doesn't seem to be an uncommon thing with demons."

She raised a brow. "Can you blame us?"

"No," he admitted. "He does strike me as the kind of person who would try to deal with his issues all on his own, though. I've heard a few stories about him."

Rain shrugged again. "Most Hunters are like that, and the better they are the worse it gets. Any elite Hunter is going to be bad for it, it just comes with the job." What made an elite Hunter wasn't necessarily years of experience, but the caliber of Fiend they could kill without sustaining a mortal wound. Elite Hunters spent their careers hunting the worst and the scariest of the monsters, those no other Hunter could face and return alive. They saw more tragedy, more heartbreak, and more death than the others. They were the Hunters who had a tendency to outlive their friends and eventually it seemed to get to a point where most gave up on forming new friendships or keeping old ones going because those people would inevitably die. Her uncle had managed to stay out of the latter group, luckily, but Rain could count the number of people still alive that he cared about. "A lot of Hunters build walls around themselves, either the older or stronger they are. It's just not that easy always having friends and family members dying around you."

He thought about that for a moment. "There's a lot of soldiers like that too."

"You both look rather cheerful," Schuyler said as he rejoined them. "The shopkeeper said that there's a really good bookstore down the road, and after that we can head back."

"Oh fuck," Warren and Rain groaned in unison. Having grown up with a scholar she knew better than to unleash one in a bookstore without strict time constraints.

"How's your family doing?" Schuyler asked a little while later as leaned against the bookcase beside her. Surprisingly it was Warren who was taking the longest, despite his earlier words.

"Pretty good," she replied. "Storm started her work on tracing magic and Dad was hurt pretty badly in a hunt but will make a full recovery, so for now he's a guest lecturer for some Academy classes."

"What about Damien's family? I don't know if either of you have mentioned them. I know you're his family, but did he ever marry or anything?"

"No..." Rain wanted to hit her head against one of the bookcases. Her uncle hadn't married, but Raven had died around this time of year and every year on the anniversary of her death he was a mess. Raven was the only woman he'd ever fallen in love with. "Fuck." It was a tragic love story: Damien had met Raven not long after Storm was born, a brilliant herbalist and part-owner of the apothecary in Lysee, though as far as their people went she'd been frail, not much stronger than a human. So when a plague struck the territories that was actually strong enough to infect her people, Raven had succumbed and the healers had been powerless to save her. Damien had had to watch the love of his life slowly waste away and die. Usually her father tried to keep Damien in the city for this, but where he'd been injured... "Fuck."

"Rain?"

"I have to go."

What's wrong? Can we help?"

"You remembered why you're worried?" Warren asked, returning to them.

"Yeah, look, I'll see you guys in the morning. This... it's a family thing," she told them.

The prince frowned. "You sure?"

"I can tell you right now whatever bar he's in is one that you two wouldn't come out of alive."

"Why?" The humans followed her out of the store.

"Generally because the kind of people who go there just want to drink in peace and are extremely dangerous and not accepted by polite society. You know, like me and Uncle Damien."

"But there's also going to be thieves, assassins, mercenaries, and the like," Warren pointed out.

"The rules are different for us *demons*," she reminded him, the word like ashes in her mouth. "We're like them, people you don't want to fuck with." People who looked scary and had the weapons to back it up. "With people like that, like us, there's a kind of understanding, a kind of respect that as long as no one tries to start shit we can all coexist and get drunk peacefully."

"Okay," Schuyler said, accepting her decision. No one brought up the bandit incident, but then again, she had saved them before that had happened and demonstrated just how dangerous she could be.

"We'll see you later, or in the morning," Warren said, leading Schuyler down a street that would take them directly to the inn. Rain pulled her medallion out of her shirt and followed the silver dot, hoping she wasn't too late to keep her uncle from doing anything destructive. He was more of a cynical drunk than an angry one, but given his mood and the grim expression her father always had when he went to peel her uncle off the bar stools in Lysee and haul him home she knew it wouldn't be pretty. By the time the two men had arrived back home Uncle Damien had been passed out or on the verge of passing out, and dawn usually wasn't long off. By the next afternoon he was back to normal, if a little subdued for the day.

She made her way through the streets quickly but without running, especially when she got to the older parts of town, were the joys of a burgeoning city weren't felt and the darkness showed through. Here she attracted less notice than in the markets though she knew there were eyes on her, taking in the differences that marked her for what she was. She encountered no trouble, and the expression she kept on her face would dissuade most. She and Kestrel had practiced it until they could make their classmates scramble back from them.

The Golden Fiend was not a name she'd ever expected to see on a bar, but the place looked about right, every bit as run down as *The Bloody Goose* in Ankira had been, if not worse because this was no hidden gem. Actually, it reminded her more of *The Fallen Guardian* in Lysee. She walked up to the door, which was guarded by a rather large and muscular human who looked like a prize fighter.

"Aren't you a bit young to be 'round this kind of place?" He asked as she drew close, giving her a slightly disapproving look. "This ain't a place for kids, even if you are a Hunter."

"Good thing I'm not a kid," she told him, resisting the urge to find out how good a fighter he was. She was eighteen now, an adult in the eyes of her people and humans alike. "I'm looking for another Hunter: silver eyes, dark hair, drunk." She knew he was there, but it seemed like the better idea to play up to the guy in front of the door who may or may not try to stop her from entering. Not that he'd succeed; it would just make everything a little bit harder.

"He's here," the man confirmed. "Don't know if I'd advise you get too close to him. He looks dangerous, even for a Hunter. Damn near slit a guy's throat an hour ago"

"The sentiment is sweet, but he's both my uncle and my mentor," she mentioned, giving him a saccharine smile that barred her fangs.

"Fine then," he surrendered, shaking his head as he stepped back slightly. "Let me know if you need help when you have to carry him out of here." Rain nodded even though she could have easily lifted the human.

The bar was what she'd expected, quiet and in disrepair, patrons either drinking themselves into oblivion, quietly playing cards, plotting some sort of crime, or a mix of all three. Her uncle sat at a table in the corner, a half empty bottle on the table in front of him, staring at the ceiling. He hadn't noticed her yet, so she went and sat down across from him. It was a moment before he looked at her.

"Tempest?" He asked, his expression hopeful for the barest moment before it turned to heartbreaking sorrow. He covered his eyes for a moment, then took a long drink from the bottle. Rain suspected it wasn't the first he'd had. "Rain."

"Sorry," she said, only now realising that she was in over her head. She didn't really know what to do or say. Things like what had happened in the hotel months before were one thing, this was a whole other kind of battle. She didn't know how her mother and later her father had managed to get him home.

He shook his head. "S'not your fault," he slurred, letting his hand fall to the table.

"Raven died fifteen years ago today, didn't she?"

"Yup. Exactly fifteen, as of an 'our ago, just after sunset," he confirmed, taking another drink. "So, you're here, what're you gonna do?"

"Mostly I was thinking of keeping you from doing anything stupid," she said carefully, keeping her tone light.

"Ha!" He barked out a laugh and waved his hand. The bartender quickly appeared with another full bottle of deep amber liquid. "Yer here, you migh' as well drink."

"Someone has to carry you back to the inn," she pointed out. She didn't think she'd ever seen him quite this drunk. "Is Raven why you do this every year?"

"Just once a year and no more. Give in once to hold it back." It sounded like he was quoting someone. "And no, it's not just for her. She's part of it, but she's not the only one."

"Hold back what?" She thought she knew the answer. Her uncle had been a Hunter for over twenty years and had lived on the streets before that. Like she'd told Warren, the old and the powerful saw a lot of people they loved die and elite Hunters always got to see the worst of the world.

"Trying to distract me to slow down my drinking?" He asked with a slight smile that still failed to reach his eyes.

She shrugged. "I don't know... I just know that Mom and Dad never left you alone on the anniversary of Raven's death. Plus," she added, trying for levity, "you're my mentor, I need you so I can graduate." He gave her a wry grin.

"Don't worry," he told her, toasting her with the bottle. "I'm an ol' pro at this." He tipped it back and drained half of what was left.

"But why?" She asked. "Raven's been gone for fifteen years."

"And your mother for almost twelve, and Hiroma for twenty, and Skylark, Steel, and Forest for eighteen, and Isabella, York, Meadow, and Jet for sixteen, and the list just goes on, and on, and on, and it won't end until the day I die," he said, his tone bleak. "Not to mention the fires, the ruins, the screams, the blood and the shredded bodies I've walked around or on trying to fight to stay alive." He laughed suddenly, but it was a hollow sound. "This is what you have to look forward to, kiddo, this is the big reward for being one of the best. You'll get to join the ranks of the consummate survivors, the ones who'll always get to watch everyone else die." He drained the bottle. Raven might have been the catalyst for this yearly ritual, but his grief for her wasn't the only thing he was trying to drown. It was how he kept his darkness at bay, by holding it all back except for one day a year. Now she understood how he managed to keep skirting the edge everyone expected him to fall from.

"So you're drinking the rest of the year?" She asked, trying to hide her fear at his speech. It rang too true for comfort.

"Just enough to dull the edge and no more," he replied, pushing the empty bottle aside where it was quickly whisked away and opening the next. Again it sounded like he was quoting someone. "Some days it takes a bit more than others."

"Did you come up with those rules?"

He shook his head. "No, it was Tempest." He sighed and ran his hand through his hair, pushing it back. "Wanna hear a story, kiddo?"

"Okay," she agreed cautiously, earning another wry grin.

"Y'know how I disappeared for a while when Raven died?"

She nodded, brushing her hair back from her face. "Amber thought you went to find her family."

"Yeah, I did that, and then I spent several weeks getting fucked up by night and hunting by day, then I just wandered, doing the same damn thing wherever I wound up. I was almost suicidal," he admitted with a dark laugh. "Then your mom found me rottin' away in a bar one night, I don't remember where. I still don't know how she did it, never thought to ask." He went quiet for a minute, then took a drink. "Anyway, she said that she'd had enough and it was time for me to come home." He shook his head. "Like I was going back to that empty flat, full of memories, full of *her*, full of the future with her that I was never going to have." He drank and closed his eyes for a moment, either chasing memories or running from them, Rain wasn't certain. "Tempest said that I wasn't going back there, I was going to my other home, with her, Ash, and you two little devils. She said I was going to sober up, go hunting and be the best damn babysitter in the territories." He shook his head again. "Your mom could be some fuckin' stubborn when she wanted to be. She told me that we would have that night to get spectacularly drunk, then at dawn we were going home whether I liked it or not." He grinned slightly. "You can bet your life that we were on the godsdamned road at dawn, hangovers and all."

"When did she make the rules?"

"On the way back. She told me to pick one night of the year, just one, to remember everyone who's been lost to me, who's gone on before me. One night a year to give into the darkness, to remember and to grieve. Let off some steam, I guess you could say. Then the rest of the year, drink no more than what it takes to dull the edge of the pain." A heavy sigh. "I never could fight off the darkness, not like she did, I just learned to live with it. And after Tempest died, well, I wanted to break the rules, I could barely take it, but you needed me, and so did Storm, and your father. I had to keep it together, and after a while, I just couldn't bring myself to break that promise to her, no matter how hard it was to keep." His eyes were wet with tears and she was having a little trouble seeing past her own. She had no idea what to say, and she knew that if Uncle Damien had been sober he wouldn't be telling her any of this. This was her uncle, her mentor, someone she'd always looked up to and looked to for strength. She wanted to do something, say something that would help or at least not make things worse, but she didn't know what to do. She didn't know how to deal with this kind of situation. He looked at her and laughed slightly. "Don't worry about me, kiddo. I've lasted this long, I'll keep going until long after it's my time to stop."

"Do you think you'll ever find anyone else?" She asked, toying with her medallion.

He shook his head. "Raven was one of a kind. She's the only person aside from your parents who ever really knew me and accepted me for who I am. She never asked me to change, but she still made me want to be a better person. She wasn't perfect, hell, no one is, but she was perfect for me, like what your parents had. It's just not something that can be recreated, and it wouldn't be fair of me to try to put that on someone else. No one deserves to be in second place, not like that."

"Oh."

He sighed and rubbed a hand over the stubble on his jaw. "You'll find your own way to make things work. I just want you to promise me one thing, just one, and then we can go."

"What?"

"If you ever feel the darkness creeping up on you, you'll ask for help. Anyone, I don't care who, as long as you trust them to do right by you." World-weary and bloodshot quicksilver eyes locked onto hers and she knew that no matter how drunk he was right now, he would remember this. "Promise me that you won't be like me and let it eat you alive until someone has to hunt you down and drag you back. You'll ask for help, like I should have."

"I will, I promise."

He nodded slowly. "Good, good." He took a deep drink, then put the stopper back into the bottle, frowning at it. "You didn't drink anything, did you?" It was more than half empty.

"Nope."

"It's for your own good." He lurched to his feet, still clutching the bottle. "This stuff'll rot your brain."

"Sure," she drawled as she moved to help him when he stumbled slightly. "Let's get you back to the inn." She had no illusions that he was going to stop or that their talk had changed anything for him except allowing him to vent a little.

"That's a good plan," he agreed. "This way I won't have to worry about where I'm gonna pass out." He let her take most of his weight as they went back to the inn. She waved at the muscular human as she glanced at the sky. She'd been in the bar for longer than she'd thought; it was well into the night.

"Just how much have you had to drink?" She wondered after she got him into his room.

"No clue," he told her, shrugging "'lot."

"Okay, see you tomorrow," she said, leaving him to grieve in private. She went to her own bed and lay staring at the ceiling for a long time, wondering if that was truly the destiny that awaited her, the bitter fate of the consummate survivor. It was scary. She didn't want to drink herself half to death once a year to try and control the pain, didn't want to end up like the empty-eyed Hunter they'd met on the road who was only fighting until she could die. She knew she risked it, knew all Hunters risked it, but she didn't want that fate. In the end, as she drifted off to sleep while the sky outside slowly grew lighter, she knew that only time would tell what would become of her. If she wanted to be the best, she had to be willing to pay the price.

11
The Village

"How'd it go last night?" Schuyler asked when she went downstairs to the tavern late the next morning. She'd neither slept well nor for very long, constantly interrupted by awful dreams that weren't quite nightmares. It was almost funny, because while becoming an embittered and suicidal Hunter was something she was afraid of, it wasn't her worst fear. As long as she was on her guard, she was certain she would know when she risked drawing close to that line, and as long as she made sure to keep people who cared about her in her life she wouldn't fall.

"Fine," she said. She wasn't sure if it was a lie or not. Sure, she'd managed to get him to the inn safely and without any murder, maiming, or destruction, but she'd also seen how deep her uncle's damage went, and she wasn't sure he'd ever recover from it.

"So, you're a Hunter," one of the Rangers who was escorting the prince and Warren came over to join them. She wasn't sure where Warren was.

"An apprentice," she answered, showing her medallion. "For a few more months, anyway."

"You ever been to Kelaroon?"

She shook her head. "I know a few who have." Some of them hadn't returned alive.

"How would you like to come with us?" He asked. "Of course, you get to keep what you kill, but the way things are going a few Hunters at our backs would make things this a lot easier. The others and I were talking, and we'd all feel a lot better if you came with us, especially seeing as you already know our charges. I'm Rick, by the way." He held out a hand.

"I'll have to talk to my mentor about it," she said, gripping his forearm in a warrior's greeting.

"The one who thinks we're useless?" He asked dryly. "Though I believe the exact words he used were 'live bait'."

"That'd be him."

"Was he just saying that because he was buzzed?" So that must have happened before he went to *The Golden Fiend.*

"No, he'd say that sober. We get why you guys do this, but what's merely extremely dangerous for us is completely suicidal for humans."

"Yeah, I get that a lot. Anyway, if he can keep his opinions to himself for a while," Rain and Schuyler both burst out laughing. "Okay, if he can tolerate us for a short time, he'd be a welcome addition," Rick said with a slight wince.

She couldn't help a slight grin. "I'll talk to him. When were you planning on leaving?"

"Either today or tomorrow morning," he replied.

"We're not in a rush," Schuyler added, "especially when it's going to start getting far more dangerous soon enough."

"We were planning on leaving early tomorrow anyway." Her uncle was definitely not going anywhere today. She turned as Damien sat heavily beside her. He looked gaunt and his eyes were bloodshot. He wasn't wearing his armour, just a loose shirt, pants, and boots. "You look like hell."

"Aren't you a ray of fucking sunshine?" He said, drinking from his flask.

"Hey, I got you back here alive," she reminded him, pushing an empty glass in front of him and filling it with water she drew from the air. "Water will help more than hair of the dog."

He glared at her. "You sound like your mother."

"I'll take that as a compliment." Uncle Damien shook his head but drank down the water, glaring again when she refilled it. "So, how much of that did you overhear?" She asked, aware that the Ranger and Schuyler were watching them.

He closed his eyes for a moment and rubbed at his temples. "Not a fucking thing, too hungover."

"Does he do this often?" Rick wondered, apparently rethinking his offer. Damien opened his eyes to glare at him. "Ah, okay... I was wondering if you and your apprentice wanted to travel with us to Kelaroon. Things have gotten pretty damn bad around there and we need to make sure the prince arrives safely."

"Fine," Damien said and turned to Rain. "At the very least it'll help you save up for that tattoo." Rain had started saving up for an armour tattoo, for all she'd have to wait another three years to get it. It was a powerful spell and therefore extremely expensive, but worth the money.

The Ranger winced. "I don't know how you guys do it, tattoos hurt like hell."

"Not really," the Hunters replied in unison. Uncle Damien turned to Rain and raised a brow. There were a few exceptions to the 'three years' rule.

"That's what I hear from everyone," she said quickly. No one needed to know that she and Kestrel had both gotten anti-fertility spell tattoos almost two years before.

"Right," her uncle said, brow still raised. "Anyway, I know the Council doesn't want neophytes around Kelaroon right now, but I think you've proven that you can handle yourself, and I'll be around anyway."

"What do you consider a neophyte anyway?" The Ranger asked. "I mean, even the younger Hunters and Guardians seem more than capable of fighting Fiends."

"Three years or so after graduation," her uncle replied, pushing the empty glass towards her to refill again, which she did. "Now, that's three years actively hunting. For Guardians it's more like five years, because there's legal shit they have to be able to handle as well." He drained the glass and waved down a maid to order food. "What about your lot?" He nearly managed to keep his disdain for Rangers out of his voice. Nearly.

"Five years," he replied, "and we don't have an Academy or anything like that, not that a few of us haven't tried to get in."

"You'd die," was the blunt reply.

"It can't be that brutal," Rick protested.

Rain put her hand flat on the table. "Stab me." He looked aghast. "Really, stab me," she insisted. Rick looked at her uncle, who shrugged. Rain sighed and took one of her own knives and brought it down hard on her hand. She felt the subtle fizzle of the impact of the blade against her protection spell, but that was it. The humans' eyes went wide. "All students have armour spells, we learn and practice with live weapons."

"And we can't use those spells," Schuyler remarked absently, staring at her hand.

"Fine, you win," Rick surrendered, holding up his hands. Talk changed to travel plans, arguments about what route to take. Other Rangers and soldiers joined them, and Warren returned from wherever he'd been. Damien wasn't as familiar with the Kelaroon region as he was with other places, but he knew enough to make some suggestions. Eventually, they settled on a route that would take three days and they would be able to avoid camping.

"What about weather?" One soldier asked. "I know its spring, but there's still a risk of a storm."

"Water magic," Rain told them, waving her hand through the air and creating a mini flurry. "I have a limited influence on the weather as well." The soldier nodded as the plans were finalised and they figured out what they needed to acquire.

"I'm going back to bed," Damien decided when Schuyler and Warren's escort left them alone with the two humans. Rain nodded as he walked away. She'd have an early night as well.

On second thought, maybe early wasn't early enough, she decided as she covered a yawn. "You know, I think I'm going to get some sleep as well. We're all going to need our strength."

"Isn't Kelaroon where your friend died?" Warren asked as she stood.

Rain nodded, swallowing hard. "Aiden was talented, and his mentor was a highly respected Hunter who barely made it out alive." She didn't mention that Jerek refused to talk about what had happened and had nearly quit hunting. Hell, she'd seen him just before they'd left and he still didn't look right.

"We've heard rumours about what's out there," Schuyler said grimly. "What do you think are our chances if we come up against something like that? I mean, so far everything I've read said that the normal Fiends gather around them."

"Do exactly what Uncle Damien tells you and the losses will be minimal," she said. "But I really don't think everyone in this party is going to make it to Kelaroon alive."

It only took until sunset on the first day for them to see just how bad the situation was. Two of the soldiers were dead and one Ranger had suffered major wounds that had two other comrades taking him back to Avern for treatment.

"Hellfire alive," Rain swore as they arrived at the village where they'd planned to stay the night. It was destroyed. Villagers stumbled across corpses and still-smoking ruins as a cold spring rain fell around them.

"Rain," her uncle said, glancing up at the sky. Rain nodded and closed her eyes for a moment, gathering her magic and drawing power from the rain. She thrust her hands up and apart, scattering the clouds and stopping the rainfall, the effort leaving her breathless for a moment

A Guardian spotted them and stumbled over, clutching the bloody stump of her arm close to her body. "Go north," she said. "The Fiends were headed that way and there's another village not half an hour from here. We have everything under control."

"I'm not staying behind," Schuyler said before anyone could say anything. "I'm as good as a battlefield medic."

"But-" Rick started to argue.

"No time, let's go." Damien kicked his horse into a gallop and Rain followed right behind him. She heard cursing, but soon the rest of the group was close behind. They hadn't gone far when her warning charm began to heat up, so she pulled the water on the ground around her, forming it into deathly sharp icicles, quickly destroying a Fiend that came at them. She caught Damien's gaze and glanced back at the humans. He nodded and she dropped back, circling to the rear of the group. The Rangers didn't argue, just moved up to the middle while soldiers drew their bows.

They were almost there when the screaming started.

Somehow the scene was always the same in these situations: villagers ran, trying to escape the Fiends, some valiantly tried to help others, some just tried to save themselves. Guardians fought or directed villagers to safety, another Hunter fought nearby. The screams, the scent of blood, the ring of steel against rough hide, claw, and bone would have overwhelmed her six months ago, but not now. Later she would let herself feel empathy for the survivors and pity for the victims. She'd fought battles like this twice, and she'd had nightmares for weeks afterward, the present and past colliding in vicious and cruel ways.

"Don't take any stupid risks," Damien ordered as they separated to cover more ground, operating like Hunters were trained to do. She went after the closest Fiend; it was roughly her height and a strange lavender shade. It turned away from the human it had cornered to face her.

"Hey fucker, come get me!" She called out. The Fiend lunged and she stepped out of the way, slicing its head off with a clean stroke. The human barely looked at her and ran. She could see two Guardians as well as the fighters from their group. Two more Fiends rushed her. Rain jumped, landing squarely on the hunched back of the smaller Fiend and throwing herself past the larger, taking its head as she flipped over it and kicking its body at the other. She lunged and killed the smaller in a single blow before a rather large set of claws struck with bruising force, throwing her into the side of a stone building, the wall buckling. While the armour spell protected her from any true damage, it still hurt like hell as she slid to the ground, rolling as the Fiend punched through the wall where she had been. She severed its legs before removing the head. She didn't collect any fangs, though. It wasn't the time or the place to be concerned about that. Now she just had to focus on the fight, on where her enemies and allies were, figuring out her own place in the space of a heartbeat. The Rangers fought as a group, working to take down the weaker Fiends while the soldiers went to help the Guardians, leaving the average and strong Fiends for the Hunters. Rain suspected her uncle's hand in their actions, but didn't dwell on it as she cleaved a Fiend in half.

She fought, time fading away until it didn't matter, along with any aches, fatigue, the splatters of blood that soaked through her clothing. She fought with ice and steel, ruthless and fast. Every Fiend that fell beneath her blade was one more person that would survive. Something shifted and snapped beneath her boot as she ran towards another enemy, the sensation strange enough that she looked down. It was an arm. There was nothing attached to it, no body, just an arm, lying on a patch of stained earth.

"Rain!" She looked up in time to drop into a roll, narrowly avoiding a fist like an anvil aimed at her head. She came up jumping, stabbing her sword high into the Fiend's back and using it to lever herself up, a second blade made of ice forming in her other hand to take the head. Ragged claws dug into her sides, dragging her back as the body fell. She jerked her blade free and thrust it back over her shoulder, feeling a grim kind of satisfaction when the Fiend shrieked, dropping her as it reared back. Her boot went through what had been someone's ribcage, but she didn't let herself think about it, just kicked free and jumped back to avoid another strike as Uncle Damien came up from behind to make the kill.

"There's four left," he said, frowning as she retrieved her sword from the fallen Fiend's eye socket. One of the first rules of combat was to never let go of her weapon, even if she could create one out of ice. "Let's go." She took off after him, jumping to the roof of one house to get a better view and to avoid the bodies that littered the roads. Damien joined her. "I told Ranger Rick and the others to help deal with the survivors and the dead."

Rain nodded as she assessed the remaining Fiends with a quick look. One of the two on the left looked like it might be real trouble, and she could only see one to the right, meaning the other was likely smaller or inside one of the homes. "I'll take the two on the right." Damien could handle the other two without any trouble. He nodded and took off again. Rain leaped from rooftop to rooftop until she could drop onto her target, plunging her blade through its skull as she landed on one shoulder, throwing the Fiend off balance. She jumped again as the Fiend stumbled and she struck as she landed on top of it, slicing halfway through its thick neck. She moved fast and finished the job before it hit the ground. Standing, she looked around for her last target when the scream of a child drew her attention.

Rain didn't hesitate, running in the direction of the screaming. She lunged through the doorway, her blade outstretched, and had to pull back before she skewered a young boy. The Fiend had the child in its claws and was about to rip his head off. She thrust outward with her power, freezing the Fiend. Changing her grip on her sword, she brought the hilt down on the hand that held the boy with all her strength, shattering it. The child was screaming and sobbing as she picked him up and sliced the Fiend's head from its shoulders. She looked down at the boy and realised that he had slight frostbite from her magic.

"I'm sorry," she said as he cried. "Let's find your people." She didn't want to say parents, not when she didn't know if they were alive. She carried the child out to a Guardian who quickly took charge of him, looking from the frostbite to her. "He was about to be killed."

"That'll heal," the woman told her. "Thanks for your help."

Rain nodded. "Have you seen my uncle? He's a Hunter, tall, black hair with some grey, silvery eyes."

"*Silver* hair, thank you very much, it's a metal mage *silver*, not grey, and there's not much," Damien insisted as he came up behind her, "hardly any at all." The Guardian snorted and walked away.

"I can see it from here," she pointed out as the adrenaline faded, leaving her tired and aching. Dawn wasn't far off, so they'd been fighting through the night. No wonder she was exhausted.

"Shut up," he said without heat, rubbing a hand over the stubble on his jaw. "Deal with the Fiend corpses, then we can find some place to rest."

"Sounds good, *old man*," she said with a cheerful mock-salute, ignoring his glare as she started retracing her path and burning corpses as she went. She was probably going to need a new fire spell soon, she could feel it starting to wear out.

Now that the fight was over the humans were venturing through the village again, searching for survivors and loved ones. Some just stood still, staring at severed limbs and ruined buildings like they couldn't quite understand what was going on. She tuned it out, especially the desperate voices that carried through the air, calling out names. She tried to block out the memory of her uncle's rough, hoarse voice yelling for her as he trailed blood through their home. She'd already been down the rabbit hole of 'what if' questions over the years: What if her uncle had died? What if he or her mother had been away? What if her father or sister had been killed? Would anyone have found her? She refused to fall into that trap again, like the first time she'd had to help save a village. Like her uncle had pointed out then: there was little sense in dwelling on what hadn't happened, not when the future would hold more than enough horror. Hunter wisdom had a tendency to be rather grim.

"Never gets any easier, does it?" She looked up to see Rick leaning heavily against a building, examining a shallow wound on his arm.

"Nope," she agreed, casting fire at the withered body of a Fiend beside her.

"Need help with that?"

She shook her head. "Uncle Damien and I have it covered, and I think I saw another Hunter around here somewhere."

He nodded. "Yeah, Hannah Coal, I think."

She hadn't seen Hannah in a while. "I know her; she's one of my sister's friends." Rain also knew that she was one of the many potential apprentices that Uncle Damien had turned down over the years. She'd ended up with Amber and had actually introduced Kestrel to her.

"Cool. I'll go see if the Guardians need help," he said and walked away. Rain moved on, working until she saw Warren and Schuyler standing in the cracked doorway of a home, just staring inside. She sighed and walked up beside them to look inside. The body of a small child lay in pieces.

"What are you supposed to be doing?" She asked gently. Warren jumped and swung his sword at her but she blocked it easily with a dagger.

"Sorry," he mumbled, pale and shaken as he sheathed his sword.

"What are you supposed to be doing?" She repeated the question, her tone calm and firm.

"We… we're looking for wounded survivors," the prince said. "To bring to the medics."

"She didn't survive, so you need to keep moving." She gently pulled the humans to face her.

"How do you do this?" Schuyler demanded. "How can you stay so calm and…" he trailed off, looking around them.

"Exhaustion helps," she replied with a wan smile. "You just… just focus on the task at hand and keep moving. That's all you can do, really."

"Does it get easier to deal with?"

"Not really, you just get better at dealing with it, or you break." She put a hand on his shoulder and squeezed gently while she pulled him away from the door. "There's nothing you can do here, so you need to move on. It's pretty damn cold for spring and any wounded survivors need help *now*." He nodded and left, Warren at his heels. Rain took one last look at the child. "I'm sorry," she told the body, and then she moved on.

12

Final Test

It was well into the morning when Damien looked around and realised there were no more Fiends left to burn. He glanced over at Hannah, who'd appeared around a corner. The redhead with dark tear-filled eyes looked exhausted and defeated, shaking as she approached him.

"What happened?" He asked. She'd been a full Hunter for two years, she shouldn't have been this affected by a village getting attacked by Fiends.

"Fern is dead," she replied in a hollow tone, naming another of Storm's friends he'd seen a few times over the years, a quiet girl with green hair and pale brown eyes. "I'm bringing her home."

"I'm sorry to hear that. Did she die in the fight?" He couldn't remember anyone mentioning a fourth Hunter in the village, and he definitely hadn't seen the other young woman.

Hannah shook her head, tears falling. "Two days ago... I barely got away." Damien frowned, she didn't look injured to him. "I grabbed her and fled. She died a few hours later."

"What were you running from?" He didn't know her well, but he did know that she was no coward.

"It was awful," she said, shaking harder.

"What could it do?" He asked. A normal Fiend wouldn't leave a Hunter wrecked like that.

"It... it makes you into what you fear most," she explained, tripping over her words as she tried to get them out. "If you make eye contact with it, it'll take what you fear turning into most and make it real, and there's no way to fight it."

That was rather detailed information for having encountered something once. "How did you find out about that?

"We heard other Hunters talking about it. That's why the Council put out the order against neophytes entering the region, because it's responsible for half the Hunters and Guardians who've died in around here. Fern and I thought we could take it." She started to weep, wrapping her arms around her body. "We were wrong."

"Did you make eye contact with it?"

She shook her head. "Fern stepped in front of me. We didn't even last a full minute against it. She was afraid of going mad, like her aunt. She ended up killing herself a few hours later to escape it."

"And the Fiend just let you go?"

"It wasn't like the others, it was smart, it knew that there was nothing we could do to fight it," she cried, falling to her knees. "There's nothing you can do, and you're completely aware of what's happening the whole time. Fern fought against it so hard, but there was nothing she could do."

"Okay." He didn't bother trying to offer words of comfort or to convince her that what happened wasn't her fault; he knew it would do nothing. That Fiend was one possible explanation for what was going on in Kelaroon. The powerful Fiends, the truly sentient and intelligent ones, could exert kind of control or influence over the others that drew them in, made them even more aggressive than normal and set them to targeting villages, towns, or even cities instead of travelers. He'd seen it before and could only thank the few mercies of the gods that they weren't common.

"I have her ashes," Hannah said. "I'm bringing her home."

"We have everything under control here. If you leave now, you can make Avern before nightfall and rest there for a day or two before you keep going. Does Storm know?"

"I sent the message to the Academy yesterday, along with her medallion." Damien nodded. "I don't know how I'll ever forgive myself for this," she said, looking skyward.

"Just try to remember that as much as it was your choice it was also hers. It was her decision to protect you. She wanted you to live, so honour her last wish if you can't do anything else. Now, I need to know where the Fiend is." No wonder they didn't want neophytes out here. Hell, if the Council found out what this thing could do they would likely bar a number of more experienced Hunters as well, himself included.

"Half a day's ride north… I've got a map." He waited while she went to get it, considering the situation. If the Fiend was having success with Hunters and Guardians it likely wasn't going to move much. The intelligent Fiends tended to target his kind over humans, as though they knew who the real enemy was, or like they knew who would put up a real challenge. Possibly even to the point of letting one Hunter get away in the hopes of having stronger prey come forward. Not exactly the kind of thing he wanted to think about, but he had to consider all options. When Hannah returned she showed him a spot in the forest, burning a slim line into the heavy paper to show the path she'd taken.

He had a choice to make: either go after the Fiend or hope someone else would do it and succeed. He'd fought similar Fiends on his own before and won, but he had the scars to prove that it wasn't easy. Rangers and soldiers were useless at best, and the only other Hunter around who could help was Rain. This was one of the reasons he'd avoided being a mentor for so long: having to deal with the line between teaching someone and throwing them into a dangerous situation. He was already skirting it by having her with him in this region. Despite a certain distaste for authority, Council decisions to keep Hunters below a certain level of experience out of certain regions had been something he and Tempest had mostly obeyed. At the very least they'd taken the decisions into account when preparing to enter those regions. Right now, Rain was the only kind of backup he had, he didn't know where the other Hunters in the region were, let alone who they were. He knew damn well that if he went after this thing Rain would follow him. She was too much like her parents that way. He also had no doubt that Hannah would give her the same information she'd given him because Rain would ask, and his knew too much to trust him on his own against this particular Fiend. Hell, she'd be right not to. But if he took her with him and something happened… he didn't know what he'd do. He'd already come close to losing her with the bandits, he didn't want her in that kind of position again. Was it such a bad thing that he wanted her to be safe for as long as possible?

"Well?" Rain asked, coming up beside him after Hannah had gone, already on the road again. It was obvious she'd spoken to the other Hunter.

"I don't know," he admitted. "This thing… it's going to be far more dangerous than anything you've ever faced."

"But it probably won't be the most dangerous thing I'll ever face." He leaned against a wall with a sigh. "I swear I'll do whatever you say." He could see the determination in her eyes.

Fuck, he was going to go to Hell a thousand times over if this went badly and maybe still if it went well. "You don't go after it head on," he said in a low, intense voice. "Hell, you don't even go near it. You stay back and attack it from a distance unless you have no other choice." He could at least make certain that he took the greater risk. "And if I tell you to run, you run like hell and don't look back. No matter what."

She hesitated for a moment, but nodded. "Understood. I'll tell Schuyler and Warren." They could decide if they wanted to stay and wait for them or keep going. He didn't really care which.

He nodded. "Consider this your final exam. No one will be able to question if you've earned your medallion after this." If she lived.

They rode hard, pushing the horses through the rain as they made their way to the spot Hannah had pointed out on the map. Rain drew in all the power she could, using it to re-energise herself. She knew Uncle Damien was doing the same thing using magic he stored in his blades and armour. She was afraid, terrified, but all the more determined for it. This was her chance to prove to herself that she had what it took to stand with the best of her kind. Of course, there were of students and apprentices who took down an army of powerful Fiends wielding nothing but magic and a dagger, but she wasn't so foolish as to aspire to that. If she could help her uncle take this thing down, then she felt that she'd earned her place, earned the right to hold onto her dream of being an elite Hunter. Her warning spell went off and she looked around, but saw nothing.

"Remember, the stronger Fiends attack the weak but won't always let them close," Damien said. "I wouldn't be surprised if we don't see another until we get to the bastard's clearing."

"Right." They'd learned about that at the Academy.

It wasn't long before her mount reared back, almost throwing her. It wasn't a horse trained to bear a Hunter, just an extra that the soldiers had brought along. She managed to get the animal under control and hopped off. There was no point in forcing the poor creature to go any further. Uncle Damien also dismounted, his horse shaking, the whites of its eyes visible. They tied both horses to a tree and continued on foot, going deeper and deeper in to the forest until they reached a thicket of trees that surrounded the clearing they'd been looking for. The Fiend stood in the middle of it. It was a few inches taller than Uncle Damien, its eyes closed, and Rain could see a third eye in the middle of its high forehead was also closed. That aside, it was one of the more humanoid-looking Fiends she'd seen. It wore rough-looking pants, though its heavily muscled torso was bare. She looked at her uncle but didn't speak. Fiends had even better hearing than her people did. She held up her ring and he nodded. She twisted it and watched as the Fiend's three eyes glowed a malevolent dark red. She twisted it back and managed to relay the information with hand signals. Its eyes were the source of its power, which what they'd expected because of Hannah's information. He nodded and drew his sword, motioning for her to stay, that he would go around and try to attack the thing from behind. Rain nodded and waited for him to move before she climbed the nearest tree, using the foliage as cover to get right to the edge of the treeline where she would have the best view and remain hidden. She was absolutely still as she waited, afraid to use her magic until the fight began in case the Fiend could sense the shift in the air or her power itself.

Damien burst out of the trees at the Fiend's back, his daggers flying ahead of him like deadly silver butterflies. The Fiend turned, eyes opening, but her uncle was careful about not meeting its gaze, trying to direct his blades at the eyes filled with a malevolent cunning that sent shivers through her. Rain worked from her hiding spot, sending spears of ice that froze to the Fiend's skin on contact and spread, trying to weigh it down or just slow it down. It just flexed its muscles, shattering the ice as it swiped the blades out of the air. She had to be careful not to affect her uncle as she created a sheet of smooth ice beneath its feet, but the claws on its toes dug in. Damien managed to score a deep wounds in its side, but the Fiend was unaffected as it lunged, knocking him aside. Rain pulled up the ice into a battering ram as it tried to pin her uncle to the ground, slamming the monster into the trees. She winced at the loud crack as one fell to the ground and turned back to Damien. Tiny bolts of silver lightning started running along the length of her uncle's sword. If he could touch the Fiend with that blade, it would be very dead. It was something that took a lot of skill and a lot of power to maintain for even a short time, making it a skill that was saved for more dire times and one that set him apart from other metal mages and Hunters. Rain shifted to get a better view so she could wrap the Fiend in ice, keeping it still for the killing blow, maybe covering its eyes or putting them out with icicles. But she stepped wrong, and the branch beneath her foot broke, sending her falling to the ground. She managed to catch herself on a low branch and drop unhurt, but she'd saved herself just a moment too late to stop what happened next.

The Fiend had risen once more, its back to the Hunters. Her uncle lunged, swinging his glowing, lightning-shrouded blade. Then faster than anything she'd seen, it turned and grabbed him by the neck with one hand, breaking his arm with the other. Damien went rigid, and she knew he'd met the Fiend's gaze. She surged forward, screaming as the monster tossed him back. She just barely avoided making eye contact as it turned its attention to her.

"Uncle Damien!" She screamed as her uncle shifted and stood. He met her gaze, a wild desperation in his quicksilver eyes as he pulled a dagger from his boot with his good hand, though it trembled. She shrieked as he raised the blade towards his own throat, ducking an attack by the Fiend as she barreled into him, knocking the blade away as she forced him to the ground.

"Killing it is the only thing that's going to stop me," he hissed, breathless as he struggled against himself. Rain jumped to her feet, keeping her eyes on the Fiend's shoulders as she lunged, sending a barrage of ice spears in front of her. It kicked with blurring speed, connecting with her side and sending her flying. She pushed off the ground with one hand, cartwheeling to her feet. It was on her again, relentless. She barely managed to avoid or block the blows while keeping from meeting its gaze and watching her uncle. He was kneeling, head in his hands, fighting his own battle. She did a backflip to avoid a hit, cursing silently. How the hell was she going to do this when she had to focus way too much on where she was looking? She knew the Fiend was watching for an opportunity to look her in the eyes, and she knew what the consequences would be. What she feared becoming most was a failure, watching as everyone she loved get killed because of her incompetence. She had to do what her uncle was trying to do initially, and blind the fucker so she could have a chance. Fiends could heal from anything short of a fatal blow, but it took time. More than enough time for her finish things. She turned and ran towards the trees, trusting it to follow her since it would have written Damien off as a threat.

Rain took a deep breath to help her focus. It may have stopped raining while they were on the road but there was more than enough water to draw into the air until it was like there was a heavy rain, if raindrops hovered in place. Every drop was tied to her magic, and she knew the tiniest twitch the Fiend made. It had stopped moving, waiting, watching with inhuman intensity. She twisted, the movement a distraction as she made the droplets freeze over its head and sent spikes of ice through all three eyes before it could free itself. It screamed, clawing blindly at the ice. She quickly stepped aside, but not fast enough. While its powers may have relied on sight, it was still a Fiend. It broke the ice apart and lunged, pinning her down. Rain twisted onto her front, reaching for the sword that she had dropped and now lay just beyond her outstretched finger tips.

"Help!" She screamed, hoping her uncle could fight off the magic long enough to help her, long enough to *live*. "Uncle Damien!" She cried out as razor claws began to break through her armour spell, raking down her back, though corset saved her from the worst of the damage. She twisted back around and reached up to shove daggers in the Fiend's eye sockets, driving them deeper as she kicked hard, shoving it away enough to struggle free.

"Move!" She jumped back as silver lightning arced past her and the Fiend's head exploded from its shoulders the moment the blade touched its flesh. Uncle Damien fell to his knees beside the smoking body, breathing hard. Rain wrapped her arms around herself, shaking. He looked up at her and stood so he could pull her into a tight hug, and he was shaking just as badly as she was. "It's okay," he murmured against her hair. "It's okay, we're both fine." She realised then that she was crying. "You did great."

After a while she managed to calm down enough to stop crying. She stepped away to look at the Fiend, now a withered, blackened corpse on the grass. She reached down and snapped off a fang, stepping back so her uncle could burn it, something vicious in his gaze as he did. "How much do you think we'll get for this one?" She asked, voice cracking slightly as she got her emotions under control.

"You'd be able to afford that tattoo even if we split the take," he said wearily as she put it in a pouch. "Turn around; I want to see where it got you."

"It hurts, but it's not too bad," she told him, turning and wincing when he prodded the wounds.

"Shallow scrapes, they'll heal in no time."

"What about your arm?" .

"Yeah…" He held it out with a grimace and she watched as the metal plates in his vambrace shifted and moved out from under the leather to form a splint that forced the bones back in place. He pulled rolled up bandages out of a pouch on his belt and handed it to her so she could wrap it and make a sling while he took a deep gulp from his flask, his face almost grey. "I think after this we deserve a nice long stay home. Hell, once the Headmistress is done yelling at me for bringing you out here we should be able to just sit out the next few months."

"Can you sit around for that long?" she asked, tying off the bandage. He held his arm gingerly against his stomach, recalling his dropped daggers with a wave of his hand.

"Well, we'll take a break, anyway," he said as they started walking back to the horses. "I'd like to turn around and go home, but I think we should keep going to Kelaroon. They've got the closest healer and just because this fucker is dead doesn't mean it's safe on the roads."

"Okay, but then we go home and I'm going to sleep for a week." She paused, about to ask something, but stopped herself.

He noticed. "What?"

"How bad was it?" Her uncle looked away from her.

They made it back to the horses before he answered her. "It was... awful. I just..." he paused, and she had the sense he was trying to decide how much to tell her. "I knew it was magic making me want to do it. I knew it, but in a way it didn't matter." He didn't say anything more about it and something told her not to push him on it. She glanced up at the sky.

"It can't be just midday," she complained. "It feels like it should be night. Late night." She was certain she was going to crash soon. "How long have we been awake?"

"I don't want to think about it. If those humans want to travel any more today, I will stab them." Rain couldn't tell if he was joking or not.

The journey home was far less exciting, for which Rain was grateful. Apprentices and mentors were supposed to be back in the territories by the end of the eleventh month, and then the final assessments took place. It was a short process that mostly consisted of the mentor telling the Academy officials if they believed a student was ready to graduate, and the officials looking through the student's records to make sure there was nothing that stood out as a red flag. Once that was done the mentor created their apprentice's insignia and their new medallion was made. During this time most of the students started forming groups and making plans for their first independent hunts. When Damien returned from the Academy he found Rain and her friend Kestrel with a map spread out on the table. For a moment he stood in the doorway, watching them as they planned a route. He could still remember when that had been himself and Tempest arguing over where to go first.

"Can you believe it?" Ash asked quietly, coming up behind him. "Time's gone by so damn fast."

"No shit." It seemed like just yesterday Rain was racing Storm to meet him when he came home after a long hunt. He didn't really know how he felt about the year ending. It would be a lot of responsibility off his shoulders, but he couldn't say that he hadn't enjoyed it. It wasn't even like it was truly over, considering they lived in the same house and most apprentices kept in touch with their mentors. Hell, he'd been hunting with Ember more than once in the intervening years and still went to her for help sometimes. It was the way Hunters worked, trying to keep each other alive and fighting.

It seemed like no time passed before Rain was on the stage in the Guardian Academy auditorium, facing a crowd of families, younger students, and people from around the territories. On one side of the sat the students about to graduate. There were less of them than there had been a year ago: four were dead and three had quit. There were also more scars and metal limbs than there had been, but less than there would be in a few years' time. On the other side were the mentors, the full Hunters. The differences between the two groups weren't quite so obvious anymore.

The Headmistress went to the front of the stage and read out her end of year speech, about the bravery of the class, the sacrifices they had made, the experiences they'd had and the promise they showed. Like her speech before, this was the same one she made every year, though the names of the fallen were different. Rain glanced around and caught her uncle's eye. He winked before turning to look ahead, and she did too, looking for her father and Storm. She found them, and Phantom was there as well. She and Kestrel had a bet going on how long it would take for him to propose.

At last the names were being called -in alphabetical order, of course. Rain sat and waited with growing impatience, watching as her friends walked up to the front of the stage. This time things were a little different. Mentors still rose and went to the front as well, only now they took the apprentice medallion from the student and once the student said the oaths of service to their people and the world the magic on the apprentice medallion faded, allowing their mentor to replaced it with their Hunter medallion. These medallions had their personal insignia on one side and that of the Academy on the other, along with the Hunter's name. Like the apprentice medallions, they were spelled to stay around the neck of the Hunter until their body was burned to ash or they rescinded their vows. Once the student received the medallion, they followed their mentor to sit with the rest of the full Hunters, a student no longer. Rain clenched her hands into fists, watching as Kestrel went up. Soon. Soon it would be her turn.

Just a few more people to go. It took everything in her to sit still and wait. She hadn't been sure how she would feel about this, she thought maybe she would be nervous about leaving the Academy and being a true Hunter, but she was excited. This was what she'd been working for her entire life. This was the moment she'd been waiting for. In a few days she and Kestrel would be heading out, Hunters at last, ready to teach the Fiends the meaning of fear.

"Rain Undine."

Rain stood and walked slowly to the front of the stage, like she'd been told, though she wanted so badly to run. Uncle Damien went to stand opposite her.

"Do you hereby vow to not only stand against the Fiends, but also to seek them out and eliminate them from all corners of the world?" The Headmistress asked.

"I do." She answered.

"Do you hereby vow to act in a manner befitting a Hunter, as you have been trained?"

"I do."

"Do you hereby accept the responsibilities and the burdens that all Hunters must bear?"

"I do." A final answer.

"Then, Rain Undine, by the will of Hunter Damien Lance, by the will of the Academy, and by the will of the Council I grant you the title of Hunter." Rain had to supress her elation as Uncle Damien stepped forward and lifted the apprentice medallion from her neck, grinning with a fierce kind of pride as he replaced it her Hunter medallion. She felt a slight tingle over her skin, magic settling deep within her, binding the medallion to her.

"You did it, kiddo," he murmured before stepping back.

The Headmistress addressed the crowd now: "To all here, I present to you Hunter Rain Undine." Rain faced the audience and stepped forward. She could hear her father and sister cheering loudest of all. After a few seconds she stepped back and walked with her uncle to the other side of the stage, sitting down with the other Hunters. Not with *the* Hunters, with the *other* Hunters, because she was one of them now. She lifted the medallion to see what her insignia was. There were three raindrops side by side, the middle one larger with a simple snowflake at its heart. The medallion was slightly larger than the signet rings human nobles used, made of silver, the raised edges etched with ancient runes.

"What do you think?" Damien asked in a low voice only she could hear.

"It reminds me of Mom's insignia," she realised. Her mother's had been a snowflake inset with a raindrop. "I like it." He grinned, but didn't say anything as the next student had been called up. After the last graduate had joined the ranks of the Hunters they stood as one to thunderous applause. The party tonight would by far eclipse that of the year before, because now she and her classmates were no longer students, no longer children. They'd proven themselves as capable warriors fit to join the ranks of the Hunters as peers.

Now the real work began.

Rain couldn't wait.

Part 3
Heart

1

Broken

Damien wasn't sure what he would find when he walked into *The Fallen Guardian*. He paused for a moment, the dread that had been growing for the last year a heavy weight on his heart. He'd had a feeling it would come to this, though he would have given anything to be wrong. Maybe he should have been happy that she'd finally decided that she wanted to be found and that she wanted help, but it was hard because he'd never wanted this for her. He'd never wanted her to be in this position. Never wanted her to be like him. He took a deep breath and walked inside.

"Hey kiddo," he said quietly, slipping onto a barstool beside her. This bar was the haunt of the fallen, the broken. It shouldn't have been the place to find a twenty-four year old.

"You know, I was almost temped to just wait and see how long it would take for you to show up," Rain said. She was clearly well past her first drink even as she downed the liquor in front of her and signaled the bartender for another. As soon as the man saw Damien he brought over a second glass and filled both, leaving the bottle. "Did you know that seeking spells have a distinctive glow, especially when they're bright pink?" She tapped the magic ring she'd inherited from her mother.

"I'm sure Yasia will find that amusing." He didn't bother denying her implied accusation. She'd vanished before she was fully healed and then barely wrote back for a while until the letters stopped altogether. They'd all been going insane with worry so he'd gone to the Finder for help and had been keeping tabs on her for the last six months. She hadn't been home in over a year.

"Is Dad here?" Rain looked like hell. She was almost gaunt, her bloodshot eyes ringed with dark circles and her skin had an unhealthy pallor, a far cry from the last time he'd seen her two years ago. There were wounds visible on her skin, cuts and bruises that were the signs of a recent fight. He wondered when she'd last seen a healer, since any of them would have reported her to the Council as unfit for duty and they would have tried to bring her home to get help. Damien wished he'd gone after her, but he'd known that dragging someone back before they were ready often made things worse.

"No, he was getting ready for work when I left."

"I'm shocked," she said with a mirthless, hollow laugh. "He was threatening to tear up the countryside looking for me a few months ago." Likely around the same time Ash had begged him to do something. Unfortunately Damien had been trapped in northern Phasoia by a hard winter, fighting the whole time. Over the last five years the number of Fiends in their part of the world had exploded and too many Hunters and Guardians were dying while Keepers struggled to figure out what the hell was going on.

"I didn't show him the note. He has no idea you're anywhere near the territories." It seemed like the best decision. Rain's message had asked for him specifically and while Ash was an amazing father, he was still a father. This situation required something different.

"He also threatened to send you after me."

"I had faith you would you would reach out when you were ready. I was also just as worried as your father, so Yasia kept tabs on you to make sure you were alive once in a while." She finished off her drink and poured another, her movements stiff and slow. He could see tears in her eyes that she didn't bother to hide. Her left arm was heavily bandaged, a faint blush starting to seep through the linen, and he wondered just how badly she was hurt. He waited, sipping his whiskey as she downed that drink and another. Tempest had had it easy all those years ago, he realised as he watched Rain. It was one thing to watch a best friend fall apart and quite another to watch a niece, especially a niece he'd had a hand in raising since she was small. He wanted to hug her and yell at her for running away all at the same time, for making her family and her friends worry about her and for letting herself get so fucking close to the point of no return. He could see how close he'd come to losing her forever and it terrified him. What the hell had happened? He had to be missing something here, something no one had thought to tell him, or something that she had never told anyone and it was slowly killing her.

"I thought I could handle it. I just needed to get away after..." Her voice was barely audible as she poured herself another glass. She didn't drink it right away, just toyed with it, watching the whisky swirl around. "I thought I was doing okay, surviving. I really did. I just... I don't... know. I don't know." Her voice cracked and she took a deep breath. "I was in a fight a few days ago. It was bad... really bad. My magic had no effect on the Fiend, and it had claws like fucking razors. I won. Barely. And I was just lying there..." She took a drink, swallowing hard. "I was just... lying there, bleeding, and... I-I thought that... all I had to do... all... I just... if..." She started crying, her shoulders shaking. "If I just made the cuts a little deeper... I wouldn't have to feel like this anymore." She covered her face with her hands, trying to muffle her sobs. "I need help."

Fuck.

He wasn't ready for this. He'd known she'd had it rough, but he hadn't realised it was this bad. She was supposed to be like Ash, supposed to be able to deal with the harsh realities of their world and career path. Hell, up until about a year and a half ago she had been. Then her lover of four years had been killed by a Fiend. While she was still getting over that, she and eleven other Hunters who were her former classmates and close friends had been called on to clear out an area in western Glask where Fiends were destroying everything. Two had come out alive, including Rain. Well, most of Kestrel had come out, anyway. She'd left as soon as she was mobile, before her wounds had healed, and she hadn't returned. He downed his drink and leaned on the bar for a moment, head in his hands, his heart breaking. Then he turned so he could pull her into a tight embrace, letting her cry into his shoulder like she hadn't done since she'd been a small child, since that blood-soaked night when he'd found her in that closet and had to tell her that her mother was dead. He'd had no idea what to do then, either. He'd been badly wounded, he'd just watched his best friend die while he tried to fight his way to her, not to mention the state Storm had been in, covered in so much blood… Ash trying to fight off another Hunter to get to Rain though he could barely move for his own injuries. He felt as helpless now as he had then.

"I've got you," he murmured, just like he had all those years ago. "I've got you." He just let Rain cry, gently rubbing her back and trying not to think about the wounds beneath the bandages he could feel through her shirt. He didn't tell her that everything would be okay, because that would have been a lie. Things were not okay and likely never would be again, because that was the world they lived in and the path they walked. Their friends would keep dying around them and loved ones would never truly be safe. There were no happy endings for Hunters. Either they left the world too young or they were left behind.

"You were right," she said a while later, when she'd quieted down, though tears still fell from her sapphire eyes. "Being one of the best is a curse." He could remember when he'd said that to her, and while he had regretted his words when he'd sobered up it hadn't changed the fact that they were true. "Everyone else dies before me and I can't save them. Even when I do… I don't. I just don't want to feel like this anymore." She pulled away to wipe her eyes. "I don't want to kill myself, but I can't take it anymore." She took a drink from the bottle, ignoring the glass altogether now. "I couldn't tell Dad, I couldn't. If he knew… if he found out… I think it would destroy him and Storm's not a Hunter, so she wouldn't understand, not really. Kestrel… Kestrel has her own problems." And she blamed herself for them.

"You know I'm not the best person at dealing with the darkness inside." He was careful to keep his tone even. He'd never been good at fighting the monsters that lived in his head.

"Maybe… but you know how to live with it." It was impossible to miss the desperation in her eyes as she looked to him for guidance. He closed his eyes for a moment, covering his face with a hand. Rain was truly no longer a child, and he had to recognise that. The little girl who'd followed him around, who'd tried to copy him when he practiced, and who giggled when he swore was gone.

"I'm sorry, I know this can't be easy for you either, but you're the only person who can understand. Uncle Damien, please..."

He took a deep breath and looked at her. "You know I'm here for you."

She nodded and drank, the bottle of liquor over half empty when she spoke again. "Did you know that he proposed to me?"

"Blaze?" She nodded. "No, I didn't." They'd all known things were serious, but hadn't realised they were *that* serious. After seeing what had happened to both her uncle and her father Rain had been very guarded about her own heart.

"I told him I'd think about it." She wrapped her arms around herself again. "He died never knowing the answer." He didn't need to ask what it would have been, that much was obvious from her tone. "Why did I do that?" She murmured, looking down at the rough wooden counter, confused.

"Because you know far too much about how relationships usually end for Hunters?" He finished his drink and signaling for another bottle. It was hard to fall in love when there was a pretty fucking good chance that someone was going to be left heartbroken and grieving. Guardians tended to fare better, but right now everyone was fighting a losing battle unless they could find out what was causing the problem.

"Will it get any better?"

He closed his eyes for a moment and let out a slow breath. "You'll have good days, but you'll also have other days that are a fucking nightmare." He took a drink. "I know that's not what you want to hear, but that's how it is."

"I figured as much." She drained the bottle as the bartender put two more on the counter in front of them without a word. Good man. "Fuck, I can't even say no one warned me it would be like this. She opened the next bottle. "I thought I could handle it. Everyone thought I could. Oops." She laughed and drank. It was a hollow, broken sound.

"I thought you also knew that knowing and experiencing never quite match up," he said, giving up on his own glass and opening the other bottle. It wasn't his one night, but he could make an allowance for when he had to pull another Hunter out of the darkness, and right now Rain was drowning in it as she reached for a lifeline.

"I'd be surprised if ten of the Hunters I graduated with are still alive, let alone active right now. How's that for skill? We only graduated six years ago."

"Sometimes that happens," he said. "Wouldn't be the first time, won't be the last. The year after your dad finished was bad, only one Hunter is still alive. Everyone else was dead by the time they were twelve years out."

"Who?"

"Amber." He'd always wondered if the loss of her classmates had helped push her into being not only a consistent mentor, but a damn good one.

Rain gave him a sidelong glance. "I didn't realise Amber was older than you."

"Thanks," he said dryly, but she didn't smile or grin, and she certainly wasn't cackling like an imp the way she would have before.

"She's kinda like Dad, isn't she?"

"You mean a Hunter who's actually well-adjusted?" She nodded. "Yeah." It helped that she had Willow, but he felt it was best not to mention lovers.

"How do they do it?"

"If you ever find out you'll have to let me know. I've been wondering the same thing for years." He sighed and drank.

She was quiet for a long moment, swirling the whiskey around in the bottle before taking a drink. "So, what happens now?"

He was far gone enough that he didn't feel the burn of the whiskey going down his throat anymore, but he was still too sober for what he had to deal with. "Now we drink. We keep drinking until you don't feel anything anymore. Then at dawn we go home. You start sleeping right, eating right, seeing a damned healer when you're hurt, and exercising. Then we go out hunting again. We go for a week or two, and we go home. And we're going to keep doing that until you can do it on your own." He would do for her what Tempest had done for him two decades before and pray that it worked.

"How long do you think that'll take?" Her opinion on the matter was obvious and fell somewhere between never and forever.

He would be as stubborn as she was depressed. "However long it takes for you to get into a better headspace and you're going to be following the same rules I am: you pick one night of the year when the darkness can have you. Just one night a year and no more to remember those you've lost, to think about the horrors you've seen, and to grieve. One night and no more. The rest of the time you can drink enough to take off the edge, but no more than that. Just enough to keep you functional and sane."

"I don't know if you've noticed, but none of us are sane," she remarked in a dark tone.

"No shit. We go out and look for monsters to fight. No one who does that is sane. Can you live by those rules? I'm not going to lie, it's not easy; some days are going to be fucking impossible."

"Yeah, I can do that," she said after a moment. He knew it was just desperation that made her agree to this, the need to see some kind of solution, some kind of hope. But maybe it would be enough. It had been for him.

He signalled the bartender, who brought over two more bottles. Damien watched as she opened another and he started pacing himself. While the main roads were regularly patrolled it was still dangerous out there, stronger Fiends slowly creeping closer than they'd ever dared to the heart of his peoples' lands. In the morning Rain would be drunk, hungover, and still badly injured. Someone needed to be able to fight and it was going to have to be him. As it was they were going to be at the bar for a while; he'd never met a water mage who was a lightweight, and if right now was any indication Rain had been getting a fair amount of practice over the last year.

They didn't talk much for the rest of the night. When Rain started tipping over on her stool he brought her upstairs to one of the rooms where regulars could sleep off the night. Then he went back downstairs, filled both Rain's flask and his own from what remained in the bottles and waited for dawn to come, though he knew it would bring no reprieve. Not for him and not for her, not anymore.

2

Reunion

When dawn came Damien didn't want to move. If he stayed where he was he could pretend that none of this was real, that it was all just a dream and he'd had far more to drink than he'd thought he had and soon Ash would come drag his sorry ass home where Storm and a healthy, whole Rain would be sitting at the table, laughing. But he knew better.

"Hey Damien, looks like you've had a rough night," the day bartender, Brian, said as he stepped behind the counter. Unlike most bars *The Fallen Guardian* never closed.

"You have no fucking idea," he replied darkly, raking a hand through his hair. "I need my horse and another from the Academy." Even if Rain wasn't going to have the hangover from hell, he didn't think she'd be able to walk very far with her wounds.

"Waiting on someone?"

Not anymore. "Just have to wake her up."

Brian looked at his face for a moment and his expression fell. "Don't tell me it's Rain."

"Then I won't."

"Ah fuck, I thought she'd make it."

"Shit happens, you know that." Like the way everything had gone to hell over the last few years. More than a few good, stable Hunters and Guardians had broken under the strain, and the Keepers were starting to feel it as well after three years of trying to figure out what was going on.

"D'you think she'll be okay?" Brian asked after sending someone to do as Damien had asked.

The Hunter didn't answer as he rose and went up to the room he'd left her in. "Rain," he said, gently shaking her shoulder. She was awake in an instant, slashing out with a dagger. He'd expected as much to happen and had already moved out of the way. "It's time to go."

"I think I'm still drunk," she said, her voice hoarse.

"I think you're probably right." He helped her to her feet. "But look on the bright side: you're not stiff or sore."

"That's a good point," she agreed as she managed to find her balance. Then she stopped. "I don't think I'm ready to go home."

"First we're getting you to a healer, so you still have some time." He understood her trepidation, had felt the same when he was only a few years older than she was now. He could remember the fear of how everyone would react when he walked through the door, the guilt of having abandoned them a heavy weight that made him want to run again. In the end it hadn't been so bad, his nieces almost knocking him over when they threw themselves at him, both beyond ecstatic that he'd returned. Ash just said 'Welcome back' and let that be the end of it. Despite the fact that after Amber he was probably the most well-adjusted Hunter alive he still understood that not everyone could fight back the darkness.

There wasn't much early morning traffic in the city, but both Hunters kept their hoods up. Damien was fairly certain that Ash should have been on his way home, but there was no guarantee. They made it through the Academy gates and to the hospital without running into anyone they knew. Damien helped Rain dismount and they both went in, running into Willow, Amber's wife and a healer before they were two steps past the door.

"Rain!" She exclaimed, eyes wide at the young Hunter's appearance.

"Hi Willow," she mumbled, looking away from the critical gaze that took in every bruise, every scrape, her awkward posture, and likely a hundred other things only a healer would notice.

"You're coming with me." Her tone was harder than any diamond and allowed no dissent.

Damien waited for Rain's nod. "I will leave her in your capable hands." Willow waved him off, her attention on her patient. He shrugged and started walking back down the hall. If there was one person in the world he would be afraid to cross it was Willow. She was one of those rare people who could be both the kindest person in the world and the most terrifying, and that she was one of their best healers only added to both extremes. He quickly moved aside as Roderick came around the corner and nearly ran into him.

"Sorry. What've you done to yourself this time?" He asked, looking the Hunter over. Damien was well aware of the fact that he probably looked like shit.

"Not me, Rain," he replied. "She's back and she was hurt pretty badly."

"And you found her in a bar?" From the healer's tone Damien knew it wasn't that Roderick didn't believe him, it was that he didn't want to.

"Yeah. Willow's got her right now."

"I'll go see if I can help. Do Ash or Storm know she's here?"

Damien shook his head. "I'd rather keep it that way for now."

He paused. "I understand. No one will find out where she is from us. I'm going to see if Willow needs assistance."

Damien grabbed the healer's arm as he started to walk away. "She's hurting." Her wounds weren't just physical, they went down to the very core of her being.

Roderick nodded slowly. "I understand," he said and Damien released him. He went back outside to wait, needing the fresh air.

"What happened to you? You look like hell." Fuck. Of course Ash would be here and would find him. He sighed. "Damien, what happened after you ran off?" Damien considered his options and decided that now really wasn't the time for surprises.

"The message was from Rain." Ash looked from him to the hospital and started forward, but Damien stopped him with a hand on his shoulder. "I need you to listen. Do you remember when Tempest dragged me back here twenty years ago?" Ash's head snapped around like he'd been struck, green eyes wide. "Yeah, it's like that. It's as bad as we thought it could be."

"Fuck." He ran a hand over his face, closing his eyes. The fine lines in his face were suddenly in sharper relief than normal. In that moment he looked as old as Damien felt. "How… how bad is it?"

"From the way she was moving it was pretty bad, but Willow's got her now, and Roderick's going to do what he can as well."

Ash nodded, opening his eyes after a long moment. "She's back. That's all that matters. Anything else we can deal with."

"It's not going to be easy," Damien reminded him.

"I remember," Ash assured him. "But what about you? Are you going to be able to handle this?"

It was a fair question, more fair than Damien would have liked to admit. "I'll be fine." He just had to watch one of the few people he cared about struggle to survive the same crushing darkness that had almost finished him. Couldn't be that difficult, right? "I taught her to be one of the best. I guess it stands to reason I'll be the one to teach her how to survive it." No matter that he just barely managed it himself some days.

Ash took a long look at the hospital and sighed. "I'm going to go. Storm and Phantom need to hear about this. I'll see you later?"

"I'll bring her home." Ash gripped his shoulder for a moment and headed off. Damien watched him go. He wished once more that Tempest were still alive, though for the first time he wondered if she actually would have been able to make a difference in what had happened.

Rain walked out of the hospital moving easier than she had in months. She hadn't waited for her wounds to heal when she'd run away and the last year had been hard. Willow had not only had to deal with her fresh wounds, she'd had to deal with the damage Rain had accumulated since leaving. As Willow had pointed out more than once Rain was damn lucky she was quite powerful; otherwise there would have been lasting damage that would have shortened her career considerably instead of just gaining new scars. As it was it would take weeks of proper care to ensure that she fully recovered. Her uncle was waiting outside, leaning against his horse. She paused, wrapping her arms around herself. She didn't want to go home, didn't want to face the rest of her family.

Not yet. She tipped her head forward so her hair fell over her face, hiding the tears in her eyes. Willow and Roderick hadn't said much, just remarked that she'd lost a lot of weight and would have to work if she didn't want to have to deal with questions about how fit she was for the field. She got the hint; they were giving her a chance because they knew Uncle Damien was going to help her pull herself back from the edge. One effect of being healed was that her body had burned through the alcohol much faster than it normally would, so she was more sober now than she'd been in a long time and less hungover. While she appreciated the latter she could have done without the former. Sobriety hadn't been her friend of late.

"Ready, kiddo?" He asked as she drew up beside him.

"No, I can't do this." She started to panic. "Dad's going to be pissed, isn't he?"

"He was pissed a year ago. Now he's worried and just wants his daughter home safe." Well, if that wasn't a knife to the heart. "He was here and he knows you're back because I told him. Notice that he didn't go charging into the hospital to find you or anything? Your dad is your dad, but Ash is also a Hunter. He understands better than you think."

Something occurred to her then. "Are *you* angry with me?" She hadn't thought of that before. After all, Uncle Damien was the one who'd taught her the most about being a Hunter, about trying to deal with the shit that came with it. She didn't know what she'd do if the man who'd been her hero for as long as she could remember was angry with her, and he had every right to be. She played with her medallion as she waited for his answer.

"No," he said after a moment, taking a drink from his flask. "I hate that things turned out this way and I'm worried about you, but I'm not mad. If Ash understands better than most, I'm one of the reasons why."

It was funny; back in her field year she'd thought she'd been experiencing the real world, finally out and in the fight. But that wasn't it. Even for the first year after, while they were all still riding the high of graduating and finally being full Hunters, reality didn't set in. It didn't until the envelops with the black seals kept coming, kept finding them wherever they were, until the third village in a row they reached had been massacred, and until no matter how many Fiends they killed, more kept coming. That was when reality finally sank in. The Academy never lied about it, their instructors never lied, other Hunters were brutally honest about it, no one tried to sugar coat or glorify the job, but somehow something was lost in translation until the second or third year after graduation.

She'd have given anything to go back to those days. Most of her class, the people she'd known since her first days at the Academy and earlier, were gone. The Guardians and Keepers who'd finished that same year had fared better, with more than half the Guardians still around and only two or three Keepers had died. Only a sixth of her class was still breathing, let alone active as

Hunters. The class that had come after hers wasn't much better off, but at least they hadn't lost ten people in a single night

A shout had her turning as she drew her sword, but it was just a student running after friends. She put it away, looking at the ground. This was one of the reasons why she hated being sober. She pulled out her flask and drained half of it, her uncle watching her.

"What?" She asked, feeling defensive. He shrugged but didn't say anything. There was no judgement in his gaze, just a sad kind of understanding.

"Do you remember what happened when I came back home after Raven died?" He asked after a moment.

"Some of it." She'd barely turned four when he'd returned, but some moments still stood out, or else had been retold when she was older until they felt like memories. "Storm and I were so happy to see you again, you'd been gone for six months and didn't even write to us."

"Yeah, the two of you threw yourselves at me and wouldn't leave me alone for the rest of the day." He grinned slightly at the memory, shaking his head.

"Our favorite uncle disappeared for six months, what did you expect?" Oh. "Are you trying to say it'll be the same when I go home?"

"Well, there won't be two shrieking little monsters trying knocking you over and clinging to you for the rest of the day. They want you home, Rain, that's all. I'm not saying there won't be consequences or that it's going to be easy, but you need to trust them. They were there for you when Blaze died and they'll be there for you now."

"But I fucked up so badly."

"And now you're trying to fix it."

Rain looked away for a moment. She knew she had to go home. She would have to face her family, just like she would have to face the few of her friends who were still alive. She missed them so much, but... "I'm scared." Every day she spent away made it a little bit harder to go back. Just like it had grown harder to write back, then to open the letters or even look at them. She hadn't thrown them out, she'd kept them in her bag, first pretending that she didn't have the time. Now she forced herself to admit that she hadn't had the courage to do it.

"Yeah, it's scary," he agreed. He waited for her to make up her mind, doing nothing to push her along.

"Let's go," she said after a long moment.

Uncle Damien let her set the pace, for which she was grateful, though what was normally an hour-long trip took closer to three hours. They were attacked by two Fiends that Damien dealt with easily. That scared her. Even a year ago she would have seen one or two in a month, if that in this part of the territories. Their village was close enough to both the city and the Academy to benefit from their protections.

"How does it keep getting worse?" She hadn't returned to the territories since she'd left home, but it was abundantly clear that things were getting just as bad here as everywhere else, and the territories had once been one of the safest places to travel.

"That's the question worth a thousand gold, though a few days ago Storm said she was definitely onto something." Storm had been made a member of the Council three years before to no one's surprise and with everyone's support. Her work with magic had very quickly caught a lot of attention. Once they'd realised that the growing numbers of Fiends weren't normal many people had turned to her for answers. She'd been trying to find them for three years.

"Do she and Phantom still have that flat in the city?" It was and would always be difficult for her sister to travel so instead she and her husband of two years split their time between home and the city.

"Yeah, but they'll be home today." Rain gripped the reins tighter, forcing herself to relax when her poor horse started fidgeting. She could see the village now, the smoke from the chimneys rising above the wall that protected those within. She wanted to stop, to turn around and run, but she forced herself to keep moving forward. She wanted to get better, to get some kind of life back. That meant having to do difficult things and facing what she'd left behind. It didn't make going through the gates any easier.

Nothing had changed. Everything was exactly the same as when she'd left, barely able to move. She'd waited until there had been no one home to stop her. Once she was far enough away she'd written letters explaining that she just needed time. For a while she'd even thought that was true. But then… it just got too hard to write back or read about news from home, just like it got harder and harder to only drink herself into a stupor once in a while.

Her home looked the same as ever. She didn't realise that she'd stopped until her uncle reached over and gently squeezed her shoulder. She gave a slight nod in response to his silent question and they kept moving. She led her horse around the back of the house, where three others grazed contently. Later someone would bring them to the stables in the village for the night. No one came running out to meet her, but that wasn't a surprise. Even if her father was the only Hunter inside, her sister and Phantom both had a lifetime of experience dealing with them, and Storm had also grown up with Uncle Damien. Her older sister remembered when their uncle had come back better than Rain could; she and Storm had watched their mother and Damien ride up the path that led to their house. They'd wanted to run out to meet him, but their father had stopped them and made them wait until Uncle Damien came in. They were giving her time to make the decision on her own, trying not to pressure her. She dismounted and took her bag, gingerly slinging it over her shoulder. While her wounds weren't in danger of reopening again, they still ached. She swallowed hard as she looked at the door.

"Do I have to?" She asked, looking over at her uncle. He was leaning against his horse again, watching her.

"No," he replied quietly. "It's your choice." His expression and tone were both carefully neutral. She thought about it. She felt guilty as hell, but she still had to think about it. She was ashamed of how she'd just run off and left everyone, how she'd abandoned her best friend, how she couldn't fight off the darkness that threatened to drive her mad. She took a tentative step backwards, then stopped, her hands clenching into fists.

This wasn't how it was supposed to be.

None of this was what she'd wanted from life, what she'd imagined her future would be. What she had wanted would never be, and she had to learn to accept it.

She forced herself to move forward again, hating that it took so much effort for something that should have been easy, that should have been a happy moment. Not something riddled with doubt, despair, and guilt. How had she fallen so far? Her uncle followed, appearing as relaxed as anything, though she was certain it was an act to try to help her stay calm. He didn't try to manipulate her as other people would have done, no matter how good their intentions were, nor did he try to pressure her into making a decision. She was in control here. That helped give her the courage to open the door and cross the threshold.

Storm jumped to her feet the moment Rain was inside and hugged her tight. "I'm so happy you're back," she said, her voice cracking. It took a moment, but Rain returned the embrace just as tightly, feeing tears start to fall again.

"I'm sorry… I'm sorry, I'm sorry, I'm sorry." She couldn't say anything else as cried, her whole body shaking.

"It's not your fault," Storm told her, holding her even tighter. Rain's sister only let go when their father came over.

"I'm sorry Dad, I…"

"I understand," he said, his voice tight with barely controlled emotion. When he opened his arms Rain went into his embrace. For a moment she felt safe, protected, which made her cry even harder. He just held her, rubbing her back. When she'd gone to those ten funerals she'd just been kind of numb, her ability to feel and process emotions crashing under the weight of everything. Afterwards she'd done her best to stay that way, relying on fighting, exhaustion, and liquor to keep her going, to keep her moving, because she knew that if she stopped she would shatter.

She was right.

Rain didn't know how long she stood there sobbing, and she didn't care. It was like a dam inside her had broken and all the misery was spilling out, a hemorrhage she couldn't stop. All of the pain, all of the grief she'd refused to feel, it was all coming back now. Eventually her father got her seated at the table and she calmed down a little.

"We'll get through this, kiddo," Uncle Damien said, squeezing her shoulder as she used her sleeve to wipe her eyes.

"Welcome back," Phantom said.

"Thanks," she managed to say, her voice rough.

"Did you have that breakthrough you were hoping for?" Damien asked Storm, breaking the awkward that had fallen and giving Rain the illusion of a reprieve from being the center of attention.

"I'm definitely on the right track," she said after a moment. "But there's a lot that isn't making much sense." She frowned, toying with her fork. "Or at least, it *shouldn't* make sense."

"You'll get it," he said and Storm smiled slightly. Their uncle, a renowned cynic, had always put so much faith in them. At least Storm deserved it, Rain thought as she stared at the plate of food that her father had put in front of her.

"I don't have much time, though; a Summit has been called for the nations most affected by this, which is to say us, Landai, Glask, and Phasoia. It's in Ankira in the spring, though that could change." She sighed, leaning back. "Basically the goal is to find some way to address this and work together so that we can limit the amount of damage done while we put a stop to this. I want to be able to give people some hope that this *can* be stopped."

"What if it can't?" Rain wondered, meeting her sister's eyes. They were ice blue, several shades lighter than her own sapphire eyes, and right now they burned with determination.

Storm's lips pressed into a thin line. "There is a cause." Her hands clenched into fists. "This is deliberate. Something has an active role in all of this and maybe if we can take it out we can stop this."

Rain felt sick. Before she'd left Storm had just started toying with the theory that there was something actively causing the Fiends to migrate to their corner of the world. Back then it had been a question of 'what' and not 'who'. The idea that a being, a living, sentient being was at the center of this… it was almost too much. Could all the Hunters put together fight a Fiend with that kind of power? She could hear the others talking, but Rain could barely hear her over the sound of her thundering heart, her breathing too fast…

"Rain!" Her uncle's voice brought her back, and she was once more safely in the kitchen of her family's home. She leaned forward and covered her face with her hands, trying to hide. "Rain, look at me." Reluctantly she met her uncle's quicksilver eyes. "You are home. Look around." She did, trying to avoid the looks of concern from around the table. "Now, take a deep breath." She did, trying to slow her breathing and her heart. "Another." She forced herself to relax. "Good. Just keep breathing." She nodded. "You've watched me do this before, you know the drill." She had seen it, not often because Uncle Damien had tried to hide it when he could, especially when she and Storm were younger. She put her hands down on the table and took a deep, shuddering breath. "Better?"

"Yeah." Suddenly she felt exhausted, like something had sucked away all of her energy. Being healed earlier likely didn't help.

"Good. Now, you're going to need to heal up fast, kiddo, because you're going to be back out there in a few months. We've got a job."

"What is it?"

"Just like our first job back when you were just a starry-eyed apprentice: we're going to play escorts. Only this time, we're going to take your sister to her Summit."

"Are you sure I'll be ready?" She asked. "'Cause so far I'm batting zero against the monsters in my head." The darkness inside of her was still winning the battle and the war. One of the reasons she'd become a Hunter in the first place was to protect the people she cared about. It wasn't working out so well for her.

"You will be, because you won't let anything happen to Storm, and you won't trust anyone to look after her as well as you can," Damien replied easily. She knew he was right. Deep down, some part of her believed exactly that. She just had to find it and bring it to the surface.

"Please Rain," Storm begged. "You're my sister, I trust you more than anyone." Their father, uncle, and Storm's husband wisely said nothing.

"Okay," she said, relenting. She just had to think of it as a step on her path, a goal to reach for. She just had to work her way up to it: recover, train, hunt, stay sober enough to be reliable. Maybe keeping someone alive for once would help. After... after what had happened, and Kestrel, after that... she needed it. Maybe it would be just the thing to help her move on. She hoped it was, anyway.

3
Steps

Rain woke with a gasp, paralysed for a moment by terror before her nightmare released her, leaving her shaking. She twisted, curling up beneath the sheets, tears falling as she tried to keep quiet as flashes of it ran through her mind; the fear and desperation, the blood on her hands, and that last quiet breath. This was one of the reasons she'd avoided sobriety for a year. If she passed out drunk she didn't have nightmares. If she wasn't sober she didn't have to remember. She closed her eyes against the nightmares made of her memories, but that only made it worse. Most of the time they were true, sometimes they were mixed with her fears for a hellish vision. Some nights it took her a few minutes to remember what had actually happened and what hadn't. She curled up tighter, arms wrapped around herself, face turned into her pillow to muffle the sounds and she tried to ignore the pain from her wounds. She hated this. She hated it so much. The guilt, the grief, the horror… it was too much and she was afraid that it would never, ever go away. She felt so small and alone. There was one person who could have made that feeling go away, who would have wrapped himself around her and held her until she was ready to let go of the nightmare and who would have warmed the ice in her soul. But Blaze was dead, just like so many others. Dead and gone, his ashes cast out to the winds. She'd done that, thrown his ashes, let the soft grey powder go even as she so desperately wanted to hold on to him. She cried harder.

Uncle Damien had warned her about this, that it wouldn't be the first or second night that got her. It was the fourth. The first night she'd been too exhausted to dream, the second and third nights she didn't know why except that maybe she'd been so damn hopeful about getting better. Then tonight had come. She knew that the next few weeks were going to be pure hell while she tried to recover and adjust her way of life. Not back to what it was, not to what she had wanted it to be since that wasn't possible, not now. It just had to be something better than what she'd been dealing with for the past year and a half. She had to create a new normal that she could live with, just like her uncle had years before, and she had to fight to keep it, had to fight against the darkness that threatened to drown her. Then the night before winter began she could take a breath. She'd had to choose one day a year, so she chose the day before the winter equinox, when everything was darkest and dying. Uncle Damien hadn't said anything when she'd told him, but he'd chosen the anniversary of his fiancée's death, so he could hardly comment on how morbid she was being. She had been tempted to choose the anniversary of the day when life had finally broken her, but it hadn't felt right. To her it felt like that should be a day spent fighting like hell. Then again, maybe the depression was making her masochistic. It was hard to believe over a year had passed since she'd carried Kestrel's ruined body from the battlefield, screaming for help until her voice gave out, since… since that.

She reached out, unable to stand it anymore, her fingers quickly finding the cool surface of her flask. She drank deep, relishing the sweet burn of liquor down her throat and glanced at her window to see that dawn was still a long way off. She knew she wouldn't get to sleep now, not after that. So she rose and went downstairs, treading quietly to avoid waking anyone. Her father was at work, guarding the borders of their village against Fiends, but it was his last night. He was switching back to being a Hunter once more, since she and her sister were grown and because Hunters were desperately needed. Rain felt a stab of guilt knowing that she had taken herself and her uncle out of the field for a while, because Uncle Damien wasn't going to trust her on her own for a long while. She couldn't say he was wrong about that.

Rain made it to the kitchen and rummaged through the cupboards until she found a full bottle of whiskey, her flask having been emptied on the way down. It was stronger than the stuff sold at *The Fallen Guardian*, so if she drank the bottle she would be able to sleep soundly, without dreams, without worries, without guilt. But doing that would break the rules she'd promised to keep. She was still staring at it when Storm came down, pulling a robe tighter around her body as she touched the spell that turned on the lights in the room.

"Rain…" She sighed as she took in the sight at the table. She looked exhausted, working hard on trying to figure out what the hell was wrong with everything. Rain didn't say anything, didn't try to explain or defend herself because she had nothing. "Rough night?"

Rain nodded. "Yeah."

Storm sighed and got two glasses from another cupboard. She handed one to Rain and opened the bottle to pour a measure of liquor into her own. Rain copied her when she got the bottle back, though she was far more generous about it. "What happened?" She asked, settling herself into a chair. Rain knew she wasn't just asking about tonight.

"I really don't want to talk about it." Because her sister was intelligent, smart enough to ask all the right questions that Rain didn't want to answer or to buy any bullshit, and unlike their uncle she wouldn't wait for Rain to decide to tell her on her own.

But maybe Rain was underestimating her sister, because Storm didn't push now. "Have you thought about talking to a counsellor?" The Academy had several who were available at all hours to any Hunter, Guardian, or even Keeper who needed them.

"I did after Blaze died," she replied choking on the name because it always brought pain. "I just felt even more helpless than I did at the start." She knew people who'd gone to the counsellors and it had worked for them, but it just wasn't what worked for her.

"Okay. What about talking to Kestrel?" Rain looked away, ashamed. She hadn't left the house since she'd returned, and she'd be lying to herself if she said that wasn't part of the reason why. "Rain, she wants to see you." Rain only knew that Kestrel was in the city and working at the Academy because she'd read it in one of the last letters she'd opened from Storm. She'd never written to Kestrel, hadn't read any of the letters she'd sent since she'd fled. She was too ashamed and afraid.

"Something wrong?" They both looked up to see Damien leaning against the doorframe, sleepily rubbing his eyes.

"No, just some sister talk," Storm told him.

"M'kay." He turned around, leaving them once more. The consequences of living in a house with Hunters: the tiniest noises woke most of them.

"So, back to Kestrel, you should see her."

"I don't know if I-"

"Bullshit," Storm said before Rain could get the excuse out. Then she paused and lowered her voice. "Bullshit. Rain, you don't get to wallow in misery anymore. She's gone through hell as well and she didn't have the luxury of being able to run away." Or run at all. "It'll do you both some good."

Rain toyed with her glass, swirling the liquor around. "You sound very certain of that."

"I am, and unless you can give me a very good reason of why I shouldn't be, I'll keep being certain." She gave Rain a piercing look and for a moment she was worried that her sister would see what she was trying to hide. But then Storm's expression softened slightly. "I thought so. Look, you two need each other, you always have. She's teaching a class in the morning, but nothing in the afternoon. Don't you need to get your armour repaired?"

"That sounds more like an order than helpful information." Her sister was right, it was just... she was afraid. That was it. She was afraid of what would happen. But the point of coming home was to face those fears, wasn't it?

"Your powers of observation are as acute as ever."

"Bitch." But there was no heat in the insult, and her sister just smiled. Rain drank the rest of the liquor in her glass.

"Phantom and I are leaving early," Storm told her, taking both their empty glasses to the sink. "I suggest you get some sleep."

"You seem awfully certain that I'm going."

"You will, because you want to but right now you need someone to force you into it. Aren't I a good sister?" She gave Rain a saccharine smile.

"I won't be going back to sleep, I'll just have more nightmares."

Storm's expression softened again. "Just try, maybe it'll be different."

"I doubt it." But she preceded her sister up the stairs anyway and went back to her room. She noticed it as soon as she walked in, leaning against the wall by her door. Uncle Damien's sword. He must have realised why she was up and put it there. Though she was too old to have him sit by her bedside to keep away the nightmares, the sight of his sword was enough to give her the courage to go back to bed and fall into a mercifully dreamless sleep.

A sharp knock on the door woke her up. She was on her feet in an instant, blade in hand before she remembered she was at home and safe. "Get ready," Storm told her when she opened the door, hiding the knife behind her back. "We're leaving in an hour." Rain closed the door with a sigh, leaning against it for a moment before she went to get dressed. Her armour needed serious repairs after the last year and she'd put them off, trying to avoid going to the Academy for fear she'd see someone she knew. Hell, that was why she'd spent most of the last four days in the house, since the whole damn village knew her. But now time had run out, so she packed up her armour into a bag and pulled on leggings and a simple dress that fell just past the top of her calf-high boots, regular leather since her armoured boots also needed to be repaired. Wasn't that just a metaphor for her life right now? Every damn thing was. She felt naked even though she had her armour spell that usually made the rest redundant, though her body's current state proved that that wasn't always the case. The only things that didn't need to be repaired were her weapons, thanks to the work her uncle had put into them over the years. She quickly got everything together and headed downstairs to find that her father had returned and was laughing at something her uncle had said.

"Are you coming too?" She asked Damien as she poured a cup of tea from the kettle on the stove.

He shook his head. "I ran into Emerald the other day and she said that Hawk is already out for mentors for next year, so I'm going to avoid the Academy for a while. I also told him that the next time he asked me I was going to stab him, but he doesn't always have the best memory." He stared at her until she also grabbed a piece of toast and some fruit. Her father's magic was in plants so they always had fresh fruit. Rain sat down beside her sister and forced herself to eat.

"I don't know if we'll be back tonight," Storm said. "It depends on how the Council meetings go and if I can make any progress with my work." She sighed and Phantom put an arm around her shoulders. A pang went through Rain and she looked away. She didn't begrudge her sister her happiness, but still... it had taken a long time before she found someone she could open herself up to, and she didn't know if she would be able to again. Not with... not with everything that had happened.

It wasn't long before they were getting ready to leave, her father gone up to sleep. He would stay home for a few days before deciding what paths he would take hunting, but Rain was certain he wouldn't go far. Her uncle had retrieved his sword and didn't say anything about putting it in her room the night before. She tried to focus on the task at hand, refusing to let her mind wander to the reasons why he'd put it there. She would go to the smiths first, then the hospital to see if anything more could be done with her wounds yet. By then Kestrel would be done with her class. She wouldn't keep avoiding her best friend.

Two hours later she found herself walking down familiar hallways looking for Kestrel's office, her armour to be picked up in a week and her wounds healed a little bit more. Storm had given her directions before they'd parted ways, so it didn't take long to find the right door. She stood in the hallway for a moment, bracing herself. Then she knocked.

"Come in!" She pushed the door open with a shaking hand. "Rain!" Kestrel cried, standing and all but leaping across the room to hug her tight. Rain returned the embrace, trying to ignore the burning sensation in her eyes. Her old friend looked a lot better than the last time she'd seen her. Of course, Kestrel had been covered in bandages and barely clinging to life. Now she wore a wide black patch over where her left eye had been, the scars stretching from her hairline down her neck, and Rain knew there were plenty more scars under her friend's clothing. One of the arms wrapped around her was metal above the elbow, and both her legs as well, one close to the hip and the other below the knee. If Rain hadn't learned how to keep blood circulating through wounds Kestrel would have died long before help arrived. As it was, it had been a near thing. Rain had been exhausted, barely able to manage it and deal with her own wounds. If she hadn't been so hurt, if she'd just been a little bit quicker, if everything hadn't gone so wrong, a lot would have been different that night.

"How's it going?" Rain asked, dragging her mind back to the present. She wasn't going down that rabbit hole, not now.

"Pretty good, finally got used to the new body," Kestrel replied, releasing the Hunter to show off her new limbs. "Storm got the mage who did her leg to help me out, though they haven't managed to find a way to replace eyes."

"I like the patch, very badass," Rain decided. Somehow there was no awkwardness, but then she and Kestrel had been friends since before they could walk. She still felt guilt, so much guilt, but she couldn't let that stand in the way of their friendship, she needed it too much. It felt selfish, but it was true.

"Yeah, I debated going the glass eye route, but I like this look better," Kestrel agreed, her remaining eye bright as she pushed Rain into one of the chairs in front of her desk and took the other for herself. She looked good, far better than Rain did.

"So, you really are a teacher," she remarked, looking around the office. It was nice, with a large window that overlooked the courtyard.

"Yeah, I'm just as surprised. So far it's going pretty well; they're keeping me on for a whole year anyway. I did some tutoring over the summer with air mage students."

"Always a good sign."

"Yeah, how about you?" Kestrel's expression made it clear she wouldn't accept any bullshit from Rain.

"I've been better." It was honest enough.

"Do we need drink it out?"

"Not for a while," Rain replied with a sigh. She should have picked a closer date. At Kestrel's look she explained the rules.

"Ah. Sounds like a way to manage things, I guess," she said after, though Rain could tell she didn't fully approve. Before everything Rain wouldn't have thought it was a good idea either, but things changed. "So, what happens after you get completely wasted?"

"Dunno. Either someone will be with me who stays sober enough to get me home around dawn or someone comes to find me and peels my drunk ass off the bar stool." She hadn't really thought that far ahead.

"If you want company I'll be your sober-ish person, though we'll still need someone to get us afterward. I haven't actually gotten drunk with the new limbs; Storm said it would be better to wait until I really got used to having them." Kestrel frowned. 'But wasn't she seven when she got her leg?"

"She still had to get replacements as she grew," Rain reminded her friend. "I can say that she knows about the drinking from first-hand experience. I was there and had to carry her home."

"Ah, that explains her tone," Kestrel grinned for a moment before her expression turned serious. "Please don't tell me that you still blame yourself for what happened that night. I know that's why you left. I don't remember much of it. Mostly I just know what other people have told me, but I do know that there's nothing else you could have done."

"Be grateful for that," Rain suggested, taking out her flask and drinking. "I doubt anyone kept anything back from you." Not a lie if she didn't include herself.

"Why the hell did we survive instead of the others?" Kestrel's gold eye shone with tears.

Rain shrugged instead of answering. She was certain she had the same curse as her uncle, just like he'd predicted seven years before. She was one of the consummate survivors. "Do you still have nightmares about it?" She asked instead.

Kestrel nodded. "Often enough, even though I only remember flashes. I wish I were still able to hunt, then at least I'd have some variety."

"You can't hide what you fear most from your own subconscious," Rain reminded her darkly. "Maybe you'll add a new flavour to the nightmares, but your mind will always know the best fuel." She took another drink and handed the flask to Kestrel, who also drank, grimacing.

"Fuck, that's strong," she gasped, handing it back.

"Have I mentioned it's been a really, really bad year?" It felt good to be around Kestrel; somehow she'd forgotten that. Things didn't seem quite that bad when she was around, maybe because she'd lived through the same hells that Rain had, even if she hadn't fallen quite as far.

"Growing up sucks," Kestrel said with a sigh. "Do you know what you're going to do now?"

Rain shrugged. "I have to wait until my wounds heal, then get back to some kind of routine, I guess. Get my head in a better place." She leaned back, kicking her boots up onto Kestrel's desk and ignoring the glare her friend leveled at her. "After that, who the fuck knows?"

"They've been getting closer to the city and I've that even outside the territories they seem to be targeting us over humans." That seemed to go with Storm's theory, and Rain had noticed something similar over the last few months.

"Storm to think that she's on to something, and hopefully she'll figure it out soon. Otherwise this could turn into a war."

"They're still talking about that?"

Rain nodded. "The only thing that's changed is that they're debating involving human forces with the Hunters and Guardians in their imaginary army that's going to clear out the Fiends."

"But they tried that before and it didn't work." Neither of them had been involved in that effort.

"I know it's an awful plan, but at the very least it would by us time to get to the bottom of this."

"Yeah." Kestrel leaned back for a moment before getting to her feet. "Come on, it's too stuffy in here."

Rain shrugged and followed Kestrel outside, wandering the cobblestone paths and passing Rain's flask between them. It was sunny but not hot, the cool bite of fall noticeable in the air.

"Watch this!" Rain and Kestrel jumped at the shout and turned as a student did a series of backflips across the grass to the cheers of her friends.

"It'll get easier," Kestrel said and Rain wasn't sure if she was talking more to herself or to Rain.

"Time makes for stronger liquor," Rain murmured. It was something she'd heard her uncle say when people talked about time healing all wounds because he knew it was utter bullshit, just like they had learned over the last six years.

Damien didn't look up from his book as Ash came down the stairs. "Sleep well?" He asked, turning a page as the other Hunter paused and stretched, yawning. Most people were surprised when they found out he enjoyed reading, especially if they knew about his past and how he'd been illiterate until he'd arrived at the Academy. He and Tempest had worked bloody hard at it and it had become something to bond over, sharing books and helping one another with the more difficult words, trying to hide their trouble from their classmates. Ash moved to sit on the couch across from him with a sigh. "Is it important? Shit just got real here."

"I could always tell you how it ends," Ash offered.

"I could always tie all the utensils into a knot," Damien returned, though he did mark his place with a scrap of leather and shut the book. It only took one look at Ash's face for him to figure out what the topic would be. "You're worried about Rain." Ash wasn't the only one.

The other Hunter nodded. "She's... she's different. I know, I know, we knew that was going to happen after everything she's been through... but still." He was still a father who wanted his little girl to be happy.

Damien tapped his knee with the book for a moment, thinking it over. "Something is missing."

"What?"

"She's hiding something."

"Aside from the last year?" Damien looked at Ash, who sighed. "Fine. What?"

"You're sure you didn't leave anything out about the night her friends were killed?"

"I'm positive. I was there when she told the Council what happened. But obviously you don't think she told them everything." He put his head in his hands.

"Think about it, Ash, Rain is a very strong person. Losing so many people in one night is traumatic, sure, and on top of losing Blaze not long before that doesn't help. But it still doesn't account for her running away like that, not when she's barely able to move, or for her to become an alcoholic." There had to be a catalyst, like Raven's death had been his. Granted, he'd been well on his way to drowning in darkness so it hadn't taken much to push him over the edge.

"She took loosing Blaze pretty hard," Ash pointed out, but Damien could see that things weren't adding up for him either.

"I know I wasn't around for any of this, but she still wrote to me. She was dealing with Blaze's death. This... there's something more."

"Okay, but there's a problem: Rain's the only person who knows it. Kestrel doesn't remember much, especially after she was the target of the most powerful Fiend's attack, and only two people left that field alive."

"I know."

"We need to do something or..."

Damien raised a brow. "Or what? She'll end up like me?"

"I would rather she end up like you than Siobhan or Wolf." He named two other elite Hunters. Siobhan was a suicidal recluse fighting to die and Wolf was truly insane. The rest of the elite weren't in much better shape. It was part of the job, part of the burden they carried by being the best at what they did. Rain was well on her way to becoming one of them, just like she'd always wanted to be.

"Fair enough, always go for the best of the worst." He kept talking before Ash could say anything else, "I'm going to see if Ember's around. She might know something that'll help. Hell, she knows more about dealing with traumatised Hunters than the Academy ever did." She was one of the Hunters who'd actually made it. She was in her late eighties and had only just retired a year before. Lucky for him she'd decided to spend much of her retirement teaching at the Academy.

"She's gone right now," Ash said. "She went to see her great-granddaughter but she's supposed to be back in about a week. Should we see if she'll come back sooner?" If they wrote to her and explained the situation Damien knew she would return as fast as she could.

"No. I don't think that's necessary. It took me a few years to get my shit together, and it's only been four days for Rain. Well, I'm as together as I'll ever be at this point."

"I bet that if she's going to tell anyone the deep, dark secret she's hiding it'll be you."

"Does that bother you?"

Ash gave him a wry grin. "If it were anyone else it would. Hell, I think I'd rather it be you than me; you understand this better than I do."

"You know, I always told her that if she had to be like any of us to pick you."

"Freakishly well-adjusted?" Ash used Damien's words. Well, he might have left a few out.

"I still stand by that," he said, leaning forward and bracing his elbows on his knees. "For now she's following the same rules that Tempest gave me, and I think that if she can stick with them it just might be the thing that'll work."

"Tempest did always have good ideas." Damien could hear how much Ash missed her. "Do you think things would have gone differently if she was here?"

He shook his head slowly. "Not this time. I don't think even Tempest could have prevented this." The only thing that could have changed what had happened was if they knew what was causing all the Fiends to converge on their corner of the world. He sighed heavily, knowing that things were going to get worse before they got better.

4

Stumble

Rain spent the next few weeks learning the meaning of 'tough love'. Every morning she was all but dragged from her bed and forced into a morning workout, fed three meals a day with at least one person watching to make sure that she actually ate, and made to go to bed at a half decent hour. She was making progress, physically at least, her wounds healing quickly as she started taking care of herself. A few autumn storms didn't hurt either. Mentally... things weren't going nearly so well. Nightmares plagued her sleep and more than once she woke screaming and sobbing, that last shuddering breath echoing in her head. Stupid things made her jump, others gave her flashbacks to horrors she wished she'd never seen. It was like everything she'd managed to deal with over her six years of hunting was coming back to haunt her. It made the 'limited alcohol' rule hard to follow, not when all she wanted was to sleep through the night, to escape for just a little while back to that numb state where she could pretend that nothing hurt. Not even her uncle's sword against the wall was enough to chase away the monsters in her head some nights.

"Sometimes I think I'm doing better and then it's like I take two steps back," she told Kestrel as they walked through the campus. She spent a lot of time there or in the city, reconnecting with friends she'd fallen out of contact with. Most of them understood, and others... well, she was probably better off without them. "I feel like I'm going to go insane." She played with her medallion, half surprised that the surface hadn't been worn flat yet.

"Well, you were gone for a little over a year and you've been back for all of a month. You knew it was going to take a while to get back on your feet."

"Still, I nearly stabbed Hawk a few days ago because he came up behind me." She couldn't let it go, though Academy administrator had taken no offense.

"So? Wolf actually stabbed Adrian, remember?"

She snorted. "You know, I'd forgotten about that. Weren't they sparring?"

"Yeah, then Adrian tried to throw in some illusion magic and got stabbed when Wolf figured out where he was." Adrian had been a shadow mage, like Phantom.

Rain looked skyward. "I wonder... if he'd lived, would he have been there that night?"

"Don't go there," Kestrel said, putting an arm around her shoulders and squeezing gently. "Not now. You only have to hold out for two more months, and then you can take a break, go down the rabbit hole and drink it all away."

"That shouldn't make me feel better." She took a drink from her flask.

"No, but that's what we're dealing with."

Rain sighed and wrapped her arms around herself. "Uncle Damien said that once I get cleared by a healer we're going hunting."

"What do you think of that?"

She took a deep breath and let it out slowly. "I don't know. I mean, I'm happy to get back out there and fighting, doing something, but at the same time I'm scared of what will happen. I can't afford to have a panic attack in the middle of a fight."

"Isn't that why your uncle is going to be there as well?"

"Yes." She kicked at the ground as they walked, scattering leaves that had fallen. "But how long will I need a babysitter before I can deal with this on my own?"

One of Kestrel's eyebrows went up. "You must be feeling off if you're calling your hero a babysitter." Rain gave her a look. "Come off it, Rain, I know you better than that."

"Rough night," she said. It was an excuse, but it was true.

"Nightmares?"

"Always."

"Consider it paying the piper," she suggested. "You did avoid them for a year."

"That really doesn't make me feel better." She drank again.

"It won't last forever. I don't have nightmares every night," Kestrel said. "It took a long time, granted, but they do become less frequent."

Rain kicked at another leaf that had fallen from its tree. Most of them still clung stubbornly to their branches, their fiery hues almost glowing in the sunlight. "It's easier to keep burying things." Besides, Kestrel didn't have her nightmares, and Rain would make damn sure that she never did. It would kill her friend to find that out.

"Now I know you paid attention in all of the classes every year where they said that was an awful idea that doesn't work for anyone because I copied your notes."

Rain shrugged. "It's not as easy in practice."

Kestrel sighed. "I know... How's Storm doing?"

"I haven't seen her for two days because she's been working in the city. I do know she's getting closer to some kind of breakthrough. Uncle Damien and I are going to see her before we go home," Rain replied, grateful for the change of subject.

"Really?"

She nodded. "She wouldn't say anything more, but... well, we already knew that there was no good answer to this."

"Did she mention anything about the weird flashes we saw?"

"Sort of. She kind of mumbled something as she was walking away when I asked her." Before everything had gone to hell Rain had used her mother's ring during a fight and saw odd flashes of light around a Fiend. Since it had been trying very hard to kill her she hadn't thought much of it until later, when she started looking. Not all Fiends had them, but enough had that she'd mentioned it to Storm and a few older Hunters. She'd completely forgotten about it when her world had come crashing down around her in the space of six months. She did remember that it hadn't been anything like the magic she was used to seeing in them. "I'll ask her again when I see her. You okay?" She asked when Kestrel stretched her arm with a wince.

"Fine, this happens sometimes for a day or two after I get an adjustment done," she said, flexing the metal limb.

"Ah. Do you want to find a place to sit down? There might be space by one of the smaller fountains."

She shook her head. "I'll be fine. What about your wounds?"

"Willow said that I should be good to go in the next week or so. The problem is the wounds that accumulated over the last year without a healer's attention. It takes more work to set that damage to rights than healing fresh wounds." The newer wounds she'd had when her uncle had found her were now pale scars. There were a few going down her left arm, one across her stomach, another across the middle of her back, and a few lines down her left leg, adding to her collection.

"Then you have that Summit in Ankira, don't you?"

"Not for a while, it's set for late winter or early spring, though that could change if Storm figures things out sooner. I do know that Forest Meadows is going, and Amber and Nadina are his escort." Forest was a member of the Council and a retired Hunter. He wasn't as strong as the elite Hunters, fighting on the same level as her father, but that was probably a good thing, considering the mental states of the elite Hunters. She didn't think she'd met Nadina before, though when Storm had listed her she'd done it in a way that made her wonder if she should remember the Hunter.

"Oh, did you hear the rumour going around about Amber?"

"That the Headmistress is retiring and Amber's first in line to take her place?" Her friend nodded. "Dad mentioned it a few days ago, but he didn't know a whole lot about it."

"I asked Amber about it yesterday, but she said she didn't know any more than I did."

"Did she say if she'd take it?"

"She said she'd have to think about it. But really, who else would be better suited?"

"Dad said that Hawk's wanted the job for years."

"He'd do well, but I think Amber's better suited. Besides, we need Hawk where he is." Aside from being a perpetual thorn in her uncle's side,

Hawk was the one who ultimately decided if a mentor-apprentice pair would be a suitable match. He'd taken the position after the whole debacle with her mother, uncle, and their mentors had gone down. In the thirty years since he hadn't made any mistakes and the last five years aside, student mortality rates had gone down.

"I agree, but I don't think he would try to fight it if she was offered the position."

"I thought I heard your dad's name thrown around too."

"Dad won't take it," Rain said, shaking her head. "I think they just need names to make a list, but I'd say Amber's got it and it would only take minimal begging to convince her to take it."

"I'd say you're probably right."

Something rushed past them. Rain and Kestrel turned to see the Fiend take a few running steps. Rain lunged at it, her blade poised to strike when it vanished for a second to reappear a meter farther away, facing them. It charged. Rain lunged again, but it flickered and when it reappeared she wasn't ready for it to be so close, too off-balance to move away. Its claws were going to go through her. Kestrel barrelled into her, knocking her out of the way. Again. It was happening again. She shook her head to clear it, to focus. Something wasn't right. Her warning spell should have gone off. Someone else should have noticed it before it got this close to the Academy. But it was hard to think when Kestrel was lying on the ground. The ground beneath her was wet. She knelt to touch the stones and her hands came up red. But that made no sense, she wasn't bleeding. She looked up. The Fiend flickered a few more times and vanished.

"Oh shit," she heard someone say. That wasn't the right reaction to this. There should have been panic, a call to arms at least. She turned and saw a group of students, but her mind turned them into the dead. She shook her head again, trying to clear it.

"Shit, I'm sorry, I didn't realise there was someone there," a young woman was saying, but it sounded like she was speaking from the other side of the world. Rain closed her eyes for a second. Shadow mage. The girl was a shadow mage. The Fiend had been an illusion, nothing more.

But why couldn't she catch her breath? Why wouldn't her heart stop racing? She tried to take a deep breath but the air choked her. She opened her eyes and all around her was blood. Hers, theirs, it didn't matter, it was blood. She looked at Kestrel, who was getting to her feet. But how could she move when she was bleeding so badly? Blood flowed from around her eyepatch, from where her metal limbs joined her body. Rain felt like she was going to be sick. No…. no, no, no. That was the past. That was the past. It was over. It was over and done with.

"Rain," Kestrel said her name, reaching for her with a blood soaked hand. Rain jerked back, away. If only she could *breathe.* Kestrel said something she couldn't hear over the roar of her own heartbeat. She looked down at her hands. They were soaked with blood, but just like then it wasn't her own, but the bloody dagger was. No, not again. Not again. She couldn't have done that twice, wouldn't have even then, not if there'd been another choice. She'd begged, she'd argued, but in the end... She kept shaking her head, trying to clear it, but the past and the present wouldn't unravel. She felt like she was going mad. "Rain!"

Damien looked out the window as he finished speaking. Ember's office faced a courtyard and was high enough that he could see all of it. It had been a popular place to relax when he'd been a student, and evidently that hadn't changed. Small groups occupied much of the space, some students lying back in the grass while others read or practiced magic. They all looked young, so very young. It made him feel old and tired. He took a drink from his flask. It was funny though, because he would still be in his prime for another decade or two. If he were a human he would already be slowing down, feeling the effects of years fighting on his body as more than scars. Actually if he were human he would be little more than a skeleton in a grave somewhere, and would have been that way for some time.

"Well, this is quite the problem," Ember said, leaning back in her chair, her fiery red eyes thoughtful.

"I don't know how to help someone fight a battle that I've been losing for decades," he said, turning back to face her. "I don't know what I'm doing, and it's not like I can just copy everything Tempest did for me; Rain's my niece. Tempest was my best friend."

"Yes," Ember agreed, "there's different dynamics at work." She sighed. "I don't know Rain all that well, so I'm not sure how much help I can be."

"Anything would help." He couldn't keep the pleading tone out of his voice.

She was quiet for a long moment, thinking it over. "The only way to mess this up would be to abandon her or let her use you as a crutch, and you wouldn't do either of those. What worries me more is whatever she's hiding, but I've found that secrets like that don't tend to stay hidden for long, and they have the power to break people, especially if you try to force it."

"Even though it seems to be stopping her from getting where she wants to be?"

"You know more than most about the kinds of secrets that Hunters guard closely," Ember reminded him in a pointed tone.

"Which ones are you referring to?" He asked mildly. He'd always wondered how much she'd guessed about what he and Tempest had done.

She gave him a slight smile. "I think you know, but that's not important right now. You need to let her come to you. She's smart and she's always looked up to you. I'd be shocked if she doesn't already know that you see far more than you let on."

"Maybe being back on the road will help," he said, running a hand through his hair. "Fiends will give her an outlet for her frustration."

Ember nodded. "What do you have in mind?"

"There's some trouble around Cortia, it's not too far away so I figure it's as good a place as any to start. If I just took her around the territories she'd feel like I was treating her like a child, and she'd be right. If I take her somewhere where there is real danger then maybe she can face some of her fears without the danger of having a panic attack."

"Sounds like a good idea to me."

"Then I must be on the right track," Damien remarked with a slight grin, taking another drink. He was about to say something else when there was a knock on the door.

"Yes?" Ember said, raising her voice enough that it would carry through to the hallway.

A lanky youth opened the door, looking nervous. "Kestrel sent me, there's a Hunter who needs help, they're by the lake." Rain. He glanced at Ember and saw that she'd drawn the same conclusion. They were both out the door before the youth could say anything else. They raced to the lake by the northern end of the Academy. A Hunter caught in a panic attack could be dangerous, unable to tell a friend from an enemy. He'd nearly killed a maid at an inn once. Rain had been the one to stop him that time.

They slowed down when they saw Kestrel. She was standing on her own, her arms wrapped around herself like she was trying to literally keep it together. She hurried over to meet them when she saw them. "I can't get near her," she said, weeping. "I just make things worse." Ember reached out and gently gripped her shoulder.

"You did the best you could," she said softly. "You've both been through a lot."

"A shadow mage was practicing by the East Tower, she made a Fiend that reminded us of… of the thing we fought." A shudder ran through her. "Rain figured out it was an illusion. She knew it, but…"

"We get it," Ember said, and Damien nodded.

"She started running; I followed her here and sent someone to get you because I knew Damien would be with you." She looked out towards the water and Damien followed her gaze. Rain was sitting by one of the trees that guarded the edge of the lake, her knees drawn against her chest and her hair hiding her face. Damien braced himself and walked over, moving slowly and deliberately making noise so he wouldn't catch her by surprise.

"Hey kiddo," he said lightly, sitting down beside her. She didn't say anything, just sat there shaking, almost hyperventilating. "It's okay, you're safe, there are no Fiends here." The standard things to say to any Hunter having a panic attack, taught to all Academy students. They were worthless statements, things no Hunter would ever truly believe and often mocked, used in jokes or said sarcastically over a mug of ale until they did have some kind of meaning; that there was no immediate danger and the Hunter was among friends. It was funny how that worked, Damien mused as he watched his niece. Rain made a sound somewhere between a sob and a snort. "Exactly," he said, leaning over and gently bumped her with his shoulder. "Relative sobriety sucks, doesn't it?" A slight nod. He leaned back, stretching out his legs as he looked at the water, watching the ripples made by the winds that were always present this close to the ocean. "That Fiend you fought last year, the one that could turn invisible, that's the kind of thing you see maybe once in a generation. It's a miracle anyone survived, let alone two of you." She flinched. "I don't know what else happened while you were gone, but I think I can guess, and it's a lot of drinking, fighting, and watching people die while you pretend that you're completely numb to it all but you really aren't." Out of the corner of his eye he saw her raise her head just a little, though her hair still hid her face. "If you're numb then nothing can touch you. Nothing can hurt you, nothing can break you." He debated calling her out on keeping secrets, but decided against it. She didn't need that right now.

"What if this happens when I'm out hunting?" She shifted so that her chin was resting on her knees, her hair falling back enough that he could see her tear-stained face. She flinched when she looked out at the water, closing her eyes.

"It's blue," he said firmly. "The water is blue, just like the sky." She took a deep breath and opened her eyes again, nodding slowly. "My bet is that it's because there were no Fiends that you panicked. If there were enemies you'd deal with them, and maybe panic after, but that's not important." She gave him a side-eyed glance. "I mean it, and I'll prove it to you because once you're cleared we're going to Cortia for a week."

She looked like she couldn't decide if she was surprised or not. "You really don't believe in easing people into things, do you?"

"I thought you learned that as an apprentice," he remarked, putting an arm around her shoulders. "Getting out will help keep your mind off things and you can start to figure out a new kind of normal."

"That doesn't sound so bad," she agreed reluctantly.

"Now, I'm going to get Kestrel to come over here." Her head dipped forward, hair hiding her face again. "Kestrel understands what happened, Rain. Just remember that only the scars are left." She nodded, so he stood and went back to where Kestrel and Ember were sitting.

"Is Rain okay?" The younger woman asked, looking up at him.

"Eventually." He held out a hand. When she took it he pulled her to her feet. "How are you?"

"Alright, I guess. If Rain hadn't had a panic attack I probably would have," she admitted, following him back to where Rain was. "Hey," she said. Rain looked at her and went pale, clenching her hands into fists and squeezing her eyes shut for a moment.

"Remember what I said," Damien said softly. She took a breath and opened her eyes.

"Are you okay? You fell when you knocked me aside."

"Still got my armour spell," Kestrel said with a small smile. Rain nodded, pushing her hair back. He saw that her other hand held her medallion in a tight grip. With any luck, she wouldn't let it go.

"Uncle Damien?"

"Mhm?"

"Roderick thinks I'll be okay to hunt in a week." She didn't look as afraid of the prospect as she had when he'd brought it up before.

"Good." He waited until Kestrel sat down next to his niece before going back to Ember.

"Well?" He asked as she gave him a considering look. He spoke quietly enough that neither of the young Hunters would hear him.

"I think you just might do," she told him with a small smile.

A week later they left at sunrise. It was funny how, in spite of not seeing her uncle for two years they still fell into the same easy rhythm they'd always had.

"One," she said, spearing a Fiend the size of a house cat with an icicle. She didn't get a fang off it. She'd come across similar Fiends and they'd all been poisonous. It just wasn't worth the risk, even if both she and her uncle did have vials of antivenin in their packs.

"Are you sure you want to start this?" He asked. "You haven't won against me yet."

"It's been over two years, old man," she said. "I've gotten better." Small steps, doing the things she used to enjoy until they had some kind of meaning once more. Building something she could accept and live with, that's what she had to do.

"Seriously? You do realise that this means war, *kiddo*." She was pretty sure that her uncle saw the game for what it was, but was willing to play along without comment.

"So how bad is the situation in Cortia?" He'd done a supply run the night before and mentioned that he'd talked to a few people about it.

"I'd say pretty damn bad, they've lost four Guardians in the last week. I knew some of them in passing and they were all good, strong fighters"

That was very bad. "Do they think there's a stronger Fiend pulling in the numbers?" Great. Just great. Just what she wanted to deal with her first time back out in the field.

"I'd say chances are good."

"How long before there isn't anyone left to fight?" Rain wondered. They were all getting killed so fast. "What would happen then?"

"Whoever is left would be fucked. The humans aren't strong enough to fend for themselves. Unless someone manages to prove that the legend of our ancestors giving up their souls is true and then figure out how they did it and then repeat it, everyone is doomed. One." He'd speared a squirrel-sized Fiend with a dagger then gave her an arch look. "No old man has reflexes like that."

"I think your hair is greyer than the last time I saw you," she remarked.

He glared at her. "It's not grey it's *silver*. I'm a powerful metal mage. I should have some *silver* hair, it's appropriate and has *nothing* to do with my age."

"Sure."

"It's true!"

"Okay." His glare deepened. Keep pretending until things start having meaning again. "Two!" She announced, dismounting to collect a fang.

"When I win I am going to be drinking top shelf whiskey tonight."

"What you decide to spend your own money on is of little concern to me," she said as she got back on her horse. The shadows were lurking around the edges of her mind and heart, looking for any way to get in, but she was feeling a little bit better for being out in the field and getting ready to hunt the monsters again. She'd never have the normal she'd wanted, too many people were dead for that, like Blaze, and there was too much guilt, too many situations where she'd been forced to make an impossible decision that would haunt her forever. But she couldn't have it, so she had to find something else, no matter how hard it was to let go of that dream. She was lying to herself if she didn't admit that she still clung to it, that she couldn't let go of what could have been instead of accepting what was. Maybe once this was all over; once whatever was causing the Fiends to kill off her people in increasing numbers was dead she could start accepting it and move on. Vengeance wasn't sweet, she knew that. It wouldn't bring the dead back to life and it wouldn't make her happy. But she could make damn sure that whatever being or beings were responsible for her friends' deaths couldn't get anyone else. Maybe, just maybe, that would be enough for her.

5

Normal

"Maybe next time," Uncle Damien said with false sympathy as they sat in a tavern. It was their third night on the road, and so far they hadn't faced more Fiends than she would have expected to see five years before. She suspected that was mostly thanks to the fact that they'd decided to stay as close to the coastline as possible for the trip. On the way back they might consider the inland roads, depending on the weather. At the moment the biting winds were preferable to the low visibility of the thick forest. Rain was certain that the ease they'd had would slowly vanish as the horde of Fiends gained ground in the territories, but for now she was grateful for the respite. There were Fiends in the ocean, truly nightmarish creatures of myth and legend that lurked in the darkest depths of the waters, but so far they didn't seem to be affected by whatever was pulling in the Fiends. Or was it pushing them?

"Definitely next time," Rain informed him. "You only won by two kills."

"Still a win," he said with a shrug, waving down a servant for more ale.

"Damien, got a letter for ya!" The innkeeper said as he approached their table. Both Hunters tensed until they saw that the seal wasn't black but a bright sky blue. Then again, the innkeeper was one of their people and would have known what a black seal meant.

"Thanks," he said as he took the letter with a passing glance at the Council seal. Her father's insignia was an ivy-wrapped rose and Kestrel's was a stylised version of the bird that was her namesake. She waited as he read it and sighed. "Looks like their calling in the powers for whatever's wrong in Cortia."

"What?" He handed her the letter. It was a request for Hunters in the area to head to Cortia and deal with the Fiend that was drawing in the others, as Rain had suspected.

"Any elite Hunter known to be within a few hundred kilometers of the town will be getting a letter like that," he said, taking a drink. "That's what the blue wax means." Rain knew that dark green was just a general request for any Hunter. "Right now that's us and maybe Emerald, as far as I know, anyway."

"Us?"

He looked at her for a moment. "The unofficial requirements to be considered an elite Hunter are having been active for at least ten years and having the power and skill to take down basically anything. Right now you have two out of three, and I expect you to survive for far longer than the next three years. Your dad, in comparison, has the years of service and he's very skilled, and hell, he could figure out how to beat almost anything, but he lacks the power to do it."

"Mom had all three, didn't she?"

He nodded again. "Luckily things get a bit fuzzy when it comes to requirements for sanity. Anyway, what do you say, are you up for a serious fight?"

She thought about it for a moment. Sometimes one had to throw oneself to the wolves. She nodded. "Let's do it." He grinned and went to reply to the letter, leaving her alone for a minute. She took a deep drink of her ale. She'd been doing well so far –nightmares aside- but who knew how long that would last? When her uncle returned they played a few rounds of cards with an off-duty Guardian who knew better than to play for money against her uncle.

"I might only know you in passing but I've heard the stories," Cloe said with a grin.

"That's no fun," Damien sighed. "What if we promised to play nice?" She gave him a look.

"She has a point," Rain remarked, laying down a card.

"Oh shush," he said without heat. She shook her head and eventually headed up to her room, falling asleep soon after her head hit the pillow.

"Apparently you do know how to play nice," Cloe remarked as he got up and started searching for his clothes. He could feel her eyes on him and wondered if she was staring at the scars that turned his body into a roadmap or at the tattoos that decorated his arms and torso, plus one that was placed high on his inner thigh. Of course, there was something else she could have been staring at in that region of his body.

"Glad I had a chance to prove it," he said with a grin as he found his underclothes and pants. "Having a wonderful partner helps too." She laughed and tossed him his shirt.

"Good night Damien, and happy Hunting," she said as he left to go to the room he'd rented. He had lovers, short term flings that were more about sex than anything else. He always slept alone, though. Part of it was courtesy, he was often restless and nightmares weren't an uncommon thing for him. The other part was more complicated and –if he was being honest- more pathetic. He didn't want to wake up next to someone who wasn't Raven. She'd been dead for over twenty years, but that was one step he just couldn't take. He knew Ash was just as bad. With any luck in the world, Rain wouldn't be the same. Of course, they all seemed to be rather short on luck these days. He made it to his own room and checked the lock before undressing and getting in the bed. He'd had his night of mourning already, to mourn her and everyone else who had left him behind. Raven wouldn't have wanted this for him, hell, he didn't want it for himself either, but it was all he could handle. He turned onto his side and closed his eyes, letting sleep steal him away.

"Gods damn it all to hell!" Rain growled as the fortified town of Cortia came into sight the next day. The town was on the edge of where the forests thinned out into rocky barrens before the mountains. The Eskaven Mountains stretched most of the way across the continent in a crescent, wrapping around the northeastern part of Landai and creating a natural northern border for Phasoia.

"Maybe next time." How many times was her uncle going to say that?

"You're only ahead by one."

"Still a win," he reminded her. "Let's see what we can find out about that Fiend."

The atmosphere in the town was both tense and bleak, but that was to be expected. Guardians in the territories usually grew up in the towns and villages they protected and were fairly well-known. The inn wasn't very busy either, only a pair of Hunters in the tavern.

"Jerek, River, it's been a while," Damien said, going to sit across from them as Rain dealt with getting rooms and hauling their gear up. She'd been here before, the last time a little over a year and a half ago, just before Blaze died. Actually it had been the last time she'd seen him alive. He'd been heading farther north while she'd gone east to meet up with Kestrel. A wave of sorrow went through her, but she only allowed herself a few moments of it, sitting on the bed. She had to hold out for the night before midwinter. Then the three hundred and sixty four after it, but hopefully they would be easier, though she doubted it. She stood and went downstairs.

A Guardian had joined the three Hunters, looking weary and defeated. "I don't know what's going on," he was saying as Rain sat down at the table and took a drink from her flask to hold the sorrow at bay. "We've tried to find the Fiend, but anyone who goes after it either dies or comes back with nothing."

"This is my niece, Rain," Uncle Damien told the group. She knew Jerek, but the others were strangers to her. "The Hunter is River Cobalis and the Guardian is Jack Green."

"We had a little luck today, a lot, actually, otherwise we'd be dead right now." Jerek sighed before turning to her. "How're things going?" She'd crossed paths with him a few months ago, and she could see from his expression that he was worried about her.

"Better," she said. It was true enough. "You?"

"Grateful to be alive," he replied with a wry grin.

"We got close, so we know that it's big," River said. Rain figured he was using a similar trick to one of hers, where she could determine the size and shape of something from the water in the air around it. "Unfortunately as far as magic goes I'm not that powerful, just strong enough to survive as a Hunter."

"Well, Rain is shaping up to be one of the elite," Jerek said. "Maybe she and Damien will do better than we could." While Hunters were trained to favour cooperation over competition, no one was perfect. In cases like this, however, only a fool wouldn't admit that they were in over their head. Why take a risk when someone else was far more likely to survive?

"It's about time a water mage joined their ranks," River said with a small smile.

"Does it have a general territory?" From her uncle's tone she figured this was what they were talking about before she'd sat down.

"Right. The times we got closest were when we headed north-east. I'd probably give it a ten kilometer radius?" Jerek glanced at River for confirmation, and the other Hunter nodded.

"It doesn't attack like almost every other Fiend, which is strange," River added.

"So we're dealing with one of the intelligent ones. Great." Damien sighed and took a drink from his flask. Rain swallowed hard. This was going to be a hellish fight.

"Should we head out and see what we can find now? There's still plenty of daylight yet," Rain said as she took a drink from her flask. She'd have to refill it before they left.

"You up to it?" He asked, pushing his hair back from his face.

No. "Yes."

"Then by all means, let us hunt this bastard." Rain quickly went to the bar and got her flask filled and then they left. Villagers waved as they walked past, a fleeting and desperate kind of hope on their faces. They likely knew the Council had decided to send someone in to handle the problem, and she could tell that some of them recognised her if not her uncle, and knew what they were capable of. No pressure.

"Do you think we'll have to watch for a swarm?" She wondered as they reached the town gates.

Uncle Damien thought it over for a moment. "Depends, I've seen it go both ways. Sometimes there's a swarm, sometimes it's just looking for a bit of fun."

"That's a hell of a thought," she muttered uncomfortably.

"I try not to have it often." They headed northeast as soon as they passed the gates.

"Stop here," Rain said after an hour. "I'm going to see if I can sense anything."

"How far can you get?" Damien asked. It was the latest in a string of cloudless, sunny days; a rarity for the middle of fall.

"Probably a few hundred meters and nothing finite, not without actual rainfall or fog, but there might be something." He nodded and drew his blade, positioning himself to stand guard as she sat down on a flat rock and closed her eyes. She drew in a deep breath and let her power wander outward, connecting with any drop of water she could find in the air or on the ground. They were still fairly close to the town, so she didn't expect to find much, and if they had no luck at all by tomorrow night she would have to see if she couldn't bring on some rain. It took a fair amount of power she wouldn't have considered using without someone as strong as Damien around. Her eyes snapped open. "There's a body and a lot of blood." She stood and ran, her uncle a step behind her. They found it not five minutes away, torn to pieces and scattered across the ground.

"One of the villagers," he said, kneeling down, careful of the blood and chunks of flesh scattered around. Rain took a deep breath as she tried not to put other faces on the mangled corpse, though it felt like the eyes stared straight at her.

"It's fresh," she said, forcing herself to look at it as a clue that would help them find the Fiend. "The thinnest layers of blood have only just started to dry."

Damien frowned. "It won't be far away then; this looks like bait to me." But for who?

"But wouldn't our warning spells have gone off?"

"If it evaded Jerek and River but River could still find it with magic then I'd say it's learned how far away it needs to be to avoid tripping the spells." That was a terrifying thought.

She looked around, though she was quite certain she wouldn't see anything. "Could it get *past* our warning spells?"

"Now there's a thought," he said, rising. "But I don't think so. They can't use magic the same way we can, not in any way that would let them hide. It's also why the radius for the warning spells is small, so that it's strong and nothing can slip through." She didn't get how he could always seem so calm and collected. He didn't looked even mildly disturbed by the idea that a Fiend could conceal itself from the spell they relied on the most. "Want to try again here? The Fiend should still have some blood on it, unless there's a river or creek nearby." Chances for all three were good, though she knew the town relied on a river south of their walls for water.

Rain nodded as she got to her feet. "I think I have something, or it could be a tree, and maybe even an injured animal in a tree."

"Lead on," he said with a dramatic wave. She nodded, drawing her sword just in case.

They didn't get far when she was pretty damn sure it wasn't an injured creature or a tree. "It's moving."

"Towards us or away?"

"Away." They sped up, keeping a careful watch around them. It wasn't long before they reached a large clearing surrounded by thick bushes. Somehow they always found a clearing. Then her warning spell went off. She and her uncle moved so they were back to back, watching carefully. But nothing happened. "What the fuck is going on?" She hissed, looking around.

"It's toying with us," he muttered. Rain created a ring of small ice spears around them and sent them flying in all directions.

Then she saw it. It wasn't much shorter than the trees, easily three times her height, with a slighter build than she would have expected. She turned and lunged into her uncle, dragging him down with her as it moved past them with incredible speed, narrowly missing them with its claws.

Heart thundering in her ears, Rain jumped to her feet. "Hellfire, it's fast," she said. As fast as the last one had been. *Focus!* She ordered herself sharply. Focus on right now. It wasn't the same fight and it wasn't the same Fiend. That Fiend was dead, she'd made damn sure of it.

They jumped apart as the Fiend went by again. She twisted the ring on her finger, but it wasn't using any magic. She rushed at it with a cry, blade poised to pierce its flesh. It moved and struck as she went past. She managed to step aside, but still felt razor sharp claws against her armour spell, right at the top of her spine where the tattoo was. Like the Fiend knew where to aim. Damien rushed it as she turned, grateful it couldn't negate her magic, though that didn't mean it couldn't kill her.

"No!" She screamed as it struck, sending him flying. Damien went *through* one of the trees, a thunderous crack echoing through the forest as it fell. Rain jumped out of the way. She barely had time to scream his name when the Fiend was on her, moving with a speed she could barely match, a flurry of strikes and steps that gave her no time to collect herself, no time to come up with a plan of attack, just blind panic as she moved to survive. She had to push back memories of the last time: tripping over Malachite's severed head when she jumped back to avoid a blow. She could still remember the feeling of his jaw dislocating under her boot heel. Now she ducked, rolled, then jumped, managing to land on its arm and using it to propel herself at its head. It shifted just enough for her to miss, and she saw the other arm rear back, ready to strike. Something shoved her aside with a flash of silver and she fell unharmed to the ground, flipping to her feet the moment her hand touched the ground and leaping back. Damien stood braced against a tree, one hand outstretched. He'd used the metal in her armour, which shouldn't have been possible for anyone or anything, except that her own sister had designed the spells that strengthened them, so she would have made sure that either their uncle or father could save her life. Blood trickled down the side of his face, but otherwise he looked fine. She jumped and attacked, scoring a long cut on its shoulder. She rolled as she hit the ground, twisting when she came to her feet so she was facing it. The thing was fast, too fast for its size.

Damien threw daggers at it, the silver wires attached to them glittering in the sunlight as the blades stabbed through its shoulders and legs. He made the other end of the wires wrap around trees, boulders, anything that could possibly help restrain it, and the Fiend roared as it struggled to get free, trees bowing. She had no doubt he changed the blades to be barbed the moment they sunk into the Fiend's flesh. "Little help here, kiddo," her uncle said tightly, straining to hold the Fiend. He wove more wires into a thick rope and tried to bind it further, but it was clear it wouldn't last. The Fiend was too strong and too fast. They had to end this *now*. "We got this, it won't be like last time."

She knew what she had to do. The last time she'd done it had been a year ago and it had been a last-ditch effort to survive that had nearly killed her. She'd been certain that she would die. Now she had the proper spells to protect her from the most dangerous weapon a water mage could draw on, though she was one of very few who dared. She pushed her right sleeve up over the tattoo that wound around her hand, wrist, and forearm. "On my mark let it go," she called out. He nodded and she thrust her hand in the air, her skin tingling as her magic worked, trying not to let her fear distract her. Lightning was a friend to no one.

She shrieked in pain as the lightning struck, her tattoos glowing as they tried to contain the electric power, to stop it from killing her. She only had seconds before she lost control of it. "Now!" Damien released the wires and the moment he was clear she let lose, directing the blast at the Fiend. It was incinerated instantly, a pile of blackened bone and ash crumbling to the earth. Rain fell to the ground, clutching her arm as agony radiated out through her body, staring at the ashes that blew away with the wind. It was dead, and she and her uncle were not. Her lips turned up in a smile she knew looked slightly manic, but she didn't care. For a moment, for the barest moment, she'd felt alive again.

The air was still charged from that blast, prickling against his skin. The wire and daggers Damien had thrown were gone, charred and twisted hunks of metal too brittle for even him to salvage. He was cautious as he approached Rain, unsure of her state of mind. She'd looked clear-eyed when she'd attacked, but he knew how quickly that could turn. "Hey, kiddo," he said, sitting down beside her with a groan, holding his side. She was pale and trembling, but that could be the magic she'd used as much as anything else. "How're you holding up?"

"Everything hurts," she said. "But I didn't panic."

"Nope," he agreed, "and we're both still alive. Just remember that the panic usually hits when you think you're safe. Are you hurt?"

She shook her head. "You? That thing threw you pretty hard."

"Let's get going, we'll stay the night and head back." He stood and winced as several muscles protested loudly. "Also, if anyone tries to tell you that using your body to cut down a tree is a good idea, just stab them. I'm going to be every colour of the fucking rainbow tomorrow." He held out a hand and pulled her to her feet.

"Oh fuck," she cursed as she nearly lost her balance. He helped her get stead and then she went to grab a piece of bone before they started walking back. He could see that every movement hurt and recalled the few times that Tempest had used lightning. Even with protection spells she was going to feel that for a few days. "You're bleeding."

He raised a hand to where she was looking and found a cut on his temple. "Splinters are a bitch." He pulled a handkerchief out of his pocket and dabbed at the spot. It stung, but the blood seemed to be mostly dry. Fiends were often attracted by the scent of blood, but with that one around, they likely wouldn't see another before they got back inside the town's walls.

"What about the body?" She asked, rubbing a hand over her face.

"We'll send someone out to get it when we get back," he told her. "Probably Jerek and River. Let them do some of the work." Rain just shook her head and drank from her flask. The last year was showing; she'd always been a talented fighter, flowing and graceful. But now there was a brutal edge to each movement that hadn't been there before, turning her from a talented fighter into a killing machine. He couldn't say it was a bad thing, not in their line of work. It was the changes in her personality that saddened him more, even though he'd known they were inevitable. Panic attacks and depression aside, she was colder, harder than before. But again, those changes were necessary for Hunters to survive and stay as sane as possible. It didn't mean that he didn't regret the loss of the days where she'd scrambled after Tempest and himself whenever they practiced, her toy sword in hand as she tried to copy their movements, laughing with glee when she did it right.

"So this whole 'one night' thing, does it actually help?" She asked, examining her chunk of bone as they walked. Normally they would have taken fangs, but that was only because they were usually easy to get and carry. It didn't actually matter what part of the Fiend they brought back. Some Hunters made it a game to bring back the most disgusting bit they could find, though he and Tempest may have won it for all of time two years before Storm was born.

"I find it does," he replied as she fell in step with him. "It's not the healthiest coping mechanism, mind you, not by any stretch of the imagination, but it's hard to work through things and find closure when you know that the next day or week or month you're going to see the same damn thing or worse, or you're going to be sent to deal with it, especially when you're like us." The elite, the strongest and most damaged of the Hunters.

"Don't you get tired of it?"

"Yeah, I do. It's been over twenty years. But the way I see it, I'm still holding on pretty damn well." Even if it was only by a thread some days.

"And what if this doesn't work for me?"

He forced himself to shrug and kept his tone light. "Then you'll find your own way."

"You sound pretty damn sure about all this."

Damien sighed and stopped. When she turned to face him, he made sure she was looking him dead in the eye. "I helped raise you, I trained you to be the best damn Hunter there is, I put you in situations that no other apprentice would be expected to handle and you not only won but you saved my sorry ass at the same time. I read your letters after you saw horrors that no one outside our line of work, not even Guardians, could imagine. So even if you've forgotten, I know exactly what you're capable of." She stood there for a moment, stunned. "And you know what else? When I die you are going to be standing on that fucking cliff with that medallion around your neck and you're going to throw my ashes to the winds. Not Storm, not Ash, *you*. You will outlive me and I don't give a shit if you're cursing my name as you send me off." She swallowed hard. He had no illusions that Ash would outlive him, even if by some miracle Damien didn't die at the claws of a Fiend. "Do you understand me?"

"Yes." The slightest shadow of a smile flickered on her lips. He wasn't entirely sure she believed him, not yet, but it was a start. Just like killing that Fiend was a start.

"Did I ever tell you it would be easy?"

"Nope, you made it abundantly clear that it was not." She sighed and they started walking again. "You know, that was even better than some of Dad's rants."

"Eh, I had to have at least one in me." He wrapped an arm around her shoulders, careful not to put any weight on her. "Just don't make me do it again. I'm supposed to be the drunk cynic. I like being the drunk cynic. I've turned it into an art form that is sadly underappreciated, please don't take that away from me."

"I'll try," she said, the shadow of a smile becoming a little bit deeper. "And I'd rather you not die for a very long time."

"I'd like that too." But sometimes things didn't always work out that way.

6

Fall

Rain woke screaming, slashing at monsters that weren't there with her dagger before she remembered where and when she was. She dropped the blade and hugged her knees to her chest, sobbing and shaking.

"I got this," she heard her father say before her door opened. She figured her uncle was out there as well, all part of living in a house of light sleepers. "Nightmare?" He asked, carefully looking around the room. It was a reflex developed by all Hunters; check everything at the sound of a scream.

"Yeah," she managed to choke out, the memories still threatening to drive her mad, playing over and over in her mind. The blood on her hands, the desperate, gasping breaths, arguing in the dark as the pool of blood grew.

He sat on the edge of the bed and held her close. "Take a deep breath," he told her. "Just breathe through it." She tried, taking a long, shuddering breath that did little to help, so she took another.

"It was just like I was there again," she said after a while, when her shaking had faded to slight tremors. Her hand was pressed against her stomach through her loose shirt, over the scars that ran from the bottom of her ribs on the right side of her body down to her left hip. The magical dagger that had bound her powers and punctured her lung had put her in serious condition, but this wound along with the others she'd received had very nearly killed her. A sob escaped her. "I wish it had never happened." Then she wouldn't be a suicidal alcoholic at twenty-five who could barely hold herself together, Kestrel wouldn't be a broken ragdoll of scars and spelled metal, the rest of her friends would still be alive, and she never would have... that wouldn't have happened. She wouldn't have been forced to make a decision that had left her broken. Hell, she'd take it a step further and wish that she'd been there when Blaze faced that Fiend in the north, then he would still be alive, sitting with her and Kestrel in some run-down tavern, laughing over a pint as they lost track of time. He would be shaking his head over their antics, Rain cleaning out anyone foolish enough to play a hand of poker against her and Kestrel drinking hardened soldiers under the table. "I wish none of it had happened."

"I know, Rain, I know. But it did happen, and we have to learn to live with it." He sighed. "Survivor's guilt is a terrible thing."

"Yep." He stayed for a few minutes longer until she calmed down. When he left, shutting the door quietly behind him, Rain curled up under the sheets, one hand still over the rough scar tissue. Survivor's guilt was a bitch. She reached for the flask on her bedside table and drank half of it at once. Tomorrow she would sleep; she planned on being too wasted to dream. Hell, she might actually manage to sleep a night through for the first time in months. Or was it tonight already? She glanced over at her window and through the crack in the blinds she could see light slowly overtaking night. It was now the day before midwinter.

This was the day she was allowed to stop trying and let herself feel the pain she kept shoving deeper and deeper into the recesses of her broken heart. She could think about how things should have been so different than they were, could miss the people her heart ached to see just one more time. Eventually she rose and showered, using her magic to heat the water until it was almost scalding. She dressed and went downstairs. Her father had already left, heading to the city with Storm and Phantom. So it was just Uncle Damien in house, and she found him in the kitchen, nursing a steaming mug of tea.

"Did you stay to play babysitter?" She asked, refilling her now-empty flask.

"Nope," he said, drinking from his mug. "Of course, you will see me some time before dawn to peel you and Kestrel off the barstools of *The Fallen Guardian*."

Rain frowned as she sat across from him. "I never told you our plans."

"I've known you your whole life," he reminded her, frowning at the tea and adding a few drops of whiskey from his own flask.

"Can you guess where I'm headed now?"

"The Cliff, but that one's obvious. If you're going to have a day of mourning and regrets, of course that's where you'll start."

"Fair enough," she allowed, taking a drink. She'd been avoiding that spot since she'd returned, but it was time to face reality. "It's going to snow later," she remarked, glancing out the window.

"Very appropriate," he said, drinking his tea.

Rain knew that The Cliff had to have changed, battered as it was by the winds and the raging sea, but it didn't look any different now than when she'd watched her mother's ashes scattered from its edge. Grass and a few hardy types of plants clung stubbornly to the rock along with a few trees, though few grew close to the edge. If she looked over it she would see a craggy surface that was constantly battered and blasted by the ocean and the wind. The only changes she could see were the number of weapons thrust into the ground close to its edge, embedded deep swithin the stone by magic. There were a few other mourners, some openly weeping while others just stared in silence, either at the markers or the distant horizon. She didn't recognise any of them, but could pick out a few Guardians and at least two Keepers in the mix. First she went to her mother's marker. After twenty years her sword was still straight, still a shining silver with a razor edge. The only marks were from the battles she'd fought, including her last, and at some point the leather that wrapped the handle had been replaced with a dark grey wire that reminded Rain of storm clouds. She knew that once the snows were gone there would be flowers that would bloom without anyone taking care of them. She didn't know how often her father came to this spot, but she was certain it was at least as often if not more than her uncle, who made a point to visit it whenever he was home, just like he went to the spot where Raven's ashes had been scattered farther south, where citizens of the city were laid to rest. Those places had no individual memorials, just an altar-like monument. She wasn't sure what to call it, but they were usually quite pretty.

For the most part Keepers held the duty of preserving these funerary sites, a difficult task here since the coastline was constantly battered, though that was part of what made it a truly fitting place for the warriors of their kind. Still, she knew the earliest weapons, those swords, axes, scythes, bows, and others that had belonged to Hunters from eons past had been taken by time. She couldn't help but wonder what The Cliff, the territories, and hell, the world would look like when she had turned to dust. She reached out and touched the pommel of her mother's sword. It was a little shorter than what she favoured, though she knew she was also a little taller than her mother had been. She knelt and saw that there were still two runes near the hilt, the clumsy marks made by the hands of a child; her and Storm, actually. Their father had shown them the runes for luck, and one day when their mother was visiting someone in the village she and Storm had taken the sword and used one of their uncle's metalworking tools to etch them into the blade. Her mother hadn't been angry when she'd seen it, she'd just laughed and asked Uncle Damien to make sure the marks would never wear away. If only they'd worked.

"I'm sorry I couldn't be more like you. I wanted to be. But I'm not. Everyone used to say that you would have been so proud of me, of my skills and how I was a credit to you, Dad, and Uncle Damien. But what about now? Would you still be proud of me, even when I've fucked everything up so badly?" The sword wavered in her tear-filled vision. "I'll try to make you proud again." She stood and blinked away the tears. She had no idea what lay beyond this life, if the legends about her kind were true. Some part of her hoped they were, because that would mean that her mother and her friends weren't truly gone, that they were in a better place where there was no fighting no Fiends, where there was peace. The other part didn't believe a place like that could exist.

Taking a drink, she went down the rows, each weapon placed with care, close to those on either side but not touching. She walked until she came to Adrian's marker, two short swords. If he had lived through their training year she knew he would have been there last year and fought alongside them. Maybe it would have made a difference. Then again, maybe she would have just put off mourning his death for six and a half years. Who the hell knew?

Blaze's scythe stood, the wooden staff no worse for wear, and she knew that if she twisted her ring she would see her father's spells and magic preserving it. Blaze had no plant mages in his family that she'd known of, and she'd wanted to make damn sure that it would withstand the test of time. She hadn't been to his marker since his funeral, had actively avoided it since then because she couldn't bear to face it, to face the fact that he was gone.

"I would have married you," she whispered to the winds, tears falling now. "I never got the chance to tell you, but I would have said yes." She took another drink, almost impossible to swallow past the lump that had formed in her throat. She lingered for a few moments longer, unable to say anything else. She had loved him. She did still, and likely a part of her always would. He hadn't been perfect, but he'd been perfect for her. He hadn't balked at her hesitation to answer, hadn't even looked surprised. He'd kissed her and told her to take her time, he wasn't in a rush, they had all the time in the world.

Except they hadn't, because he'd died a few days later. She couldn't even wonder about what would have happened had she gone with him, because she knew she wouldn't have made a different decision. Kestrel had been in a dangerous situation, and while Blaze was going into a troubled area, he was a strong Hunter and he should have lived. She still didn't know what happened, but in the end, it didn't really matter. Knowing wouldn't bring him back to life, nor would it mend the hole in her heart.

She went a little further, to ten weapons that were clustered closer together than most of the others to show that these Hunters had fallen together. She just broke down at that point, falling to her knees in the snow, sobbing, the guilt overwhelming her. There was no way she could have saved any of them, not then. She'd tried so fucking hard, but she just hadn't been able to do it. There had been more than just the invisible Fiend; there had been a swarm of other Fiends along with it. So many of them…

"I thought I'd find you here," Kestrel said as she stood beside Rain. She'd heard the other Hunter approach, the soft whir and slide of Kestrel's metal leg unmistakable. She wondered how long it had taken Kestrel to get used to it since her friend used to be able to move in absolute silence. "I still can't believe they're all gone."

"I know." Rain got to her feet. "What the hell did we do that we deserved to survive?"

"Dunno, I didn't think I ever did anything that bad." Tears spilled from Kestrel's eye, the normally vibrant gold turned dull. They stood in silence for a long moment, then moved on to visit the markers of the other friends they'd lost. There were a lot of them, far too many.

"Do you really think they found peace?" Rain wondered, taking a drink as she looked down at a scimitar that had belonged to a Guardian who had nearly been able to best them in poker. She handed her flask to Kestrel.

"That's what they always told us, isn't it?" She took a drink before returning it. "When we die we've paid the toll for our powers, so we regain our souls and can find peace." She snorted. "You'd think we'd be more religious with a story like that."

"Hard to believe the gods care most days," Rain said, drinking.

"True, but that doesn't seem to put the humans off any. Then again, they seem generally less cynical than we are, the lucky bastards."

"Yeah, lucky." Lucky little sheep, sitting prey for the monsters and crying for the wolves to protect them since the shepherds did fuck all to protect anyone. But what would happen if the Hunters vanished? What would happen if there was no one left to answer their cries? The sheep would be utterly helpless.

Of their class of over sixty graduates, only ten were still alive, and of those ten, Rain would be surprised to find out that half −including herself- were still active Hunters. The rest were either like Kestrel, forced out due to injury, or quit, unable to take the strain of the last few years. Rain couldn't even say that she blamed them, not after the way she'd spent the last year. Some might gradually get back out there or become Guardians, but most wouldn't. They would try to find a way to build lives that didn't revolve around fighting and pray that their children didn't want to fight monsters. Hell, most active Hunters wished their children wouldn't join the ranks. Her own father had admitted it once a few years before, pointing out that he wanted her to be happy and Hunters don't get that option.

It was inevitable that they would end up *The Fallen Guardian* drinking away their sorrows. Well, Rain was trying to find solace at the bottom of a bottle; Kestrel was doing a much better job of pacing herself. Rain knew she was mostly there to be supportive because while Kestrel did share most of her pain, she was out. She could find some kind of peace in her life, some kind of escape, closure. But that wasn't for Rain. Not now, not until her own sword stood among the other markers and her ashes were scattered across the sea, and that would be a long time coming yet. She had that kind of luck, just like her uncle.

She had vague recollections of Uncle Damien coming to get them at some point and being carried up the stairs. The next thing she knew for certain was that she was waking up in her own bed with a vicious hangover. From the light filtering through the curtains she could tell that it was roughly mid-morning, far later than she normally slept, which made her wonder when she'd gotten home. She rose slowly, fairly certain she was still quite drunk. The world around her shifted and lurched with each movement but she managed to get to her feet, holding onto the wall for balance. Somehow she'd managed to get her weapons off and get out of her armour, a boon because as comfortable as her corsets were, it sucked to sleep in one, which she had done on a number of occasions. She grabbed her flask but knew from the weight that it was empty. She tossed it on her bed with a curse and staggered out into the hall, somehow making down the stairs without incident. There were people in the kitchen, though they were making an effort to speak quietly.

"A targeting spell would make up for the lack of depth perception, d'you think?" Kestrel was asking.

"You'd need a tracking spell mixed with it," Rain's father answered after a moment. "It's been done, but not on a human weapon." Any weapon made by their people was made to withstand their strength and magic. There was also the fact that the craftspeople could bring out more of the natural strengths and inherent magic of their materials to help with that.

"Hey kiddo," Damien said when Rain lurched in. "How's the hangover?"

A groan was all that came out when she tried to speak, and it was probably for the best. Her father rose and handed her a glass of thick, unnaturally blue liquid.

"Drink all of it," he ordered, steering her to the table. She sat with a nod and downed half of it before she realised how awful the taste was. She paused, coughing as she tried not to vomit. Since her head was already starting to clear she drank the rest as quickly as she could before filling it with water to wash away the taste. By the time she put the glass down on the table she felt better than she had in a while, no hangover and no residual drunkenness either.

"Why did I never know you could make that?" She demanded, seeing that Kestrel also had an empty glass in front of her. It would have come in handy a number of times over the years.

"Because I believe in consequences."

"He makes it for me once a year if I'm in town," her uncle said. "It's a recipe he learned from Raven, though she refused to teach it to your mother or me. I have no idea why." He tried and failed to look innocent at that last remark.

"Right... doubtless it's the same reason why the only person I've taught the recipe to is Storm."

"Wait, Storm knows?" Rain was going to have words with her sister.

"I only taught her recently, once she was old enough that you couldn't talk her into telling you what it is or making it for you." It was impossible to tell if that was directed at her or her uncle, but she figured it was most likely an even split.

"Your father is a cruel man," Uncle Damien said with a sigh.

"You know how all these years I've been saying that you're the worst?" She wondered.

"Yeah."

"I've changed my mind," she said, looking at her father.

"Do you see what I've had to put up with the last few weeks?" Her father asked Kestrel, shaking his head in mock despair.

"I'm not taking sides." Kestrel had been around long enough to know better.

"Probably for the best," Damien agreed. "Anyway, back to your question, I think that if we got the schematics for the human design but had one of our own make it, then it could work."

"Are you talking about a bow?"

Kestrel nodded. "Now that I'm used to the new limbs and the limits of my body Nadina's said that she'll help me get back into archery."

"I've heard that name before," Rain said, trying to remember.

"She's one of the Hunters escorting Forest Meadows to the Summit," Damien reminded her. "She graduated in your year."

"Why don't I remember her?" She thought she remembered everyone, living or dead. She'd made a point of learning the names and faces of everyone in her class and remembering them.

"Because until six months ago she went by Nathan," Kestrel said. "You'd have known this if you read the letters we sent you."

Rain frowned for a moment before clueing in. *"Oh.* Okay. But why is she down here? I thought she was planning on staying around the far North since she's from there." There was a small village of their kind in the glaciers just past the Eskaven Mountains that created Phasoia's northern border. There wasn't much past the range except more mountains, ice, snow, and glaciers.

"She had to come to the Academy to finish up the paperwork to change her name and decided to stick around and help out since things are going to hell. She's been coming around every few weeks since then to help with archery lessons since I'm down for the count." Rain recalled the oddly intense yet friendly rivalry they'd had going on since day one at the Academy, and it clearly hadn't ended.

"Weren't they getting hit hard three or four years ago?" Right around the time they realised that something was off about the way the Fiends were moving.

Kestrel nodded. "Right, it was like every Fiend in the north suddenly decided to head south."

"And surround Phasoia, Glask, and Landaia, slowly moving inward," Rain said, thinking.

"Well, Storm did say that it was manufactured." Damien said.

"But there are far richer lands to conquer than Phasoia, Landaia, and Glask. Like Mysk," Kestrel pointed out. Mysk was a huge kingdom further south, beyond the Great Woods.

"You're forgetting that we're also in the mix," Rain's father spoke up

Damien frowned. "But it would take a special kind of idiot to try anything with us, not after the last time."

"Wasn't that eight hundred years ago?" Rain wondered, trying to remember her history lessons.

"Exactly, it resulted in eight hundred years of peace for us. Besides, they need us too much, without our kind it would be a massacre, they'd have no defense against the Fiends." Sheep at the slaughter.

"But how the hell is this working? It'd have to be the Fiends themselves making the move and I don't think they're that politically capable." This was giving Rain a headache; she pressed her fingers against her temples, trying to think it out. She really didn't envy her sister's position.

"No one ever said any of this made sense," her father sighed, shaking his head.

"Well, I should probably get back to the city," Kestrel said eventually. "There might not be classes today but unfortunately papers won't grade themselves." Midwinter was a holiday of sorts, but any kind of festival had been very quiet the last few years, people either in mourning or afraid of attracting attention and bad luck.

"Let me get ready and I'll go with you," Rain said. She went upstairs to shower and dress. She was just sliding her boot daggers in places when there was a knock on the door. "Yes?"

Her uncle entered. "How do you feel today?" She knew he wasn't asking about her hangover.

She thought about it for a moment before answering. "Better." It almost felt like she could breathe easier, like the weight on her had shifted a little. She wasn't fine, but she could last a little longer, which she supposed was the point.

"It's like an infected wound, sometimes you have to drain it," he said. "Maybe it'll heal, maybe it won't."

"And maybe you'll carry scars that leave things unable to work the way they should ever again?"

"Sure." She wasn't certain what category he would fall under. Somewhere between scars and open wounds.

She stood, checking that everything was in place. "From now on just enough to take off the edge."

"For another year. Think you can make it?"

"I don't know." Right now it seemed like she could, but who would know in a week, a month, the next time she faced something that brought on flashbacks or a panic attack?

"How about this: do you want to make it?"

That was much easier. "Yes."

"Okay." He seemed happy enough with her answer.

"Are you going to come to the city with us?"

A slight grin. "Nah, I'm too old to play babysitter again." He had far more faith in her than she had in herself. "Besides, constantly hanging out with you kids is bad for my image."

"Because people might remember how old you are?"

"Now that's just unnecessary." He gave a small, hurt sigh as she walked past.

Damien watched as she and Kestrel rode off, leaving him and Ash. "You going to follow?" The other Hunter wanted to know.

"Nope," he said, though part of him wanted to. "She's not a kid anymore and she's just getting her confidence back." Especially if she was making jokes about his age. Besides, the last time he'd done that had been at the start of her third year at the Academy. As for yesterday, he might have sent a message to let Kestrel know that Rain had left, but he hadn't followed her.

"Why do they have to grow up?" Ash wondered with a sigh.

"Because we need people to take our places when we fall," Damien said, turning away from the window and taking out his flask.

"That's pretty fucking dark."

He raised a brow and didn't back down. "Well, it's true. We won't live forever."

7
Means to an End

Damien checked the edge on his daggers as he packed for a hunting trip. In the few weeks since midwinter Rain had been doing alright. There'd been a few rough moments, some near backslides, but she was holding on with a dogged determination that made him proud. It was strange how time passed, though. When he was twenty-five he'd moved in with Raven and Rain had been a newborn, so tiny and helpless, and two-year old Storm was always getting into something.

"How many days?" Rain asked, poking her head in his room.

"Ten. We're basically going to do a loop." It wasn't the worst winter they'd had, but there had been a few nasty storms. One upside to the storms was that they usually inconvenienced the Fiends as much as the Hunters.

"Damien, message for you!" Ash called from downstairs.

He was tempted to ask the other Hunter to bring it up, but there were far too many wooden objects in his room, never mind the floor, walls, ceiling, and bed among them, so he went downstairs. The message Ash handed him bore the seal of the Council. Frowning, he opened it. They required is presence as soon as possible. The fact that they were summoning him to meet with them instead of merely directing him meant that this was going to be a shade of dangerous that fell far closer to deadly than normal.

"What's wrong?" Ash wondered from where he was checking on the herbs he was coaxing to grow despite the fact that they were deep into winter.

"I have to meet with the Council to find out what my next brush with death will be." He set the letter on the table.

"Sounds fun." Damien snorted and went back upstairs.

"Do you have any more of that balm for bruises?" Rain asked, leaning out of her doorway walked past, frowning when she caught his expression. "What's going on?"

"I have to go meet with the Council. Something came up, and it's going to be extremely dangerous." There was no reason to hide it from her.

"Can I go?" She asked. He wondered if that wasn't a reflex at this point, she'd been asking that question since she was a child.

"I don't know what's going on," he hedged. "I'll be back in a few hours, and there's a big jar of balm under the kitchen sink." He had no idea how it kept winding up there. He readied and left, taking the horse Ash had left in the yard. It only took half an hour to make it to Lysee, the roads miraculously free of Fiends. He made his way through the streets to the Council building with ease. It was a little smaller than the hospital, standing in defiance of the giant and overly ornamental style humans favoured for government buildings or palaces. Still, it was beautiful, built by mages who were masters of their arts. It was made to be a welcoming place, even to an orphaned street rat who'd grown up among humans in a foreign land. He could remember the first time Tempest had dragged him inside, a few months after he'd first arrived at the Academy. He'd been worried about getting kicked out of the building, since their kind weren't welcome in such fine places in Ankira. He'd still been learning about demons, about his people. Tempest had wanted to help him and to show him that the 'demons' weren't the monsters humans made them out to be. They weren't perfect, no culture was, but it was far better than where he had been. He'd been tense the whole time, expecting at any moment that someone would order them out, but even though they'd deliberately dressed in ragged clothing –so Tempest could make her point- no one had. The Keepers had simply nodded as they walked by or asked if they needed anything. To him it had been surreal. It had also marked the end of Damien referring to himself as a demon for the most part. Demons were monsters the humans created. His people were just trying to make sure everyone survived as best they could.

Now his boots tread familiar paths over the brightly coloured rugs that decorated the smooth stone floors with confidence. He made it to the meeting room and entered without knocking since they were expecting him. The five members of the Council sat around a table, and the atmosphere was alarming: a decided mix of rage and despair as he sat in a sixth chair that had been pulled up. Storm looked exhausted, despair and guilt adding a century to her eyes. He knew three things at that point: they'd figured out what the hell was going on, they were going to count on him to fix it, and it was going to be bad.

"So, what's going to try to kill me this time?" He asked without preamble, leaning back in his chair and kicking his boots up. Garnet glared at him so he gave her his most charming smile in return.

"This is serious, Hunter," she said, her tone as biting as always.

"I assure you, I am being serious." They had never really gotten along. Actually it was fair to say that they hated each other. She had been a year ahead of him at the Academy. There was just something about her that rubbed him the wrong way, and the feeling was mutual. "What's going on and what do I need to do to deal with it?"

"We know what's causing the Fiends to attack this part of the world," Storm spoke up, her voice ancient and brittle. "It's our own people."

"What?" His feet hit the floor as he sat up. To suspect it was a possibility was one thing, but to hear it was the case was another. "But our people are being targeted."

"That's what makes this particularly abhorrent," Aria said. She was the oldest serving member of the Council, well over a hundred years in age though her pale grey eyes were still razor sharp.

"We have reason to believe that this is a precursor to someone trying to build an empire. If they take out our kind they can easily take control of any country they wish using Fiends, and Landaia, Glask, and Phasoia are a pretty good start," Forest added, "not to mention our own lands."

"One person couldn't do this alone, could they?" He asked, leaning back again as he rubbed a hand along his jaw.

"Possibly," Storm replied. "It seems like the spells are made so that the casters control the more powerful Fiends, who can in turn control or influence average Fiends. But with the area being covered there have to be at least two people behind this, we don't believe a single person could keep this up for a long time. You will have to kill everyone who has a hand in the spell to break it. Do you remember the story of the Keeper who wanted to control the Fiends?"

Damien had told that one to Storm and her sister years ago. "He wanted to be able to control the Fiends so he could turn them on one another, so that Hunters and Guardians wouldn't have to take such risks. He went away so he could work on his spells where they couldn't hurt anyone else. Some say he succeeded, but died of old age before he could find an apprentice to whom he could entrust his life's work, others say the work drove him mad and he threw himself from the tower, more say that the magic backfired and he was killed by Fiends he tried to control, his spells either faltering or not working at all."

"I traced the magic to the Eskaven Mountains in northern Phasoia. We managed to get a hold of a map that shows there's an old fortress there, though that's all we know about it." A lot had been lost when the kingdom that held the territories that now belonged to Phasoia and Glask fell two and a half centuries before.

"Do you have any idea who's behind it?" He asked, running a hand through his hair. He wasn't sure he wanted to know the answer.

"We know one and have an idea for a second," Storm said. "Gold Tailor is the one we're certain of. There were traces of metal magic, and he's the only metal mage powerful enough that we can't vouch for." Metal magic wasn't the most common and Damien had always been more powerful than Gold, even when he'd only been an apprentice not quite grown into his magic. There were four or five others who were even stronger, but they worked as smiths and weapons-makers, mostly in the city or at the Academy. He doubted, as Storm likely did, that anyone weaker than Gold would have been able to manage a spell like that for any amount of time, let alone roughly half a decade.

"And the idea?"

"No one who is supposed to be living," Garnet began cryptically.

Damien sighed. "Now is not the time for riddles, Garnet."

She pursed her lips, but dropped the act. "The only person we can think of is supposed to have been dead for thirty years, so we think she had an apprentice we didn't know about. Do you remember hearing about Shade Perrela? Of course, we have no idea what kind of mage her apprentice might be, which makes everything a little harder." Damien nodded, remembering the stories. He'd been in the Thieve's Court in Dagani at the time so he'd only heard about it after everything had ended. Wolf had been sent to kill a Keeper who'd gone rogue and it had cost him his sanity. Given some of the things shadow mages could do, like the idiot who'd caused Rain's panic attack a few months before, he wasn't surprised.

It still didn't make sense. "They wouldn't be looking to build an empire, though. Would they?"

Forest shook his head. "No, we believe they are either working with or for someone else, but we don't know who."

Damien shrugged. They would be human, nothing he was worried about. "Will I be doing this on my own?" It was almost like a bad joke: some demons, humans, and Fiends walk into a bar... Still, not bad for a day's work, though traveling in winter was a bitch and a half, especially going northward. On the other side of the Eskaven Mountains it wasn't a long trek to reach permafrost.

Aria raised a white brow. "Are you asking because you want to be on your own or because you have a team in mind already? Either way, we're leaving it up to you. Anyone and anything you require will be made available to you. We want this dealt with as quickly as possible." From her tone Damien knew that he wasn't being sent to capture the rogues, this was going to be an execution. Sanctioned murder. It didn't bother him nearly as much as it should have, likely remnants from being raised among humans. Demons saw killing one of their own as the highest crime. Humans didn't value the lives of their own people nearly so much. At least, not that he'd ever seen.

"Excellent." He could feel Storm's eyes on him as she realised what he was going to do. "My niece, Rain Undine, will be my partner in that case."

Forest frowned. "I heard the girl had become unstable."

"She was. She's made significant progress over the last few months," Damien replied honestly. "She's skilled enough for the task and I believe that mentally she can handle it." It would let him keep a bit of an eye on her while he threw her into real danger again, and she was also one of the few people alive he trusted at his back. The others were Amber and Ash, and Rain was far stronger and better suited to this than either of them.

"No one doubts Rain's talents," Garnet said. "But if she panics at the wrong moment... perhaps someone who just has more experience would be a better choice."

"She won't, and I believe this will be a good opportunity for her, since I expect she will be able to undertake such tasks for the Council in the future." She was following in his footsteps and in Tempest's, though hers would go on long after theirs ended.

"He is correct in that," Aria agreed. "This is a chance for her to prove herself." The others nodded slowly, though Storm looked like someone was forcing her head to move. He knew it couldn't be easy, balancing her duties as a member of the Council and as both his niece and Rain's sister when she was sending them into danger by doing her job correctly. But it was something that she had chosen, just like rest of the Council. Like Hunters, they had no illusions about the darker aspects of their duties. He was proud that she could deal with it and do her job well.

"What of the Summit?" It made no sense to put it off until spring now.

"We've moved it up, since we're more aware of the nature of the threat," Aria replied. "Storm and Forest leave tomorrow by Guardian Ship with their escorts, and ships have also been sent for the Phasoian and Landaian delegates." Damien's brows went up. This was unprecedented. But then, so was everything about this situation; unprecedented and urgent.

"Might Rain and I accompany you as far as Ankira? We'll head north from there."

"Of course," Forest agreed, frowning slightly. It was still quite a trek from Ankira and the weather wouldn't help. Damien hated travelling any kind of distance in the winter. It sucked.

"I know some people in the city who might be able to shed more light on this now that we have real information."

"Can you trust that they won't be spies?" Garnet demanded. "The nature of those acquaintances gives us reason to doubt how trustworthy they are."

"They know better than to cross me," he said with a cold smile.

Forest spoke before Garnet could say anything else. "How long do you plan on staying?"

"We'll leave the next sunrise. I'll make sure that any new information gets passed on to you or Storm."

"Very well. I believe that's all?" Aria looked around at her colleagues.

"One thing," Storm said. He looked at her. She wasn't happy with him, but she had to know that Rain would have been begging to go anyway and he was certain that even if he said no she would follow. "In the fortress there should be information about the spells, notes and the like on how to use them. We either need them brought here or destroyed."

He canted his head slightly. "Which would you prefer?"

"I would prefer they be destroyed. As useful as the spells could be, they've already proven to be far too dangerous. The risk of the wrong person finding them again is too high."

"Very well," he answered, proud of her.

"The route and everything is left to you to decide, you'd know best," Forest added. "If there's anything you need let us know, and if you're on the road send a falcon, we will ensure that it gets to you as soon as possible. I believe that's everything?" He glanced at Storm, who nodded. "Very well, that'll be all." The others stood and left one by one.

"Do you need an escort back home?" He asked Storm when she stood.

"Yeah, I'll be going now since I need to pack, and Phantom still has a few hours of his shift left. He's coming, but he doesn't have to figure out how to fit a thousand pounds of paper and books into a saddlebag." He nodded as he stood, stretching. Forest was still there as well, and met his eyes.

"I'll catch up to you in a few minutes," Damien said, able to take a hint. She nodded and walked out, leaving him with the other Council member.

"This is something I never saw coming," the retired Hunter admitted, drumming his fingers on the heavy wood of the table.

"I don't think any of us could have," Damien replied with a grim smile.

"You know, I'm surprised that Gold lived this long," he said, drumming his claws against the heavy wooden table.

"Yeah," Damien agreed, shrugging. "But he's been living in the shadows for years now, he's quite good at it."

"Did you know that I was the lead investigator in Eida's death?"

That was an odd comment to make, though Gold and Eida had always been very close. "I didn't realise you were a detective."

"I happened to be the closest one to the scene, and it's not like it was overly complicated. A perfect suicide." His tone hinted at his suspicions.

"She always was rather methodical, except when it came to gambling," Damien said.

"I imagine that Tempest was glad to hear of it."

"She'd gotten past everything by the time word reached us." It wasn't a lie, technically speaking.

"What about you, are you past what Gold did?"

"Are you trying to make sure I'm not going to make this all about revenge?"

"If we're being honest, very little about this won't be about revenge," the older man admitted. "For you, your niece, for all of our people. If I had any concerns you would take a stupid risk to get that revenge, however, you would not be standing here."

"Alright, but I get the sense that there's more to this than reminiscing over traitors."

"Make the bastards pay, Damien."

Damien smiled; a cold, cruel expression. "Bet on it."

He left in search of his eldest niece and found her in her office filing a bag with books and papers. "Do you really need all of that?" He asked, brows raised. There was a lot.

"I don't know," she said, more than a little frantic as she moved around, adding more to the pile.

"Why the worry?" He moved to lean against her desk so he'd be out of the way, careful not to knock anything over.

Her expression was bleak. "I have no experience with this kind of thing and they're all counting on me. Not just the Council, everyone. Our people, the humans, everyone is counting on me for answers, and I get to be the one to tell them that even after the spell is broken it could take over a year for things to go back to the level of nightmare that we've enjoyed for eons as well as a possible invasion."

"Don't worry; the minute you tell them that there's a couple of Hunters going to deal with the spell the pressure will be all on us and you'll be their hero," he said with a wry grin. "Forest will have your back and Rain's friend Schuyler will support you. As for the invasion, they've probably pinned everything on this working, especially since it came pretty damn close. Breaking the spell could very well destroy them."

"And I agreed to send you and Rain into dangers unknown." Ah, yes, he'd been wondering when that was going to come up. "What if we're underestimating the danger?"

"That's our job, Storm." He took a drink from his flask. "Normally we don't even have this much information when we get sent out to do something. I've faced some real nightmares that I didn't expect to deal with over the years. That's just how things are, and it's why Hunters like Rain and I get sent out to deal with them, because we're the most likely to survive the worst case scenario."

"Right," she said, leaning against a bookcase with a sigh.

"We'll be home before you can miss us."

"Then you'll be gone again."

"Right." They were Hunters, it was what they had done for generations and what they would keep doing for generations more, long after he was dead, long after the girls were dead. It would just go on and on and on until everything turned to dust. He took a drink.

"I wish we could do something more, something that would make a real difference," she said wistfully, wrapping her arms around herself. Damien held out his arms and his niece stepped into his embrace. "I don't want things to just go back to the way they were before. I want them to be better."

"So do I, but that's not going to happen." Reality was a harsh and unforgiving thing.

After a while she stepped back and emptied the bag of books to reorganise it. When she was done the pile was much smaller. "There, that's everything."

"Alright, let's go," he said, taking the bag for her. "Are you ready?"

"As ready as I'll ever be. Thanks."

"It's what I'm here for," he told her as they walked out.

Ash and Rain were playing cards when they got back, though the game was quickly abandoned when Damien and Storm walked into the kitchen.

"Well?" Rain asked.

"You and I won't have to worry about any fancy parties," he answered. "We have to go save the world. Well, four countries, anyway." Storm quickly explained the situation. While Rain looked more and more eager, he could see Ash growing increasingly concerned.

"I also have a map," Storm said, bringing his full attention back to the conversation. "Since we didn't actually talk about exactly where you were going."

"That is kind of important," he agreed as she pulled it out of her bag and spread it out on the table. The map was of northern Phasoia, the Eskaven Mountains curving around the northern border. "I spent almost half a year trapped there," he said, pointing to one spot near the top of the crescent. Storm looked over at him.

"The fortress is around here," she said, pointing to a spot that would have been roughly three days' ride away from where he'd been.

So close. He'd been so fucking close. He pounded his fist on the table, the wood nearly giving way. "Fucking hell, I could have ended this already?" He snarled as he stared at the spot.

"And done what Damien? They would have caught you by surprise and killed you," Ash said as he ran his hand over the table, fixing whatever damage was hidden by the map with his magic. Damien forced himself to sit and took a huge swallow of whiskey.

Storm looked at her sister. "We should go pack."

"Re-pack in my case," Rain said almost absently as she followed Storm out. Damien moved to stand, but from the look on Ash's face, they weren't done.

Ash waited until the girls were upstairs before speaking. "I don't like this. I really don't."

Damien sighed. "What part of it?" He could guess several things his old friend might object to aside from everything.

"The part where you and Rain are going on a revenge quest," he replied, started to pace around the room.

"Things turned out okay last time I did something like that, and Tempest and I were younger than Rain is now."

The other Hunter's frown deepened. He hadn't been pleased with Damien or Tempest then, either, though he'd kept his mouth shut when he'd found out what they'd done. "Maybe, but there wasn't nearly as much danger. What if you kill the mages before the Fiends? They'll rip you apart."

"You say that like the mages won't order them to anyway."

"The fight will be more controlled because they won't want to die."

"I'm hardly helpless and neither is your daughter."

"What about the part where one of the mages likely has a connection to the Keeper who drove Wolf mad? And need I remind you that we have no idea what actually happened that day?"

"Wolf was never all there to begin with," Damien argued. "Shade was a shadow mage; they're even less common than metal mages. There's not much chance that a powerful shadow mage would be born and vanish without word getting around." Which was lucky for them; Damien would have preferred to take on an army of powerful Fiends to one powerful shadow mage. At least he would die knowing what was real.

"True," Ash agreed reluctantly. "Still, there's so much about this that's just not right."

"I think you mean everything."

He snorted. "Pretty much…" Damien could see there was something else on Ash's mind.

"What is it?"

"I need you to promise me something."

He had a few guesses as to what that could entail. "What?"

"I want you to promise me that Rain will come back alive. That whatever happens, whatever goes wrong, she will come back alive." Ash's bright green eyes never left Damien's mercury gaze.

"I swear I will do everything and anything in my power to make sure that Rain returns alive," he vowed, not looking away. The implications of those words weren't lost on either Hunter.

The next morning they set sail just after sunrise. Rain and Nadina stood at the bow of the ship, Nadina plucking nervously at her bowstring while Rain watched what was going on around them and occasionally drinking from her flask. Normally there wasn't any trouble on the water, the ships moved quickly and the water mages were powerful. But these weren't normal times. The night before had been hellish, with awful nightmares that left her screaming as she woke. She should have expected it after everything they'd found out. She also thought she'd heard more than one shout from the direction of her uncle's room as well.

"Nervous?" Rain asked the other Hunter. She hadn't seen Nadina in roughly three years, and the other woman looked happier and more confident than she'd been back then.

"I'm pretty sure I should be the one asking you that question," Nadina said ruefully.

"I only have to deal with Fiends and a few crazy bastards hell-bent on genocide. You have to deal with humans who pay too much attention to titles and power and largely both fear and despise us."

"I don't know what it says that you managed to make the humans sound worse."

Rain gave the other Hunter a crooked grin. "I can kill my problems. You can't. Well, it would be frowned upon, anyway."

Nadina snorted, relaxing a little. "Doesn't your uncle call them 'venomous sheep'?"

"He does think that is funny," she said dryly. Much to her despair he'd never forgotten it.

"You have to admit that the analogy isn't inaccurate."

Rain sighed. "That makes it worse."

Nadina's grin widened for a moment. "Hey, it works. Most of what I know about nobles I learned from the people around the thieves' courts, and a lot of it wasn't pleasant by any stretch of the imagination."

"And I'll bet that that stretch wasn't very far from the truth either." Rain leaned against the wooden railing. "I haven't dealt with many nobles, luckily."

"Though I have to say, I'd rather deal with the human thieves than our own. Vine is one scary bastard," she remarked.

"He does tend to inspire that emotion in a lot of people," Rain allowed.

Nadina frowned. "Have you ever met the guy?"

"He's my uncle. Didn't you know that?" While none of them advertised the connection it wasn't a secret.

"If I did I've forgotten it," she admitted.

"Don't worry, most people do," Storm said as she joined them. "Actually, I think most people get him mixed up with Uncle Damien."

"So how's he related to you? Damien, I mean, not Vine."

"He was Mom's best friend," Rain said.

"Oh, I get it" she said. "It's hard to believe that Vine and your dad are brothers."

"I know, and I'm pretty sure they feel the same way about it. We don't have much to do with him, I used to think it was because he was mean, but he's just not much of a family person." Unlike Uncle Damien, who'd spent a long time dreaming of being part of a family. "I also think he doesn't want Dad's name to get dragged through the mud in connection to him."

"He actually admitted to that the last time I spoke to him," Storm said.

"When was that?"

"A few months ago. I'm in the city a lot, remember? We run into each other from time to time."

"So the rumours are true then?" Nadina asked in hushed tones.

"That he's got a finger in basically every criminal operation on the continent? Yeah." Rain didn't lower her voice.

Nadina glanced around. "Should you say that so loudly?"

"I've called him out on it more than once," she replied. "He doesn't scare me." Part of it was because while Vine had little interest in family, he wouldn't hurt them. The other part was that they both knew who would win if it came down to a fight and it wasn't Vine.

"You know, he actually offered to help find you," Storm remarked.

She raised a brow. "Really?"

"Yeah, but Uncle Damien was already on it, and Dad figured you wouldn't respond well to the kind of people Vine has at his disposal."

"He wouldn't be wrong," she agreed, turning to look back out at the water. "Storm, doesn't Phantom get seasick?"

"Yeah, it's funny. I mean unfortunate. It's unfortunate." Rain glanced back to catch her sister's grin. "Dad made him some kind of remedy to keep him from suffering, though." They all looked over at Storm's husband. While he didn't look green he was holding the railing with a white-knuckled grip. When he glanced over Storm blew him a kiss and he glared at her, inciting a laugh.

"Are you ready for this?" She asked Storm.

"Not in the least, but I need to do this. There's too much at stake and we need to use everything we have and do anything we can to end this." She turned her ice blue eyes northward. "Are you ready?"

"I am." Rain hoped she wasn't lying.

8
Long Live the King

Early the next afternoon they saw smoke rise over the treetops.

"Where is that?" Rain asked the ship's captain, watching as the dark cloud rose into the clear winter sky. Nadina and Amber were looking as well.

"Port Lacoren," he replied grimly as he turned to the mages. "Speed up!" The ship sped up, until it was difficult to see anything but a blur of colours and even Rain had to hold onto something to keep her feet under her. The Hunters rushed below to don their weapons and armour.

"What's going on?" Storm asked, pale as she looked up. The sisters were sharing a room with Nadina and Amber. Storm had stayed to work on something while the others above deck to give her some peace and quiet.

"Port Lacoren is probably under attack," Rain told her when the others hesitated. Storm froze and went dead white. Rain wasn't surprised; while Storm may have gotten over her fear enough that one or two Fiends wouldn't send her into a catatonic state she was still terrified of them. There was a knock on the door and Nadina opened it to let Phantom in. He went to Storm and wrapped his arms around her.

"The ship's air mage has been able to confirm that it's Fiends and that the attack is still ongoing," he told them as Storm hid her face against his shoulder.

"Can we get anything on how bad it is?" Amber asked as she ran a hand over the jeweled studs that lined her pointed ears. Rain knew she was checking the spells she had stored in them.

"No, sorry."

"Are you going to stay here?"

"Unless you really need help…" he glanced at his wife.

Amber considered it for a moment. "Between the Guardians and the Hunters here with wounded companions we should be fine."

"Won't they want to stay with those friends to make sure they live through it?" Rain wondered as she braided her hair. Generally speaking, Hunters didn't go near the Guardian Ships unless they were almost dying, like the other two times she'd been on one.

"Some will, but most will fight. Wouldn't you?"

"Fair enough." She wanted to say she'd have to think about it, but realistically she knew that wouldn't happen. She would always fight the Fiends. She glanced at her sister, hoping that the fact that they were being casual about it would help her calm down, which meant she had to keep her worries that this was a deliberate action by their enemies to herself for now. Still, it was looking like it might be a better idea for her and Uncle Damien not to stop in Ankira and keep going north as fast as they could.

"They'll likely have the docks set up as a shelter for non-combatants," Nadina said as she strung her bow. "I overheard the mages talking about the port emergency protocol. Anyone who's injured will be put on a ship and the ships will move out to the middle of the river, along with any non-combatants they can fit." Aquatic Fiends generally stuck to deeper waters than the river they were on.

"We're nearly there." Rain's father said as he came into the room. "Storm, you okay?"

"I don't want to be here," she said in a small voice.

"It'll be like any normal day," Phantom told her in a soothing tone. "I'll be by your side and your family will be fighting the monsters. Your sister and uncle will probably get into some insane contest that we'll hear about when they come back and your dad will just roll his eyes while they argue about stolen targets or Fiends that should count as two kills instead of one."

"He's not wrong," Rain added, keeping her tone light. "Except for the 'insane' bit, anyway." The others just looked at her for a moment, even Storm. "What?"

"I'll act as your spotter," Nadina offered. "Insane or not."

"Sweet!"

"That'd be cheating," Uncle Damien said from the doorway. "We're all needed above deck. Come on Storm, you're needed too." Phantom helped her stand, but she managed to walk up on her own. The smoke was much closer, its scent heavy on the air now. Rain could hear the sounds of a battle.

"There's one upside to this," she remarked, watching the plume draw closer.

"What?"

"A fast-moving river is a pretty good source of power." She'd been drawing on it since they'd set sail, using spell beads to store what her body couldn't hold right away. Since she'd switched to spell tattoos for her more important enchantments she'd found a new use for the beads. The power of a fast-moving river like this one was better than a pond or lake, though she was hoping for a good storm before they had to face their enemies.

The ship slowed as they reached the docks, which were set in a crescent that Rain wasn't sure was natural. With their kind involved it could be hard to tell. Crude tents lined the wooden walkways; people crowded them as screaming could be heard from behind the wall created by the buildings set near the harbour. It was hard to see how far along the fight was from their position.

"I'm going over," Rain decided, unable to wait any longer. The captain nodded without looking at her. She leaped overboard, turning the water beneath her feet to ice as she landed. She wasn't surprised when the other Hunters joined her, thought Forest stayed behind. They ran to the docks and Rain melted the path behind them to keep it from getting in the way of any ships.

"What do you need?" Rain's father asked a Guardian who waved to them.

"We need Fiends dead," she replied grimly.

"We can do that," Damien said, giving the Guardian a mock-salute.

"I'll take the high road," Nadina said. They quickly chose their directions and split up. She watched as her friend leaped to the rooftops, an arrow already poised to strike. Her warning spell had gone off a few minutes before, but she'd turned it off because there would be danger all around. A roar was all the warning she had before a young woman came running around the corner, a Fiend only steps behind her. Rain took a running leap and took the Fiend's head off in a smooth cut.

"Head for the docks," she ordered. The human nodded and changed direction. Rain kept going, searching for Fiends and keeping out of the way of other fighters. Port Lacoren's high concentration of her people meant there would be more fighters and fewer casualties than other human settlements. As it was, she did intervene when the fighters looked like they weren't even of an age to attend the Academy, ordering them to head for safety while she dealt with the Fiends. While she understood the driving need to fight–she felt it herself- an untrained fighter was just more work for the gravediggers after the battle was over.

She turned as a Fiend came running at her only for it to fall as an arrow exploded in its neck, taking its head off in a brutally efficient way. She raised her sword in salute to Nadina, who waved as she leaped to the next building, her magic allowing her to all but fly across the distances.

"There's some trouble over this way," she called out. Rain nodded but kept to the streets in case she met other foes. She reached an open space with a fountain, the whole area painted red with blood. Fiends were still feeding from the remains of the group they had trapped, bits of flesh flying. Rain had to stop and take a deep breath, but the dark memories stayed at the edge of her mind, promising to come out in full force once she thought she was safe. She drew water from the fountain and the snow on the ground, sending it out as a barrage of lethal icicles. The Fiends who weren't shredded were pinned to the sides of buildings, easy pickings for her and Nadina.

The last Fiend had fallen when she saw a green explosion erupting in the sky, followed by others. Archers signaling that the fight was over. She took to the rooftops, stopping beside Nadina. "We need to keep moving," she said.

"I agree," The other Hunter said tightly and they took off, leaping from rooftop to rooftop. Rain wasn't an air mage, but she could still clear the distances with ease. After all, she wasn't human.

"Do you think…" she began, but didn't know how to word it.

"That this was deliberate?"

"Yeah."

"I want to say that's crazy."

"But you aren't going to."

"Unfortunately." They soon caught up with Amber and Damien, dropping to the streets so they could join the other pair.

"Where's Dad?" Rain asked her uncle.

"He went back once he saw that everything was being handled to help with the injured." A plant mage was handy to have around in those situations – especially in winter- and Rain knew her father always carried the seeds of medicinal plants with him. "I don't think we're going to be able to stop long in Ankira," he warned her.

"I figured as much. Do you think they found out the Summit got moved ahead and decided to try to stop us?" Like Nadina, neither her uncle nor Amber looked surprised at her suggestion.

"I don't know," he replied after a moment. "It could be, or it could be something random. Since it's not going to be an issue much longer I wouldn't worry about it."

"I should have checked for magic, like with the other Fiends," she said, annoyed with herself. "I know it wouldn't have made a difference, but what if they decide to hit Ankira next?"

"They wouldn't," Amber said. "It would be foolish to attack a capital city first. It might be a human city, but it's still got Guardians, plenty of military resources, and traveling Hunters."

"Not to mention the thieves with all their little forbidden magics and tricks," Damien added. "The only places safer than a capital city would be Lysee or the Academy."

They reached the docks and Rain was surprised and proud to see her sister moving among the tents with their father, helping him. She couldn't see the ship that had brought them, but she figured it was safe to assume they'd either turned around to get reinforcements while the port town recovered or were among the ships holding the wounded and non-combatants. Forest confirmed the former when they found him.

"We can't stay here," he added. "We have to keep going."

"Yeah, we figured as much," Phantom said as he led Storm and Ash over. They collected their things from one of the tents and managed to acquire enough horses for their group. They found no resistance as soon as they explained why they were there, and by the time they got on the road they'd only lost a few hours of travel time.

They set a fast, hard pace to reach Ankira as quickly as possible. Amber and Phantom took the lead while Rain's father and Nadina guarded the rear. Rain and her uncle flanked the group on either side, ranging along the group and off the road, making sure that nothing could get close. It was a tense ride and they were all relieved to be inside the gates as evening fell, bringing snow with it.

"I still need to see if any of the smugglers know about that fortress," Damien said quietly as they rode past the line of people waiting to get into the city. There were some glares cast their way, but even if the humans didn't recognise anyone in the group they would still know them for Hunters by their clothing, so no one tried to stop them.

"Soulless monsters," someone muttered.

"Haven't heard that one in a while," Rain muttered quietly.

"No, those insults seem to be coming around again," Nadina said.

She shrugged. "Could be someone's brushing up on their legends and fairy tales again, humans get into that every few years." Unless someone chose to say something to her face she let the weak barbs pass. They would eat their words when one of her people had to save their sorry asses from monsters that wanted to rip them apart and feast on their flesh. She glanced over at her sister to see how Storm was doing with this. Of the group Rain, Storm, Nadina, and Amber stood out the most. The sisters both had unnaturally vibrant blue hair and eyes, though Storm's hair and eyes were several shades lighter than Rain's, while Nadina had white hair and eyes, and Amber had amber eyes and ruby red hair that was just starting to have strands of white running through it.

"They look so... fragile," Storm said quietly when she caught Rain's look. Rain understood her tone; for most of their life Storm had been considered fragile due to her physical limits even though she was quite powerful magically.

"Yet still so destructive," Uncle Damien added as they went through the gates. He didn't lower his voice. The others shook their heads as he led the group through the streets and to the palace.

Storm moved until she was next to Rain. "Take this," she said, handing Rain what looked like a silk handkerchief. Rain frowned but took it, her eyes going wide as she felt the magic in it.

"What is this?"

"I was trying to think of something that could help you," she said, keeping her voice low so that only Rain could hear her. "This was the best I could come up with." Rain opened the square. It was the size of a handkerchief, the spell drawn out in Storm's neat and elegant hand. Runes went around and through what looked like an elaborate knot of a design. She recognised a number of them, but some she'd never seen before.

"This is for a storm?" She asked, looking back up at her sister.

"Remember how they told us never to mess with weather magic?"

"Because it's stupid and dangerous."

"Well, we're messing with weather magic. If you burn that it'll create a massive thunderstorm; lightning, rain, wind, the whole bit. The only thing is that once it gets released you won't be able to control it and its as powerful as I could make it and still keep the spell stable." So it'd probably put a hurricane to shame.

"And all I have to do is light it on fire?"

"That's it. As soon as it takes effect there'll probably be enough lightning to blow up a building, so get away fast," she added. Rain nodded and carefully folded the silk before she tucked it into one of her belt pouches. "Don't use it unless you absolutely have to. I've never done the spell before and I don't know how well it'll work, and even if it works perfectly it'll be dangerous."

"It'll work." Rain had no doubt about that. Storm was brilliant and meticulous. If she said a spell would do something then it would do just that. "Who knows, I might finally beat Uncle Damien with this spell." She grinned when Storm rolled her eyes.

It wasn't long before they reached the palace, and goodbyes were said before they split up. There was an awful tension, an unspoken fear in everyone's eyes that made Rain relieved when she and her uncle rode off towards the darkest parts of the city.

"It's almost like they don't expect us to come back in one piece," she said as they turned away from the main thoroughfare to narrower streets that were far less crowded. She smiled at a man who pulled a knife from his ragged clothes while advancing on them, flashing her fangs. He paled and ran off.

"Well, we are both known for being a touch reckless, so their concern isn't without reason or precedence," he pointed out as they reached the decrepit-looking building that served as the court of thieves in Ankira. She couldn't argue against that, so she just shrugged.

The night was getting started when they entered. The first thing Rain noticed, however, was that Dagger wasn't on the throne. His granddaughter Laverna was. Rain looked at her uncle to see that he'd noticed as well, dread tightening his features. When she'd been here in the past, even if Dagger was off somewhere else and left things in Laverna's control, she might have been around the throne but never on it. Never. Only the Thief King sat on the throne. She followed her uncle as he went straight for the throne. Laverna saw them and rose to meet them before they reached the shallow dais.

"Granda's not dead," she said quickly. "But he's not long for it."

"How long has this been going on?" Damien asked, suddenly looking a hundred years older.

"He got sick over the summer and decided to step down. He's over sixty now, so I guess it shouldn't be that much of a surprise. He's lived far longer than most Thief Kings," she explained, though Rain could see the sorrow in her eyes. She knew that the other woman had been raised by Dagger. "I'll have someone take you to him, if you'd like. I know he'd like to see you." The 'one last time' went unspoken.

"Sure."

"I'll stay and see what I can find out," Rain offered.

Her uncle nodded, but she wasn't entirely sure he'd heard. "Thanks," he said as he followed the burly human that Laverna waved over.

He should have known this was going to happen at some point. He should have known it a long time ago. *Maybe I just never thought I'd live to see him die of old age,* he thought. Humans aged faster than his people, and they deteriorated far faster as they aged. When he was Dagger's age he would still be in his physical prime, maybe with a few lines on his face. Hell, Ember could have easily spent several more years in the field if she'd chosen to, and she had a decade on the former Thief King.

The thug brought him upstairs to the suite of rooms that Dagger had occupied since taking the throne almost forty years ago. They were in immaculate condition considering the look of the building, but he knew the decrepit façade was part of the front that it was an abandoned building of no interest. Dagger's rooms were hidden for the few times the police dared to raid the court. He was left in the sitting room while the human went to talk to Dagger. Damien could hear his friend coughing and speaking in a thin, frail voice that sounded nothing like him.

"Dagger will see you now," the thug said as he left. Damien nodded went into the room, trying to ignore the faint scents of disease and blood. Dagger was reclined on his massive bed, far thinner than when Damien had seen him just a few months before when he'd passed through Ankira on his way home.

"I was wondering when you'd show up," the former King of Thieves remarked. "Did my granddaughter send for you?"

"No, I'm on my way to deal with our Fiend overpopulation issue," he replied, forcing himself to sit down in the chair that someone had put by the bed. He hated disease. He couldn't stand to be around anyone who was sick, and it had nothing to do with catching it, because he was too strong for most illnesses to infect him. "I see you've finally handed over your crown."

"She'll rule for a long time," Dagger predicted. "I'm happy I lived long enough to see it." He had a coughing fit then, and the handkerchief he used to cover his mouth came away red. Damien gripped the arms of the chair to keep himself from bolting. In his mind it was Raven lying there, too weak and fevered to move, too delirious to know it was him at her side.

"Surely you're not going to give in so easily, old friend," he said tightly.

Dagger wheezed a laugh. "Yes, I am old, but you're no spring chicken either, not anymore. I've had a good run of it, but I think this is of the road for me."

Damien's eyes burned. "No one can live forever." The old thief had said that to him the day they'd met. His mother had died not long before and he'd been trying to figure out how to survive. It hadn't been long before Dagger started looking out for him even as he aspired to rule the thieves.

"Exactly, and I don't want to either. Now tell me, how's that niece of yours doing these days?"

"She's doing better. Right now she's downstairs trying to see if anyone knows anything useful to us." Someone would, someone always did in these places. It was just a matter of asking the right people the right questions, and he was sure she could manage it.

"How much longer do you plan on Hunting?" Dagger wondered with a slight grin.

"Don't know. I'll find out when I die," he replied with a slight smile. Dagger just shook his head. It was an old conversation. If he was a thief it might have made sense to retire, or even if he'd been human, but he wasn't. He was a demon. He stayed for as long as he could, even when their conversation inevitably turned to reminiscing about the past. When Damien had first left the city he hadn't returned for almost a decade, though he had kept in touch with Dagger sporadically. He lingered far longer than he should have, but he knew Rain wouldn't object to delaying their departure until morning under these circumstances. He tried to ignore the coughing and wheezing as well as how very thin and grey his friend had become.

There was a knock on the door and a human mage walked in holding a glass of honey-coloured liquid. "It's time for you to get some rest," she said. Damien glanced out the window and saw that it was well after dark now.

"I can sleep when I'm dead," Dagger replied. Damien covered his face with his hand as he slowly shook his head and the mage just looked aghast. "What? Too soon?" The old thief barked a laugh that quickly turned into another coughing fit.

"I should let you get some rest," Damien said reluctantly. "You need your strength to be a thorn in everyone's side for a little while longer." He leaned over the bed to hug one of his oldest friends, trying not to think about how emaciated he was, how frail the once-strong arms that returned the embrace were. "Fare well, you old bastard," he said, forcing a crooked grin. Dagger smirked and Damien could see that they both knew what this was, and it became hard to leave, to turn away and walk out. But he did. Even though he knew that this was the last time they would see one another. No one could live forever.

He needed a drink.

He made it back down to the great hall with some kind of composed façade in place. After all, it wasn't his time to give into the darkness, the whispers of a hundred departed friends. What was one more to that list? Just a drop in the fucking ocean at this point.

"I'll have whatever's strongest," he told the woman behind the bar.

"Your funeral," she said, pouring an almost clear liquid into a glass and sliding it over. He took a sip and coughed. It burned like the spirits he used medicinally, but it wasn't quite as strong.

"Not bad," he said, taking a deeper drink.

She looked impressed. "Most of 'em are praying for death after a drop." He forced a grin, flashing fangs. "Ah, demon. That explains it."

"Sure." It explained so much and so very little. He finished the drink and she refilled the glass. He hated being around sick people, hated watching them fight against an invisible force and fail. He'd watched Raven waste away to little more than a shadow, barely aware of what was going on. He couldn't handle it again. He would rather be ripped to shreds by a Fiend's claws than die from a disease.

"Hi," Rain said, hopping onto a barstool beside him.

"Did you find out anything else?" He decided to seize the distraction.

"Yeah, actually. Do you remember that little kidnapping stunt with Schuyler and Warren seven years ago?"

"They're connected," he guessed.

"Yeah. Apparently that was part of some giant plot to take over the three kingdoms but we managed destroy it, though now they've managed to find an alternate plan, which is what we discovered."

He sighed and took a drink. "Were you able to get anything on numbers?"

She shook her head. "Only that it's a small group, likely made up of either disgraced or disgruntled nobles who think they can do a better job of ruling and want more power. They aren't big on letting outsiders in and do tend to stay at their base."

"Which would be the fortress. Do they rely on hired swords?" He was certain that at least half the people they'd killed that night had been mercenaries.

"Some," she replied. "What is that?" She indicated his glass. He held up his hand and the woman gave Rain a once over.

"You a demon?" She asked, taking in Rain's age and slender build. Rain raised a blue eyebrow at the question. "Just wanted to make sure," she said, pouring the drink. His niece tried it and coughed, then glanced up at him as she realised how strong it was.

"Don't worry, just a few edges," he told her, correctly interpreting the look. She nodded slowly. "We'll leave at dawn and see how far we can get by sunset. If we go straight north it should take us roughly two weeks without any additional problems."

"With additional problems?"

"Months, easily."

"Right. Luckily blizzards are as good as thunderstorms," she murmured, taking another sip of liquor. "So I can have the best of both worlds." She showed him a spell crafted by Storm that would cause a massive storm.

"If I didn't know you were a water mage I'd have to wonder where you got your insanity," he muttered as he finished off what was in his glass and signalled for another. "We'll get a message to Storm and the others on our way to *The Bloody Goose.*"

"Already did it."

"Aren't you on top of things tonight?"

"You were busy," she said with a shrug.

"Thanks." They both drank, and Damien wondered again why he was cursed to always be the one left behind.

9
Mercy

The rich scent of blood filled her nightmares.

"Rain, please, we both know how this is going to end." An agonised rasp in the night.

"No, don't talk like that!" Rain begged, though she was at a loss. She had no idea how she was going to manage this. He was even worse off than Kestrel, and she had no idea how she was going to get the three of them out of here alive. She turned to make sure Kestrel was still breathing, silently begging her to wake up as she ignored the pain from her own wounds. She was seriously injured as well, but she was the only one even remotely mobile. She was shocked to be still alive, had been certain that using lightning would be the last thing she ever did. But she was alive. In absolute agony, but alive.

"You can't save all three of us. You know she has a better chance of surviving than I do." He coughed, blood misting the air.

"I can't just abandon you here to die!" That wasn't an option. "Who knows how long you'll live? You could be like this for hours. More Fiends are going to come, not to mention wild animals."

"You can't afford to wait." There was something in his expression, a decision he'd made.

"Tristan…"

"Then help me die now."

"What? No!" She couldn't kill one of her friends.

"I can't move, I can't feel most of my body. I am not going to make it out of this alive. I'm not and I know it, and you know it too."

Tears blurred her vision. "I can't."

"Then leave me. Kestrel is going to die without help. I'm beyond it."

"Tristan…"

"Please, Rain." Tears fell from his eyes as well. "I'm done. Let me go and save her."

She tried to argue, but in the end…

She woke up sobbing.

The sun's light hadn't yet reached over the walls of Ankira when the Hunters rode out. Rain pulled her cloak tighter around her, feeling raw after her dream. Uncle Damien didn't look much better, but knowing a close friend was going to die soon would do that to a person. The only person she'd seen die from sickness was Raven, and that happened too long ago for her to remember. She imagined it would be something like watching someone dying slowly of their wounds, clinging to life as their broken body gave out. Doubtless that was what had brought on her nightmare, one that had been all too true.

There hadn't been two survivors that awful night, not initially. There had been three; three survivors bleeding out in a ruined field far from help. Kestrel had been clinging to life, and Tristan had been slowly dying. Rain couldn't have left him like that, but there was nothing she or anyone else could have done to save him, and he'd known it. He'd had little chance of surviving more than a day or two, let alone recovering. When Rain mentioned that Kestrel was still alive he'd asked if she had a chance to survive, and Rain had known what was coming next. They'd argued about it, but in the end he'd won. She'd ended his life, somehow getting it right the first time even though she was sobbing, shaking, and badly injured. Then she'd picked up Kestrel and managed to get to help, though it was a blur of pain, panic, and guilt. The guilt had never faded.

She took a deep drink from her flask, tears blurring her vision.

"What's wrong?" Her uncle asked when she wiped them away.

"Nothing," she lied. She'd never told anyone about that, not even Kestrel. After all, it wasn't a lie to say that everyone else had died. She'd made sure of it after all. She just couldn't say it, couldn't tell them, and maybe, just maybe, if she didn't say it out loud she could pretend it never happened.

"Something about Dagger's condition is reminding you of whatever's been weighing on you for the last year and a half, isn't it?" She looked away, focusing intently on her horse's mane. Sometimes it was easy to forget just how much her uncle noticed because he didn't pry unless he felt there was a damn good reason. "If you ever decide you want to talk about it I'm here for you." She wasn't so sure. This wasn't something that was talked about, even at the Academy. It wasn't taboo so much as something that no one wanted to consider. Murder was an abhorrent crime among her people –especially those who dealt with Fiends- and even when it was sanctioned it wasn't something done lightly. Humans were included, unless they attacked first. To take the life of another Hunter… whatever Tristan had said, Rain still believed there had been a chance he would have survived. Not a great chance, but still a chance. She shouldn't have given in.

"I don't want to talk about it," she mumbled, still refusing to look at her uncle.

"Okay." He didn't push, didn't argue.

"Have you ever killed anyone out of mercy?" The words came out before she could stop them.

He didn't answer for a moment, and she risked a glance at his face. He looked surprised. "Mercy killing…" A knot formed in her stomach. "I've never killed anyone out of mercy. Not a human, nor one of our people," he said slowly. "Though I came close, once."

"When?" Raven was her best guess, but Uncle Damien had been through a lot of tough and fucked up situations. She knew that he'd kept most of them from her and her sister.

"It was Raven," he replied, taking a drink. "Near the end, when… anyway, I thought about it. I thought long and hard about it. The others who'd gotten sick and died, well, they hadn't died easily or peacefully. It was at the point where we knew that nothing could be done, that she was going to die. But… I couldn't do it. I just couldn't bring myself to do it."

"Do you regret it?"

He gave her a wry grin. "That's the kind of situation when it just doesn't matter what you do. You'll be damned for the rest of your life." He took a drink. "It'll mess you up pretty bad, even if you know it was the right choice, which is what I'm going to guess is your case."

"I don't know," she told him, taking a deep drink from her own flask.

He sighed and ran a hand through his hair. "Did you know if he would survive?"

"Maybe if I hadn't been hurt, or if-"

"Not what I'm asking," Damien cut her off.

She closed her eyes and swallowed hard as she tried to push back the images her mind tried to torture her with and recounted the full story, from coming around after she fried the Fiend with lightening to discovering that Tristan and Kestrel were both a live but badly injured, and then the argument. "Then I killed him." She finished in a whisper. "He was my friend, and I killed him."

Uncle Damien was silent for a long moment. "It was an impossible situation, but I think that he was right. If you'd done anything different there would've been two, maybe three more bodies to bury."

Part of her knew he was right, but the part that felt guilty didn't want to accept that. "So how do I get past this?" She wasn't sure if she ever could.

"Take a drink and put that shadow with the others."

She took another drink. "What about Mom or Dad? Did either of them do it?" She couldn't bring herself to say the words. It was pathetic, she knew it was, but she couldn't do it in that moment.

He thought for a moment. "Your dad, actually. Before your mom or I met him. He only mentioned it once, and he was pretty drunk when he told us about it, but I'm sure if you asked and explained why he would talk about it."

"Okay." She thought about that as they rode in comfortable silence. She'd never have guessed that her father would be the one to bear that kind of burden, but apparently he had and had somehow come to terms with it. She would have to have a long talk with him when she got home.

The lands surrounding Ankira were mostly plains with low, rolling hills and farmland that continued south and west through part of Landaia as well, though at the moment everything was covered in a thick blanket of snow. In a day they would be back into the dense forests until they drew nearer to the mountains and thing began to thin out. She thought there might be marshlands in there somewhere, but she thought those were further west of where they were headed, then again, in the winter it wouldn't matter, since they would likely be frozen.

They did fairly well for the first week, covering more ground than they'd thought they would, but their luck ran out nine days in, when the village where they'd intended to spend the night was in ruins.

"Looks like they were hit almost a month ago," Rain said as they picked their way through the rubble. She couldn't see any full corpses, just the occasional limb peeking out of the snow.

"I think you're right," her uncle agreed, looking around. "Still, we don't have much choice at this point." Her warning spell went off and she turned, but Damien already had already cut the Fiend down. They'd given up on competing for the moment; there were just too damn many of them to keep track.

"How do you think the Summit is going?" She asked as they looked for a building that was still intact. She wondered what hell had descended upon this village to leave it in this state. Fiends weren't generally interested in buildings unless there was someone inside of them, and then they tended to use doors or windows instead of bashing down walls.

"They're probably having a far easier time of it than we are; the kingdoms want answers, solutions, and someone to blame. She and Forest are handing them all that and more."

"Fair point."

"Won't change anything though, I can tell you that now. They won't change their minds about us. Hell, they won't even stop to think that we've suffered too." He shook his head and sighed.

"What about over there?" She pointed at a building that didn't look like it was on the verge of collapse. She couldn't think of anything else to say. He was right. They headed over and found that while the windows were broken it was still sound. Damien started a fire while Rain set sheets of ice to replace the windows, etching spells into them so that she could see through them as clear as if they'd been glass. Then she pressed her hand against the door, using a touch of magic to activate a spell tattoo on her left shoulder. Power flowed down her arm and glowing runes spread from her palm over the door. It would keep the door from being opened, either by lock picks or a battering ram. Of course they could just take out the wall around the door, but Fiends didn't usually think of that. "I'll take first watch?" She didn't want to face the dreams she knew she would have. Not yet.

"Sure," her uncle gave in without argument as they ate and fed the horses, deciding to keep them inside where it would be safe and warm. She heard a howl outside as snow started to fall again.

"It's a wonder there are any animals left in the wild," she remarked, drawing her cloak over her shoulders like a blanket, more for comfort than warmth, unlike her uncle who hated the cold.

"They have the sense to run like hell the moment anything dangerous draws near," he pointed out. "So it's not much of a surprise."

"I guess." She leaned back against the stone wall. "You'd think we'd have figured out where they come from, though. The Fiends, I mean." She remembered one day back when she was a student and someone asked if Fiends reproduced. Their instructor had just said that if that was the case then he really didn't want to think about it.

Her uncle thought about it. "Maybe we will someday; there are Keepers trying to figure it out. Hell, maybe we used to know, back before our ancestors gave up their souls, but they couldn't get to the source of the Fiends to destroy it and over time the knowledge was lost or forgotten."

"So we have traumatic or depressing. Lovely."

"That's life," he reminded her as he tapped his warning spell bead to alter its radius before stretching out on the floor, using his pack as a pillow. "Wake me up when it's my turn." He turned his back to her. Rain gave a quiet sigh and looked out the window at the snow. In five days they should be at the base of the mountain where the fortress was. Soon this would be over or she would be dead.

Her warning spell went off a few times, but she didn't go out. If something were to try ripping the building apart she would do something, but until it got to that point she was going to stay where she was. It was generally considered bad form to leave a hunting partner alone while they were sleeping. She pulled a book from her bag and started reading; it was a story that she'd read before, but it was good and sometimes the familiarity was comforting. In the story she knew everything would turn out okay; that the good people would win and find the happiness they deserved, something that happened so rarely in real life. A few hours later she heard a gasp and Uncle Damien sat upright, blade in hand.

"You haven't missed anything," she said while turning a page, though she did watch him out of the corner of her eye. A moment later he relaxed, ran a hand through his hair and drank from his flask.

"Good to know. Your turn to sleep." She nodded and tapped her warning spell bead to narrow down the range while he widened his again. Unless something broke into the building it wouldn't go off. It was one of the benefits to hunting with a partner or in a group; if she were camping on her own she would never be able to take the risk, so she would have woken up any time a Fiend drew near. It was beneficial when one was actively trying to avoid sleeping and dreaming, but not healthy and another reason to avoid camping as much as possible. He held out his hand for her book and she it tossed over before laying down, taking a moment to find the least uncomfortable position in her armour and weapons, ensuring that everything was within easy reach. Armoured corsets were still not the most comfortable things to sleep in, but after the last six and a half years she'd become used to it and was able to fall asleep quickly.

She woke to a sky nearly as dark as when she'd fallen asleep, tears streaming from her eyes. It had been a long time since she'd had a dream of Blaze that wasn't some horrific reimagining of his death, but she would have chosen even the worst of those instead of this. She'd dreamed of the good times they'd shared, of the affection and love, his deep laugh, the warmth of his arms around her as she fell asleep, the way his eyes glittered when he told her that he loved her. All her favorite moments, all moments that she would never ever have again, and she'd known that even in the dream; she hadn't felt happy, she'd just felt a deep, hollow ache that lingered still and hurt worse than any physical wound.

"Fun dreams?" Uncle Damien asked when she sat up.

"The best," she replied, her tone harsh as she wiped away the tears. But they just kept falling. She wondered if the dream was made worse by the fact that she hadn't thought of him much in the last month or two. Part of that was just trying to deal with everything going on and the other part was trying to avoid the pain and the guilt that came with avoiding it. Figuring out how to help the living had to come before mourning the dead for someone in her line of work, and it was something she'd had trouble with over the last two years.

"There's a few Fiends out there," he said lightly as she readjusted her warning spell. "They've been around for the last few hours." She stood and wiped away the tears once more as she looked out the window. There were two Fiends watching, only moving occasionally. She twisted her ring and looked past them, focusing on part of a wall that stood alone.

"I see flashes of magic." Her hands clenching into fists as her sorrow turned to anger.

"Most likely their orders are to target any of our kind they come across," he said as he started packing and readying the horses.

"And if they're after us specifically?" She wished she were just being paranoid, but they both knew it was a possibility. The Summit hadn't been a secret, so it was possible there were spies waiting for news of anyone moving against them, and more than enough time had passed to get word to the fortress of who to watch out for. All they could do was prepare for the possibility they would be targeted.

"Go on, kill the fuckers," he said, waving her on.

She picked up her sword and walked out, feeling the brush of magic over her skin as she passed through her barrier. The Fiends were on her in an instant, but she was faster. She killed one within seconds but the other put up more of a fight, actually throwing her into a stone wall with a wild punch. Its head soon fell from its body all the same and she collected the fangs and burned the bodies as Damien led the horses out. Then she dealt with removing her spells from the doors and windows. Without a tie to her the ice would eventually melt.

"Feel better?" He asked as they mounted.

"A little," she replied, watching the withered bodies burn to ash.

"Uncles always know best," he said with a slight smile. "I'm thinking we should push our luck and see if we can make it to Alcara instead of Yakema."

"What's the difference?" She asked, trying to picture the map in her mind.

"Five or six hours."

"The sooner we get to Eskaven Mountains the better," she said as they took off. If it hadn't been cloudy she would have been able to see them, their snow-capped peaks looming in the distance.

Damien signaled for Rain to be cautious as they approached the village nearest the fortress a few days later. As far as he knew the group they were dealing with hadn't had anything to do with it, but he knew very little. Rain flipped up the hood of her cloak to cover her hair. Nightfall was drawing close, but it was still light enough to tell clearly that it was deep blue. Damien had half a mind to attempt passing as a Ranger until they knew what was going on. He said as much to Rain, who raised a brow.

"Would that even work? We're not as, well, as soft as humans." She had a point. He remembered thinking that the Guardians in Ankira looked strange, their features a little too sharp, their eye colour too vivid, never mind that many of those colours would never be found in human eyes. It had taken a while before he realised that he looked the same, even though he'd known they were demons like him. Then to walk in a whole city of people who looked like him... Gods, that was so long ago. Now, while humans didn't look nearly as odd to him as they would to his territory-born and raised niece, there was a certain something, a difference he saw but couldn't describe.

"True," he agreed with a sigh. "Still, we should be careful until we know what's going on."

They made their way to the gates, guarded by humans. He couldn't see any of their people.

"Hello strangers," the older guard greeted them warily. "What brings you to our village?"

"We're passing through and want to avoid camping," he replied. "Surely you've seen a pair of Hunters before?" Out of the corner of his eye he saw Rain lower her hood again.

"We have, but most of them head farther east where the mountain passes are easier to get through," he replied. It was the truth; Damien himself had gone that way whenever he'd had to cross the mountains.

"Might I ask what reason you have to be so mistrustful of the people standing between you and the Fiends?" Rain wondered, canting her head slightly.

"Our reason is everything we've learned about that old fortress and the folk in it," he replied bluntly, carefully watching for their reactions.

"About a day's ride from here on the mountain? I'm guessing the people around it are somewhere between sketchy, corrupt, and straight-up evil?" He nodded and Damien relaxed a little. These people were on their side. "Good, because we plan on ending them." It wasn't the phrasing she used that bothered him, it was that she said it with a casual air and a promise of death in her eyes, two things that were never a good mix and ended with good Hunters getting killed for stupid mistakes.

"Maybe we can help," the guard offered after a moment, nodding to his partner. They opened the gates to show a small village. Damien estimated only a few hundred people lived there, and while it wasn't derelict it obviously wasn't prosperous. He didn't know much about the noble who held these lands, only that it was a duchess and she lived a few days ride to the south-east. The more talkative guard joined them, signaling for someone on the wall to take his place.

"Where are the Guardians?" Rain wondered, asking Damien's next question. He decided to just let her do the talking for now, though the human looked more frightened of her than Damien. It was probably because there was no way for him to pretend that she was human.

"Dead," he told her. "We sent their ashes back with a Hunter who passed through four years ago, but no replacements were ever sent and we were assured that any who did come would be killed, so we didn't press the issue."

"Probably because they would report anything off to the Council," Rain said. "Crooked Guardians are hard to come by and most don't last." They ended up working for Vine Glade instead, trading their careers as Guardians for careers as thugs. "Who was the Hunter?"

The guard frowned as he tried to remember. "Name of an animal, can't remember which one. Strange bastard, crazy, I'd say –no offense."

"Wolf?" Damien supplied. He actually liked Wolf, but he could understand why others might not feel the same.

"That sounds right," the human said as he led them to a tavern. From the outside Damien could see that there were a few rooms above it, likely in case of any travelers or visitors. It wasn't surprising to hear that Wolf hadn't mentioned anything. Not for lack of care or conscience either. He'd likely been distracted by something and had forgotten. He truly was insane. Shade had really done a number on him thirty years ago.

"Daxon!" The tavern owner greeted the guard with the enthusiasm of close friendship. "And guests?" He took in the Hunters and paled, shifting back to put more space between them. Not that it would have done any good against Damien and Rain.

Daxon was quick to explain. "They're here to help."

The other human's trepidation turned to open relief. "Thank the gods!" He ushered them to a table and had food and ale brought over.

"What do you know about the fortress?" Rain asked after she took a drink.

"We stay far away from it. Our folk are coal miners and the entrance to the mines is a ways away so we have a camp that's close by. It's close to the fortress too, so we see more than we'd like to." Then he kept talking and Damien got an idea of how bad things would be. There would be around thirty humans, ten of them the bastards behind this whole shitshow and the rest were skilled mercenaries, plus untold numbers of Fiends, most of who were of the more powerful variety. He ordered something stronger than ale when the humans were done talking. Rain looked tense as well.

"How's your village still standing?" She asked.

"I guess they figured we weren't a threat once the Guardians were gone," the tavern owner replied with a shrug. He'd sat down with them once he'd arranged for their rooms for the night.

"It's possible, and if they have a powerful mage they would use magic for a lot of things coal would normally be needed for," Damien said, taking a drink. "Exactly how far away is the entrance to the mine?"

"A day's walk from here, or thereabouts. The fortress is another five or six hours beyond that, and there's a lot a climbing as well." That'd be nothing to them, so he figured it at one or two hours uninjured even with the snow, though there wasn't as much as he would have expected to see in the mountains in winter, which was a welcome surprise. "As for the camp it's an hour from the mine entrance and by a lake. Things are pretty empty since its winter, but there's a few families that stay year 'round to keep things in working order."

Rain looked over and Damien nodded in answer to her silent query. They would head to the camp next, and it would be far easier to get back to when injured. He had little doubt that getting out of this unscathed was impossible, if both of them even survived. "Do they have messenger falcons?" Rain would have to get a message home, however things ended.

Daxon nodded. "The camp falcons can only make it as far as here though."

"Our friends at the fortress?" Damien guessed.

He nodded. "Here we have a few that can go further, we learned to be careful about it."

"Could they make it to the Guardian Ships in…" he looked to Rain when he couldn't recall it.

She paused for a moment. "Port Atrixa?"

"That's it, it's three days' ride west." It didn't connect with any waterways leading to Ankira, otherwise they would have been able to make the trip much faster.

"Should be fine. Jack here is in charge of 'em, he'll make sure the messages get out."

"I wasn't expecting help so easily," she said, leaning back.

He shrugged. "You demons are scary, but at least you're on our side."

"Most people aren't willing admit their dislike comes from fear," Rain remarked.

"Does it bother you that we're afraid?"

She thought it over for a moment. "Better to be hated and feared than just hated." It was something Damien had said more than a few times. Fear offered some protection where hatred invited aggression.

"Fair," the human allowed.

A little while later Daxon left with a promise to meet them in the morning and lead them to the camp while Jack went to deal with other patrons who'd come into the tavern. "By morning the whole village will know that we're here," Damien remarked. He could feel the other patrons looking at them.

"Is that good or bad?" Rain wondered as she took a covert glance around them.

"We'll be gone before anything can be done to affect us so I don't think it'll matter. We'll take the horses to the camp and go the rest of the way on foot. If humans survive there it should be safe enough for the horses."

"So we storm the fortress on foot then?" she asked.

He leaned back in his chair. "Seems like the best option."

"Did you decide how we're going to destroy any evidence of the control spells?"

He rubbed at the stubble on his jaw and decided that he needed to shave soon. "No, not really... Why?" The question was prompted by her expression, a mix of mischief and glee he'd seen mirrored on Tempest's face when she was about to do something particularly insane or brilliant. More often it was a mix of the two. It was slightly unsettling to see it on her daughter's face.

"Storm said there would be a lot of lightning when the storm spell is cast. More than enough to fuel a decent explosion that could reduce a fortress to rubble."

"There's a risk of avalanche you need to consider," he reminded her.

"It doesn't actually take all that much to direct an avalanche if you get at it early enough," she informed him. "I wouldn't be able to control it, exactly, but I can pull it towards the fortress and leave the village and mine clear, especially with the storm going on."

"How many times have you dealt with avalanches?" He knew of one, had been there when she'd told Ash about it and had laughed when the man nearly went up the wall. More than one water mage had gotten overconfident dealing with such things in the past, and not even the distant past at that, less than ten years ago if his memory was accurate. But it happened to mages of any type; they might have magic and power, but in the end they weren't gods.

"Three, and I caused two of them."

"And your father knows about how many?"

She grinned. "One."

He mulled it over. "We'll wait and see how things are. If you're absolutely certain you can control it, we'll do it. Otherwise we'll figure something out." As it was, he had half a mind to send her home. This situation was far worse than he'd anticipated, and as good as Rain was, as much as she was the best person to have at his back, and as much as she had a right to be involved, she was still his niece. He still wanted her to be safe.

"Okay."

But that clearly wasn't how things were going to work out. "Forest did want us to make an example of this, anyway." There were a number of ways to destroy something, and this time he wouldn't have to worry about covering anything up. "Let's focus on survival for now and worry about that after."

"Sounds good."

10
All that Glitters

Daxon met them at the tavern before sunrise and they started off towards the camp. According to him it hadn't been discovered by their foes, thanks in part to the fact that it wasn't readily visible, half-hidden by the mountain in a measure that had initially been for defense against Fiends. The villagers had never seen a reason to tell 'the bastards in the fortress' about it. Rain and her uncle rode with their weapons drawn, ready to fight whatever may come. Snow fell lightly around them, but she hoped that they would soon be in the middle of a wild, raging storm. She couldn't wait, though she did hope that the other mage they'd be facing wasn't a water or air mage, either of which could draw on weather systems for more power. Since they were on a mountain an earth mage wouldn't be all that great either. A fire mage could use lightening as well, but would be no match for her. "You've seen the Hunter, but have you seen the other of our kind that's helping these people?"

"Another demon? No, but I heard their people talk about her though, the few times they came through the village when they first took the fortress. They said she's batshit crazy and powerful."

"Did you get a name?"

"Dunno, your names are odd enough that I wouldn't have noticed." The Hunters let that slide as they rode.

They were attacked by Fiends twice but killed with relative ease, though Rain was almost thrown off a cliff. She was saved by one of Damien's wires wrapping around her wrist and hauling her back.

"You two sure are something to watch," the human remarked around midday. "Like you were born for this kind of thing."

"If you listen to the legends we actually were," Rain said.

It was early evening when they made it to the camp, though Rain wasn't sure that 'camp' was the right word, as a number of the buildings looked like permanent fixtures. Daxon introduced them to the people there, all of whom looked relieved to hear that they would soon be somewhat safer.

No pressure.

"When do you think we should head out?" Rain asked as they stored their bags in an unoccupied cabin. It was made of stone, not wood, which would have been a strange choice had they been anywhere else, but coal dust tended to get everywhere and that didn't mix well with fire. Or maybe it mixed too well. Aside from a small bathroom set apart from the rest of the space everything was in one room, including two sets of bunk beds.

"Nightfall," Damien said. It made sense; many of their opponents would be human and most of the Fiends would be controlled by the spells, unable to take advantage of their ability to see in the dark unless they were ordered to attack. "Until then I'm going to get some rest." He gave her a considering look. "You should too." She nodded but stepped outside for a moment, too full of nervous energy.

The humans were preparing for a storm to hit, bringing things inside, checking windows and doors. Rain had warned them that one would be coming, certain she would use the spell. Restless, she started doing some light exercises that wouldn't tire her out but would make sure there was no lingering stiffness from a day spent riding. She didn't do anything with her magic, unwilling to waste what she might need later. There was also no need to terrify the humans they might need to rely on for a few days while they recovered. At least she hoped it would only be a few days.

"Do you really think you can win?" She stopped as Daxon walked over. The sky was finally starting to grow dark.

"Well, it takes a monster to defeat a monster," she said.

"Do you really see yourself that way?"

She shrugged. "It sounds cool so I run with it." She didn't tell him that while her people had the strength and magic of monsters she saw humans as the real monsters.

"Well, best of luck to you."

"Thanks." She grinned and went back inside the cabin. Damien was still asleep, so she quietly closed the door and checked over her weapons.

"Hand 'em over," she looked up to see him sitting up.

"Did I wake you?" She asked as he stretched, but he shook his head. She handed over her blades and he sharpened them for her. She twisted her ring and saw the shining silver of his magic flow over each one, ensuring that the steel would take a hell of a beating before it started to warp and had an edge that would slice through flesh like air. He handed back her last dagger when night fell.

"Ready?" He asked. She took a deep breath and nodded.

"They won't know what killed them." They both did one last check to make sure everything was in place. It was now or never.

The trek wasn't too difficult. She leaped from ledge to ledge, Damien behind her as she moved ice and snow out of the way, though sometimes she used ice to widen them or her uncle used wires to get both Hunters to higher ground, though they were still careful about conserving power for the moment. Still, they made good time and were soon at the base of the fortress walls. It was clearly old, crumbling in places. They hadn't been attacked but her warning spell had been going off for a while. She turned it off now; it would be more of a nuisance than a useful tool since they were about to be surrounded by Fiends. Out of the corner of her eye she saw her uncle do the same.

"Anyone on the walls?" He asked. She closed her eyes, feeling she shape the snow took as it fell and shook her head.

"Fiends are on the other side though," she answered as she twisted her ring. She could see that the wall was etched with a spell to sound an alarm when magic was used around it, though something like her ring wouldn't register. She relayed what she saw, but they'd both expected it.

"Need a hand over?" She nodded and went back as far as she could while he crouched and cupped his hands in front of him. When he gave a sharp nod she ran at him and the instant her boot was in his hands he launched her upward. She grabbed the edge of the wall and pulled herself over before taking the wire that had wrapped around her belt and nodding to her uncle as she braced herself. Damien scaled the wall and quickly wound the wire by hand as they assessed the situation, staying low to remain unseen. The Fiends wandering the courtyard hadn't noticed their presence yet, most were trying to duck away from the snow. She looked at the fortress itself. It was small, consisting of a tower detached from the mountainside but it looked like it would have thick walls. There might have been more to it once, but the rest had been reduced to snow-covered rubble over time. Lights flickered in the small windows.

"Wait!" Damien hissed, holding out his hand to stop her from moving. A figure walked out of the building.

"Gold." Rain hadn't twisted her ring to turn the spell off, so she could see the fine strands of gold magic that connected the figure to the Fiends. She wondered briefly who was the worse monster, the ex-Hunter or the Fiends.

"He's mine," Damien snarled quietly.

"Do you think he's brave enough to face you on his own?" Rain asked. There were at least ten Fiends, and with the traitor occupied they likely wouldn't cause her too many problems.

"If you lock that main door from the outside he won't have a choice unless the other mage wants to come out and fight us as well."

"Got it."

They both leaped from the wall. Gold stared at Damien as Rain made it to the door and pressed her hand against it. There was a brief flash and she turned to go after the Fiends as a thick sheet of ice grew over the wood, an extra irritation for those inside that Damien approved of.

"It's been a while, Gold," he remarked in a mild tone. Gold looked older, but even their kind aged in thirty-odd years. He had to be in his eighties now and he looked like he'd lived a hard life. It was funny, for all he'd wanted to plunge a blade into the man's chest he'd never really thought about what would come before that.

"I suppose I shouldn't be surprised to see you, you've earned quite the reputation for yourself," Gold said as he glanced between the Hunters and saw that they'd come alone.

"You flatter me." Damien noticed that the snow was receding around him even though Rain was fighting. She'd been practicing.

"So, how do you want to do this? Make some grand speech about how sweet revenge will be after all these decades? How you've waited for this day for years, hunting me down?" Gold wondered, smirking.

"If I *really* wanted you dead you wouldn't be in front of me now. I'm just going to put a blade in your heart and call it a day well spent." He shrugged as he drew his sword.

"No gloating about Eida's untimely death?" From his tone Damien was sure he'd guessed what had really happened to her, that it hadn't been a suicide.

He didn't rise to the bait. "One thing we haven't figured out is who you're working for."

"What, you don't think I could be behind all of this?" Gold was stalling; glancing back at the door. Damien could hear people struggling to get it open, though without the help of someone powerful they wouldn't. His niece knew what she was at, and had learned from her sister, one of the most brilliant minds of her generation.

"No, you never were the mastermind of anything." Damien lunged and the battle began. Gold had experience on his side, but Damien was an elite Hunter for a reason. Blades sparked as they struck and he twisted to avoid a dagger while sending off one of his own, either hoping to stab through Gold's defenses or get the wire placed to trip him up. True fights between Hunters were rare and hard battles. It was as much a battle of wits as of weapons, since most experienced Hunters had their armour spells as tattoos and often came down to what the fighter chose to prioritise, since the tattoos relied on one's own strength for power. Concentrate more power into the spell and have weaker attacks, or put less into the spell and risk injury but be able to attack with more power and magic that could potentially get through a stronger shield. Fiends howled in an eerie, hair-raising cry. He lost track of time as he attacked and defended, using every underhanded technique he knew to conserve power and deal more damage to his enemy. It was kind of ironic, the treasonous bastard fought like an honorable warrior. His loss.

He bent all the way back as Gold's sword swung above him and kicked his feet over, catching his opponent in the jaw and sending him sprawling on the flagstone that covered much of the area around them.

"Who else are you working with?" Damien asked as he skipped out of the way of an arrow shot from a window. Rain was still occupied with the Fiends.

Gold just laughed, spitting blood as he stood. Damien moved like he was pushing his hair back and tapped his spell to reveal magics. He assumed the Fiends were partly connected to Gold, and though his spell wasn't strong enough to show him the connections it would be helpful in other ways. He lunged, feinted, then cut into Gold's side. The shield spell flashed and rippled as it absorbed the hit, and Damien could tell that Gold was putting more power into the control spells and on his defensive spells than any attack. It was clear that the older man knew who the better fighter was. Still, Damien had to act fast, there were bigger fights yet to come. He ducked to avoid another blow and pulled out a special blade, one that he'd initially intended to melt seven years ago.

"I see you've only lost some of your edge," Damien observed as he skipped away from a thrust to his heart as he sliced with the dagger, cutting a long deep line down Gold's arm. The other man wasn't wearing any other armour. He stared at the cut, then the blade in shock.

"What the hell?"

"Interesting blade, isn't it? Cuts through magic just like flesh," Damien said. "Don't worry, it's the only one of its kind. The maker met a bad end a few years ago." He'd made damn sure of it.

"You know, I'd heard that the hot-headed street rat had turned cold," Gold remarked. "Never thought it might be true." He sent blades spinning like throwing stars, but Damien managed to alter their course just enough that they went to either side of him, a show of power that had Gold backing up a step, which brought Rain to his attention. She was on the other side of the courtyard now, and Gold sent a blade flying at her. Damien shouted a warning, praying he wasn't overestimating her skill. She twisted and jumped at the last second so that the Fiend she was fighting was nearly cut in half. She landed on its torso and took its head with barely a glance.

"How about we keep this between us?" Damien suggested as Gold's quickly bruising jaw slowly closed again. He didn't wait for an answer, attacking. The older man fought with a kind of desperation that allowed Damien to get in a few more hits that caused real damage. It was disappointing. He'd expected something... more. This was the monster who'd sold two young Hunters to a Thief King, who'd been exiled and yet managed to survive for decades. He was a good fighter, but only good, and in all other facets of his being he bordered on pathetic. Damien heard the door burst open and Rain scream, but the sound was abruptly cut short. He tried to see what was going on, but Gold chose that moment to launch a flurry of attacks. Damien fought to find an opening, and when he saw it he struck, plunging the magic blade behind Gold's collarbone and using it to yank the other Hunter into his sword. He twisted the blade and watched the life flee from the traitor's eyes. Damien withdrew the dagger and kicked the body off his sword as he turned and looked around. One of the double doors was off its hinges and the courtyard was devoid of anything living aside from him. They must have taken Rain. He turned back toward the tower and saw a shadowed figure was watching him from one of the highest windows just before a thick forest filled his vision. Cursing as he realised what was going on, he tapped his spell bead and saw what he'd expected: shadow magic surrounded him like a fog. He tried to run, but it was like trying to move through thick syrup. Fuck. Fuck. Fuck. A grave mistake had been made, and they'd all been tricked. A group of humans came out then, and he was far too slow to stop them when a damp cloth was pressed over his mouth and his magical dagger taken and stabbed into his shoulder. Everything went hazy, and then everything went dark.

It was hot, so very hot, and dry... the perfect hell for a water mage. They'd put a blindfold over her eyes before throwing her onto a floor, shutting the door, and then it felt like everything in the room caught fire. She'd just finished killing off the last of the Fiends outside when a dense fog had filled her vision and she couldn't dispel it. Fucking shadow magic. It had made it impossible to fight back when the humans had grabbed her. She coughed, her throat painfully dry and her lungs burning. There wasn't a single drop of moisture in the air. Rain twisted, using the floor to push her blindfold down enough that she could see, ignoring the minor protests of the small handful of wounds she'd acquired. None of them were severe enough to require immediate attention.

"Fuck," she coughed as she could finally see. The walls and ceiling burned with fire. "Fuck. Fuck. Fuck." This was not good. Her wrists and ankles were bound with a heavy rope. They were probably worried about her uncle's metal magic, trusting this fucking fire trap to keep her from using magic.

Fools.

They hadn't even thought to remove the spell beads from her earrings, let alone her armour or weapons. Apparently they hadn't consulted with their ex-Hunter or pet shadow mage on how to incapacitate a Hunter. She twisted back onto her side, almost wishing she hadn't worn her fingerless gloves since her claws couldn't slice through the combination of leather and chain mail, would have made things easier. She sliced the back of her middle and used the blood to create a sharp blade to slice through the ropes. She then used it to etch a spell on the floor, one she'd actually from Ember a few years before. Once it was done she activated it with power she'd stored in one of her beads. The runes and symbols lit up and the fire died a moment later, revealing the spells drawn into the walls and ceiling. She stood and found herself in a small room that had a single small window set high in the wall. Rain tested the wall carefully and when she found it wasn't hot she jumped, catching the windowsill and pulling herself high enough to smash it with the hilt of a dagger. Cold air rushed in and she could breathe again even if she couldn't use the window to escape. It felt so damn good. She debated using the storm spell, but decided to wait a little longer, in part because it was likely to blow up the tower, and it wasn't quite time for that.

She tried the door and found it locked, but that was little trouble for someone who'd learned to pick locks from thieves. She drew her sword as she opened it, twisting her ring for good measure. A Fiend came charging down the hall and she swept it against the wall with a blast of water and froze it there so she could cut off its head. One benefit to winter: places that weren't properly heated got damp, which meant more water for her. She moved forward, trying to decide if she needed to go up or down. She came across a window that overlooked the courtyard and saw that her uncle wasn't there, though a group of Fiends feasted on a gold-haired corpse. She moved on, facing a few more Fiends she dealt with quickly, heading up since the first staircase she encountered led that way. She smashed any windows she came across, allowing the cold air and snow inside. It would attract attention, hopefully drawing enemies away from her uncle. They might have drugged her, but she knew she hadn't been out long, though evidently it had been long enough for her uncle to finish the fight and move on, unless they'd also managed to get him. She had a feeling it was the latter.

She made it up two more floors before she encountered humans. Two women rushed her, holding their weapons with the same ease that Rain did. She exchanged a few blows and found that they were very good, but in the end they were only human. She wasn't. She cut the sword arm off one opponent before turning to run the other through, her own sword able to slice through their armour with ease thanks to her uncle's magic. Then she turned to finish the first off.

"Soulless bitch!" The woman snarled for her final words.

"Words hurt," Rain told the corpse lightly as stepped over it to get to the staircase. She really needed to find her uncle, and she was pretty sure the next floor was the top of the tower, and most of their enemies were likely holed up in there. She wished she had the tracking spell she'd used as an apprentice, but she didn't. She did, however, know something that would work almost as well in this case.

Silently thanking her sister for using her as a test subject over the last decade she pulled a stream of water out of the air and used it to etch a spell in ice on the stone floor, placing one of her daggers in the center of it. All of her blades carried traces of her uncle's magic and after he'd sharpened them just a few hours before she would have no trouble tracking it. A touch of magic and the spell activated, a slim quicksilver thread appearing from the dagger and leading towards the next staircase, going up. Three more runes and the spell appeared mirrored on the blade so she could pick it up and still follow the thread. As long as the spell remained in place and her uncle remained alive she could follow it to him, though she had a feeling she was going to find him with their enemies. As a last measure against shadow magic she carved a spell Phantom had shown her into the leather of her vambrace. It wouldn't stop her from seeing illusions –she had her ring for that anyway- but it would protect her from the physical effects of the magic. Apparently they had been wrong and it *was* possible for a strong shadow mage to be unknown.

She killed four more humans and three Fiends before she made it to that last staircase. She created a light mist that was just enough for her to get a sense of space and set it ahead. There were two guards in a short hallway and a set of double doors. The guards seemed like humans, so she ran up the stairs and froze their heads into blocks of ice, catching the bodies as they fell. That was going to create one hell of a mess when they thawed, but that wasn't her problem. There was only one entrance, and that was a problem since there was no way she wasn't going to get caught and her uncle was in there, meaning he was captured and could therefore be used against her. There was no magic on the doors, but that meant little given what was on the other side. The voices were still muffled but she could hear someone yelling within. If she remembered correctly from what she'd seen outside, this floor was lined with larger windows that she could use those to escape or to dispose of her enemies. Taking the glass out in advance would have to be a priority the moment she entered. She created a barrage of ice spears, took a deep breath, and shoved the doors open with all her might, sending the ice in ahead, aiming for windows and enemies.

This was it; this was her chance to end this nightmare.

11

Choice

She got the chaos she'd wanted: windows shattered as humans and Fiends fell. She saw her uncle, his standing between two guards with his hands bound behind his back. A familiar hilt stuck out of his shoulder and she repressed a shudder. The Fiends in the room suddenly multiplied, but she was ready this time and her magic ring was still active, so she knew them for the illusions they were. She deliberately stepped through one to throw a dagger at a human fighter. As she was unhindered by the shadow magic the human had no time to dodge and the blade struck him squarely between the eyes. The shadow Fiends dissipated a moment later, the humans reaching for weapons. Some were dressed in human court finery while others wore the rugged clothing and armour of mercenaries.

"Well, well, well, the little Hunter got free and she knows some tricks. Looks like you were right, Damien." An older woman stood leaning against a table. Her complexion was pasty rather than pale like Rain's, her hair and eyes were a dark charcoal and Rain put the her age over ninety, older than Ember or Forest, far older than she had expected. "I know I heard rumours about her; she would have truly been one of the greats. It's a shame, really, that it has to end here."

"So you're Shade's apprentice," Rain guessed.

She laughed. "Poor girl, you also believed the stories, didn't you? I do suppose it was my own fault; I didn't exactly correct anyone when word of my death reached me."

"Rain, this is Shade Perella, the rogue Keeper who drove Wolf insane," Damien told her in a tight voice, his expression haunted. So insane he wouldn't have remembered if he'd actually killed her. Rain felt dread knot her stomach and glanced over at him, wondering what she'd made him see. Later she would try to figure out how no one had thought of that, for now she had to figure out how to survive. The room took up most of the top floor, though a fair bit of the space was taken up by roughly thirty Fiends lining the walls. Experience led her to the conclusion that most –if not all- would be of the strong variety, so the Hunters would be in for a lovely time when all hell broke loose. She could still see the flashes of magic around the Fiends, but they were barely visible now, likely because it was only shadow magic holding them. She could also see small, restless movements among them and from the look on the face of a mercenary nearby it was a new development, though Shade didn't seem to have noticed it yet. Or maybe she didn't care. Rain wouldn't be surprised to find either to be true.

"You flatter me," Shade told Damien with a smile made creepier by its sincerity. "That he grew so confused over that particular detail of our encounter was a useful coincidence. I was truly surprised to hear the news of my death a few months later. I didn't actually expect him to survive the rest of the day, let alone the next thirty years. He's far stronger than I gave him credit for." Once again, she utterly sincere and all the more creepy for it. "Do you want to know what I did to him? I gave Damien a little taste of it before you got here." She asked with a conspiratorial grin.

"No," Rain replied, grateful that her voice didn't falter.

Shade looked disappointed, like Rain had taken away a treat. "Are you certain? It was quite ingenious, if I do say.

"You won't get the chance," Rain said, raising her sword point until it was level with the shadow mage's heart.

"Fine then, but wouldn't you like to know why all this is happening?" Rain had no idea what the woman was trying to do. She wouldn't have expected Shade to listen when she said no or try to bait her with information. It had to be some kind of sick game. Or Shade was completely twisted. Once again, neither would surprise her.

"I know enough." She knew enough to know that she didn't want any answers, not about what had happened to Wolf, not about why Shade and Gold had turned on their people. Knowing wouldn't change what had happened. Nothing could do that. Nor would it change what was going to happen.

"Spoilsport. So you can counteract my magic. What are you going to do now?" A challenge.

"I'm going to make sure that you die this time." She made the grim promise as she lowered the temperature of the liquids in the room, including the water in the air. It wasn't long before she could see her own breath and hear the humans' teeth chattering. It would be harder for them to interfere if they were freezing. Shade's eyes went wide with surprise at her words, but she laughed.

"I don't know if you're very brave, very confident, or very stupid. Of course, it could very well be a mix." The human mercenaries moved toward Rain but Shade sent them back to their positions with a wave of her hand. "No, it's fine." She turned back to Rain. "You know what? Go ahead. Kill me. Do it." She held her arms wide open. "I won't stop you. But remember this: if I die, the spell breaks. The Fiends will be free. You may be good, but do you really think this is a fight you can win? And when you lose –because you will– everyone here will die. You, the humans around you, that handsome Hunter behind you who is so very attached to his darling niece. They'll all die by your decision. This will be your fault and their blood will be on your hands. Can you do that? Can you make the decision for everyone here to die?"

"Rain," her uncle started, but she heard someone hit him and he grunted in pain. She wanted to look back but resisted. She had to keep her eyes on Shade.

"Hush now, she has to make this decision on her own," Shade chided before turning back to Rain again. "Tell you what, I'll even let the two of you live and I will let you go. You'll be free to keep trying to oppose us. At the very least it will be amusing to watch you try and maybe I'll even be surprised by how long you live."

As awful as it was, Shade did have a point. Rain was about to take all of their lives into her hands, even Shade's life. Sanctioned or not, this was going to be murder, and it would be done by her will and by her hand. She shifted slightly, the movement appearing unconscious, like she was indecisive. Shade's grin grew wider.

"Take all the time you need, because this is a choice you only get to make once. By all means, stab away, but you can't pretend you don't know the consequences to your actions. Can you live with them?" Rain could feel her uncle's gaze on her as he waited for her to act. She'd learned about being a Hunter, about living as a Hunter from him, however the last year and a half turned out. He knew what she was going to do. She waited a few more moments, letting the point of her sword waver slightly. The humans started to relax. *There we go*, she thought.

"I've made up my mind," she said at last.

"You're a clever girl, I'm sure you've made the right decision."

"I have." She stepped forward and ran the mage through, meeting Shade's gaze as she twisted the blade before yanking it free and turning, ready to fight for her life. She could live with a little more blood on her hands if it meant that the people she cared about had a greater chance of survival, if it meant that *anyone* had a greater chance of survival. That was part of the job she'd chosen, to sacrifice her mind and body to keep the world safe from the Fiends, no matter the outcome.

As Shade's corpse fell to the floor the threads of shadow magic vanished. Rain leaped to pull the magic dagger out of Damien shoulder as the humans stepped away, more concerned for their own lives as the Fiends began to move. He freed himself from the rope binding his hands and drew his own sword. Everything shrank down to the time between one heartbeat and the next as the battle began. Blades of ice and metal spun through the small space, wreaking havoc and spreading carnage. Rain ignored the screaming, the blood and limbs, the smoke as one of the few candles still lit fell over and papers caught fire, the flames quickly spreading over corpses and anything else it could consume. She didn't care what she stepped in or on in those moments, it didn't matter as long as she didn't lose her footing. A Fiend ripped off a human's head; she took its head a heartbeat later. There were just too many of them and not enough room to fight. The humans weren't even trying to kill her or Damien for ruining their plans; if anything they were trying to move behind the Hunters. Some tried to fight, but either they fell quickly or they tried to flee as soon as they realised how outmatched they were, adding to the chaos. She needed to get out of here and hopefully a number of Fiends would follow her.

She made her way over to Damien. "I'm going outside and setting off the spell!" She called out when he made eye contact with her. He nodded as he cut the arms off a Fiend.

She turned and ran for the door, several Fiends on her tail, hoping her uncle wouldn't be far behind. As far as she could tell most of the humans in the room were dead. For her own injuries she had at least one broken rib and she was pretty sure her wrist was sprained, but there was no time to worry about that. The Fiends who'd followed her were only a little bigger than a normal human, but all had that malevolent intelligence in their eyes. She managed to cut off a hand, decapitate another, and then cried out when a third scored the back of her shoulder. She threw herself forward, rolling to put more distance between her and them. The Fiend that had caught her back tried to do so again, and she realised with horror that it was going for her armour spell. With her skills her physical armour would have been enough against one of these Fiends, but no more than that. She saw a few more humans running towards her. They backpedaled when they saw the Fiends, their eyes wide with fear. One Fiend got past her and went straight for them.

She could see the plea for help in their gazes but she had five other Fiends hell-bent on shredding her and she was barely holding her own. She tried freezing them against the wall, but that only worked twice before they caught on and just attacked constantly, never giving her time or space to do it again. She needed to cast the storm spell and get outside. Through a window she could see her uncle had somehow made it out there ahead of her and was still fighting; he'd likely jumped through a window, using his wires to lower himself to the ground. She ran down another floor and had just enough time to get the square of silk out and light it on fire. She threw it into an empty room and leaped out of one of the windows she'd smashed as the Fiends caught up to her. Lightning came out of nowhere, bombarding the tower with explosive force as black storm clouds radiated out across the sky, the wind picking up and rain falling in sheets. She managed to get a chunk of ice beneath her feet and pushed off, turning her fall into a slightly controlled descent as she kept creating ice platforms to jump to until she could drop safely to the ground, avoiding chunks of tower as the stone gave way under the onslaught. Fiends leaped from the windows, trying to escape the destruction, and more poured out the door or clambered over rubble, seeming to appear out of nowhere. She couldn't help a wild laugh as she drew the power of the storm into her body, her aches and pains fading as her exhilaration grew. Her sister had been right; this was far more intense than anything she'd ever experienced.

She couldn't think about who may or may not have been alive in the tower. Maybe she would think on it later, when she was trapped in another nightmare, but not now. Now she had to focus because powerful Fiends were converging on her and her uncle in a scene lit by brilliant lightning as thunder exploded around them. She ducked around one Fiend only to have another make a grab for her and succeed, grabbing onto her leg. She screamed; it felt like her leg was on fire. She killed it, jumping back as it slumped over. Another tried to pull her close, its jaws opening far too wide, so she cut off its bottom jaw and an arm in the same slash and danced away, trying to ignore the pain, ignore the memories of her last desperate fight. This wouldn't end the same way. They'd won, the villains were dead, and now it was a matter of getting out alive. Even if they didn't, even if they both didn't survive, they'd won.

She tried to hold that in her mind as she raised her hand to the sky, absorbing lightning until she couldn't see for the pain, until she thought the protective spell on her arm was going to give out and she would be incinerated. She pulled from the energy of the storm, using it to act as a counter to the lightning so she could hold more of that wild electric power. She needed to kill as many as possible now or they would have no hope. When she was on the verge of passing out she released it in a burst of raw power. Several Fiends were incinerated instantly. She took a deep breath as more converged on her, now the biggest threat, and raised her arm again. She'd never done it a second time before, but now she had no choice. It was so much worse, her body feeling like it was going to be ripped apart. She couldn't hold as much power, but she still took it as far as she could before letting it loose, her heart stuttering briefly before it regained a normal rhythm, her vision fading for a brief moment. But few Fiends were left unharmed.

Barely holding on, she jumped out of the way of another attack only to realise that she'd made a grave error. She tried to twist away but she was too close. The Fiend that had been after her armour spell had managed to get behind her. Claws sliced through her armour and skin and she cried out. The armour spell lasted long enough to ensure that the Fiend only did surface damage rather than cleaving through her spine, but it was enough. She felt the spell flicker and die as blood ran down her back. She spun away, putting up a wall of ice before the Fiend could get in another hit. She was in trouble now, deep, deep trouble, even with the storm to draw power from. A bony fist caught her side, ribs cracking as she flew. She managed to turn her landing into a handspring, slicing a Fiend down the moment her feet touched the ground. She had to get to her uncle. The Fiend who'd destroyed her spell raised its head and let out an eerie cry. All of the Fiends turned their gazes towards her. She managed to make eye contact with her uncle for a brief moment before more of them went after her. The already difficult fight turned into an impossibly desperate battle for survival as she put all of her skills and powers into lasting another breath.

History was repeating itself. Damien fought like a madman to get to Rain; he'd seen the Fiend strike her, knew from her expression what had happened. He knew because he'd seen it before, twenty years ago, moments before Tempest had died.

He couldn't let it happen again.

It couldn't happen again.

It couldn't.

He threw all of his power behind his attacks, trusting that she could use the raging storm to protect herself just a little longer. Back then, with Tempest, the rain had come too late to save her. He made a slender thread of copper wire wrap around his sword and one of his daggers; the dagger he stabbed into a Fiend with shapeshifting abilities and thrust his sword into the air. Attracted to his magic and the metal of his sword, the lightning struck his blade, following the copper wire instead of going through his body. He couldn't generate lightning, but if it was there he could make use of it, though not nearly as well as Rain. The Fiend was lit up from the inside for a moment before falling over, dead and smoking. He recalled the dagger, making it go through the eye of another Fiend while he made two more blades spin like throwing stars, slicing through a Fiend's thick neck and discouraging any from attacking his back as he tried to get to his niece. She was trying to get to him as well. It was just like last time. She used the rain to create a pillar and thrust herself into the air, trying to go over them, but another Fiend leaped, grabbing her ankle and pulling her to the ground. She screamed and made the pillar fall on her attacker, but it was too late. She landed wrong and the Fiends converged on her. He shouted her name and tried to push down the panicked desperation that threatened to swallow him.

History wasn't going to repeat itself.

History wasn't going to repeat itself.

History couldn't repeat itself.

He struck and blocked with a single-minded focus, ignoring when a Fiend clawed his side, leaving deep cuts. That didn't matter. He twisted and decapitated it before thrusting his blade through another Fiend as he turned back. Now there were only the Fiends that surrounded her. He threw his sword, making it spin like a disc to take all their heads at once, twisting the metal whatever way he had to in order to kill them all. The bodies fell away and his blade returned to him. He kicked the withering corpses away and found a mound of blue and red ice that was scored with deep marks from the Fiends' claws. Clever, clever girl. But he had no idea how badly wounded she was underneath it. He dropped his sword and pulled out a dagger with a narrow blade, using his magic to heat it just enough that it could make a mark in the ice. With shaking hands he etched out the spell to melt ice and waited, rocking back on his heels. The marks glowed red for a moment before the ice began to melt. He wanted to speed it up, but he didn't want to burn her, especially not now when she had no defenses aside from her physical armour. Slowly, too slowly for his liking, the ice melted away, revealing his niece. She was so pale, so very deathly pale. Shallow cuts marked her face, and he could see deeper wounds, one crossing her collarbone. He caught her as the ice that had been holding her up melted away. She was cold, so cold. He held her tight, struggling to breath past the lump in his throat.

"No... no... no..." She was barely breathing, her pulse a thin flutter under his fingertips. He held her close. There was nothing he could do. He wasn't a healer, help was too far away, and there were more enemies, between the fortress and the camp there was a fair amount of ground to cover that would be made treacherous by Fiends and by the storm. His vision blurred with tears, and for a moment the blue hair spilling over his arm was lighter in colour, the body smaller, and the armour different. So cold. So very cold, even for a water mage. So cold and so still, just like Tempest. "Please... please don't die," he begged again, rocking her back and forth gently. "You have to stay." He'd promised to bring Rain back. He'd promised to do anything to bring her back home, anything in his power. He'd have done it, gladly. He would have given his life for her. She deserved better than this.

He was supposed to be the one to die on this trip. He was supposed to die, and Rain was supposed to bring his ashes to The Cliff to scatter to the winds and sea. It wasn't supposed to be like this. Not like this. Not again... Every. Fucking. Time. Every time he was supposed to have died, someone else died in his place, like the universe was trying to drive him over the edge. This time it might have succeeded. "I'm so sorry," he said in a ragged voice, not sure who he was speaking to. Was it Rain, dying in his arms? Was it Ash, to whom he'd promised Rain's safe return? Was it Storm, about to lose yet another family member because he wasn't good enough? Or was it Tempest, his oldest, dearest friend, the first person he'd really trusted, the first he'd been able to call family? Was he apologizing to her for his repeated failures? He hadn't been able to save her, just like he hadn't been able to save her daughter. It was just like Shade had said, just like the bitch had shown him.

He bowed his head as the storm raged around him, wondering what the hell he was supposed to do now. Sit here and die? No. He couldn't. He had to bring Rain home. He had to bring her home where she would be safe from all harm, though he knew she would soon be well beyond that anyway.

12

Onward

Everything hurt. She felt like she was dying and everything hurt. Something warm dripped onto her face, and she hoped it wasn't saliva, because she didn't want to be eaten. The ice was supposed to have been her shield, but with her injuries she'd passed out as soon as it closed over her head. Her heart was an unsteady beat in her chest and she knew she'd lost too much blood, was still losing a lot of blood, but the storm still raged on, so she managed to pull a little more power from it, just enough to keep the rest of her blood in her body and to keep her body going for just a little longer. Fucking hell, it hurt and she had no idea how long she could keep this up. She forced herself to open her eyes and saw her uncle's saturated leather vest. She managed to tilt her head back and saw that her uncle's head was bowed towards her, tears dripping along with raindrops. She was a water mage, she knew the difference.

"Uncle Damien?" She said, barely able to speak. His eyes flew open and he stared at her for a few moments.

"You're alive?"

"I think so?" She wasn't entirely certain, but that likely meant she was alive. For now, at least. She was in bad shape and she knew it.

He held her tighter. "Fucking hell, kiddo, you scared me half to death." He took a few deep breaths. "Fuck. Rain, don't ever do that again."

"I don't want to," she replied. "I don't want to die." Not when she was just getting her life back.

"Not for a very, very long time," Uncle Damien promised her. She felt something around her wrist, a tug on her vambrace. She looked down and watched as the silver wire coiled and twisted, forming a bracelet of runes and symbols. She'd never seen that combination, but she knew each part and could tell what it was meant to do.

"You can't do that!" She protested, though she could understand the logic of it.

"I can and I am. Your armour spell is toast and we still need to get off this godsdamned rock." The spell was meant to act as her armour spell had, only instead of drawing power from her it relied on her uncle's magic. A spell like this would drain his power reserves far more quickly than the spell the Hunters used to protect themselves.

"You could die."

"Any more injuries and you *will* die," he reminded her as he detached the wire and quickly bandaged her wounds. "Let's just focus on getting somewhere safe. Can you stand?"

She didn't want to. "I have no idea." He managed to get to his feet and helped her stand up. It took everything she had not to fall over, but once she made a staff out of ice it was a little easier. "Can we actually make it down to the camp?"

"All the bodies are going to attract more Fiends. We don't have a choice right now." She tapped her warning spell, almost fainting from the movement. "You're bleeding," she pointed out, aware that her own words were starting to slur from shock and blood loss.

"I know." He glanced down at his side and shrugged, holding out a hand to steady her as they started walking. "This is going to be hard."

"Uncle Damien, when you were up in the room, what happened?"

"An offer to join their group and live, and then Shade demonstrated her powers when I refused. Don't ask about it," he added quickly. "They didn't bother trying to explain what the hell they were thinking in doing this, probably for the best."

She decided do as he asked for once. "I saw Gold's body."

"Yeah, I think there may still be a few pieces scattered around," he said, helping her when she stumbled.

"Did it feel good to get revenge?"

He took a moment before answering. "I'm happy enough that he's dead, but I wouldn't say it was satisfying. Revenge never is. What about you?"

She also took a moment to think about it. "I guess I feel relieved that they can't do anything else, but I thought I would at least get some sense of closure."

"Did she get under your skin with that little speech about murder?"

"A little," Rain admitted.

"Do you remember what I told you after I asked why you wanted to be a Hunter?"

"At Mom's funeral?" He nodded. "You told me..." she paused, trying to figure out which bit he meant. "You told me that I can't save everyone."

"Exactly."

"Then I told you that I would save as many as I can."

He nodded. "That also means being okay with the fact that sometimes people are going to die no matter what you do."

"I know."

"Then prove it," he said, squeezing her shoulder gently. "Do your best to save people, mourn those who are lost, but don't let it consume you."

"That's awfully philosophical."

"Blame the blood loss," he said with a wry grin.

Damien was almost right: the trip back wasn't hard, it was nearly impossible. It took them three times as long to make it down the mountain, and they didn't dare stop to rest because they wouldn't have been able to start again. Every step was agony, even worse than when she'd had to carry Kestrel to safety while keeping herself alive.

"Come on, kiddo, we're nearly there," Damien said, gently pushing her forward. He was struggling too, keeping one hand pressed against his bleeding side. Eventually he paused to bind the wound with a length of bandage. "Just a little farther."

"But we still need a healer." She certainly did. The power she was siphoning from the storm had gotten her to the point where she was stable, but she couldn't do better than that, especially since she was on the verge of crashing.

"We'll figure it out when we get back, and we'll also figure out how we're getting back home. This storm is going to mess everything up for a while, and I don't know about you but I'd really rather not be stuck in the mountains for several months. I just did that last year and it was awful."

"I need a drink," she decided a while later, "and the healer. Preferably at the same time."

"That does sound wonderful," he agreed, glancing up at the sky. The storm had just started slowing down, the sky still heavy with malevolent black clouds. "I have no idea what time of day it is."

"Me neither." She stumbled and grabbed onto him for support. "I don't know if I can make it back." She was starting to crash, even as she tried to draw more power from the storm.

"We really don't have a choice, and look, we're close." He pointed to the rocky outcrop that partially hid the entrance to the mines. "Not far now."

"What do we do after?"

"Pass out for a while and then figure it all out."

She shook her head. "I mean when we get out of here."

"Go home, recover, maybe take a few extra days to relax once our wounds heal and then go hunting again."

"So we just carry on like nothing's changed?"

"Has it?"

She opened her mouth to say that of course things had changed, but then she actually thought about it. The Fiends were still there, Hunters and Guardians were still needed to risk their lives to protect everyone, and they would keep dying as they tried to do so. The numbers of Fiends would go down, perhaps, but they wouldn't go away, and even then, the concentration of Fiends in a given area changed all the time. "No," she was forced to conclude. Hell, it had taken long enough to figure out that there really was a problem in the first place. "We averted a crisis, but it didn't change a damn thing."

He nodded. "Nothing really changes, not for us. In a few decades there'll be another group of bastards who are going to try something or there'll be some insanely strong Fiend that lures in the others. Maybe you'll be one of the people who have to put a stop to it, maybe you'll just hear about it after the fact because you're busy somewhere else, but nothing is going to change."

Nothing would change, her friends would keep dying. Children would grow up orphans because their parents were killed by monsters, and sometimes they wouldn't get to grow up at all. Their relationship with humans would be tenuous at best as most humans continued to resent and fear them. "When you think about it that way Hunters really do sound insane."

He raised a brow. "I'm shocked you would ever think otherwise."

"No, sometimes it just hits me again."

"Ah, yeah, that happens."

"So... what happened back there... was that like what happened to Mom?" She'd never really heard too many details on what had happened, just what her father had told her and Storm. Damien would talk about her mother's life but never her death. Once she'd been out in the field for a little while she'd understood why and stopped asking, but now... that had to be why he'd reacted so strongly.

"It was just starting to get cloudy," he answered. "Then... it was just overcast."

"So if there'd been a storm..."

"Maybe." He grabbed her when she slipped and helped her steady herself, though it clearly caused him pain as well. "Maybe it would have turned out differently. Then again, maybe not." He shrugged sadly, grimacing at the movement. "We can't change the past."

"Or the future, apparently, because nothing changes."

Damien looked over at his niece. Despite her words she looked resentful, angry even, but not hopeless. That was a good sign, a better reaction than he would have expected despite the progress she'd made over the last few months.

"Do you want to quit?" He asked, helping her down the last rocky slope.

"No! I'm not going to give up." He heard the 'anymore' that she didn't say. In a few weeks, few months, she would be able to stand on her own again, would be able to handle whatever came along. Maybe not perfectly or even well at times, but she would be able to handle it. Soon he wouldn't have to keep such a close eye on her. She wouldn't be cured though, wouldn't be fixed. There would be times when she would stumble and fall, when she would need help getting up again. Something would happen that would threaten to drown her once more. At least now she would know what to do, wouldn't let herself get pulled so far down again. She would live, and gods willing she just might find some kind of happiness in life again. He reached reflexively to his belt and found his flask was still there, and it was the one with the special liquor. He took a drink and handed it to Rain.

"Seriously? After everything you still have that?" She drank and handed it back as she coughed. "Damn."

"I take drinking very seriously," he replied, taking another swallow. It burned like fire but it helped push back the pain and clear his head, so he got her to have another drink as well. He could see smoke rising from the camp, and not in a 'everything has gone to hell' kind of way, which was a nice surprise given their luck so far. He'd seen both enough to know the difference at a glance. "Look, we've nearly made it."

"Yippee," she drawled.

"Come on, you can do better than that," he said, and she glared at him.

They made it safely to the camp and while Rain all but passed out Damien made sure the messages that needed to be sent out were sent out, to the Council, Ash, and the nearest Guardian Ship. Rain wasn't at risk of dying, but she still wasn't in any kind of condition to travel much farther without help, and he wasn't in the best shape either. If he hadn't been in so much pain the expressions on the villager's faces would have been far more hilarious when they saw the Hunters. He was sure they expected him or Rain to fall over dead at any moment, but that was part of the reason why they were the ones out fighting Fiends and the humans were discouraged from doing the same.

He groaned as he finally lay down on one of the bunks and tried to get comfortable, though he didn't want to sleep. He didn't want to dream of Tempest's death again, and he knew that's what would happen, likely for the next few weeks. He also expected Rain to wake up screaming for the next while. Even if she seemed okay for the first night or two, it was inevitable. They would go home and life would go on, and then one day he would die and the Hunter asleep nearby would be the one to scatter his ashes and live and fight a long time after he was gone.

He heard a gasp and turned quickly as Rain woke up and couldn't hold back a groan of pain. "You okay kiddo?"

"I'll be fine," she said, starting to sit up and then apparently realising that was a bad idea and lay back down again, her face almost grey. "Say, how many Fiends did you kill?"

He frowned as he thought it over. "Ah, I don't know, at least twenty?"

Her face lit up in a huge grin, the first genuine, happy smile he'd seen since he'd found her in the tavern. "Finally!" She crowed. "Finally I win!" She thrust her fist in the air. "Fucking hell that was a bad idea," she groaned as her arm fell back.

He finally caught on. Between the tower and the lightning blast she'd killed a lot of Fiends. "For fuck's sake, really? Now?"

"Hell yes! It counts."

"Fine, fine, you won," he said, shaking his head and unable to hold back a grin. "It took you seven years, but you finally beat me."

"The student surpasses the teacher!"

"I wouldn't go that far. I still have seven years' worth of wins on you."

"But I have one, the first of many."

He just shook his head again. "Go back to sleep, *kiddo*."

In the end Rain had a number of new and impressive scars, but once again managed to escape any lasting damage when her wounds were fully healed weeks later. She was doomed to survive, after all. Nothing would stop her from hunting short of death, and that end wouldn't come in a battle. Not for her.

"What'd the mage say?" Storm asked, looking up from a book as the younger woman walked through the door.

"The armour tattoo had to be redone," she replied with a sigh. "The scarring would force her to alter it too much to just fill in what was destroyed. She just removed it and did it over again." It stung a little but would be fine by the time she and her uncle left in the morning. She turned around and took off her corset to show it off. She'd worn an off-shoulder shirt for that reason.

"That's annoying, but at least it can go over the scars," her older sister said, standing to take a closer look, her hand going over her stomach. "She did good work." Rain still couldn't believe her sister was going to have a baby. She would never be able to have kids, not with what she did and what she saw all the time. Her parents had done it, and so had other Hunters, sure, but she just couldn't. At least Storm got to have something of a happy ending, though. Kestrel too, as she regained her archery prowess with Nadina's help. The other Hunter had decided to stick around since things were going to be rough for a while yet.

"I would hope so, it took her long enough to do it," she grumbled, stretching.

As for herself, well, Hunters didn't get happy endings. They just tried to make sure that other people could, taking the hard roads and the scars, skirting the edge of madness and trying to stay ahead of the darkness that threatened to swallow them. It wasn't pretty, it wasn't easy, but it was what she chose to do, and she would live with the consequences and burdens that came with it.

"Where's Dad?" He'd been home when she'd left that morning.

"Dad wound up having to teach a class for Amber, she's got a meeting with the Headmistress about taking over." Storm grinned. Everyone was thrilled that Amber had accepted the post without argument. "He'll be back later. You know, I still can't believe you and Uncle Damien picked your travel route by throwing darts at a map."

Rain turned to face her sister, frowning. "How would you have done it?" Storm rolled her eyes instead of answering. "Anyway, I'd better finish packing; we're supposed to leave tomorrow." They both looked over as their uncle came into the room, drinking from his flask.

"Hey kiddo, you good to go?"

"I am." It was time for the Hunter to get back to work.

About the Author

Stacey Oakley lives in Newfoundland enjoying the weather that most people hate. She has a BA in Art History & Visual Studies from the University of Victoria and is working on finishing a post-grad diploma in Cultural Resource Management. When not explaining what those mean she can usually be found either reading a book or writing one. Other hobbies include swimming, knitting, reading, and playing the clarinet. *Hunter's Soul* is her first novel to see the light of publication.

9 781775 040705

THREE DOG KNIGHT

COLDSTONE CASE FILES

BOOK THREE

JASON GILBERT